THE
DAGGER
AND THE
FLAME

PRAISE FOR
THE DAGGER AND THE FLAME

'Sizzling romance, stunning world-building, spectacular writing.' – Lauren Roberts, author of *Powerless*

'Packed full of Doyle's trademark lush description and snarky banter, *The Dagger and the Flame* is a sprawling adventure through the treacherous streets of Fantome. Enemies to lovers, sworn-to-kill-each-other-but-let's-kiss, swoony romance, perilous mystery, cute animal sidekicks – it ticks every romantasy box and will delight fans everywhere.' – Melinda Salisbury, author of *The Sin Eater's Daughter*

'Fast paced, and exciting and clever, and because it's Catherine Doyle, it's beautifully written, too. Oh, and did I mention it's really, really hot?' – Louise O'Neill author of *The Surface Breaks*

'Gorgeous and ruthless: stand back everyone, the true rivals to lovers has arrived.' – Sarah Rees Brennan, author of *Long Live Evil*

'Stunning, thrilling, and devastatingly romantic. *The Dagger and the Flame* is guaranteed to be your new obsession.' – Katherine Webber, co-author of *Twin Crowns*

THE CITY OF FANTOME

THE
DAGGER
AND THE
FLAME

CATHERINE DOYLE

SIMON & SCHUSTER

First published in Great Britain in 2024 by Simon & Schuster UK Ltd

Text copyright © 2024 Catherine Doyle

1 3 5 7 9 10 8 6 4 2

Simon & Schuster UK Ltd
1st Floor, 222 Gray's Inn Road
London WC1X 8HB

Simon & Schuster: celebrating 100 years of Publishing in 2024

www.simonandschuster.co.uk
www.simonandschuster.com.au
www.simonandschuster.co.in

Simon & Schuster Australia, Sydney
Simon & Schuster India, New Delhi

A CIP catalogue record for this book
is available from the British Library.

HB ISBN 978-1-3985-2837-6
eBook ISBN 978-1-3985-2845-1
eAudio ISBN 978-1-3985-2844-4
PB ISBN 978-1-3985-2838-3

Printed and Bound in the UK using 100% Renewable
Electricity at CPI Group (UK) Ltd

MIX
Paper | Supporting
responsible forestry
FSC
www.fsc.org   FSC® C171272

For Rachel Denwood, who turned the spark of this story into a flame

THE CITY OF
FANTOME

Valterre

EVERELL
VILLAGE

Hugo's
Passage

Primrose Square

OLD
HAVEN

Our Sacred
Saints'
Cathedral

SAINTS'
QUARTER

BRIDGE
OF
TEARS

THE VERNE

Grand
Versini

SOUTH
QUARTER

To the Plains

Traveller's
Arch

NORTH
QUARTER

SCHOLARS'
QUARTER

LAZENNE VILLAGE

THE
HOLLOWS

House
Armand

Rascalle
Marketplace

THE
SOUTH SEA

LIST OF PLAYERS

ORDER OF THE DAGGERS

Hugo Ralphe Versini, *Founder of the Order of the Daggers*
Gaspard Dufort, *Head of the Order of the Daggers*
Ransom Hale, *Dagger*
Lark Delano, *Dagger*
Nadia Raine, *Dagger*

ORDER OF THE CLOAKS

Armand Versini, *Founder of the Order of the Cloaks*
Madame Cordelia Mercure, *Head of the Order of the Cloaks*
Madame Josephine Fontaine, *Former Head of the
Order of the Cloaks*
Valerie, *Cloak*
Sabine Fraser, *Cloak*
Theodore Branch, *Shadowsmith*

Sylvie Marchant, *Shade smuggler*
Seraphine Marchant, *her daughter*

HOUSE OF RAYERE, THEIR ROYAL HIGHNESSES

Bertrand IV, King of Valterre
Odette I, Queen of Valterre

SAINTS OF VALTERRE

1. Calvin, Saint of Death
2. Celiana, Saint of Song and Poetry
3. Frederic, Saint of Farmers and Hunters
4. Maud, Saint of Lost Hope
5. Maurius, Saint of Travellers and Seafarers
6. Oriel, Saint of Destiny
7. Serene, Saint of Animals
8. Alisa, Saint of the Sick
9. Cadel, Saint of Warriors
10. Calliope, Saint of Beauty and Youth
11. Placido, Saint of Peace
12. Jasper, Saint of Artisans
13. Lucille Versini, Saint of Scholars

Part I

'Take only what your cloak can carry,
and your conscience can bear.'

Armand Versini,

FOUNDER OF THE ORDER OF CLOAKS

'Those who refuse to wield the dagger are
doomed to die by its blade.'

Hugo Versini,

FOUNDER OF THE ORDER OF DAGGERS

Before

Out beyond the glittering city of Fantome in the wild heart of the plains, the midnight moon hung like a lantern in the sky, bathing the farmhouse that belonged to Seraphine Marchant's mother in a soft silver glow. The light crept in through Seraphine's window and danced along the pages of her book, and for a moment, she imagined the curious moon was reading over her shoulder. She turned a page, the words blurring as her eyelids grew heavy. She should be asleep but she couldn't rest at such a crucial point in the story. Even if she had read it eight times already. Even if, at seventeen years old, she was too old for fairy tales.

Pippin slumbered at her feet, warming her toes. As a dog of considerable age and with only three legs to carry him, he had no interest in the inky whispers of imagined adventures. He cared chiefly for naps, river sprats and, on occasion, Farmer Perrin's chickens.

At the sudden sound of swearing, Seraphine turned her face to the window. Out in the garden, Mama was on her hands and knees hissing at the lavender, whorls of her thick black hair veiling her face. Unusual behaviour, even for Sylvie Marchant. Seraphine frowned, closing her book. Down below, a cat darted from the bushes. Mama pounced, snatching up the startled tabby. It was Fig, so named because Seraphine often found the stray napping in the fig tree behind their house. Not that Mama had ever taken the slightest interest in him until now.

Seraphine watched as her mother pulled a familiar glass vial from the pocket of her cardigan before removing the stopper with her teeth. The cat yowled as Mama tipped the contents into his mouth. Pippin raised his head, a growl rumbling in his throat. Unease rumbled through Seraphine, too.

Mama set the cat down. Fig scampered a couple of steps, then jerked. Another step, and a howl burst from him. It was not a sound Seraphine had ever heard before, and the agony of it raked claws down her spine. Pippin's hackles rose.

She pressed her nose to the window, watching in silent horror as Fig's little body thrashed. In a matter of seconds, he grew to twice his size, then larger still. Soon, Fig didn't look like himself at all. Not a cat, but a beast. His fur was so black it seemed to join with the darkness. Strange shadows poured from his barrel chest like tentacles, some sweeping through the low bushes, others lashing out, high and fast. Mama jumped backwards to avoid one, a laugh springing from her as though it was a jump rope.

Seraphine's blood ran cold.

The moon dipped behind a cloud and in the sudden dark, Fig disappeared entirely.

'Pss pss pss,' hissed Mama.

A deafening roar cut through the night. As the cloud passed and the moonlight returned, Fig lunged from the bushes, with saliva dripping from his fangs. He cornered Mama.

Seraphine leaped to her feet, the book tumbling from her lap as she bolted for the bedroom door. Behind her, she felt, rather than saw, a snap of bright golden light, and then heard Mama's shout rising in the dark. Seraphine took the rickety stairs two at a time, grabbing the kitchen broom at the bottom. With Pippin barking at her heels, she burst out into the night.

And ran head-first into her mother. She stumbled backwards, broom raised, eyes wild. The beast was nowhere to be seen, but Seraphine kept her guard up. 'Get behind me, Mama!'

Mama's bronze eyes were wild, too. 'What are you doing out here, little firefly?' she demanded breathlessly. 'You should be asleep.'

Seraphine blinked, then stared hard at her mother. Sylvie Marchant was uninjured, grinning with two neat rows of pearly teeth. But there was an edge to that smile. A faint smell of burning lingered in the air, and beneath it, Seraphine scented a strange citrus tang, like lemon blossoms. She craned her neck, searching the darkness. Pippin was already tramping through it, inspecting the bushes.

'Where is Fig?'

Mama cocked her head. 'Fig?'

'The cat,' said Seraphine, her heart beating so loudly she could scarcely think. 'He changed. He charged at you. I saw him.' She was still brandishing the broom. 'I thought you were hurt. I came to rescue you . . .' she trailed off. She felt unsteady on her feet. Unsteady in her mind.

Seraphine knew Shade magic. She had grown up with it, watching Mama grind and bottle it long before Seraphine started helping with the task. She had washed the dust of it from her fingers more times than she could count, but what she had seen just now . . . *that* was something else. Something bigger. A dent in the rules they had followed so very carefully, for so very long. *Touch, but don't use. Never taste.* The thought etched a scowl on her face. 'What are you up to, Mama?'

Mama gently flicked her on the nose. 'Watch that frown before the wind sets it. Or we'll have to start using you to frighten off the crows.'

Seraphine tossed the broom aside. 'You know we're not supposed to mess around with—'

'I know the rules,' said Mama, swishing the words away. Refusing to be interrogated. Or scolded. 'I think you've been reading too many stories, darling girl. I only crept out to look for my ring. I thought I dropped it in the bushes when I was gardening this afternoon.'

The lie was so effortless, so comforting, that Seraphine felt herself leaning into it, like a slant of sunlight in winter.

'Come,' said Mama, nudging her back towards the house. 'Let's put some colour back into those cheeks. It's nothing a little sugar won't fix.'

As Seraphine watched her mother bolt the back door behind them, she tried to unpick the strange smile on her face, the spring in her step as she went to the kitchen cupboard and retrieved the remaining half of yesterday's sugar loaf. A rummage in the drawer produced a candle and then the cake was between them, the lone candle alight.

She stared at Mama through the flame. 'Do you have a secret birthday I don't know about?'

'It's after midnight,' said Mama, gesturing to the clock on the wall. 'Which means it's the birthday of Saint Lucille.' Mama's favourite saint. She didn't give a rat's ass about the other twelve – the ancient original ones, who once stalked the length and breadth of the Kingdom of Valterre with true magic in their veins. Lucille, the last of them, was young and clever and almost recent enough to touch. She was the Saint of Scholars, and Mama saw herself as a scholar, too.

For her part, Seraphine preferred the allure of stories over the mercurial nature of philosophy. She rarely prayed, and only ever to Saint Oriel of Destiny. Seraphine was a dreamer, not a scholar. But that was not the fault of Saint Lucille. Or the cake. 'Make a wish, Seraphine.'

Seraphine frowned again, but this night was so utterly baffling already, she didn't see the harm in making a wish. So, she closed her eyes and made the same one she always did. For a grander destiny, for the freedom to go far beyond their little farmhouse in the plains, to hurl herself headlong into the kind of adventures she read about in her books. A life that made her heart gallop, that made her feel like she was truly *living*.

She blew out the candle and she and her mother perched on the countertop, setting the strange incident in the garden aside and devouring the remains of the sugar loaf. But when Seraphine went to wash her plate in the sink, she saw Mama's ring sitting in the soap dish.

She held it up, suspicion nagging at her once more, but Mama only laughed as she snatched it from her. 'There it is! It looks like *my* wish came true.' She slipped it onto her finger. 'Now, to bed with you before we push our luck.'

Seraphine was too tired to press the matter. If she was honest with herself, a part of her was too frightened to prod at the lie until it fell apart. There had always been a darkness in Mama, and Seraphine feared that if she looked directly at it, it might become a part of her too. It might destroy their careful little life.

'Goodnight, Mama.' As Seraphine pressed a kiss to her cheek, she swore she saw a spark in her mother's burnished brown eyes. The sign of a different, secret wish that had yet to come true.

'Sweet dreams, my little firefly.'

That night, Seraphine sat on her windowsill, waiting for the tabby cat to return, but as the full moon gave way to the blushing dawn, she nodded off, dreaming of terrible beasts with sharp fangs leaping at her from the shadows.

One year later

Chapter 1

Seraphine

It was midnight in the city of Fantome, and Seraphine Marchant was running for her life. Pippin was doing his best to keep up. They were following the Verne, the pebble-grey river that wound through the heart of Fantome like an artery. From the arched stone entrance on the outskirts of the city, it led them through the north quarter and onto Merchant's Way, where the taverns were lit and bustling, echoing with the caterwauls of drunk sailors.

Seraphine barely noticed them. It was the beginning of autumn, and a light rain was falling. It kissed her cheeks, mingling with her tears. Her chest burned, as though a fist was closing around her heart, but she didn't dare slow down. She could still smell the smoke that had driven them from their farmhouse only hours ago. It coiled in her hair and sat heavy in her lungs.

Keep moving, she told herself. *Don't look back.*

Every time a memory of the fire reared up, Seraphine shook it off violently, but the flashbacks were becoming harder to ignore. The shock was fading. Beneath it waited a rising swell of grief and anger. Questions tumbled over one another, demanding to be answered.

Don't stop. Don't think.

Beside her on the street, Pippin was splashing in and out of puddles, trying to cool his singed tail. Soon, his shaggy grey face was sopping. Seraphine tried to pick him up, but he wriggled free.

'Little gremlin.' She sniffed. 'Have it your way.'

Saints, her legs ached, and her body was so tired all her bones felt like lead. She wished she was riding Scout, the dappled mare's strides sure and quick beneath her, but the fire had sent Seraphine's beloved horse fleeing through the fields and there hadn't been time to look for her. It was too late to turn back now. Seraphine herself should have been dead by now. But Saint Oriel of Destiny clearly had other plans for her.

Though Seraphine hadn't grown up in the bustle of Valterre's capital city, she had visited Fantome so many times that she knew the street layout like her favourite constellations, and knew how dangerous they became when the sun went down.

When she was a little girl, Mama used to bring her into the city every Sunday. They would set out from their farmhouse in the plains at first light, taking a wagon to arrive in the city by late morning. At the harbour market, Mama would buy a pocketful of jam-and-custard pastries and they would wander along the Verne, giggling as they licked the sugar from their fingers.

Afterwards, they would browse for hours at Babette's House of Books, Seraphine selecting a well-thumbed fairy tale, while Mama – always clever, and forever straining beyond the reaches of her imagination – pored over yellowed encyclopaedias about alchemy and invention, with text so small Seraphine had to squint to read it.

When the street lanterns flickered to life and the air chilled, they would head home, Mama's hand tight around Seraphine's as they left the darkening city behind them. For it was in the falling shadows of Fantome that the Cloaks and Daggers roamed. The rival guilds, one of thieves and the other of assassins, were both powered by Shade – the only magic the once-blessed Kingdom of Valterre had left at its fingertips. Shade was a substance, controlled by those brave enough to step, or foolish enough to fall, into the underworld. The fine black powder was a mundane substance, unworthy of the divine majesty of Valterre's long-dead saints, those twelve magic-borne figures who had founded the city over a thousand years ago, filled it with life and beauty, made it glitter like a sea of stars.

Shade was the dust that lost golden age had left behind. A volatile substance that bent shadows to the will of man. For those skilled in the art of dark magic and trained by the Orders, Shade could be used to steal. To spy. To kill. To avenge. To survive.

The Daggers consumed Shade in small doses, temporarily turning their bodies into deadly weapons where one touch alone could kill. The Cloaks never consumed Shade. Rather, they wore it, allowing them to blend in with the night and take from it whatever they wished. They might have considered themselves nobler than their rivals, but to dance with Shade at all was to tempt fate.

Mama's job as a smuggler meant that Seraphine had lived in close proximity to Shade her whole life. Both as the boneshade plant, raw and trailing roots when it arrived from the far hills of Valterre, and as the fine black powder it became once Mama had painstakingly baked and ground the plant into dust.

Seraphine had filled more vials with Shade than she could count, but she had never dared experiment with it herself. Even the touch of the glass felt like ice against her fingers. A cold breath of warning. Then there was Mama's guiding voice, always close to her ear as they worked side by side at their workbench, reminding Seraphine that while Shade was what they did, it was not who they were.

We are merely the go-betweens, little firefly. Nothing more, nothing less.

But that wasn't really true. There was no in between with Shade. Playing with magic was like playing with fire, and in the end someone always got burned.

The Age of Saints was long over.

At night, the Cloaks and Daggers owned the city. Mama always knew to keep well away from them and having grown up in her shadow, never far from the cold slick of Shade, Seraphine did too.

As she got older, their trips to the city became fewer and less frequent, as though Mama feared they might be snatched off the street, even in daylight. Better not to be there at all, if they could help it. Better to be nestled in a faraway farmhouse than darting through murky, shadow-swept streets, where anyone – even one of the king's nightguards – could find themselves in the wrong place at the wrong time.

Mama had spent most of her life looking over her shoulder, and yet, in spite of all her caution, she had run afoul of the guilds at last.

But why now? The question nipped at Seraphine's heels.

Stop, she hissed to herself. *Don't look back.*

The night had fallen silent, and her thoughts were too loud. Memories crowded in on her, catching her by the throat. She slowed down when she reached the Scholars' Quarter, fighting the rising urge to retch. Towering, opulent buildings peered down at her, their beautiful stained-glass windows like wide, prying eyes.

What are you running from, Seraphine Marchant? she imagined them whispering.

She hated hearing the thunder of her own heartbeat, the chatter of fear in her teeth. In the main square, she slumped onto a bench under a pear tree, clutching the armrest with whitened knuckles. The fire was still crackling in her head, and there, between the violent whips of red and gold . . . lay Mama.

The memory rose like a tidal wave, and in the sudden stillness, Seraphine could do nothing but yield to it.

The setting sun gilded the cornfields as Seraphine and Pippin trudged home without a single measly rabbit to show for their hunt. Not that they hadn't enjoyed themselves, racing each other through the hills. Seraphine had stopped to tumble down the highest of them just to see if she could roll faster than Pip, and find out how much grass she could collect in her teeth. A lot, as it turned out. In her fist now, she clutched a bouquet of bluebells, a gift for Mama, to thank her for giving her the afternoon off. A bribe, perhaps, for tomorrow's freedom.

They turned at a familiar bend in the road, and at the sight of smoke pluming in the distance, Pip set off into a run. Seraphine laughed at the mutt's sudden sprightliness, sure she had run him ragged in the fields. But the sound died in her throat as she ventured closer, into the thickening haze. The cloud was too dark for chimney smoke, too high and black and choking and— Seraphine dropped the flowers.

She bolted for home, lungs aching, heart pounding. As she cleared the last of the low hills, she saw the flames that brewed the smoke. They made a violent ring around her house, like a dragon come to devour it. There was such a roaring in Seraphine's head, she forgot to breathe.

The flames parted as though she had willed them with the strength of her horror. And there, beyond the open doorway of the farmhouse lay her mother. Already dead. Already burning.

It was no dragon that Seraphine saw standing over her, but the figure of a man. A shape she did not recognize. Tall and broad-shouldered with a sweep of wavy hair. His face was wreathed in smoke, except for a pair of violent, quicksilver eyes.

The roaring gathered in Seraphine's throat, choking her. Or perhaps that was the smoke. She didn't care as she stumbled towards the doorway, towards her mother's killer. He was already turning away from Mama's body, slipping his hands into his *pockets as though he might take a stroll in the back garden. As though he did this kind of thing every day of his life.*

And she knew, saints, she knew, exactly what he was.

An assassin, brewed in the dark heart of Fantome and sent here by Gaspard Dufort, the infamous leader of the Order of Daggers.

Mama had been marked.

If it wasn't for Pippin whining and tugging at the hem of her trousers, Seraphine would have flung herself into the fire just to claw the Dagger back. But the dog at her ankle was enough to stop her, to kindle in her some vital instinct to run.

To run and run and never stop.

Now, in the stark silence of the square, Seraphine let the memory wash over her, knowing it would return again to ravage the shores of her soul. That question, like a shark in its belly.

Oh, Mama. What did you do?

She dropped her head and tried to breathe, but she couldn't get enough air. Her head was too heavy, and her heart had been sliced right down the middle. If she stood up now, it would fall apart inside her chest.

Pippin yipped at her feet. She ignored him. He darted under the bench, and spun around so that she could see his tired little face peering up at her. She squeezed her eyes shut. 'No, Pip. I'm too tired.'

Pippin nudged her ankle, then yipped again, as if to say, *Get moving!*

Relentless little gremlin. Seraphine groaned. If she gave up now, simply collapsed on the bench and waited for the same evil that had taken Mama to come for her too, then what would become of Pippin? She was all he had left. She raised her head and raked her hands through her hair. The city blurred into focus – the soft green of the pear tree, the cool touch of the wrought-iron bench.

She gripped the golden teardrop that hung from her neck, and reached for a different memory of her mother. Not as she had been that evening but on the morning of Saints' Day a month before. Mama had stayed up all night to craft the necklace, pressing it into Seraphine's hands like a talisman just after sunrise.

Happy Saintsmas, my little firefly. Mama's brown eyes were tired, but her smile was bright.

Seraphine had been half asleep, desperately foraging in the cupboards for something to stave off her hangover. The previous night had seen far too much celebrating – wine, and lots of it. The unexpectedness of Mama's gift had surprised her. They had agreed on no presents this year, and Mama was not a sentimental sort. She valued knowledge over trinkets, and over the years, had filled Seraphine's bedroom not with pretty clothes or fancy jewellery, but with books and maps – sketches of the world far beyond Fantome. But the necklace – this necklace – was different. That morning, Mama had been different. *Wear this always and think of me*, she'd said, almost pleadingly. *May it protect you when I cannot, Sera.*

That day had come far sooner than either of them had guessed. Save for the smoke in her hair and the dog at her feet, the tiny golden teardrop was all Sera had left of Mama and their little farmhouse. A paltry flame in a world of sudden darkness. The loss made her want to scream.

Suddenly, Pippin growled. Sera looked up, to the roof of the Marlowe, the oldest museum in Fantome, in all of Valterre. It seemed taller tonight, darker.

'It's only a gargoyle, Pip,' she said, but the back of her neck was prickling. A shadow rippled near the clock tower and she swore she glimpsed a figure there, gilded in moonlight. It was gone as quickly as it came.

She had lingered too long. Tall buildings meant long shadows, and in Fantome, shadows were dangerous. Anything could be hiding inside them. Any*one*. Including the Dagger who had killed Mama.

Chapter 2

Seraphine

In the distance, the Aurore Tower stood like a proud candle casting its flickering light over the city. It was not wise to stray too far from its glare, but the glow of the Aurore never reached the Hollows, a murky pocket of east Fantome where the wretched and the forgotten made their home: thieves and troublemakers, beggars and brutes, creeps and carousers, and the orphans and runaways who came looking for a better life.

For there was magic there, too.

And, with any luck, Pippin's keen nose would lead them to it. Sera ran faster.

As the clock tower chimed one, Mama's voice rang in her head. *If anything ever happens to me, you must get to House Armand. Brave the Hollows and run until the streetlamps wink out. Pippin will show you the way.*

But Pippin had stopped to inspect a leaf.

Sera used to wonder why Mama had so readily taken in the trembling three-legged mutt five years ago. She was far from being a dog person. Or a people person, for that matter. And back then, the poor mite was so easily frightened that he barked at his own shadow. But Mama knew before his accident Pippin had been a tracker. He had a nose for magic. And a knack for survival.

Seraphine wondered now if Mama had foreseen her own grisly murder. Sylvie Marchant was neither Cloak nor Dagger, but for years, she had worked as a Shade smuggler alongside the guilds, trading magic for coin, and in doing so, dwelling in the murky haze between good and evil. All to provide a better life for Sera.

Shade was as scarce as it was dangerous. Sniffed out by tracking dogs far beyond the city, it was bought by seasoned smugglers like Sylvie Marchant, who knew precisely how to mix it, and then sold on to the few who knew how to use it without succumbing to it: the Daggers and the Cloaks. Sera always secretly feared the underworld would turn on them. After all, what honour was there among thieves and assassins?

But why now? The question nagged at Sera. *And why the fire?*

Perhaps Mama always knew that one day their world would go up in flames, and Pippin would be all Sera had left. Maybe that was why she hosed him down and put a bow around his neck five years ago, presenting him to Sera like he was the second coming of Saint Oriel.

Sera had adored him instantly.

She clicked her teeth now, shooing him along. The sight

of his burnt tail wagging as he led her through the deserted streets filled her heart with so much love it felt like pain. His little legs quickened as they neared the Hollows, the scent of Shade getting stronger.

Tucked away in the far reaches of the Hollows, House Armand was home to the clandestine Order of Cloaks. The great thieves of Fantome were always seeking to recruit lost souls tempted by the security of a comfortable home and the lure of magic, the chance to make something of themselves.

Tonight, the Cloaks were in luck. Sera was about to deliver them a fresh recruit and the cutest mutt this side of the Verne. All she had to do was remain in possession of her courage long enough to get there.

Don't stop. Don't think.

She kept a wary eye on the shadows as they ventured deeper into the Hollows. Seedy taverns and dilapidated theatres huddled along narrow streets that were strewn with broken bottles and other detritus, the well-worn cobblestones cracked and stained with vomit. Sera reminded herself that this was not Dagger territory, but she couldn't shake the sense that she was being followed.

That he was out there somewhere, watching her.

Pippin halted, a growl rumbling in his throat. His gaze darted from the roof of a nearby boarding house to the dimly lit brothel beside it. Sera gripped the rusty blade in her pocket as a shiver spider-walked her spine. She wished she had brought something sharper, but almost everything had been burning. She'd had to settle for Mama's small garden shears.

Pippin barked at a flitting shadow.

Sera brandished the shears. 'Come out and face me!'

The air trilled with distant laughter. At the end of the street, three women stumbled out of a busy tavern. A dishevelled man hobbled past, his brown eyes tired.

Not a Dagger.

Sera let out a breath, her cheeks heating with embarrassment.

But Pippin's hackles were still up.

Another shadow flitted on the brothel roof. Sera grabbed an empty flowerpot from a nearby windowsill and flung it at the slats. It sailed through the dark, before striking the roof and smashing into pieces.

She was certain she heard a low chuckle.

Her heart galloped as she hurried on, to where the streets grew quiet and the lanterns winked out. 'Follow the hedgerows,' she muttered, mentally tracing the map that used to hang on her bedroom wall.

Pippin darted ahead, tracking a scent until, at last, they came to a leafy hedge. It climbed inwards from the street, then pitched up towards the sky, where it sprawled into a mass of creeping vines that wrapped themselves around an enormous shape. In the dark, it looked to Sera like a very grand mansion. Or rather, the space where a very grand mansion might have been, if there was anything there at all.

Which was exactly what she was looking for.

After all, House Armand was cloaked. The stonework had been coated in Shade, made to melt in with the dark. She could make out the vines that hugged the house, but the windows and the front door were hidden from her.

See where the shadows ripple like drapes swaying in the breeze, whispered Mama's voice in her head. For a moment, she felt so close, Sera turned around and tried to pull Mama from the dark ... but there was nothing behind her, just a whisper of tumbling leaves, the quiet patter of falling rain, and—

Shit. A pair of quicksilver eyes halfway down the street. The tell-tale sign of a Dagger. This time, when Sera grabbed Pippin, he didn't fight. She sprinted along the hedge, desperately searching for a way in. Finally, she found a gap. Then— a gate! She shoved it open and slammed it behind her, her fingers trembling as she set the catch. It was absurd to think a gate would keep a Dagger out but Sera hoped he wouldn't readily breach Cloak territory by crossing the boundary into House Armand.

That was, by all accounts, against the rules.

Wayward twigs stroked her cheeks as she hurried down the overgrown path. Still, there was no door. No windows. No *house*.

'Come on,' she muttered, panic thick in her throat. 'I need a door.'

Patience, Sera. The light will come.

When the moon emerged from behind a thicket of clouds, she tracked a slant of light to where it bounced off a drainpipe. The shadows were rippling. For a moment, the glamour broke and she glimpsed a window. And behind it, a face peering out at her.

'Help! Please!' She paced up and down, tracking every trickle of moonlight until one fell upon a large brass doorknocker. Sera lunged before it disappeared and rapped three times. 'Hello? Can anyone hear me?'

After what felt like an eternity, the door creaked open, and the shadows that had been cloaking House Armand parted to reveal a frightfully pale old woman dressed in black. She was small and stooped, with milky blue eyes and a wrinkled, scowling face.

She took a long look at Sera, then croaked, '*No.*'

'But—' The door slammed in Sera's face. Then disappeared entirely.

'Wait! Come back!' Pippin barked raucously, but the old woman was gone. Sera whirled around, desperate. The moon had deserted them. Somewhere nearby, she could hear the creaking of a gate.

No. No way. She had come too far to give up now. Her heart thundered as she hurried around the side of the house. She followed the vines until she came to another gate that appeared to lead into a back garden. It was locked. She kicked it until it buckled, managing to squeeze through the narrow gap.

Around the back of the house, in the absence of moonlight, she grabbed a fistful of stones from a nearby flowerbed and began hurling them into the darkness.

The first three landed with dull *thunk*s – stone on stone. The next four got lost in the vines, making no sound at all. And then, just when she was about to give up, she heard a satisfying *plink!* A window. She fired off three more in the same direction.

Plink! Plink! Plink!

Before she could ready her next assault, there came a nearby *whoosh!* The back door to House Armand swung open and a shaft of golden light slipped out. She sprinted towards it.

'Sanctuary!' The word burst from her like a cry. 'I've come to plead for sanctuary!'

This time, a different woman occupied the doorframe. She was impossibly tall and slender, with deep brown skin and keen brown eyes. Her black hair was cropped close to her head and despite the late hour, her lips were painted a deep glittering red. She wore a trailing green robe, tied with a silk sash, and she smelled like tuberose and danger. Sera knew her at once. She had marvelled at her picture in the penny papers many times, but to see her towering over her in the flesh felt like a dream.

Madame Cordelia Mercure, custodian of House Armand and Head of the Order of Cloaks, pursed her lips as she looked her over. 'There's no need to make such a scene about it.'

'Sorry,' said Sera. 'I was just—'

'Trying to break all my windows?'

'Trying to get your attention.'

Madame Mercure rolled her hand. 'Well. Get on with it, then,' she said, in a bored voice.

'I'm Sera Toussaint.' A half-lie, but better to keep things simple for now. Madame Mercure might know what happened to her mother. If Seraphine revealed herself, then as Head of the Order of Cloaks, she would decline to interfere in Dagger business, and Sera would lose her chance at sanctuary. No. She had to be smart about this. 'I— well, my mother died.'

Madame Mercure arched a slender eyebrow. 'And what do you want me to do about it?'

'I ... lost.' The last word stuck in Sera's throat. She had been trying to elicit sympathy from Madame Mercure, but she had only managed to make her own eyes prickle. The sudden recollection of her loss was like a rock in her throat. 'I have nowhere else to go.'

Madame Mercure reached into the pocket of her robe. When she withdrew her hand, it appeared empty but as she moved it under the lantern and flicked her wrist, a handkerchief appeared as if from nowhere. 'Crying is such desperate business,' she said, handing it to Sera. 'It makes me terribly uncomfortable.'

Sera took the cloth and knew at once it was made with Shade. As it passed through a shadow, it seemed to disappear, only she could still feel it tingling between her fingers. She dabbed her cheeks and a smudge of soot came away with the tears. The stain melted before her eyes and the handkerchief looked brand new again. Pippin raised his head to sniff it.

Madame Mercure startled at the movement. 'Gracious. A rodent.'

'Pippin's a dog.' Sera bristled before she could help it. 'He's friendly.'

Madame Mercure peered closer. 'Mange?'

'No. He's been well cared for.'

'He doesn't look it.' She looked Sera over again, her gaze lingering on the singed ends of her hair, then the golden teardrop at her throat. Sera noticed it was glowing faintly in the dark. 'And neither do you. What did you say happened to your mother?'

Sera was seized by the image of Mama lying on the kitchen floor, her face so grey it looked like the ash falling around her. The whites of her eyes had turned black. Her lips too. It was the mark of a Dagger's kill, that shadow magic choking all the light and life out of Mama in ten heartbeats.

'Plague.' Bile pooled in Sera's throat. 'Her lungs gave out.'

Madame Mercure's mouth twisted, tasting the lie.

'And now, you wish to be a Cloak?' she said, taking back her handkerchief.

Sera nodded. What choice did she have? There was nowhere else to hide.

Madame Mercure's gaze flitted over her shoulder, her nostrils flaring as though she could sense something moving in the dark. Pippin raised his head like he could sense it, too. 'Tell me, Sera Toussaint. Do you have the nerve for thievery?'

'Yes,' said Sera, curling her fingers, crushing the lie in her palm.

Madame Mercure studied her a moment longer, as if she was making some silent calculation in her head. Then, at last, she stood aside. 'Vincent will make up a room for you tonight. He will arrange a small stipend for clothing and toiletries. Your first month of room and board is an advance on your first job. That will also be your test. All profits go to the House. Ensuing jobs will be split fifty-fifty. I'll call upon you soon for your first assignment. Be ready.'

'Thank you, *thank you*.' Sera leaped through the door, terrified the invitation might expire. As the shadows of House Armand folded around her, she trembled with relief. Pippin licked her hand to settle her, and she looked up to find herself in the grandest kitchen she had ever seen. Every black granite surface was gleaming, and the room was graced with several crystalline vases of fresh roses. The tall corniced ceiling was hung with no less than three flickering chandeliers, and there were enough priceless oil paintings on the walls to sustain an art gallery.

Madame Mercure moved in front of Sera, eclipsing the view. 'The shears in your pocket. Leave them on the back step. Weapons are not permitted in House Armand.' She removed a set of door keys from the pocket of her robe and Sera noticed a miniature black eye mask dangling on the chain, the winged tips curving into sharpened points. 'Unlike our morally corrupt brethren, the Cloaks do not dance with death. We are noble folk, you see.'

'Of course. I understand.' As Sera removed the shears and reluctantly set them down, she reminded herself that it would take more than a rusty blade to skewer the Dagger that had killed Mama.

But that would come later.

Chapter 3

Ransom

It was midnight in the city of Fantome, and Ransom Hale was on the hunt. Not that anyone noticed him, sauntering through the deserted streets in a high-collared charcoal coat, dark trousers and leather boots, his inky black hair curling in the rain.

Tonight, the mark was a girl. He had been tracking her from the outskirts of the city, long after she fled the burning farmhouse. She had been easy to spot even from a distance. Her pale face was marred with soot and the ends of her hair were singed black. Her low sobs had reached him on the wind. A wretched, sorrowful sound.

He kept his eyes on her as he stealthily crossed the Bridge of Tears. She was still crying, clutching helplessly at her chest like she was afraid her heart might fall out. In another life,

Ransom might have felt sorry for her. He might have felt the loss of her mother as keenly as he had suffered his own, but he had been taught long ago that a good Dagger did not indulge in sympathy. And Ransom was one of the best.

And yet, tonight, he felt uneasy. The girl was younger than he had been expecting. Much younger than any of his previous marks. As he followed her into the Scholars' Quarter, using the night's shadows to climb a nearby building and swing seamlessly from one rooftop to the next, he wondered if they were close to the same age.

Gaspard Dufort doesn't kill innocents, he reminded himself. The Head of the Order of Daggers might be ruthless, but he was not without a soul. If he were, he wouldn't have taken Ransom in almost ten years ago and raised him as his own son.

According to Dufort, the girl's name was Seraphine Marchant, but Ransom preferred to think of her simply as his mark. It was always easier that way. Dufort hadn't mentioned the dog. Pitiful little thing.

She collapsed on a bench in the square, her head falling like she was in prayer. Ransom leaned against the clock tower on top of the Marlowe to study her. She was a short, fine-boned creature, with large eyes and long hair the colour of summer wheat. She was wearing a dark coat that reached to her knees, and scuffed boots, laced up the middle.

For a long time, she was still.

The dog yipped and darted around her feet, trying to rouse her from her trance. The girl was unmoved. Defeated by what she had glimpsed out in the plains, or lost in the maze of her own terror. Or perhaps she was simply praying to Saint Maud of Lost Hope.

Whatever she was doing, it irritated him.

'Get up,' he muttered. 'Get up and run.'

Let me chase you.

She raised her head, as if she had heard him. She was fiddling with something around her neck, her mouth twisting nervously. She reminded Ransom of the doll his sister used to play with. Dainty, breakable. An easy mark.

But *why* was she a mark at all?

The dog growled. Right at him.

Shit. Ransom ducked behind the clock tower. If the mutt had spied him, his Shade must be wearing off. He reached into his pocket and removed a glass vial, the black dust inside shimmering faintly as he unstopped it. He downed it in one go, his eyes watering at the sulphuric burn. His throat spasmed as he fought the urge to retch. It never got easier. Some day, when his luck ran out and the nightguards finally got brave enough to pick him up, the scientists at the Appoline would cut open his body to find all his organs grey and shrivelled. Rotted through with Shade. A hollow space where his heart had once been.

That was the fate of every Dagger, sooner or later.

The fine powder worked its way down Ransom's gullet. He closed his eyes, weathering the full-body shiver as shadows unfurled inside him, flooding his veins, and lacing the bones in his ribcage. He tasted the promise of death on his lips as he flexed his fingers. The shadow-marks across his hands began to move, darting like fish in a pond. When his eyes burned silver, he knew it was done. The darkness was his to command.

He was seized by a familiar rush of adrenaline. Before the gloom came the heady rush of power. And the power of Shade was intoxicating. Night fell away like smoke clearing in the breeze until he could see as far north as the Aurore and count every merchant vessel bobbing down south in the harbour.

When Ransom stepped out from behind the clock tower, the girl was gone. Her footsteps echoed in the silence. She was heading east, towards the Hollows. He stalked to the edge of the Marlowe and pulled a shadow from the next building. He caught it like a rope, swinging himself down to the ground.

His landing was clean, soundless. He grinned, sweeping his hair back. The chase was his favourite part of a job. It turned Fantome into his own personal playground, every building a ladder, every shadow a slide.

But this one would take longer than most. Dufort had warned him not to kill tonight.

Watch her, first. I want to know where she goes. What she does.

Ransom let himself enjoy the chase as she led him deeper into the Hollows. Hell, he even enjoyed it when she flung a flowerpot at him. Terrible aim. Good survival instincts. The best way to evade a Dagger was to hide behind a Cloak. And he was impressed by how quickly she found her way to House Armand. The mutt must be a tracker.

Not that it mattered. It would take more than the pity of Madame Mercure to protect the girl now. Dufort had marked her. It was only a matter of time before he gave the final order.

Satisfied with what he had gleaned, Ransom turned for the long walk home. Shadows squirmed under his skin, his fingers itching to *kill, kill, kill.*

He dug them into his pockets, ignoring the familiar pull. In an hour or two, he'd be himself again. Magic was a game of restraint. To consume it at all was to place one foot in hell. Something the Cloaks never dared to do. There was nothing more lethal than swallowing too much Shade, or doing it too fast. Those who got drunk on their own power risked turning on their friends or themselves just to satisfy that itch: *kill, kill, kill.*

Ransom was so lost in thought he hardly noticed the man lunging from a nearby alley. His eyes were wild, his skin red and scoured. He reeked of alcohol and sweat and was brandishing a peeling knife. 'Hey, rich prick. Empty your—' The threat died in his throat when he glimpsed the silver rings in Ransom's eyes.

Big mistake.

Adrenaline surged through Ransom's body. His hand shot out, catching the man by the throat. The drunkard screamed as shadows crawled up his neck, spreading their poison. His eyes rolled, turning black.

A kill from a Dagger takes ten heartbeats.

Ransom dropped the man after eight.

He collapsed in a puddle, his hands at his throat. 'Mercy . . .' he gasped out. 'Mercy.'

Ransom's fingers twitched as he stared down at him. 'Not mercy,' he said, in a low growl. 'I don't kill for free.'

The man whimpered.

Rankled by a familiar prickle of revulsion, Ransom turned on his heel and left the Hollows behind him. *Better to be feared than to fear*, he reminded himself. Gaspard Dufort had told him that the day he took him in. Ransom had spent the first ten years of his life living in terror. He would kill a thousand times just to keep from going back to that place.

Desperation makes the Dagger.

Power keeps them.

Leaving the Hollows, he passed a pair of oblivious nightguards on patrol and took a detour through Lazenne, a sleepy neighbourhood lined with old manor houses and leafy oak trees. Sometimes, at night, he wandered these quiet manicured streets, imagining a life where he woke every day to the chorus of birdsong and the smell of freshly baked bread. He would descend a winding staircase to find Mama sipping her favourite orange-and-bergamot tea. Anouk would be browsing the penny papers in a chair by the window, reading about horrors so far from their perfect little lives, it felt like peering through a looking glass into another world.

Sometimes Ransom wandered until his heart ached, just to remind himself it was still there.

He crossed the Bridge of Tears as the clock tower chimed three. The Shade was beginning to wear off. Exhaustion would soon set in, magic giving way to an all-too familiar feeling of gloom. Sleep couldn't come soon enough, he thought, as he turned west towards Old Haven, just as a sharp whistle came from above. He jerked his head up just in time to glimpse a shape falling from the sky. It toppled him with a strangled yelp.

Ransom rolled over, swinging blindly. The shape laughed, and the sound was a familiar wheeze.

Ransom groaned. 'Lark, you bastard.'

Lark leaped to his feet, offering his hand to Ransom. 'Takes one to know one.'

Ransom kicked out, catching his ankle.

Lark caught himself before he fell. 'Nice try,' he said, fixing the collar of his dark blue pea coat. Messy waves of auburn hair stuck out from underneath a grey top hat, his normally forest-green eyes blazing silver in the dark.

Ransom rolled to his feet, assessing his oldest friend and brother-in-arms as they stood apart from each other at almost the same height. 'Where are you coming from? And why are you wearing that ridiculous hat?'

'Casimir Manor.' Lark's pearly teeth flashed in the dark. That dimpled smile was made for mischief – breaking rules, and breaking hearts. Lark was far too charming to be a Dagger, and he knew it, too. Maybe that was why he liked to flout the rules. He removed the top hat, twirling it by the rim. 'The crusty old count barely blinked. Light work. I couldn't resist the souvenir.'

'Common thievery, Lark?' Ransom's brows rose. 'Doesn't that make you a Cloak?'

'It makes me an opportunist. I would have stolen his grand piano if I had any hope of carting it out of there.'

'Good luck explaining that to Dufort.'

'I was going to say it washed up in a storm.'

Ransom snorted. 'And with that shit-eating grin, he'd probably believe you. A copper says you can't get the hat in the Verne.'

Lark threw the hat. They watched it sail across the bank and fall down, down, down into the rushing river, where it floated swiftly away.

'Too easy,' said Lark, holding his hand out expectantly.

Ransom smiled, tossing him a copper. Now, Gaspard Dufort wouldn't see that ridiculous top hat sitting on Lark's head, engraved with Count Casimir's initials, and backhand him all the way to the Aurore. The rule was simple: Daggers and Cloaks stayed out of each other's way. Daggers didn't thieve and Cloaks didn't murder. A minor distinction that had caused a family war so bloody that, over two hundred years later, the underworld still spoke of it in hushed tones.

'Was the countess there?' Ransom asked, as they turned for Old Haven.

'His wife was out of town. His mistress was warming her spot,' said Lark, with a derisive snort. 'The old dog.'

'Dead dog,' muttered Ransom, thinking involuntarily of the girl and her mutt.

'Mama will be pleased,' said Lark, patting the coins in his inside pocket. 'Twenty silvers means twice as many chickens for the farm. And just in time for winter, too.'

Ransom kicked a stray pebble, ignoring the twist of envy in his gut. Not for the provincial farm, which would soon be overrun with chickens, but for the kind-faced woman who collected their eggs and welcomed her son home every Sunday for brandy-and-butter cake. Sometimes, Ransom went along too, eagerly sharing Lark's family life, like a beggar eating the crust off a heel of bread. 'Doesn't she ever ask where the chickens come from?'

Lark clucked his tongue. 'Morals don't make soup, Ransom.'

And that was the crux of it. Lark didn't give a shit about his mortal soul. His mother was the centre of his world, and his two younger sisters were his moon and sun, and he made no bones about it. Madame Delano had never quite recovered from the same fever that took Lark's father. Her lungs were heavy and she was slow on her feet, but the bills came thick and fast, and the girls grew like beanstalks. So, at twelve years old, for the sake of his family, Lark had gone to work, telling his mother he had got a job delivering penny papers in Fantome.

Seven years later, and despite the fact his arms were now covered in permanent whorls of shadow, the painful, ever-expanding tattoo that came courtesy of the Shade he regularly consumed, she still pretended to believe him. Lark Delano was the most lavishly gilded paperboy in Fantome. They often laughed about it. Bad luck had made Lark a Dagger, but their friendship was Ransom's good fortune. He didn't know what he would do – what he would be – without it.

'Did you find your mark?' said Lark.

'She's at House Armand.'

He barked a laugh. '*Hell's teeth.* She's a Cloak?'

'No.' Ransom frowned. 'Not yet, anyway.'

'Then she's clever,' said Lark thoughtfully. 'Good luck with that.'

'I don't need luck,' said Ransom, half-convincing himself. 'I like a challenge.'

They walked on, the crisp autumn leaves crunching under their boots. The rain sputtered out, leaving behind a lingering mist. It scattered the light from the Aurore, bathing the streets in a golden haze.

'Why did Dufort burn the house?' Ransom wondered aloud. 'Wasn't it enough to just kill Sylvie Marchant?'

Lark glanced sidelong at him. The silver glint in his eyes was fading, revealing the green beneath. He looked tired, now. Tense. 'How should I know?'

Ransom ignored the bite in his friend's voice. 'And why didn't he just stay there and wait for the girl?'

'Why don't you ask him?'

'Because he'd probably set me on fire, too.'

A good Dagger did not indulge in curiosity. It was a waste of time and conscience. Worse – it encouraged hesitation. And in the art of assassination, a split second of hesitation could be the difference between life and death.

And yet, as they wandered the deserted streets of Fantome, where the rats fled at the sight of them, Ransom's mind whirred. When was the last time Gaspard Dufort had even got his hands dirty? And why would the highest-ranking Dagger in Fantome leave a fire in his wake? There was nothing quick and clean about an inferno.

Sylvie Marchant must have been important. So, what did that make her daughter?

Well, shit. Despite his better judgement, Ransom was curious.

At last, they reached Old Haven, home to the oldest neighbourhoods and most weather-worn graveyards of Fantome. Plumes of smoke curled up through the grates in the cobblestones, each one a whisper of the fireplaces that burned far beneath them, and the life that thrummed there.

They came at last to the town statue of Lucille Versini, Saint of Scholars. Carved from white marble, the young woman clutched a book to her chest as she looked north towards the Aurore.

An angel, guarding the gates to hell.

Ransom used the dregs of his Shade to pull his shadow from the cobblestones. He cast it around Saint Lucille's neck and tugged. The statue groaned as it leaned back until its unseeing eyes looked up at the stars. Beneath its pedestal was revealed the entrance to the catacombs of Fantome. Home of the Order of Daggers.

Ransom released the noose and followed Lark down the steps. Above them, the statue of Saint Lucille keened as it returned to its feet, sealing them in. They paused at the bottom of the stairwell, where an archway of skulls marked the entrance to Hugo's Passage. Above it, the immortal words of the elder Versini brother had been carved into stone:

Those who refuse to wield the dagger are doomed to die by its blade.

Ransom pressed two fingers to his chest, making a sign of respect as he ducked underneath the archway and walked into the darkness.

Home, at last.

Chapter 4

Seraphine

'Ugh. What is that rancid smell?'

'Stale smoke. She smells just like Madame Fontaine.'

'Looks like she's got a mutt, too.'

'*Aw!* Look at his cute little face, Val! Do you think he's friendly?'

'I don't know, but he reeks worse than she does.'

'You can't be rude to the new girl.'

'Hey, sometimes the truth hurts. And it's not like she can hear me.'

Sera stirred at the sound of voices in her bedroom.

'Shush, Val, she's waking up!'

'That's because you're right in her face, Bibi!'

Sera cracked an eye open to see another pair barely a foot

from her face. They were dark blue and rimmed with long lashes the colour of tangerines. They blinked, and the voice they belonged to hitched. 'Hi! Good morning! I'm Sabine! But everyone calls me Bibi.' She smiled, stretching the scattering of freckles along her pale cheeks. 'This is Valerie. But she prefers Val. Don't mind her scowl. She's not a morning person.'

'*Saints*, Bibi, let her breathe.' Bibi was shoved aside and before Seraphine could sit up, a different girl appeared before her. She had warm brown skin and brown eyes, flecked with gold. They matched her delicate nose-ring, and the three studs in her left ear. She was indeed scowling, under a generous crop of violet-tinted dark hair. 'Come on, rookie. The suspense is eating us alive,' she said, blowing a stray curl from her eye. 'Who are you, and why do you smell like a bonfire?'

'Let her sit up first, Val!' Val was tugged backwards, both girls tumbling off the bed in a scuffle. Pippin, now roused from his slumber, wriggled out from under the covers to bark at them.

Sera groaned as she sat up, her body adjusting to every new ache. For a heartbeat, she forgot where she was. Then the horrors of yesterday came flooding back. The burning farmhouse. Mama's body on the kitchen floor, her ash-grey hand flung out towards the front garden, as though to warn Sera to flee. To run and hide in the only place that could protect her now.

On Madame Mercure's orders, the manservant Vincent had shown her to a room on the fifth floor. It was just big enough for a single bed and a narrow dresser, with a woven rug on the bare boards and a mirror hanging on the wall. She had been so exhausted, she collapsed straight into bed, tucking Pippin close as they both drifted off.

She realized now she was still wearing her boots.

She kicked them off. They landed with a clatter, shaking ash and dirt across the rug. Bibi and Val were back on their feet. The red-haired girl – Bibi – was a few inches shorter than Val, her freckled face round and friendly. They glanced at the discarded boots, then back at Sera, still waiting for her to explain herself.

She cleared her throat. 'Uh, hi. I'm Sera. I came last night.'

'Boring,' said Val, rolling her hand. 'We've already figured that part out.'

'Madame Mercure stuck you up here and really thought we wouldn't notice you. But Vincent's far too much of a gossip to keep you a secret.' Bibi chuckled, smoothing her pristine floral dress as she perched on the end of the bed. She beamed at Pippin. 'He forgot to mention this little treasure, though.'

'Mutts aren't welcome in House Armand,' muttered Val, her eyes softening as she begrudgingly scratched Pippin under the chin.

'Val's just cranky because she's been trying to get a dog for ages,' said Bibi. 'I keep telling her to steal one from the shelter.'

'I'd just end up stealing all of them,' sighed Val.

'Go on, Sera,' prompted Bibi. 'We're on tenterhooks. We don't usually receive initiates so late at night. And they're rarely as . . .' Her gaze lingered on the burnt ends of Sera's hair. 'Uh, crisp?'

Sera smiled a little. Bibi's kindness was like a salve. Despite her guardedness, it made Sera want to confide in her. The trouble was, she didn't know where to begin. Not with the truth of what had happened to her mother. Or that she had been marked by Gaspard Dufort.

She ignored the chill that skittered down her spine, and said simply, 'I lost my mother yesterday. We only ever had each other. I had nowhere else to go.'

Bibi's face fell. 'So, you're an orphan, too?'

Sera flinched, the word pricking her like a pin.

'Sorry. I just meant . . .' Bibi blushed violently. 'Well, I'm an orphan. I joined House Armand six years ago, on my eleventh birthday. Madame Mercure caught me trying to pickpocket her outside the Marlowe and said I had real promise. It was the most perfect twist of fate. As if Saint Oriel herself had planned it.'

Sera raised her eyebrows. After the summer spent breaking in her horse Scout and nearly breaking all her limbs in the process as well, she'd always considered herself to be brave – daring even. But she'd sooner gnaw her hand off than try to pickpocket the most famous Cloak in Fantome.

'I've been here since I was a baby,' said Val. 'House Armand is all I've ever known.'

Bibi dropped her voice. 'Some say Val was born wearing a tiny cloak.'

Val rolled her eyes. 'You know I *hate* that joke.'

'Who says it's a joke?'

'Madame Mercure says I have to pass a test before I can stay,' said Sera, sweeping the hair from her face, and seeing ash come away on her fingers. She hastily wiped it on her trousers, hoping the girls hadn't noticed. 'I don't know how good a thief I'll be. I've never stolen anything before.'

'So, you'll learn,' said Val, with a shrug. 'Just like the rest of us did.'

Bibi was nodding. 'Mercure wouldn't have let you through the door if she didn't see potential in you.'

'That was all Pippin,' said Sera, sure Madame Mercure knew a tracker when she saw one. 'If he hadn't found this place, we would have been sleeping on the street.'

Or dead, she thought grimly, picturing those menacing quicksilver eyes. Her jaw tightened. Mama hadn't just died yesterday. She had been murdered. And for some sick reason, the Daggers had decided to make a spectacle of it. Beneath the fresh horror of her grief, rage was prickling. *Burning.* She counted her breaths, trying to quell the sudden, rabid urge to ransack the little room, to rip the mirror from the wall and pull every singed hair from her head, screaming until her voice went raw. Until Gaspard Dufort heard her all the way across the Verne.

Evil, hateful bastard.

You will pay for what you did.

'Huh,' said Val, who had been silently observing her. 'You suddenly look . . . ravenous.'

'*Saints*, you must be starving!' said Bibi, hopping to her feet. 'When was the last time you ate?'

Sera frowned. She didn't feel hungry, but now that she thought about it, she couldn't remember her last meal. Poor Pippin must be starving.

'I could eat,' she admitted.

'But first, you should bathe,' said Val, a little awkwardly. 'You don't want to put the other Cloaks off their food.'

'Val's right,' said Bibi, snooping in Sera's dresser only to find that there wasn't a stitch of clothing in there. 'You only get one chance to make a good impression. Take it from someone who tried to rob Madame Mercure.'

'That's true,' said Sera, still unsure as to whether, at House Armand, an attempted robbery created a good impression or a poor one. She rolled out of bed.

Val took one look at her filthy outfit and grimaced. 'I'll get you something to wear before your stipend comes through. Lucky for you, I have impeccable taste.'

'Thanks, Val.' Sera was glad when they both swept out of her room, so they couldn't see her eyes water at their kindness. She was a mess, filthy and bedraggled. Her heart was shredded to ruins, but it was still beating. She was still standing. Somehow.

She reached for her anger, anchoring herself to her fury, rather than her pain. She went to the window to peer out at the wakening Hollows. The dreary taverns were slowly yawning to life, the brothels going to sleep, the cracked streets thrumming with the forgotten folk of Fantome rising to sell their wares in the grey morning haze.

There was no sign of the Dagger. Morning had blanched the shadows from the Hollows and sent him scuttling back to Hugo's Passage, no doubt to lick Gaspard Dufort's boots and claim his reward. The man who had ordered Mama's death, and the burning of her house for good measure. It wasn't enough to turn on Sylvie – no. Dufort wanted to destroy her too.

Gutless wretch.

Sera would get back on her feet here. She would play

Madame Mercure's game, gather some savings and her wits, and before she turned her back on Shade and the underworld and all the strife it had brought into her life for good, she would find a way to make Dufort pay for what he had done to Mama.

A fatal parting shot from Sylvie Marchant. It was exactly what he deserved.

Pippin whined, startling Sera from her spiralling thoughts of revenge, and reminding her that they were both in need of a good scrub and a hot meal.

'Priorities, priorities,' she muttered, scooping him up.

The bathroom on the fifth storey of House Armand was almost as grand as its kitchen. The floors were white marble, the clawfoot tub so big that Sera could lie down inside it without touching the rim. The shelves were lined with expensive soaps and heady perfumes, the shampoo so fragrant she left the lather on for ten minutes. She scrubbed her face three times to get rid of every last particle of soot and smoke. She found a small pair of scissors in a cupboard under the mirror and used them to cut off the burnt ends of her hair, until it was only long enough to reach her chest.

She braided the pale strands away from her face as she stared at herself in the mirror. Her tanned cheeks were wan, darkening the scatter of freckles along the bridge of her nose. Her blue eyes were wide and intense. The fleck of bronze in her left iris was the only feature she had inherited from her mother. That, and her temper.

After she had scrubbed herself clean, Sera washed Pippin. He wriggled and squalled the entire time, so loudly that every Cloak within earshot would probably think he was being murdered. 'Such a drama king,' Sera chided, as she trimmed his tail and the scruff around his face, until she could see his beady eyes again.

Back in her room, she rifled through the clothes Val had left on her bed. She had multiple options, each outfit as beautiful as the next. It sure as hell paid to be a thief. And probably twice as much to be a Dagger. Sera tried not to wonder about the price on Mama's head. Was she worth more than Val's gold-trimmed leather boots? Less than her fox-fur stole?

Sera chose a pair of fitted black trousers that tapered at her ankles, flat black boots and a high-necked knitted cream sweater that made her feel like the wife of a rich merchant sailor. It was a far cry from the practical clothes she wore out in the plains: pale, loose-fitting shirts to keep off the heat of the sun in the cornfields, leathers to ride Scout bareback, her boots always laced high enough to protect her trousers from the mulch in the vineyards. But her rough look never bothered Sera. Lorenzo – her childhood best friend who had recently become something more – always told her she looked beautiful, no matter what she wore – or didn't wear – and judging by the way he pressed his body against hers out behind the barn, his gaze molten with desire, Sera thought it must be true.

Steeling herself, she followed the sound of morning chatter down to the dining hall, which was located on the second floor of House Armand. It had all the grandeur of a ballroom, with dark herringbone floors and corniced ceilings. The walls were adorned with gold-leaf wallpaper and hung with some of the most exquisite landscapes Sera had ever seen. The dining chairs were cushioned with velvet, while every table bore a large silver tray of fresh pastries, pitchers of orange and grape juice, heaped plates of bacon, sausages and fried eggs, as well as a steaming pot of coffee.

Yes, yes, yes.

The Cloaks knew how to eat. And steal. Every inch of House Armand dripped with opulence. At one end of the huge dining room, a row of bay windows looked over the back garden. In the morning light, Sera could see that the lawn was beautifully manicured, and bordered by magnificent oak trees. An old woman was sitting alone by the window. Sera recognized her scowling, wrinkled face from the previous night and with fresh ire, recalled the croak of her '*No!*' as she slammed the door in her face.

She glared at Sera now, through the cloud of smoke that billowed from the pipe in her hand.

Sera fought the urge to offer her a choice finger. Mama had always warned her to respect her elders. Even the tyrants. Sera turned away from the old woman, scanning the other faces in the room. There were forty or so Cloaks down here. Most of them looked around her age, but a handful were older, closer to Mama's age, and there were a pair of twin boys who looked around twelve or so. Most sat in pairs or small groups, chatting among themselves. Some flicked their gazes towards Sera when she entered but if they were surprised by her presence, they didn't show it.

Evidently, new recruits were not uncommon at House Armand. And yet, judging by the row of unoccupied bedrooms on the fifth floor, turnover must be high. Sera supposed that not everyone was cut out to be a Cloak, to live a life of subterfuge and suspicion, but as she inhaled the smell of warm bacon and freshly ground coffee, she figured there were worse things to sell your soul for.

'Sera! Over here!' Bibi waved a half-eaten sausage from her table across the room, where she and Val were in the middle of breakfast. 'Sit with us!'

Sera hurried over, tucking Pippin under the table. She slipped him a strip of bacon while the old woman continued giving her a menacing glare.

'Who is that?' Sera asked, in a low voice.

'Don't mind Madame Fontaine,' said Val, with a dismissive wave of her hand. 'The old fossil hardly ever gets out any more.'

'She slammed the door in my face last night,' said Sera.

Val snorted. 'Sounds about right. When I was nine, I nicked a peppermint from her pocket and she pushed me down the stairs with her walking stick.'

'That's . . . unhinged,' said Sera.

'Yeah,' said Val, admiringly.

'One time, when I was practising piano in the music room, Madame Fontaine came in and cut six inches off the end of my hair because I was playing an *arrogant sonata*,' said Bibi, mimicking the croak of her voice. 'She said it had too much staccato.'

Sera's eyes widened. 'Did you tell Madame Mercure?'

'No point,' said Val. 'Fontaine is part of the furniture here.'

'She used to run House Armand until she got too old and started losing her sight,' said Bibi. 'She was some Cloak, though. Rumour says the last King of Valterre once hired her to rob the Queen of Urnica.'

'What did she steal?' said Sera.

Val dropped her voice. 'The queen's first-born son.'

Sera choked on her bacon.

The other two burst into laughter.

'Val's just teasing,' said Bibi. Then she mimed sewing her mouth shut. 'Patron confidentiality. No one knows for sure what she stole. Only that the king paid so handsomely for it, House Armand was able to build a new wing. She was damn good in her day. Probably because she's favoured by Saint Oriel.'

Sera's brows rose. 'What do you mean?'

'They say Fontaine is a distant descendant of Oriel Beauregard. That sometimes she whispers to Fontaine in her dreams and speaks to her through her tarot cards. That's how she always knows so much.'

Val snorted into her coffee. 'If you ask me, Fontaine's just a nosy old bat with too much time on her hands.'

'Maybe she's both,' said Bibi.

Sera sneaked another glance at the old woman, who was now glaring at a crow in the garden. 'This place is different than I imagined.'

'Did you think we'd all be wearing our cloaks to breakfast?' said Val. 'And pickpocketing each other in the halls?'

'Well . . . yeah.'

They laughed again.

'We don't wear Shade when we're not working,' Bibi explained. 'After a while, it gives you a headache. We always make sure to remove our cloaks, gloves, boots and scarves, and leave them in the cloakroom when we come back from a job. It's the only room in House Armand that's locked.'

'How come?' said Sera.

'Because that's where the Shade is kept. And Shade leads to temptation,' said Val. 'All it takes is one taste for a Cloak to go rogue. And who knows what they might do, then?'

'Or who they might kill,' said Bibi, in a low voice. 'Not long after I first came to House Armand, there was an . . . incident. A couple of Cloaks stole a vial of Shade from the cloakroom and swallowed it, just to try it. It was too much, too soon. One of them – Phillipe – lost his senses. He tried to murder Madame Mercure.'

'*Saints*,' muttered Sera. 'What happened?'

'It took nine Cloaks to stop him,' said Val. 'But in the scuffle, Phillipe managed to grab one by the neck, killing him almost instantly. Once the Shade wore off, Madame Mercure revoked his Cloak and called the dayguards. He's been rotting in the king's prison ever since.'

Sera wrinkled her nose. 'But the Daggers can kill as often as they like.'

'The Daggers have their own agreement with the King of Valterre,' said Bibi. 'They have his coin and his ear. And besides, in Fantome, murder is only murder if you get caught.'

'Lucky for some.' Val's voice dripped with sarcasm. 'Dufort's been on a damn spree lately.' She jerked her chin towards a nearby table, where a slender bald man with thick spectacles was cutting up his fried egg. 'Griffin says the Daggers cleared out a whole sailing ship that docked in the harbour the other night. Took the bodies, left the boat. The traders are calling it a ghost ship.'

Sera had to work to keep her voice even. 'Why would Dufort do that?'

A shrug. 'Maybe he's finally lost his senses. All that Shade has eaten through his brain.'

'He probably chucked them overboard,' said Bibi, pushing her food away. 'Nothing worse than a watery grave.'

Sera could think of something worse. A burning house. A burning life. What the hell was Dufort up to? And had Mama had something to do with it?

Her thoughts twisted back to Shade. She imagined all those vials of black powder in the cloakroom, just waiting to be used. Sera had been around Shade all her life but she had never longed for the taste of it. She had never wanted anyone dead, never wanted to let Mama down. But now ...

Now ...

Sitting here, in the grey morning mist, with Dufort on a rampage and without Mama at her side, Sera wondered what she could do if she got her hands on a vial. Took just enough Shade to drown out her pain, to feel strength instead of fear. For the first time in her life, she understood the lure of that black powder.

After all, to swallow Shade was to become a reaper. And everyone feared the Reaper. If she was clever, careful, she could find the Dagger who had killed Mama and give him a taste of his own medicine. Or maybe she would follow him back to the catacombs, to face the snake that was devouring Fantome: Gaspard Dufort himself.

'Where did you say you came from?' Val's question jolted Sera from her thoughts.

'I didn't,' she replied, reaching for her cup of coffee and weaving a quick half-truth. 'I lived out in the plains. My mother had a vineyard there. Small and seasonal, but it paid the rent.'

'A farm girl. Hmm. We've had a few of those pass through here. Weak nerves. Soft hearts.'

Not mine. Not any more. Sera slipped another piece of bacon under the table, avoiding Val's probing glare.

'That's a pretty necklace.' Bibi traced the golden tear at her throat. 'What kind of gemstone is that?'

'I don't know.' Sera closed her fingers around it on instinct. 'It was a gift.'

Val laughed, brashly. 'She's not going to steal it.'

Sera loosened her grip. 'Sorry, Bibi ... It's just ... I don't know what you look like when you steal.'

'Well, here's a hint,' drawled Val. 'You wouldn't see us do it. I could nick your dog right now if I felt like it.'

Sera looked her over. 'Where would you even put him?'

A flash of pearly teeth. 'Trade secret.'

Bibi shot her a warning look. 'Val's just joking. And anyway, Cloaks never steal from each other. It's part of our code. We don't even lock our bedroom doors.'

'Right,' muttered Sera. 'Just the cloakroom.'

Bibi reached for the coffee pot, before refilling their cups. 'Val and I are doing Sleights this Sunday if you want to come along. We'd be happy to show you the ropes, help you prepare for Mercure's first assignment.'

'What's a Sleight?' said Sera, looking between them.

'A small theft. Pockets, mostly. A jam jar, here and there.

Chocolates. Perfume. Whatever we fancy,' said Bibi. 'They keep our fingers nimble in between Breaks and Heists. The jobs we undertake for our patrons.'

'Breaks typically involve houses, shops, taverns,' Val went on, and Sera got the sense she should be taking notes. 'Heists are the big ones. We're talking museums and manors, the palatial homes of some of the richest families in Valterre. They usually require a team of three or more, depending on what's at stake. Precious artwork, antique furniture. And don't get me started on sculptures.'

Sera was reminded of the giant marble statue of a naked man on the fifth-floor landing.

'It's coin, mostly. Sometimes jewellery.' Bibi grinned. 'Once, Val nearly broke her leg stealing a pouch of pebbles she swore were diamonds.'

'I was thirteen. And clearly an idiot.' Val turned to Sera. 'Last year, Bibi stole a dead ferret for a patron because she thought it was a mink stole. When she presented it to Madame Mercure, she nearly got her cloak revoked.'

Bibi scowled at her. 'You have to stop bringing that up.'

'What about the king?' said Sera, thinking of the palace that sat at the mouth of the Verne, where King Bertrand and Queen Odette often summered with their children. There must be enough riches in that place to launch a fleet of ships to Urnica, and it wasn't like the royal family, who had a hundred homes across Valterre, would even miss half of them. 'Do you ever take from—'

'*Never.*' Val regarded Sera as though she had suddenly sprouted horns. 'The Cloaks can steal on his behalf, but never *from* him. It's an accord that goes right back to the time of Armand Versini himself. To dare steal from the King of Valterre would attract an entirely different kind of trouble.'

'What about the city guards? Don't you ever worry about getting caught?'

'They can't arrest what they can't see,' said Bibi, smugly.

'And any nightguard foolish enough to try and catch a Dagger in the throes of Shade might as well fling themselves in the Verne and be done with it,' said Val.

Sera took another generous sip of coffee, if only to hide the revulsion on her face.

Val watched her drink. 'So, your mother died. What about your father?'

'I don't know him,' said Sera, her chest tight. It was easier than saying his infrequent visits over the years were like thunderstorms, that he often arrived in a fury that sent her hiding under her bed. She hadn't spoken to him since her thirteenth birthday, when he had stomped in through the back door and caught Mama by the throat. She had clawed his face bloody to get free before Sera chased him from the house with a rake, swinging with such wild abandon that she decapitated three shrubs.

They should have run that day. They should have run and never looked back.

Val let the matter rest, returning to her breakfast, while Bibi bent down to feed Pippin under the table. Sera let her gaze wander, taking in the rest of the dining hall. At the other end of the room, an oil painting of Armand Versini, the founder of the Order of Cloaks, hung above a stately fireplace. He was wearing a leather eye mask, the same style and shape as the symbol Madame Mercure kept on her key chain. A constant reminder of the importance of her role.

The menacing mask had marked the first in Armand's experiments with disguise, but the painting suggested it had done little to hide his good looks. He had suntanned skin, thick black hair and a finely trimmed moustache. His brown eyes were strangely soft, and his lips were quirked, betraying the barest hint of mischief.

Underneath, engraved into a gold plaque, was the motto upon which the Order of Cloaks was founded:

Take only what your cloak can carry, and your conscience can bear.

Sera wondered whether a portrait of Armand's brother, Hugo, hung somewhere in the catacombs, and if the air down there smelled like the rotting skulls he had buried in the walls.

'Please don't tell me you're drooling over Armand Versini,' scolded Val, waggling her butter knife in remonstration. 'Don't they have handsome men out in the plains?'

As though she had conjured one up with her question, the door to the dining hall swung open and a man stalked in, walking with the kind of lazy confidence Sera had only ever read about in books. He was tall and lithe, dressed in dark trousers and a loose blue shirt. His skin was golden tan, and his silver hair was slicked back, revealing a straight nose and strong cheekbones. His lips twitched, as though he was on the verge of smiling and his eyes were a perfect turquoise, like the south sea of Valterre.

When they met Sera's, her breath hitched.

Bibi and Val groaned in unison.

'Why do they *always* swoon?' said Bibi.

'I knew he'd come,' said Val. 'It's like he could smell her.'

'Who is that?' said Sera, tearing her gaze away.

'That's Theo,' said Val, rolling her eyes. 'And if you're wondering whether he's a good kisser, the answer is obviously yes.'

'I wasn't,' said Sera hotly.

Val smirked. 'Whatever you say, farmgirl.'

'Theo's the Shadowsmith at House Armand,' said Bibi. 'He might be a bit of a flirt, but he's a skilled artificer. He's the one who turns Shade into things we can use. Clothing. Footwear. Weapons.'

Sera stole another glance over her shoulder. Theo was now sitting with Griffin two tables over, but he was facing her. His smile was dazzlingly bright, but it wasn't directed at Sera. He was grinning at Pippin, who had peeked out from under the table to see what all the fuss was about.

'So, he's the one in charge of the Shade?' said Sera.

'Yeah,' they chorused.

She thought again of those glimmering black vials. Of what she might do with one after all this time. When Theo met her gaze again, she smiled, just a little.

Chapter 5

Seraphine

On a Sunday morning, come rain, hail or shine, the Rascalle was the busiest marketplace in Fantome. It welcomed all kinds of traders: jewellers and bakers, cobblers and hatmakers, weavers and millers, fishmongers and blacksmiths, and farmers who came all the way from the plains to sell their wares and make good coin. Nestled down by the harbour, the market looked out over the sea. When the tide was high, the wind cast the scent of seaweed and brine across the square, which added a questionable tang to the pastries.

When Sera arrived at the Rascalle, arm in arm with Bibi and Val, and with Pippin scurrying at her heels, the marketplace was so noisy she could hardly hear herself think. This was probably a good thing, because she was already having second thoughts about coming. Five days had passed since her arrival at House Armand, and though the Cloaks had been more than welcoming, without Mama she felt like an unmoored vessel, lost at sea.

Even so, she had tried to use the days wisely, learning her way around the grand mansion like an explorer charting a new continent. She introduced herself to as many Cloaks as she could find, exchanging polite greetings in the halls and idle chit-chat in the common rooms. She even spent a morning with Blanche, the old custodian of the house library, who recommended to Sera so many of her favourite novels that by the time she was leaving, she had to crane her neck to see over the stack in her arms.

She had met Rupert and Bianca, the husband-and-wife team who ran the kitchens with expert precision, and Alaina, the temperamental pastry chef who somehow always managed to look beautiful – and vaguely furious – while covered in flour. On Sera's third night, after a couple of glasses of wine, Bibi had confessed to her secret undying love for Alaina, only to staunchly deny the crush the following morning.

Sera noticed their lingering glances over breakfast, exchanging a knowing smirk with Val. In the afternoons, she walked in the gardens with Pippin, letting the mutt sniff out his own map of their new home. She was always nervous outside, even on the grounds of House Armand. She might have stopped running from the Daggers but she was still hiding from them.

Today's outing to the Rascalle made Sera feel like she was walking a tightrope over a ravine, but she knew if she wanted the protection of the Order of Cloaks, she had to start acting like one. Even if the idea of stealing mildly horrified her.

'Take a breath, rookie,' said Val, clapping her on the shoulder. 'You're as stiff as a board.'

Sera blew out a breath. 'I'm trying to look confident.'

'Great work, thespian.' Val's voice rippled with sarcasm. 'Try unclenching your jaw.'

'You don't have to steal anything today,' Bibi reminded her. 'Just watch and learn. Sleights are fun. You'll see.'

It was not so much the Sleights as her imminent death that worried Sera now. She wasn't expecting to see a Dagger perusing the Rascalle in the middle of the day but after what had happened to Mama, she couldn't be too careful.

Still, the likelihood was low. The square was too bright. Too busy. And there were dayguards milling about, conspicuous in their cornflower-blue uniforms trimmed in gold, wide-brimmed black helmets and tall black boots, the royal insignia of Valterre proudly emblazoned on their chests and on the hilt of their longswords.

They came to the edge of the marketplace, which was overlooked by a bronze statue of Saint Oriel of Destiny – a tall, beautiful woman in a veil, measuring a spool of thread to cut. Oriel had died over a thousand years ago, but during her life she had sat at the right hand of kings and queens, looking far beyond the stone walls of their grand palaces, into the future. Warning them of unseen dangers, of wars brewing like storm clouds on the horizon, alliances that might crumble, others that could be found across the sea, and heirs, both worthy and troublesome, yet to come.

Legend said if you stood by her statue and curled your finger around the bronze thread, the strands of a great destiny would find you and whisk you far from Fantome. Sera had done so many times as a child, often standing on Mama's knee to reach the thread, but whenever she pictured the sprawling landscape of their future in her mind, she had never imagined herself alone in it.

There was a ring of children around Saint Oriel now, all clamouring for that bronze thread. Sera wanted to tell them not to bother. Oriel was long dead, and their destiny was their own to muddle out. There were smart decisions and poor decisions. Luck, good and bad. And then there were depraved murderers like Gaspard Dufort, waiting in the wings to destroy your entire life.

The three Cloaks meandered through the milling crowd. There were at least fifty stalls here, and ten times as many people. Bibi and Val hadn't bothered to don their special cloaks, even though the magic-imbued material would make it easier to flit in and out of shadows and hide in plain sight. Instead, they were dressed entirely as themselves, a pair of wide-eyed innocents who had come down to the marketplace for a cream bun and a nose around.

They wandered down the sloping cobblestones, following the curve of the harbour, where the air was dusted with the scent of cinnamon sugar.

Val turned on Sera. 'What do you fancy, farmgirl? A charm bracelet? A silk scarf? Rookie's choice.'

'I doubt I'll have much use for a silk scarf.' Idly, Sera imagined strangling Mama's killer with it. 'But thanks anyway.' She looked for Pippin, and spotted him sniffing around a stall of fresh mackerel. 'I'd better grab Pip before he blows your cover,' she said, hurrying away from the girls. 'Good luck!'

By the time she had jostled her way to Pippin, he had surrendered his interest in the mackerel and was sniffing the boots of a stern-faced dayguard. 'Pardon me!' said Sera, swooping down to grab him. He yipped and wriggled in her grasp. 'You little troublemaker,' she hissed, ferrying him away. 'Can't you at least try and behave yourself?'

Pippin cocked his head, as if to say, *Define 'behave'.*

The mutt had a point. They had come here with a pair of thieves. Sera caught a glimpse of Val, giggling with a trader of fine gold jewellery. She leaned in, pointing to the furthest necklace with her right hand, while her left hand snatched a ring from the front of the stall, slipping it into the pocket of her coat. As the man turned to show Val the necklace, her fingers darted around, rearranging the other boxes to completely hide the empty space.

A few moments later, Val sauntered away, grinning from ear to ear.

Sera spun around, tracking the dayguards, but none of them seemed to have noticed anything. She moved on and found Bibi perusing a stall of trinkets at the other end of the marketplace. She was leaning over the wooden bench, as if to take a closer look at something, her long red hair making a perfect curtain to hide her free hand. A heartbeat later, the Sleight was over.

They made it look so easy.

Sera paced the edge of the marketplace, searching for a quiet spot amid the fray. There were people everywhere, children wandering about with funnel cakes and ice-cream cones.

Traders shouted over each other as they haggled, while street musicians jangled copper-filled caps, hoping for silvers.

Pippin wriggled himself upside down in protest until she relented and set him back on his feet. She wrung her hands, not sure what to do with them. Val winked at her from the middle of the square. She was eating a caramel apple, and wearing a black hat with a feather in it. Bibi was perusing a stall near the entryway, the pockets of her plum coat bulging.

Remembering not to gawk, Sera turned to face the harbour, feigning interest in the nearest boat. It had a sleek wooden hull and white sails rolled at the mast. *Mariner's Dream.*

Noticing the line of her attention, an old man in a flat cap sidled over. 'More like *Mariner's Nightmare,*' he grunted. 'I wouldn't get too close, girl. The whole ruddy crew upped and disappeared. Thirty-odd sailors and not a trace to be found.' He blew a smoke ring from his tobacco pipe, quickly chasing it with another. 'Something stinks.'

Sera raised her eyebrows. This must be the ship Val mentioned the other morning. But thirty sailors ... thirty marks in one night. Even for the Daggers, the number was obscene. 'What was the vessel trading?'

'Spices from the south. Every barrel left untouched.'

Sera frowned. Nothing taken. No bodies left behind. It didn't make any sense. 'Maybe the crew made a pact,' she murmured. 'Maybe they hated their patron or their captain, or the long, gruelling hours at sea and decided to hell with it all ... '

The man snorted. 'Ignorant little kelpie. The captain disappeared along with them. And that pretty little fairy tale don't explain all the other disappearances, does it?'

Sera's cheeks prickled. Just what the hell was Dufort up to?

'Well, what's *your* clever theory, then?' she asked, with too much bite.

The old man blew another ring. 'Badness is growing. There's a wrongness in the wind. In the water.'

Sera hated those words, and the shiver they chased down her spine. 'That's not a theory.'

'It's a feeling,' he said, wandering away. 'Just a feeling.'

Swallow it, she wanted to call after him. She barely had the space to contemplate what had happened to Mama, without adding these strange happenings at the harbour.

She turned and walked along the shop fronts, to where the crowd was at its thinnest. She lingered outside the Rose and Crown, a bustling tavern already brimming with red-cheeked revellers, and wondered if she should pilfer something, too. What if this was all a test? Madame Mercure had warned Sera that she would summon her soon for her first job, but there had been no sign or word from the Head Cloak since that first night. What if Mercure had told the girls to take Sera down to the Rascalle today to test her nerve?

What if *this* was the job? Or some sort of secret initiation rite?

Her mind reeled, a new panic setting in. Maybe she should take a peach from one of the fruit stalls. She winced at the thought. She had grown up around these farmers, probably run through their fields as a child. One cold wet spring when Sera was little and coin was scarce, she'd swiped a turnip from Farmer Perrin. By the time she got home she was crying so hard, she couldn't speak. Mama spotted the turnip and walked her all the way back to Perrin's farm to apologize. The following morning, Perrin's wife came by with a fresh pot of turnip soup, and a sack of potatoes for the pantry. Mama had cried then, too.

Sera saw no point whatsoever in stealing from good, honest people. Snatching a handful of peppermints or a jar of spice was not going to get her any closer to her goal of justice for Mama. Of freedom for herself. This was not the right way to take revenge. And yet, she feared if she didn't do it, Madame Mercure would revoke her stipend and turn her out on the streets of the Hollows, to rot in the underbelly of Fantome.

Sera sighed, laying her forehead against the foggy window. She suddenly felt exhausted. Despite the high noon sun, the tavern was draped in shadows, the dimness feathered by candles flickering from each table. An idea bloomed in her mind.

She could swipe a candle easily enough. Trail her fingers along the table, and fold it into her coat before anyone noticed. Would anyone even care? It was hardly a silk scarf, but surely a candle would count for something.

It was a notice of intent, a commitment to the life Mercure had offered her, at least for a little while. She swept the stray hairs from her face and squared her shoulders, examining the determined glint of her gaze in the glass.

Something caught her eye. An odd shape reflected behind her. Not in the marketplace, but higher up, and further back. There was someone standing on top of the sweetshop across the square. She watched them sink into a crouch, and then go perfectly still, like a statue.

Adrenaline flooded her. She spun round, frantically scanning the rooftop, but the figure was gone, leaving the brown-and-white awning of Florian's Emporium rippling in the breeze.

You're seeing things. But Pippin was growling between her legs. Had he seen it too? Or was it the street magician prancing about on stilts that had spooked him?

Forget the stupid candle. She was getting the hell out of here. She scooped Pippin up and made her way back through the square. The crowd thickened, hemming her in. Overhead, seagulls screeched, looking for scraps. Sera kept her head down, weaving her way through a mass of bony elbows and broad shoulders, children playing hide-and-seek and yipping dogs with curly white faces, until at last she reached the entrance to the Rascalle.

She heaved a sigh, setting Pippin down again.

A nearby squeal sent Sera's heart leaping into her throat. Bibi barrelled into her, pressing a wet kiss to her cheek. When she pulled back, her eyes were wild and bright. 'Don't you just *love* the Rascalle?'

'Clearly not as much as you two,' said Sera, noting Val's arrival in her brand-new hat. 'I can't believe you're just ... *wearing* that.'

Val twirled the feather. 'The best thieves hide in plain sight.'

'I wouldn't know,' said Sera awkwardly. 'I didn't get a chance to take anything. Sorry.'

'Don't be sorry. It's only your first week,' said Bibi, linking arms with her. 'And you're not even a proper Cloak yet. Did you think this was some kind of test?'

'Honestly? Yes.'

Both girls collapsed into laughter.

'I've got a better test for you,' said Val, removing a glass vial from her sleeve. She held it up, showing off the iridescent black powder. 'Why don't you try some of this?'

Bibi gasped. 'Where on earth did you find Shade?'

Sera stared at the powder as Val removed the cork stopper and tipped it down her throat.

'DON'T!' screeched Bibi, sending a nearby flock of seagulls flapping into the sky.

Val grinned as she swallowed, revealing two neat rows of blackened teeth.

'SPIT IT OUT!' Bibi lunged at her friend, but Sera caught her by the waist.

'It's all right, Bibi. It's not real. It's not Shade.'

Bibi's breath punched out of her. 'Wh-what?'

'Shade doesn't sparkle like that,' said Sera, quickly. 'Think about it. There's no light in shadow. If there was it wouldn't work. There'd be no magic at all. It doesn't stain either, not if it's prepared correctly. And see—' She gestured to the label on the bottle in Val's hand, which read *Florian's Emporium*. 'It's sherbet.'

Val glared at Sera, as she licked her teeth. 'Thanks for ruining my fun.'

Bibi pressed a hand to her heart, a relieved giggle seeping from her. 'Val, you heartless ghoul.'

Val tossed the vial aside. 'Waste of a Sleight.'

'Sorry,' said Sera, even though she wasn't. Shade was nothing to joke about, and neither were the marks it left behind, whorls of black that burrowed through your skin and bone and blood, lacing your very marrow with poison. It was a killing thing, Shade. One way or another, every Dagger succumbed to it eventually. If that really had been a vial, Sera would have snatched it from Val and shattered it at her feet. Shade was no joke. It had to be worth it – that taste. That power. It had to mean something.

Val was still glaring at her. 'You seem to know a lot about the properties of Shade for a simple farmgirl.'

Sera smiled, thinly. 'Who said anything about simple?'

There was a strained silence.

Bibi broke it by taking a small wooden box from her pocket. 'I got you something, Sera. I thought it might cheer you up.'

Sera had no interest in stolen gifts, but she didn't want to disappoint Bibi, so she took the box and opened it, expecting to find a ring or a pair of earrings. Instead, she was met with a familiar melody. It was a music box, with a tiny ballerina twirling inside.

Sera's eyes misted over. '"The Dancing Swan",' she murmured. 'My mother used to sing this to me when I was a little girl.'

'Oh no.' Bibi grimaced at the sight of Sera's tears. She took the box and snapped it shut. 'It wasn't supposed to make you cry!'

'Told you, you should have gone for brandy,' said Val, clucking her tongue.

'No, Bibi, I love it. Really,' said Sera, reaching for the box. 'Whenever I play it, I'll think of Mama. I don't ever want to forget her.'

'You won't forget her,' said Bibi, with such quiet sureness, Sera's heart ached for her too. 'Not for as long as you live.'

Sera squeezed her hand, then slipped the music box into her pocket. It occurred to her in that moment that perhaps she was not so averse to stealing after all.

'Now that we've had our fill of heart-warming thievery, why don't we stop by Marveline's Boutique on the way home?' suggested Val, as they wandered away from the marketplace. 'Let's fill up your wardrobe so I can start raiding it.'

'I suppose that's only fair,' said Sera, who, having received her stipend from Vincent that very morning, was more than eager to spend it on her own clothes.

She slowed to let Pippin catch up with her, and then realized he was missing. A quick glance over her shoulder revealed the little mutt was down by the statue of Saint Oriel, hunting for scraps.

Sera sighed. 'You two go ahead. I'll catch up.'

She hurried down the hill.

Pippin looked up at the sound of her approach, revealing a sardine hanging from his mouth.

'Clever wagtail,' said Sera, bending down to pick him up. 'I can't believe you're a better Cloak than me.' She was so busy scolding Pippin that she didn't notice the music box slipping from her pocket. She was already three steps away when she heard the soft trill of music behind her.

She spun around and nearly crashed nose-first into a broad chest.

'I think you dropped this,' said a low voice.

She looked up, past that broad chest and strong, stubbled chin, to a generous sweep of black hair and eyes the colour of autumn leaves, flickering somewhere between green and gold.

She didn't know if it was the lilting lullaby, the sheer towering height of this stranger or the way those autumn eyes were looking at her, but she felt suddenly dazed.

'Why did the swan dance?' he said, soft enough for her alone.

She blinked. 'What?'

'Your lullaby.' He offered an awkward half-smile. 'I think it's called "The Dancing Swan".'

'Oh. Yeah.' She stumbled backwards, the statue of Saint Oriel filling up the space between them as she shook herself from her stupor. Too late, of course. She had already made a prize fool of herself, ogling him like an oil painting. What was it about Fantome, and its distractingly handsome men? 'Because it was trying to fly.'

'*Ah*,' he said, as if she had answered some great confounding riddle. He stepped towards her, until she had to tilt her chin to look up at him again. 'And did it?'

'I don't know,' she said, as she took the box from him. She closed it, extinguishing the music. In the sudden silence, the back of her neck began to prickle. Pippin grew restless in her arms, and it occurred to Sera that they should leave.

'Thank you,' she said, willing her legs to work.

'It was nothing.' He was already turning away from her, stepping back into the swell of the Rascalle, like a ship disappearing in the mist. 'Have a nice day, Seraphine.'

It was only after he disappeared that she wondered how he knew her name.

Chapter 6

Ransom

'**D**ufort wants to see you,' said Nadia, poking her head around the door to Ransom's bedchamber. Her brow was furrowed, the look on her face flitting between concern and curiosity. 'Is everything all right?'

'I suppose I'll find out,' croaked Ransom, as he sat up in bed. A glance at the clock on the wall told him it was late evening. He must have drifted off to sleep. He scrubbed a hand through his hair, and cleared his throat.

Nadia lingered in the doorway, her brown skin glistening in the lamplight. Her sleek black hair was scooped into a high bun, revealing the scythes of her cheekbones and the smudge of kohl underneath her eyes.

'Heading out?' said Ransom, noting her belted tawny coat and high black boots.

She nodded. 'I need a stiff drink. Long week. Scrappy mark.' She had the scrapes on her cheek to prove it. Unusual for Nadia, who was quick on her feet, and even better in the air with shadows to swing from. Her mother had been a dancer in the Hollows, her father some rich wandering rake. If she hadn't been orphaned so early in life, Nadia might have been a dancer too. She might have had a life above the catacombs, a future far beyond the gritty underworld of Fantome.

'Who was it?' said Ransom.

'Some brainless mercenary who had the gall to blackmail the king's cousin.' Nadia never learned the names of her marks, never hesitated at the strike. She never slept afterwards, either. Not unless Lark slipped into her room and sang her to sleep. Ransom always pretended not to hear him, but sound carried a long way in the catacombs and most nights the other Daggers cracked their doors to listen, too.

'I'm meeting Lark and Caruso in a tavern over on Merchant's Way.' She bit her lip, frowning. 'Unless you want me to stay and wait for you . . . ?'

'I'll be fine.' He rolled to his feet and stretched, working out the kink in his neck. He was still wearing the navy cashmere sweater he had worn to the marketplace. It was rumpled now, and sleep had left a sour taste in his mouth. He needed to wash and change. 'Tell Lark to stay out of trouble.'

'Sure. I'll tell the moon not to rise while I'm at it.' Nadia was still frowning. She clearly wanted to stay, to dilute whatever foul humour Dufort was in. Ransom hadn't seen the fearsome Head of the Daggers since he had handed him his mark nearly a week ago.

Without warning, an image of wide blue eyes, framed by long black lashes, flashed through Ransom's head. One eye was half bronze, as though whatever divine being had painted Seraphine Marchant had run out of sky, and had to reach instead, for earth. She looked all the more interesting for it. And he was a fool for admitting it. For noticing it at all.

'Go,' he said to Nadia.

She offered a parting smile for courage.

He turned to the mirror on the wall, tracing the black whorl jutting above the round collar of his sweater. It stung faintly, reminding him of just how deep the mark had burrowed. All the way down to his soul. He was not yet twenty years old and already the shadows were inching up his chest, reaching like thorns for his neck. The marks were jet black against his olive skin, a constant reminder that no matter where he went, he could not outrun the reminders etched across his body.

This is what you are. This is what you will always be.

And one day, the poison in your bones will take you too.

He turned and peeled off his clothes, trying to ignore the desperate hum of his own conscience.

He replayed the afternoon in his head and heard himself say, like a blundering fool, *Why did the swan dance?*

Why the hell did he ask her that?

Why did he say anything at all?

He had been so surprised at coming face to face with her at the Rascalle that he had broken one of Hugo Versini's cardinal rules. *Never talk to the mark.*

Now, the mark had seen his face up close.

And he had seen the blue of her eyes, smelled the

lemon-blossom scent of her skin. Ransom had known it was a mistake, but the second he saw that wooden box slip out of her pocket, he couldn't help himself. He wanted to know what was inside, to see if it might be a clue to Dufort's interest in her, the smuggler's daughter. But it was so much worse than that. A ballerina, dancing to a sad, familiar song. The same one he used to sing to Anouk when their father dragged his temper through their house. The one she had sung back to him the night before they lost each other: 'The Dancing Swan'. It was an antidote to fear. A promise of freedom.

And Seraphine had played it for him under the Saint of Destiny. The only one of the thirteen saints Ransom ever bothered to pray to. Not Calvin, Saint of Death. Or Maud, of Lost Hope. But Oriel, weaver of fate. Oriel, cruel and cunning. What a wicked little game. And yet, in that moment, he had wanted to play it.

So, he let himself speak to the mark. And worse than that, he let her name slip.

If Dufort found out, he'd have Ransom's head on a platter.

He washed and changed in a hurry, running his hands through his damp hair to settle the unruly strands. His bedchamber was small but comfortable. He had everything he needed down here. The stone floor was covered by a fine sheepskin rug, the bed piled with woollen blankets to help stave off the chill that lingered in the catacombs. Oil lamps flickered on the walls, illuminating the framed sketch on his bedside table.

It was a portrait of Mama and Anouk, giggling with their heads pressed together. Ransom had drawn it on Anouk's seventh birthday. It was little more than a child's rough rendering but he had managed to capture the light of their smiles. On long nights, when Shade left behind its terrible gloom, Ransom held the portrait close to his heart and imagined a life where they would be together again, far from the darkness of Fantome and the long shadow of everything he had done since they left. Though he knew the shadows would never truly leave him, not now they were stamped on his body. Every kill a black mark on his skin, a fresh notch on his soul.

He shrugged on his coat before slipping out of his room. His bedchamber was located in the north-west tunnel of the catacombs, a stone's throw from Nadia's and Lark's, as well as those of a handful of other younger Daggers who had been recruited shortly after Ransom joined the Order. Around the time Dufort figured out just how malleable broken children were. What perfect weapons they made.

It was a short walk down the main north passage to the Cavern, the sprawling underhall where the Daggers congregated to eat, drink, and play games. Gamble, if they were feeling lucky. Gamble even if they weren't. Ransom preferred to spend his evenings off above ground, wandering down by the harbour to watch the night ships come in, on a rooftop with Lark or in a tavern somewhere with Nadia and Caruso.

There were other Daggers – older ones – who stayed permanently underground now, only venturing above ground when a new mark required them to. And even then, the coin had to be good. Over time, and after hundreds of vials of Shade, they had come to shun the daylight, the sun burning their faces even in winter, their eyes stinging even on a cloudy afternoon. For some, even the light of the Aurore made their skin itch. And as for summer – it was hotter than hell.

Ransom hated to think of himself becoming like that – afraid of the sunlight, afraid of *living* – but he knew all too well it was a consequence of the path he had chosen. He told himself he would stop before the shadows crawled up his neck, straining to meet the white scar that sliced his bottom lip, but after ten long years, he still couldn't find the will to leave. He didn't know where to go. There was no one waiting for him outside this life, and he was afraid of the unknown. Of his aloneness in the world.

So, he stayed and he killed, and he retched, and he slept in the smothering gloom, because that was all he knew. And in a strange way, it was comfortable.

Gaspard Dufort was waiting for him in the Cavern. The hall was empty, save for a couple of Daggers playing chess by the fire: Abel, the oldest of all of them at seventy, and his granddaughter Collette, who had joined only recently. A single black mark laced her left wrist. In time, it would grow and the song in her laugh would dull. Not Ransom's problem. He had a much bigger one.

Dufort was sitting in his favourite armchair at the back of the Cavern, one leg propped on the knee of the other. His sandy hair looked amber in the flickering light, the sides shaved so short, Ransom could see the shape of his skull, the top pulled into a loose knot on the crown of his head. His usual scattering of fair stubble had grown into a scruffy beard since Ransom had last seen him.

Dufort drummed his fingers along the armrest, the silver skull ring on his left hand catching the lamplight. It had belonged to Hugo Versini, once. Design-wise, it was a little on the nose.

'You look tired, Ransom,' said Dufort, his gold tooth flashing. 'Have I been overworking you?'

Ransom shook his head as he sank into the armchair opposite him. 'I was asleep.'

The Cavern walls were hung with tapestries for warmth, and the room smelled of pipe smoke and rum. Rows of skulls watched over them from the domed ceiling, relics from the reign of Hugo Versini himself. In the beginning, the founding father of the Daggers used to take the heads of his victims and hang them from the Bridge of Tears. Thankfully, the tradition had not lasted long beyond his death almost three centuries ago. Now, even the steeliest of Daggers could not stomach such a thing.

And yet the skulls remained, reminding them of the old adage: *Those who refuse to wield the dagger are doomed to die by its blade.*

A handful of words that had cleaved the Versini brothers apart; a story – and a warning – that Ransom had come to know almost as well as his own. The Versini boys had grown up in the northern mountain village of Halbracht, not far from the border of Farberg. A place so remote, the villagers used to cast their dead in the region's Hellerbend River. But the Hellerbend was rough, the water hardened with minerals that dissolved the bodies and their bones. Over time, strange plants sprouted along the banks, their leaves golden as the summer sun, their roots black as a starless night.

Boneshade.

It was the Versini brothers who first discovered how to dig up the boneshade root, cut it, mix it, make magic from it.

Not the magic of old, however: the force that had flowed through the blood of the saints of Valterre, the power that had built a kingdom up from nothing and filled it with light. This was merely a remnant of that power. A powdered promise of darkness. Shade, the Versini brothers called it. To swallow it was to control every shadow, to become a deadly weapon, poised to kill with just one touch. To wear it meant to disappear entirely, to blend so seamlessly with the night you could take anything from anyone.

Bored of their provincial life in the mountains, the Versini brothers were eager to make something of themselves, to climb the ranks of urban high society and amass the kind of wealth their ancestors could only have dreamed of. To initiate a Second Age of Magic, and crown themselves as gods.

They brought their new magic to Fantome, to exhibit and then sell, but the people there rejected the strange darkness, rejected the brothers and turned in prayer to their saints. The Versinis were shunned by society and threatened by the royal guard, who hounded them day and night. Over time, they grew bitter, their youthful idealism twisting into resentment.

They stopped trying to sell their magic and kept it for themselves, recruiting the damned and forgotten drifters of Fantome to their guild. And so began a year-long reign of terror, where the threat of Shade hung like a thundercloud over Fantome, fuelling hundreds of thefts and murders until the brothers brought the city to its knees.

Not gods, but monsters.

The Versinis were no longer shunned, but feared. By the people and the royal guard, and even the king himself. With such fear came power. Freedom to mould the city as they liked, so long as they kept the secrets of Shade close to their chests.

Over time, Hugo and Armand carved out a vibrant underworld, where they traded crime for coin, amassing hundreds of wealthy patrons looking to thieve and murder without sullying their own hands.

They grew richer, greedier. But power brought its own problems, and as the brothers got older, they began to argue about the limits of their magic, wondering what the Shade was poisoning in the very core of themselves, and what sacrifice it required of their bodies. Armand's guilt weighed heavy on his conscience, the pain of regret burrowing as deep as the black whorls on his skin. He no longer wished to kill for power, and to eventually give his own life for it. He wanted to live, truly and fully. But Hugo had committed wholly to the darkness, and could see no point in stopping now. To him, stealing a coin was no different from stealing a life, and indeed, it was the threat of death – of *murder* – that truly kept them in power, that kept the royal guard of Valterre from dragging them off to the gallows.

The brothers fought ceaselessly, eventually separating their followers into two different orders: the Daggers and the Cloaks, both guilds secreting themselves away to opposite sides of the city, for a while maintaining a precarious truce.

Things took a deadly turn when their sister, Lucille, a light in both their lives, and one of the brightest scholars in Fantome, tried to intervene. Ever the idealist, the youngest

Versini sought to find a way to reconcile her brothers by eliminating the influence of Shade entirely, so that she might end its terrible hold over her family. Now enrolled at the prestigious Appoline University, seventeen-year-old Lucille secretly started to study the anatomy of the boneshade plant in a bid to create an antidote to it.

But the Versinis had spies in every corner of Valterre.

When Hugo found out about Lucille's research, he flew into a rage. Fuelled by Shade and fearful of the consequences of an antidote, he hunted down his interfering sister and lashed out at her. In ten heartbeats, Lucille Versini was dead. The light in the brothers' lives was extinguished, and the last thing that bound them to each other was gone.

When Armand crossed the Verne to avenge his sister's death, Hugo met him on the banks of the river. In the fight that followed, Hugo proved the stronger. When it was over, he hung Armand's body from the Bridge of Tears for ten days and ten nights, so that every Cloak, Dagger and soldier of Valterre would know exactly who ruled the city.

For a time, all was silent in the underworld of Fantome. Until, propelled by grief and a determination to preserve his legacy, Armand's lover, Florentine, took up his mantle, and a new Cloak ascended to power. The Orders settled once more into an uneasy truce, born from a single guiding principle: *You stay out of my way, and I'll stay out of yours.*

In the centuries since, the Cloaks had been demanding the return of their founder's body, but the Daggers had sworn ignorance as to Armand's final resting place. The only grave inside the catacombs, aside from Hugo's own, belonged to

Lucille. For, in his guilt, the Founder of the Daggers had built his little sister a tomb, then did for her what he could not do for himself. He made her a saint.

Unlucky number thirteen.

Not that many in Fantome recognized her piety. After all, Lucille was not magic-borne, like the original twelve saints of Fantome. She wasn't blessed, but cursed by her brothers.

And as for the skulls – well, they were part of the furniture. When Lark and Ransom were still boys, they used to hide them in each other's beds. The night they did it to Nadia, fresh from her first kill, she got such a fright she nearly strangled both of them with their own shadows.

'Sleepwalking, are you?' Dufort clicked his fingers, snapping Ransom back to the present. 'Or am I boring you, son?'

Ransom shook his head, hating how his heart warmed at that word – *son*. 'I was just thinking about the Versini brothers.'

'Don't tire your mind.' Dufort crooked an eyebrow, stretching the shadow-mark that sliced through it. Black whorls crawled up his neck and across the right side of his face, like a hand reaching around to smother him. Tonight, the Head Dagger was dressed all in black, but his blue eyes were clear. 'We have business to discuss.'

'I know,' said Ransom. 'I've been busy.'

'Music to my ears.' Dufort raised his hand and a moment later, a tray was set down, bearing a metal teapot and two cups. Dufort poured the hot water, then removed a vial of Shade from his pocket. He tipped half of it into the first cup, then looked at Ransom, eyebrows raised.

'No, thanks,' said Ransom.

'Suit yourself.' Dufort shrugged, then added the rest to his own cup.

Ransom watched him drink. 'Are you hunting tonight?'

He smirked over the rim of his cup. 'Is that judgement I detect in your tone?'

'I don't know why you stomach the stuff when you don't have to.'

Dufort licked his teeth. 'What can I say? I've developed a taste for it.'

'I'd sooner drink sewer water.'

'Go ahead.' Dufort's eyes gleamed silver as the shadows invaded his body, pushing all the light to the surface. 'Tell me about the girl.'

'I caught up with her on the outskirts of Fantome.' He grimaced at the memory of her stricken face, how she had convulsed on that bench in the Scholars' Quarter like the grief was cutting her in half. 'I tracked her to the Hollows. She went to House Armand.'

Dufort pitched forward. 'Did she find it?'

Ransom nodded.

Dufort's demeanour shifted from calm to irritable. He tapped his right foot as he drank. 'I should have guessed. Did Cordelia let her in?'

Again, Ransom nodded. It had been a long time since he had seen Dufort unsettled like this. Usually it took the death of a Dagger, or a botched kill, to bring gravel to his voice. Perhaps that vial of Shade was stronger than it should have been.

Ransom went on. 'I followed her down to the Rascalle this

morning. She went with two Cloaks. They were performing Sleights in the marketplace.'

Dufort looked up. 'The girl, too?'

'No.' Ransom frowned, recalling the way Seraphine had shied away from the challenge, hovering uncertainly at the edge of the square, her little dog clutched to her chest like a teddy bear. 'She was way out of her depth.'

Dufort snorted, downing the last of his Shade. 'She's a smuggler's daughter, Ransom. She's not as innocent as she looks.'

'Maybe not.' Ransom recalled the way she had looked up at him in the marketplace, like a fly caught in a spider's web. How wide her eyes had been, how her voice had quivered when she spoke, a rosy hue flushing her cheeks. He didn't know if he was defending the girl, or his impression of her when he said, 'But she's no Cloak, Gaspard. She's a pussycat, afraid of her own tail.'

'Then you're the foolish mouse,' snapped Dufort. 'That troublesome urchin found her way to House Armand without any help. She's clever.' He looked away, lips twisting. 'Too clever.'

'Who is she?'

'Sylvie Marchant's spawn. A loose end.'

'Why is she so important to you?'

'Because she could end up being a thorn in my side.' There was such bitterness in his voice, his face. 'Just like her mother.'

Ransom wanted to ask about the fire at the farmhouse, but given how quickly Dufort's mood was souring, he thought better of it. The Dagger kept the shadows inside him on a strong leash, but if his temper flared, it might slip. And Ransom only had ten heartbeats to flee. 'I think the girl just wants to survive,' he said, instead.

'It's not your job to tell me what the girl thinks. It's your job to tell me what she does.' He sat back, a swarm of shadows gathering at his feet, wreathing his chair, kissing his ring. Here sat the true king of Valterre, drunk on his own power. 'I've heard enough.'

Ransom got up to leave.

'Kill her.'

Ransom froze, half out of his chair. Hadn't Dufort heard a word he'd just said?

'She's young,' he said, slowly, cautiously. 'We don't kill—'

'You kill who I tell you to kill.'

Ransom sat back down, compelled to argue despite the silver gleam in Dufort's eyes. Why was he fighting this so hard? Was it really over a music box and a shred of pity? Or because she was so far from his usual type of mark – criminals and degenerates, embezzlers and debt-ridden gamblers from some of the most entitled families in Valterre. This girl was so close to Ransom's age, they might have been friends in a different life. 'She has a dog.'

Dufort laughed roughly, as though Ransom had cracked a joke.

Ransom scrubbed a hand across his jaw.

Dufort looked him over. 'Is there a problem?'

Ransom said nothing. There was a problem, but he couldn't quite figure out what it was.

Dufort's nostrils flared. 'I've chosen to trust you with this mark, Ransom. It's important to me. Just as you are. You've shown great promise these past ten years, *son*.' That word again, like a leash. 'I see a lot of myself in you. That's why I'm close to naming you as my Second. If you play your cards right, some day the Order will be yours. The city, the king's ear, all the riches you could ever dream of … But—' He paused, twisting that thick ring around his finger, once. Twice. 'If you don't think you can do this little task, then I'll give the mark to Lisette. Or—'

'I'll do it,' said Ransom. 'Of course I'll do it.'

The truth was, there was nothing he wouldn't do for Dufort. After all, he was the one who had found Ransom wandering the streets of Fantome ten years ago, his bottom lip split open, his left eye so swollen, he couldn't see out of it.

That was the day after Ransom's mother had fled Fantome with his little sister. Papa had caught the three of them at the entrance to their village, and panic had made Ransom foolish. Slight-framed and trembling at just ten years old, he had turned back. While his mother ran, Ransom made a shield of his body and grabbed a brick, ready to fight. When he came to in an abandoned stable six hours later, he still had the brick in his hand. Mama and Anouk were long gone.

Gaspard Dufort found Ransom the following morning, sitting alone on the banks of the Verne with a gruesome split lip, begging for scraps of pastries. He looked him up and down, then tossed him a cinnamon bun. Ransom devoured it in seven seconds, wincing through the pain of each bite. When he finished the last sugary mouthful, Dufort crouched down and asked him one simple question:

What do you want to be boy, brave or broken?

That night Ransom had his first taste of Shade.

And then he killed his father.

With ten short words on the banks of the Verne, Gaspard Dufort had turned Ransom from a boy into the youngest Dagger in the history of the Order. He had been watching over him ever since, grooming him for greatness. Ransom owed his life to Dufort, and he would not soon forget it. Neither would Dufort.

'Good,' he said now, smirking. 'Let me know when it's done.'

Ransom was about to excuse himself when a shout echoed down the tunnel and exploded into the Cavern. Nadia arrived a moment later, still trying to catch her breath. Lark was behind her, wearing a look of such horror, Dufort leaped to his feet.

'Pascal Loren has been murdered,' said Nadia.

Ransom started at the name. Though Pascal himself was a brash man, with a proclivity for drinking and gambling which had more than once carried him to the brink of destitution, the Lorens were long-standing friends of the Crown as well as stalwart allies of the Daggers. They paid handsomely for the Order's services, which had ensured their protection over the years.

Dufort stalked across the Cavern, dragging his cape of shadows with him. 'Pascal is untouchable.' His silver eyes were wild, their expression violent. Nadia stiffened as she noticed them.

'We came across him ourselves,' said Lark, subtly positioning himself between Nadia and the nearest of Dufort's shadows. 'He was down by the harbour. A crowd had already formed by the time we got there. He was grey, from head to toe. His eyes were black. His lips too.'

Ransom followed Dufort to the huddle by the door. 'So, it was a Dagger, then.'

'Of course not,' snapped Gaspard.

Ransom frowned. 'Do you think a Cloak decided to try their hand at murder?'

Dufort bristled. 'Cordelia Mercure wouldn't dare move against the Lorens.' He sounded unsure, unsettled.

Nadia and Lark shared a meaningful glance.

'The locals ...' Lark began, nervously. 'They spoke of a monster ...'

Dufort curled his lip. 'What kind of self-respecting Dagger believes in monsters, Lark? Repeats the stuff of fairy tales?'

Nadia cleared her throat. 'They said it came up from the sea, crawled from the underside of that abandoned ship ...'

'That ship is none of our concern,' said Dufort, waving a hand in dismissal and sending his shadows skittering up the walls. 'Neither are its dead sailors.'

'*Missing* sailors,' said Lark. 'There were no bodies retrieved. And now we hear of this monster ...'

'Then show it to me,' barked Dufort. 'If you are so *sure* of this delusion.'

'It was gone by the time we got there,' said Nadia. 'This can't all be a coincidence. The supply chain of Shade has been compromised. With Sylvie Marchant out of action ...' She swallowed thickly. 'Who knows what happened to her store of Shade? Anyone in Fantome could have got their hands on it.'

Dufort spat, 'Do you really think I would have left an *ounce* of Shade behind at that farmhouse?'

That was clearly a rhetorical question. It occurred to Ransom that the problem might have originated with an ambitious smuggler. This wouldn't be the first time a trader decided to deal outside the ranks of the Daggers and Cloaks, despite the underworld's strict rules. But whenever that happened, it usually ended swiftly in death and witlessness. The former for the smuggler who dared to sell the Shade, and the latter for the untrained patron foolish enough to consume it. And that still didn't explain the sightings of a monster. Or thirty missing sailors.

'It doesn't matter where the Shade came from,' said Lark. 'If there's *something* out there, killing our allies—'

'*Sloppily,*' Nadia interrupted. 'And in *public.*'

'—then don't you think we should find them?' Lark finished.

Dufort clapped him on the shoulder. 'Finally. A good idea from one of you.' He took a vial from his pocket and pressed it into his hands. 'Twenty silvers for the rogue by morning. A gold sovereign if you find them before midnight.'

Lark's green eyes widened, and Ransom knew he was counting chickens for Mama in his head. Emboldened by the challenge, they both left as quickly as they had arrived. Ransom made to follow them, but Dufort pulled him back.

'*You,*' he said, raising a warning finger. 'Find the girl and kill her.'

Then he turned from Ransom and stalked out of the Cavern, dragging his shadows with him.

'What about the dog?' Ransom called after him.

Dufort's cruel laugh echoed down the stone passage. 'I could do with a new rug.'

Chapter 7

Seraphine

It was mid-morning at House Armand and Sera was half-asleep, reliving a time when Lorenzo had chased her through the vineyard behind their tutor's house. She had purposefully tripped over her basket to let him catch her. When he did, she pulled him down to the warm earth, pressing her mouth against his, raking her fingers through his perfect golden curls while his hands slid up her shirt.

How can a person taste like sunshine and feel like the finest silk? he murmured against her lips.

Sera snorted into his collar, always embarrassed and delighted by his dramatics. For her, a kiss was just a kiss – a delicious escape after a day full of lessons. She welcomed Lorenzo's needy hands on her skin but she never sought a deeper meaning in the shiver of his touch or the caress of his tongue against hers. These moments were enough as they were.

Lorenzo! Seraphine! These grapes won't pick themselves!

Somewhere at the other end of the field, Lorenzo's mother was calling them. Maria was Mama's best friend and together they ran a small vineyard. At the end of every summer, all four of them harvested the grapes, although nowadays Lorenzo and Sera always found time to distract each other from work.

Seraphine! Mama called out. *Come out before winter or our precious grapes will rot! Sera!*

'Sera?' Bibi knocked, then after a moment, tiptoed into her bedroom, rousing Sera from the dregs of her slumber. 'Are you awake?'

'Just waiting for my brain to kick in.' Sera sat up in bed, wondering about the Vergas. She had fled in such a hurry, she never thought to go to Mama's oldest friend, to tell Maria and Lorenzo what had happened. But the flames were so high and the sky so black, they must have known. Did they believe both she and Mama were dead?

A slant of sunlight slipped through the window, bathing the room in a soft honey glow. Bibi was holding a bunch of flowers wrapped in crepe paper: lilacs and irises and forget-me-nots. 'I picked these up at the market. I thought they might brighten up your ... um ...'

'Grief?'

Bibi flushed. 'I was going to say room.'

Sera smiled, her heart swelling. She might not have Lorenzo, but she had Bibi. And Val, who had come to check in on her last night with a pocket full of ginger biscuits. 'Thanks, Bibi. I love flowers.'

'I'll get a vase for them. You should get dressed. You have your first lesson with Albert this morning, remember? He'll be waiting for you down in the gymnasium.'

Sera startled at the clock on the wall, then flung herself out of bed. 'I overslept.' She rummaged in her dresser for one of the outfits she had spent her stipend on at Marveline's Boutique. She settled on a pair of loose cotton trousers and a matching short-sleeved shirt. 'Do you mind taking Pip out?' she asked, as she hastily braided her hair.

'Of course not,' said Bibi, happily scooping him up. 'I'm sure he's been dying to spend more time with me. After breakfast, we might even visit Theo to see if he will sew him a tiny cloak.'

Sera chuckled at the image. 'He'd certainly make a better thief than me.'

'You don't know that,' said Bibi, with an encouraging smile. 'Good luck with Albert.'

Sera steeled herself as she made her way down to the gymnasium, eager to throw herself into self-defence practice. It wouldn't do much for her pressing Dagger problem but it was sure as hell better than nothing. She hated feeling so nervous and uncertain, but that day at the Rascalle had spooked her.

Why did the swan dance?

She had played those innocent words over and over in her head, torturing herself with the memory of that unguarded softness in the Dagger's eyes. Was he toying with her, like a cat tossing about a mouse just to see what it might do?

Have a nice day, Seraphine.

How the hell did he know her name?

She couldn't forget those fateful words, even as she tried to convince herself he wasn't a Dagger. Not with those warm eyes and tentative smile. That low, sonorous voice. No. He was too young to be evil. Too handsome. And yet ... her name in his mouth had sounded like a threat.

She should have struck the arrogant bastard right then and there, left the imprint of her hand on his cheek as a promise of more violence to come.

Sera had spent the days since then hiding away in the library at House Armand, nose-deep in stories that cast her mind as far from Fantome as possible. At night, she sat up staring at the moon, like she was afraid if she looked away, the light would go out and the darkness would find her and finish her. Grief was a cinder block chained to her ankle, fear sitting heavy on the other. She needed to make a weapon of both if she was to survive here. She needed to stop thinking like a wayward farmgirl and start acting like a Cloak. Or better still, a Dagger.

So today, she would train.

Her first session in the second-floor gymnasium with Albert, the resident self-defence tutor at House Armand, was as gruelling as a hike in the Saravi Desert. By noon, she was bent double, desperately trying to catch her breath. Sunlight poured in from the vaulted windows, gilding the sweat on her face.

She grabbed a towel to wipe her brow, then poured herself a glass of water before downing it in one go. 'Not to be dramatic but I think I might be melting,' she gasped. 'My legs feel like candle wax.'

'Good.' Leaning against the nearby mantel of a disused fireplace, Albert grinned as he watched her, his brown eyes crinkling at the sides. He was a Cloak with such skill and leonine grace that he could ballroom-dance her across the room with six twirls and take her knees out from under her on the seventh. 'That means you're working hard.'

Despite the hours they had already spent training together, there wasn't a bead of sweat on the older Cloak's golden-brown skin.

'*Or* maybe I'm just slowly dissolving into a puddle of sweat,' muttered Sera, raking her slick hair away from her face. Daily horseback riding had made her fit, and a childhood of climbing up barns with Lorenzo just to swing from their rafters had made her agile, but self-defence was a different beast entirely. It was a kind of dance: a series of precise strikes and careful manoeuvres that worked muscles she didn't even know she had. Still, she was grateful for Albert's expert tutelage, and glad she had taken Val and Bibi's advice to schedule a session with him before her first official job. It would be a damn shame if she unwittingly stumbled into the clutches of a nightguard on her first Break simply because she didn't know how to get out of a rudimentary arm hold.

The second Sera set her empty glass down, Albert pushed off the mantel, sinking into a crouch. 'Let's move on to chokeholds.'

Sera pulled a face, glancing fleetingly at the nearest window, trying to gauge the distance to the nearest oak tree.

'Not worth the drop,' said Albert, following her gaze. 'Though you're not the first to consider it.'

She groaned in defeat. 'Fine,' she said, rolling her aching shoulders back. 'Chokeholds.'

When Val arrived a short while later, sweeping into the gymnasium in a pair of low-slung trousers and a sleeveless vest, she laughed at the sight of Sera's red face stuck in the cradle of Albert's muscular arms. 'How's training?'

'Sobering,' said Sera, still trying to scrabble free of the hold.

'Well, as much as I hate to interrupt this delightful little moment, Mercure wants to see you in her office,' said Val. 'I suggest you take a shower first.'

Sera's stomach flipped as Albert released her, and she rose on trembling legs that had nothing to do with exertion.

Madame Mercure was angry. Sera could sense it as soon as she reached her quarters in the high tower of House Armand. Val had told her this was where the ravens came to whisper to Cordelia Mercure of the nightly stirrings in Fantome, but standing here now, in a shaft of morning sunlight, the room simply looked like an office, albeit one sumptuously decorated in shades of burgundy and gold.

There was a large walnut desk littered with maps and ledgers. An ornate globe in the corner. A box of herbs sprouting along the windowsill. A row of bookshelves wrapped around the inner wall, climbing all the way to the ceiling, and on the other side of the room, two saffron wingback chairs and a small coffee table beside a crackling fireplace.

Mercure was standing at her desk, with the penny papers in her hand, glaring at Sera with such heat that she hesitated and hovered in the doorway, unsure whether or not to enter.

'Come in,' she said impatiently. 'I don't bite.'

Gingerly, Sera stepped into the room.

'Sit.' Mercure was wearing a long pewter dress that swished around her as she crossed the room. She seemed taller than Sera remembered, but perhaps that was simply because she was angrier. She settled herself in an armchair, gesturing at the one opposite her.

Sera sat. 'Have I done something wrong?'

Mercure crossed her legs. 'Why don't you tell me?'

'Is this about the Rascalle? Was it a test after all?'

'No.' Madame Mercure's voice was clipped.

'Is it Pip?' said Sera, anxiously. 'I know he relieves himself in the garden but I always make sure to—'

'It's not the mutt.' Madame Mercure sighed, bored of her own game. 'Tell me, *Sera Toussaint*, when were you planning on telling me that you are, in fact, the daughter of Sylvie Marchant, one of the most prolific Shade smugglers in Fantome?'

Sera froze. She could feel the colour draining from her cheeks. 'What—'

'Careful,' said Madame Mercure, pitching forward in her seat. 'It would not be wise to lie to my face a second time.'

Sera scrunched her eyes shut, desperately trying to think of something to say, but she had no lie big enough to cover the truth, and no excuse clever enough to banish the suspicion from Madame Mercure's face. She had been caught out. 'My name is Seraphine Marchant,' she said, in a whisper. 'I'm sorry I lied.'

'Or are you sorry you got caught?' Madame Mercure pursed

her lips. 'That's not even the part I'm angry about. You told me your mother died of the plague.'

Sera flinched. She had forgotten about that.

Mercure tossed the paper at her. It slid across the table and landed at her feet. Sera didn't have to pick it up to know what it said. It was dated last Sunday. She could see the headline from here.

FANTOME SMUGGLER MURDERED BY DUFORT'S DAGGERS.

'You neglected to tell me that your mother was murdered,' said Madame Mercure. 'The night you came to House Armand begging for sanctuary, you were running from the Daggers, weren't you?'

Sera nodded, slowly. There was no sense in denying it now. 'I didn't know where else to go.'

Madame Mercure's lips twisted. 'I read they burned your mother's farmhouse.'

Again, Sera nodded. For as long as she lived, she would never forget the sight of the smoke rising over the hills.

'Why did they burn it?' said Madame Mercure.

'I don't know.' Sera was still wrestling with the same question. 'Pippin and I were out hunting for rabbits.'

Madame Mercure's frown deepened the lines around her mouth. 'Between them, the Cloaks and Daggers trade with seventeen other smugglers outside Fantome. None of those smugglers have been murdered. Why would Gaspard Dufort choke his own supply chain?'

Sera bristled at that name. 'We— *Mama* refused to sell to Dufort. She only dealt with the Cloaks.'

All these years, Sera had never been able to tell who Mama hated more – the Daggers or Dufort himself. But one thing she knew, deep in her blood and her bones, was that no matter how many times she declared herself a simple *go-between*, Sylvie Marchant had been no innocent bystander. She hated Dufort with the kind of rage that made her eyes blaze like two bronze coins. By the end, Sylvie had been unable to stomach sight or sound of him, or tolerate anything he stood for.

Sometimes Sera had watched the way her mother looked at those vials of Shade as she bottled them and wondered just how close she had come to tasting that power, and what she would have done with it if curiosity had got the better of her. And in the endless hollow hours since Mama's death, Sera had often found herself wishing Mama had got to Dufort before he got to her.

'Why?' pressed Mercure. 'Why did your mother choose to only sell to the Cloaks?'

'Because Gaspard Dufort is a depraved monster,' said Sera. 'Mama wouldn't piss on him if he was on fire.'

A cold, yawning silence filled the room. Sera swallowed her next words: *Dufort knew that and killed her for it.*

Madame Mercure did not argue the point. There was no one who despised the Daggers more than the Cloaks, their age-old rivalry stretching all the way back to the warring Versini brothers, and Armand's gruesome death at Hugo's hands. And then there was the matter of their little sister, Lucille, the poor girl who got caught in the middle of their bloody feud simply by trying to help them. 'But Gaspard is also a clever man, Seraphine. And a clever man has a reason for everything he does.'

'Maybe he's started to lose it.'

Madame Mercure went on, as if she hadn't heard her, 'So, the question remains: what threat did Sylvie Marchant pose to the most powerful man in Fantome?'

'Mama lived in a farmhouse in the middle of nowhere. She never went anywhere or did anything of note. Unless you count making wine and tinkering with jewellery in her spare time.' Sera clasped the teardrop at her throat, wanting to defend her mother from the implication that she had somehow deserved her own gruesome murder. Banishing the fear that it might be true. 'She was hardly a threat.'

Madame Mercure pressed her lips together, levelling a hard look at Sera. 'I think you know more than you're letting on.'

Sera folded her arms, but said nothing. Of course there were other sides to Mama. She was clever, cunning, curious – not just about the beauty of nature, but about its secrets, too. She read widely and often, and sometimes, after a glass or two of wine, she experimented – with metals, plants, even rocks dug up from her own garden. And once – *only once* – with something darker, something secret and strange and deadly that Seraphine had never quite made sense of.

She still thought of Fig sometimes, the yowling tabby that had fallen victim to Mama's midnight experiment and become something . . . *other*. But over time, the memory of that strange night had turned hazy, and the more she thought about it, the less sense it made. Sera didn't like to dwell on it, to consider that her mother might have lied to her, or that there were things about Sylvie that she simply didn't know.

'Your mother was part of the underworld of Fantome.' Mercure laboured her point. 'She was part of the trade. And by the sounds of it, so were you.'

Sera glared at her. 'Mama only fell into the trade to keep us afloat. The least I could do was help her out when I was old enough.' She recalled those early years with a pang of guilt, Mama labouring at her workbench by the light of the moon, her shoulders so hunched that some nights she could barely tuck Seraphine in. Back then, they were so poor they had to share a cup of milk for breakfast, Mama pretending to take sips she never swallowed so Sera wouldn't go hungry. They often had to rely on the kindness of Farmer Perrin or Maria Verga just to survive. 'Mama did the real work. The *hard* work. I just helped her bottle it.'

'Tell me the rest,' Mercure pressed. 'What else was your mother up to in that little farmhouse of hers?'

'I've already told you everything.' Sera was seized by an image of her mother sitting at her workbench on a warm sunny day, her dark hair falling across her face as she tinkered with a strand of wire. She was surrounded by vials, as she always was, and on her left, the discarded nub of a boneshade root, its head of golden leaves still attached. There were others scattered across the table, and in the air, beneath the smell of lemon blossom, was the barest hint of gunpowder.

What's that strange smell, Mama?

Mama had set the wire down to smile at her. *That, my little firefly, is the smell of creativity.*

Sera frowned at the memory now.

'What is that thought?' said Mercure, reaching forward as if to catch it. 'The one flitting behind your eyes.'

'Mama was a good person,' said Sera quietly. 'That's all I know. That's all that matters to me.' Silence fell. She wrung her hands in her lap, waiting for Madame Mercure to decide her fate. 'She always said if anything ever happened to her, I should come to House Armand. She thought I'd be safe here.'

'That's because it was an offer I extended to her many years ago.' Madame Mercure stood up and plucked the paper from the floor. 'Back when you were small enough not to chance your tongue at lying.'

Sera jerked her chin up. 'You knew my mother?'

'I know everyone who sells to me,' said Mercure, as though it was the most obvious thing in the world. And suddenly it was. Just because Mama didn't run her own deliveries didn't mean she had never met her best customer. Her only customer. 'I liked Sylvie. She was clever, steely-eyed. She loved you very much.'

Sera swallowed thickly. She reached for those warm, gentle words, desperate to fill the yawning hollow inside her chest.

'I knew there was something familiar about you when you showed up on my doorstep. That riddle, at least, has been answered.' Mercure cast the paper in the fire. The flames hissed, devouring it. 'I must caution you, Seraphine. This is a dangerous time to be a Cloak,' she said, unease creeping into her voice. 'There are strange stirrings across the underworld of Fantome. The Daggers are getting sloppy. Reckless. First, a smuggler. And now one of their own. Pascal Loren has been found dead. And then there's the abandoned ship in the harbour. Thirty marks in one night. And many others in the south quarter unaccounted for.'

'Even so,' said Sera, rising to her feet, 'I'm a lot safer at House Armand than I am alone in the Hollows.'

Madame Mercure looked her over. 'Albert says you're a quick learner. Blanche likes you, which is no mean feat. You seem to have made friends with some of my Cloaks. But you have yet to prove yourself.'

'Then assign me a job,' said Sera, before she could second-guess herself. It was time to set aside her aversion to thievery, bury her cowardice and choose survival. Only then could she have her revenge. And after, freedom.

'Very well, Seraphine Marchant,' said Madame Mercure. 'I will send word to Theo. We will fit you for a cloak first.'

Sera smiled gratefully. 'I promise you won't regret it.'

Mercure went to the window, the frown returning to her face. 'That remains to be seen.'

Chapter 8

Seraphine

era stood outside the cloakroom in the basement of
House Armand and knocked three times. She brushed
the stray hairs from her face and adjusted the hem
of her sweater, feeling a sudden flurry of self-consciousness.
She didn't know whether it was because she knew there was
a handsome Shadowsmith on the other side of the door –
though she had only managed to steal a few passing glances at
him over the last couple of weeks – or because she was finally
getting a cloak of her very own.

There was no answer.

She knocked again, louder. 'Hello?' she called out,
uncertainly. 'It's Seraphine. Madame Mercure sent me?'

Silence.

She tried the handle, and to her surprise, the door opened.

When she poked her head around it, she expected to see someone, but the room was empty. Her heart beat fast at the unexpected opportunity. She was hovering on the unguarded threshold of the famous cloakroom of House Armand, a place full of Shade.

She slipped inside, her eyes widening at the grandeur. This was no glorified closet. Exquisite walnut shelves lined each wall, stretching up to a row of squat, narrow windows that looked out on the gardens of House Armand. It was dimmer down here than in any other room Sera had been in, but she supposed the shadows that clung to the cream walls and spilled across the floor were deliberate. They added a certain secrecy to the cloakroom, a place where all things could be hidden.

On one wall, hundreds of cloaks of every size hung from gold railings. On the next were several shelves of smart black boots, then an entire wardrobe of gloves and scarves and hats, and even face masks. Everything was black, and though they all appeared normal on the outside, Sera could sense the Shade that had been stitched into every piece of fabric. It made the air feel colder, heavier. As she moved through the cloakroom, her skin prickled in recognition.

In the middle of the room, by a leather couch and two matching armchairs, was an island covered with glass. Sera ran her fingers along the case, gazing down at a strange collection of pocket-watches, none of which seemed to have a face. There were pens and knives, masks and handkerchiefs, and spectacles made for seeing in the dark. Sera smiled. The cloakroom at House Armand was a place of true artifice and creativity. Mama would have loved it here.

She trailed her fingers along the shelves, searching for a glimpse of the vials her mother used for Shade. Something flitted across her peripheral vision. She turned, sharply, but there was nothing there. She squinted up at the windows. Perhaps a cloud had moved in front of the sun, causing the shadows to shift. But then it happened again, this time on her other side.

The hairs on the back of her neck rose.

'Hello?' she called out. 'Is someone here?'

She looked down and noticed a new shadow right beside her own. She waved her arms, feeling ridiculous. The shadow shifted, moving through hers and then across the floor, until it climbed up the side of a wardrobe.

A man stepped out of it. 'BOO!'

Sera screamed.

'*Saints!* Calm down!' He pulled his hood back, revealing a sweep of bright silver hair and turquoise eyes that were wide with horror. 'It's just me!'

Sera clapped a hand over her mouth, turning her scream to a whimper.

'That was a grave miscalculation,' he said, removing his cloak entirely and casting it onto a nearby bench. He kicked off his boots, leaving him standing in navy trousers, a pale grey sweater and a pair of stripy blue socks. No cloak, no Shade. He grinned sheepishly. 'I thought you'd find that funny.'

Sera moved her hand to her galloping heart. 'Then you don't know me at all.'

'Not yet, but I'm up for the challenge.' He stuck out his hand. 'Theo Branch. I'm the Shadowsmith of House Armand.'

Sera looked at his hand, broad and tanned golden, and was suddenly keenly aware of how sweaty hers was.

'It's just a handshake,' he said, misreading her hesitation. 'Cloak's honour.'

She gingerly took his hand and shook it. 'Seraphine Marchant.'

'The smuggler's daughter,' he said, though not unkindly. 'Mercure told me about you. I was wondering when you'd grace me with your curiosity.'

'Sera is fine,' she said, taking her hand back. 'I was just—'

'Snooping,' he said, good-naturedly. Theo had an easy smile and a pleasant voice that belied his shrewdness.

'It was more of a general wandering,' she clarified. 'I was admiring your craftsmanship.'

He rocked back on his heels, grinning from ear to ear. 'Admirers are always welcome here.'

Sera's cheeks burned. That was not at all what she meant. She turned away. 'The cloaks,' she said, brushing her fingers along a nearby sleeve. 'How exactly do they work?'

'I mix Shade in with the dye,' said Theo, joining her at the shelf. 'And I use it in the stitching too. The cloak acts like a veil of darkness. It pushes away the light, and helps you fold into the shadows.'

'And the boots, too?'

'Boots, gloves. Hats. Scarves . . .' His eyes lit up. 'It depends on how invisible you want to be. Then it's just a matter of folding yourself into the right shadow.'

Sera frowned at the sliver of darkness he had just walked out of. It was so much smaller than it had been a moment ago.

'It doesn't matter how big the shadow is,' he said, reading her thoughts. 'All you have to do is join with it.'

'You make it sound so simple.'

'Anyone can wear a cloak,' he said, with a shrug. 'The hard part is in the construction of it. It's a game of measurement and precision. Of skill.'

Sera thought of Mama, and all the hours she spent hunched over her workbench, surrounded by a mass of decapitated boneshade plants, harvesting and grinding the root until it was just so. It was heavy work, which made for long hours and aching shoulders, and a weariness that lingered long after the day was done.

'You must be very dedicated,' she murmured.

'It's my passion.' Theo smiled at her, his face so full of pride that she smiled back. She ignored the gentle fluttering in her stomach and turned to the wardrobe.

'So, when do I get mine?'

'Eager, aren't you,' he remarked. 'Right now, if you're willing.'

'I'm willing,' said Sera, far too quickly.

His eyes danced as he pulled a pinned tape measure from his pocket. He placed the pin in his teeth and unfurled the tape, talking from the side of his mouth. 'Hold still.'

She froze.

'Don't forget to breathe, Sera.'

She laughed, awkwardly. 'Sorry. I don't know why I'm so nervous.'

He winked at her. 'I have that effect on people.'

She was too flustered to think of a reply, so she stood stock still as he carefully pinned the tape to the collar of her sweater, his eyes narrowed in concentration. He was so close, she caught a whiff of his cologne, a distracting mix of sandalwood and vanilla. It made her think of Lorenzo, who always smelled faintly of sunshine and salt. She frowned. For all he knew, she could be dead.

'Are you all right?' said Theo.

She had stiffened again. 'I'm fine. I just don't want you to prick me.'

He chuckled as he knelt at her feet, running his fingers along the tape. Sera looked down at him, marvelling at the moon-silver glint of his hair. She wondered how someone not much older than her had managed to obtain such an important role at House Armand.

'Where did you come from, Theo?'

'You mean before my impressive lunge from the shadows?'

'Well, I assume you weren't born in a wardrobe.'

'I grew up near the Pinetops, the low mountains in north Valterre.' A pause, as if he was considering whether to say more.

'That's not far from Halbracht.' Sera recalled the maps on her bedroom walls. 'Just like the Versini brothers.'

'No.' The word came quick and crisp. 'I'm not at all like the Versini brothers, and that's fine by me.' He swallowed the hardness in his voice and went on. 'My father was the Shadowsmith at House Armand before me.' He paused to press the tape against her ankle, sending a shiver dancing up her leg. 'I spent most of my childhood charging through these hallways, breaking every precious vase in sight. Not exactly the most reliable apprentice.'

Sera nurtured a smile, thinking of the first time she had helped Mama bottle Shade, only to smash an entire box of vials.

'But Papa was patient,' said Theo. 'He taught me everything I know. He passed just over a year ago. They said his heart gave out, but sometimes I wonder if the Shade had seeped into it by the end.' He cleared his throat, like he was angry at himself for saying that. 'Anyway, I had learned enough by then to stay on.'

'I'm sorry about your father,' said Sera.

'So am I.' Theo pulled back, looking up at her again. 'You're shorter than I expected.'

'Won't that make me a better thief?'

'Depends how limber you are.'

She pulled a face. 'I'm a lot better on a horse.'

'None of those in here, I'm afraid.'

'Maybe you could make one for me,' she suggested.

He pretended to consider it. 'You're high maintenance for a farmgirl.' At her look of mock offence, he laughed. The melody of it was so pleasant, she couldn't help but join in.

He stood up to measure the width of her shoulders, chewing on his lip as he adjusted the tape, making another silent calculation in his head. Then his gaze fell on the golden teardrop at her throat. He gently pressed a finger to it. 'This is pretty,' he murmured. 'Did you make it?'

She shook her head. 'My mother made it for me.'

'It catches the light beautifully,' he said, turning the bead in his fingers. 'What's inside it?'

She shrugged, embarrassed not to know the answer, to have never asked. 'Um. A mother's love?'

'Powerful stuff.' He let go of the necklace. 'Right, I think I've got everything I need.'

He went to the wall of cloaks and trailed his hand along them, until he came to one hanging near the end. Sera marvelled at his sureness. To her, every single cloak looked exactly the same.

She moved in front of the mirror, while he cast the cloak over her shoulders. It fell with a flutter, the material so light she barely noticed she was wearing it at all. 'This is one of my newer designs,' he said, looking at her in the mirror. 'It's lighter. It moves with the wearer, instead of catching between their legs. We've had some trouble with that before.'

His fingers moved, brushing against her necklace as he fastened the cloak. His eyes met hers and she looked away. He reached behind her to pull up her hood, and she caught another whiff of that heady cologne. She wondered what she smelled like to him. Dog fur and anxiety, probably.

'Do you feel that?' he said, in a low voice.

For a moment, Sera thought he meant the butterflies rioting in her stomach, but then she felt the cool tingle of Shade against the bare skin of her neck. She shuddered. 'It's *cold*.'

He smiled. 'You'll get used to it.'

She winced at her reflection. 'I look like a ghoul.'

'I'm afraid you're far too pretty to be a ghoul,' said Theo, with such off-handed casualness she assumed he flirted with everyone.

'Gloves next,' he said. 'Wrists up.'

He laid his right hand against hers, dwarfing it. His lips twitched.

'They're dainty,' she said, defensively. 'Don't make fun of me.'

'I wouldn't dream of it.' She caught the rumble of his laughter as he retrieved a pair of perfectly sized gloves from a nearby drawer. They were black, made from leather and Shade. She put them on, feeling a slick of coolness settle on her skin.

'The Shade you use,' she said casually. 'Where do you keep it?'

'In the cloakroom,' he said, as he hunted for the right pair of boots. 'Where else?'

'Yes, but *where* in the cloakroom?' she clarified. 'I don't see it.'

'That's because it's hidden.' He stood up, boots in hand, and reached for a velvet hanger that protruded ever so slightly more than the others. He tugged it, and the entire left side of the wardrobe groaned as it gave way. The wood shifted to reveal a large black safe, with a brass dial.

Sera's eyes grew wide, but Theo released the hanger, and the wardrobe swung back into place. 'Why do you look so intrigued? You grew up with a smuggler. You've probably handled more Shade than I have.'

'Never unsupervised,' she admitted. Not that she had cared back then. 'I wasn't even allowed to touch the bloom of the boneshade plant. Mama said it was just as dangerous as the root. Once, when I was eight, she caught me playing kickabout with one.' She pulled a face at the memory. In all her life, she had never seen Mama so angry. 'She grounded me on the spot. I had to pick one thousand grapes to earn my freedom back.'

'Grapes, huh?' Theo scrubbed a hand across his jaw. 'What an odd punishment.'

'Mama was a winemaker,' said Sera, as she kicked off her shoes. 'It was a hobby of hers.'

'I don't know about the grapes, but she was right about the Shade,' he said, kneeling to help her with the boots. 'It can be tempting.'

Sera slipped her foot inside the first boot. 'You seem to be doing all right with it.'

He paused with his hand on her ankle. 'I have remarkable self-control, Sera.'

She watched his fingers move, as he laced up her boot, and asked him, 'Have you ever tasted it?'

He looked up. 'You mean, have I ever felt like taking a mallet to my soul?' He splayed his hands, showing her the absence of shadow-marks. 'Even wearing Shade comes with its own risks. The gloom. The exhaustion. But at least you can take it off.' He finished lacing her boots, sighing as he stood up. 'Right, then, farmgirl. Pick your shadow.'

She gripped her cloak. 'What? Just like that?'

He flashed his teeth. 'No time like the present.'

She nervously adjusted her hood. Magic prickled against her hair, making the strands static. 'Do I at least look the part?'

'If you did, then I wouldn't be able to see you,' he reminded her.

'Right. Good point.' Sera approached a shadow on the wardrobe. She pressed her hand against it, feeling the magic in her glove tingle. As shadow recognized shadow, she felt a faint pulling sensation, as though the darkness was reaching for her. She gasped as her hand appeared to melt into the wardrobe, the glove disappearing before her eyes.

'Good,' said Theo, coming to her side. 'Now step into it.'

The idea of stepping into a solid piece of wood sounded absurd to Seraphine, but when she raised her boot and pressed it against the shadow, it yielded like a cloud of dust. Suddenly, she was inside it, the rest of the shadow expanding to welcome her, and then folding around her like a blanket. She looked out at Theo and saw that he was squinting at a spot over her left shoulder.

'Ha! You can't see me!'

'You're not supposed to talk.'

'But then how can I taunt you?' she crowed. She hadn't expected it to be this easy. Or enjoyable. She turned, searching for another shadow. She found one and pounced, her cloak reappearing and then vanishing as the darkness engulfed her once more. She laughed again. 'Maybe I'll make an expert thief after all.'

'It's just a shame about those tiny hands,' he said, turning to follow her voice.

She took off her glove and flung it at him.

He caught it easily. 'Breach!'

She waggled her fingers at him. He lunged to catch her, but she hopped again, folding herself into a shadow on the wall. The darkness tickled her skin, welcoming her. A laugh bubbled out of Sera, the sound so strange and carefree, she hardly recognized it. It was followed by a twist of guilt. How could she laugh after what had happened to Mama? The underworld had claimed her, and now here Sera was, dancing inside it, playing with Shade like it hadn't torn her life apart. Killed her mother.

But no – Mama had told her to come here if something bad happened. She had told Sera it was the only place she would be safe. The better Sera hid, the better she could protect herself. The better she could sneak, and pounce. It would take more than a vial of Shade to take down a Dagger at the height of his power. She needed to be quick, stealthy. She needed to be a good Cloak. Otherwise, how could she sneak up on Dufort?

Sera pushed her guilt away, folding herself into darkness and distraction. As she hopped from one shadow to the next, playing cat and mouse with Theo, she realized she didn't want the game to end. Once it did, the spell would be broken.

All too soon, they were interrupted by an urgent knocking at the door. It swung open to reveal Valerie's ashen face. 'There's been an incident,' she said, in a strangled voice.

Theo stiffened, the game forgotten. 'What is it?'

Val's bottom lip trembled, and Sera saw her eyes were filled with tears. Her careful composure had fallen away, revealing the girl trembling beneath. There was a commotion in the hallway behind her, raised voices and hurried scuffling.

'It's Griffin. They found him down by the harbour.'

Theo followed Val out into the hallway.

Sera stumbled out of the shadows, untying the cloak at her neck. She let it pool on the floor as she scurried after them.

Out in the hallway, a group of Cloaks were carrying a body towards the other room in the basement. Sera rose to her tiptoes, straining to see over Theo's shoulder, and caught a glimpse of Griffin's greying skin. His eyes were black as ink. His lips too.

A Dagger's kill.

Theo muttered a slew of swearwords. 'What the hell are they playing at?'

'Isn't it obvious?' said Val in a hollow voice. 'They've declared war.'

Sera stumbled back into the cloakroom, trying to catch her breath. She picked her cloak off the floor and held it to her chest. As its magic brushed against her skin, she thought of Mama lying in their farmhouse, just as grey. Just as dead. A familiar heat rushed through her, the red wave of her rage scorching the fear from her bones.

Monsters, all of them. Twisted, hateful bastards. She moved her gaze from the door to the wardrobe that hid the black metal safe, to the cloaks in the wardrobes and the drawers that held every kind of weapon imaginable. She would not cower. She would not be afraid. If Dufort wanted a war, he could have it.

Chapter 9

Seraphine

Days passed achingly slowly in House Armand, while the Order of Cloaks tried to come to terms with Griffin's sudden death, and how it had happened without a word of explanation from Dufort and his assassins.

For a Dagger to kill a Cloak unprovoked broke an age-old truce that was already on shaky ground. But now it was clear the Daggers had gone rogue, which meant no one in Fantome was safe.

Then there were the rumours, though they were surely too strange to be true. And yet, as whispers of monster sightings circulated, the entire city ground to a halt, merchants closing their shops long before sunset, while children were locked inside their homes, their sticky hands pressed against foggy windows as they watched the world fall still.

Sera laughed off the rumours with Bibi and Val, but in quiet moments when she didn't have to pretend, her thoughts turned to the monster she had glimpsed that night last year in her back garden – the rabid thing that had burst from Fig's little body, pulling the darkness around it like a shroud. She could still hear its howl in her mind. This *thing* Mama had made. There and gone, in a spark of light.

Could it somehow be related to what was happening now? Or was fear stoking her paranoia?

Sera wondered if the rumours had made their way to the plains, to the people she had left behind. She thought often of the burnt shell of her farmhouse ... the burnt shell of her life. She wondered whether she should write to Lorenzo, to let him know she was safe ... to ask why he hadn't come to look for her at the one place he knew she'd be. But something always seemed to stop her.

More and more, she wanted to return to the plains to find out why Mama had been killed, to untangle what she had been doing while Sera slept in those dark hours between midnight and dawn, when she sat half-slumped and murmuring at her workbench, as though brewing something still deadlier than the black poison that kept them afloat.

But that visit would have to wait. Madame Mercure had placed a moratorium on all official Cloak activity while she investigated what exactly was going on in Fantome. And so, for the two weeks following Griffin's murder, nobody dared to venture outside.

Sera made sure her time at House Armand was not wasted. The moratorium afforded her a chance to better acquaint herself with Theo, who, as the resident Shadowsmith, was a most useful – and not at all unpleasant – person to befriend. She had quickly come to learn that the artificer kept unusual hours at House Armand, staying up for days at a time whenever he was working on some new innovation, often falling asleep at his workbench or on the couch in the rec room, or once, in his bowl of porridge at breakfast.

That spark inside him – of ingenuity and curiosity – reminded Sera of her mother, and she found that she liked being around him, even when he was half asleep or daydreaming.

The moratorium also gave Sera precious time to learn precisely how to *be* a Cloak.

After defence lessons with Albert each day, Sera, Bibi and Val took over the recreation room on the third floor to practise the art of pickpocketing. At first, Sera was woefully bad, bumbling and stuttering and far too obvious, but she was a quick learner. By the end of the first week, she managed to pilfer a gold butterfly clip from Bibi's hair *and* take Albert's watch from around his wrist.

'Nice work, farmgirl,' said Val, as she watched her. 'Ten silvers if you manage to swipe my nose-ring.'

Sera didn't dare. But her competitive streak meant she sure as hell thought about it.

Even Pippin was improving. One morning, he managed to steal Madame Fontaine's pipe while she was napping in the library, earning him such a scolding from the old woman that he had to sleep it off in front of the fireplace.

Theo didn't often join in with their lessons, but he was still drawn to their group. Perhaps it was because of all the Cloaks at House Armand, the four of them were closest in age, or maybe it was the sound of their laughter echoing through the halls that drew him out of the cloakroom most days. When he came, he preferred to sit by the window, chuckling into his coffee as he watched them. Sera tried to pretend his presence didn't unsettle her, but every time she caught a glimpse of his slanted smirk, her cheeks burned.

'*Don't* fall for those pretty eyes,' said Val, one rainy evening when they were all dressed in their cloaks. They had been flitting from shadow to shadow in the drawing room, immersed in a heated game of chase. 'He's like that with every new recruit.'

'I don't know what you're talking about,' said Sera, leaping from a shadow on the wall to catch a sliver by the window. She welcomed the cool slick of darkness, pleased at how quickly she had got used to it.

Val lunged, catching her by the hood before she disappeared entirely. 'Yes, you do.'

Sera shook her off, folding herself between the drapes. 'Nope.'

Val huffed, losing sight of her. 'You are hopeless.'

'Who's hopeless?' said Theo, stepping out from a nearby table lamp.

'*You,*' said Val, pulling her hood back. She combed her fingers through her hair, fluffing out the purple curls. 'Aren't you supposed to be working?'

He grinned lazily. 'Isn't this work?'

'This is *practice*,' said Bibi, twirling out of the fireplace. 'You never practise with us.'

'Maybe I've got rusty.'

'You haven't,' said Val. 'And you hate thieving.'

'Maybe I want to broaden my horizons?'

'You don't,' said Bibi flatly.

Sera peered out from between the drapes. 'Is anyone else hungry?'

'Starving,' said Bibi and Val, in unison.

'Me too.' Theo looked between them. 'You wouldn't deny your faithful Shadowsmith some company at dinner, would you?'

Val rolled her eyes. 'You can come, but keep the flirting to a minimum.'

'All right,' he said, dipping his chin. 'I solemnly swear not to flirt with Pippin.'

Sera laughed, before she could help herself.

'Hopeless,' Val sighed, as she swept out of the door.

Later that night when the rain finally sputtered out and the new moon peeked through a tuffet of clouds, Madame Mercure summoned Sera, Bibi and Val to her office in the high tower of House Armand.

When they arrived, she was standing by the window in a long indigo robe with flared sleeves. Even from the side, Sera could see that her face was drawn, her mouth pinched at the corners. 'Good evening, girls,' she said, turning to greet them. Her eyes fell on Sera. 'I've got a job for you.'

Sera drew in a breath. Her test had come at last, and she was surprised by the thrill of excitement in her stomach, her eagerness to prove herself worthy of the welcome she had found here, and the friends she had made.

The moratorium on theft was over. But the threat of danger remained. The Daggers had continued to kill regularly and sloppily, at all hours of the day and night, leaving broken bodies strewn like petals across the streets of Fantome. There were just as many unexplained disappearances, although most of these new horrors seemed to be concentrated down near or inside the south quarter.

This gave Madame Mercure just enough confidence to resume business. The coffers at House Armand were running low, leaving her little choice but to cede to a need still more urgent than that for caution: money. She had an Order to run, patrons to satisfy. And more than that, they couldn't afford to appear afraid of Gaspard Dufort, even if they were. It was bad for business.

And so, the Order was returning to work. It was time for Seraphine to don her cloak and earn her place at House Armand.

The job was at Villa Roman, a palatial manor on the north bank of the Verne, which had, up until recently, belonged to Pascal Loren. The largest gambling den in Fantome was finally calling in its debts and had hired Madame Mercure to help.

Tonight, they were hunting for the Rizzano tiara. Over one hundred and fifty years old, the tiara had been a gift from the King of Urnica to Pascal's great-grandmother, Edith Loren, with whom he had fallen hopelessly in love. According to Mercure's sources, the headpiece had been sitting in the safe at Villa Roman for years, gathering dust, forgotten even by Pascal himself. On today's black market, the tiara would be worth somewhere in the region of eighteen hundred gold sovereigns. Sera's share alone would be more than enough to cover her stipend five times over.

Madame Mercure had managed to procure a detailed map of the property, which was folded up in the inner pocket of Val's cloak.

'It's a soft Heist,' Val told Sera as they made their way north along the banks of the Verne. She must have noticed that Sera hadn't uttered a single word since they'd set out from House Armand just before midnight, or could sense that her excitement at becoming a true Cloak was starting to curdle into dread. Dread of stealing. Dread of *failing*. 'With Pascal dead, Villa Roman is low-hanging fruit. And it's as far from the harbour as you can get. She's making this easy for you.'

'We'll be in and out in less than twenty minutes,' said Bibi, confidently. 'I bet we could even do it without our cloaks.'

Val shot her a warning look. 'We still need to be careful. There could be Daggers about.'

'Or monsters,' whispered Bibi.

'Is there any difference?' muttered Sera, who had been so busy steeling herself for the Heist, she had momentarily forgotten all about the Daggers.

In the distance, she spied the firelight of the Aurore shining steadfastly over Fantome. A soaring three-tiered tower of pale stone, each lined with troughs of flames, the Aurore had watched over Fantome for over nine hundred years. It had been built by the people here, raised up from the rocky earth as a monument to the lost saints of Valterre. It was a tribute and a silent, burning plea. The Aurore had been a call to those long-dead saints and the magic that once blessed the people of Valterre to *come back. Come back to us.*

But the only magic here was Shade, and over time the shining tower had become the very thing people looked to when they found themselves afraid of the darkness and the creatures that stalked within it. The official symbol of Fantome – an ever-glowing flame – represented the light of the Aurore. The image of that flame hung in homes and taverns all across the city. A portent of good fortune, it had been embroidered onto wedding gowns and top hats, walking canes and baby blankets, and even carved into coffins. It had been painted and sculpted by hundreds of artists over hundreds of years. Some even wore the symbol on pendants around their necks, keeping that promise – that hope – close to their heart.

Mama never wore the symbol, but she wore the hope. Sera recalled the last time they had come to the city, bringing bread rolls and tomato soup to have a picnic under the Aurore.

Look how the flames glow all the way along the top, Mama had said, pointing high above them. *Light always burns through the shadows, Seraphine.* Her voice had wavered as she gripped Sera's hand tight, like she was trying to press the words into her skin. *Whenever you feel lost, my little firefly, you need only look to the Aurore and remind yourself how high you can climb.*

Sera had looked at her mother strangely, trying to interpret the quiver in her voice.

One day, we will be better than this life, darling girl. Better than Shade, Mama went on, determinedly. *And when the time comes, you will rise far above this wicked city and become a flame in the dark.* She had tipped her head back then, urging Sera to do the same. *You will be the Aurore, Seraphine.*

'What are you staring at?' asked Bibi, jolting Sera from the memory.

'The Aurore,' said Sera, tearing her gaze from it. 'Who do you suppose lights the troughs?'

'Who do you suppose cares?' said Val impatiently. 'Stop chattering, you two. We're almost there.'

Soon, Villa Roman was before them. Although it was still occupied, it had become a tragic husk of its former self, the gold leaf peeling from its towering façade, clouds of grime gathering across each window. Because of Pascal Loren's considerable gambling debts, parts of the roof had been allowed to fall into disrepair, and its magnificent gardens had begun to spill over the high stone walls. The façade of pale stone was inlaid with a grand stained-glass window that looked out over the Verne like an all-seeing eye. A row of gargoyles perched along the roof gutter, scowling at the river as if it displeased them.

Sera followed Val and Bibi over the iron railings and through masses of shrubbery, until they reached the back of the building. The windows there were covered in spiderwebs and the heavy oak doors were locked. Sera frowned at the metal padlock.

Val jostled her aside. 'Watch and learn, farmgirl.' She removed a pin from her hair and slid it inside the padlock as Sera kept a wary eye on their surroundings, spotting an owl watching them from a nearby tree, then a fox darting in the bushes. The back of her neck began to prickle but she told herself it was nerves, her destiny hanging on this one moment – this one lock. And the task that lay beyond it.

Hold your nerve.

She could do this. She *had* to do this.

But she couldn't stop her shiver, couldn't escape the feeling that there might be someone else here, watching them. She scanned the bushes, looking for a tell-tale glint of silver in the dark. The eyes of an all-too familiar monster . . .

Click!

'We're in!' said Bibi, excitedly.

'Get behind me,' said Val. 'I've got the map.'

Sera stepped into the dusty dimness, turning all her nervous energy towards one simple, shining goal: the Rizzano tiara.

'Do you believe in ghosts?' whispered Bibi as they made their way up the winding staircase.

'Not usually,' Sera whispered back. But something about the spiralling dust motes made her feel like they weren't truly alone in here.

'Those gargoyles outside used to give me nightmares,' Bibi confessed. Her short, shallow breaths made Sera wonder if she might be anxious too.

So Sera said with a wink, 'I think the one on the far left is quite handsome. Did you see that exquisite bone structure?'

'I suppose he does have nice horns.'

They broke out into nervous laughter.

Val stopped at the top of the stairs. 'If you two don't shut up, I'm putting you outside like a pair of naughty cats.'

There was a sudden crash from the garden, followed by a

strangled meow. They froze in place on the landing, Sera's heart thundering so furiously she could feel it in her throat.

'What was that?'

Bibi swallowed. 'A naughty cat?'

They hurried on, climbing one staircase and then another, spiralling up to the top of the house. Moonlight slipped through the windows, catching the ends of their cloaks. Up and up they went until they came to a room on the highest floor of Villa Roman. Val picked the lock in ten seconds flat. The door creaked open, revealing a beautiful library. It was bathed in a kaleidoscope of colour – blues and reds and purples and golds – the large stained-glass window casting strands of painted moonlight across the dust-laden shelves.

'How could Pascal neglect this place?' murmured Sera.

'I guess he didn't care much for stories,' said Bibi. 'Only coin.'

'What a waste of a life,' said Sera, thinking longingly of those endless afternoons in the cosy labyrinth of Babette's House of Books.

'You two are so easily distracted,' said Val, who had already found the safe under the desk, and was halfway through picking the lock. 'I could have done this entire job by myself.'

'Where's the fun in that?' Bibi drifted to the window. She pressed her palms against the coloured glass and peered out over the Verne. 'This must be the best view in Fantome.'

Sera wandered over to the desk and found a beautiful silver letter opener, engraved with the royal insignia of Valterre. Two swords crossed beneath a rose in bloom.

'Take it,' said Bibi, watching her admire it. 'Your first souvenir.'

'I don't even write letters,' Sera confessed as she slipped it into the pocket of her cloak.

'I'll write to you,' said Bibi, pilfering a fancy fountain pen and a pot of ink.

There was a loud *click*, followed by the keening groan of the safe door and then the triumphant crow of Val's laughter. 'I'm a genius! It didn't even take—'

Suddenly, a bell rang, the sound so deafening it reverberated around the room.

Sera snapped her head up. 'What the hell is that?'

Val rummaged through the safe. 'There must be a rope attached to the mechanism. The second I pulled it—'

She was interrupted by the sound of dogs barking. This time, from somewhere below.

'Run!' shouted Bibi.

But Val was shoulder-deep in the safe. 'I'm stuck!'

Sera lunged, yanking her out by the hood. Val reeled backwards with a sharp curse, and the tiara clattered to the floor between them. Sera snatched it up and jammed it onto Val's head, nestling it into the curls. 'There! Let's go!'

All three of them scrambled to their feet. They ran for the door, spilling out into the moonlit hallway. There were footsteps coming up the stairs, too quick and too many to be human. Sera spotted a shape at the other end of the hallway, and her breath caught in her throat.

There was a huge black dog prowling towards them. And three more were coming up the stairs.

'Guard dogs,' hissed Val. Villa Roman might have been neglected but its treasures had not been forgotten by the

Lorens. The girls lunged for the nearest shadow, grasping for invisibility, but the dog came right at them, a menacing growl rumbling in its throat.

'They're trackers,' Sera realized. 'Lose your cloaks! Your gloves! They can scent Shade!'

'We have to run for it!' Val ripped off her cloak and cast it over the first dog, temporarily blinding it. They made it to the second, and Bibi did the same thing. This way they managed to reach the stairs, where two more dogs were waiting for them. Sera grappled at her cloak but it was fastened too tightly and her hands were trembling wildly. In a fit of panic, she took off her glove and waved it in the air, desperately trying to distract the vicious creatures. Val and Bibi seized the chance, throwing themselves over the banister and landing on the floor below with a rattling thud.

Sera tried to follow them but one of the dogs caught her by the end of her cloak. She spun around, desperately swatting it with her glove. 'Get off me!'

'Sera!' Bibi called up in a strangled voice. 'Val's twisted her ankle!'

'Help her get outside!' she shouted back. 'I'll be right behind you.'

The lie was shrill, echoing all the way down the stairwell. She wasn't even close to getting out of here. The dogs had caught her and for all his skill and patience, Albert had not prepared her for this in self-defence class. She was screwed.

Sera kicked out and the dog growled, releasing her cloak. She ran for the library. The dogs bounded after her. She shoved the nearest shelf, sending a shower of books toppling to the ground. It bought her five seconds. She clambered over the desk, then tipped it over, buying another five.

But there was no way out. Nowhere to run. Nowhere to hide. She backed up against the stained-glass window, brandishing the letter opener.

'Stay back!' she yelled.

The dogs started to bark again, the commotion so loud she could have sworn it would wake everyone in Fantome. It was only a matter of time before the nightguards came. They would find her body ripped to shreds in a puddle of blue moonlight, the stupid cloak still fastened at her throat.

The dogs prowled towards her.

Sera closed her eyes and gripped the golden teardrop around her neck.

Mama, help me.

Suddenly, she felt something against her back. A crack in the window – a point of weakness. And there, at her side, a toppled chair.

The only way out was *out*.

The drop alone might kill her.

But, maybe . . . whispered a voice inside her. *Maybe it won't.*

Sera didn't have time to think. She pocketed the knife, picked up the chair and swung it with all her might. The window shattered in a shower of colourful glass.

Chapter 10

Ransom

Everything was going well until Ransom knocked over the flowerpot. It tumbled from the roof of Villa Roman and shattered in the garden, startling a stray cat.

Shit.

He froze, half expecting the back door to fly open and the girls to spill out in a panic. A minute passed, and then another, the slow heave of his breath puncturing the silence. He could sense them below him, winding their way through the dust-laden halls of Villa Roman, poking their heads into rooms where kings and queens had once sat.

The dirt on Pascal's grave was still wet. Cordelia Mercure was certainly quick off the mark. Ransom wondered what precious treasure she had sent them for.

Take only what your cloak can carry, and your conscience can bear. He recalled Armand Versini's famous words with wry amusement. Over the years, the Cloaks had rather stretched their founder's cardinal rule. Once, on a rainy midnight in Fantome, Ransom and Lark had spied five Cloaks carrying a seven-tier chandelier across the Bridge of Tears. And there were rumours that as a young initiate, Cordelia Mercure herself had stolen a pair of flamingos from the Menagerie Zoo.

No matter. Whatever the treasure tonight turned out to be, Seraphine Marchant would not be bringing it back to House Armand. She would not be returning there at all.

As the new moon poured its light along the banks of the Verne, Ransom sank into a crouch. His fingers were buzzing, the Shade strong inside him. It had been weeks since the incident at Rascalle, when Saint Oriel had mocked him with that lullaby, an unexpected echo of his former life. Time had blunted the sharp edge of the memory, allowing him to reclaim his senses.

Seraphine Marchant was the longest-running mark he had ever hunted, cloistering herself inside the Order of Cloaks these past few weeks, as if she knew he was coming for her. Like a fool, he'd given himself away. At least that's what he'd thought at first. But as he stalked the Hollows, night after night, waiting for the farmgirl to step out of her sanctuary, he started to hear things. Troubling things. First, news of a Cloak found murdered down by the harbour, his lips black with Shade. Perhaps Seraphine had not been hiding from him in particular – all the Cloaks were hiding from the Daggers.

Rumours were spreading like wildfire: the Daggers were out of control. Gaspard Dufort was finally losing his grip on his

Order. There were other rumours too: whispers of monsters rising from the sewers to stalk the streets at night, people being snatched from their gardens, disappearing without a trace. Ransom brushed them off. He didn't believe in monsters. *He* was the monster. But monsters or no, one thing was plain – the ordinary folk of Fantome were facing something far more sinister and dangerous than the Daggers.

Dufort, of course, was furious. The Head Dagger had become so incensed at the mounting reports, he dragged every single member of the Order in for questioning. He could be heard bellowing at them at all hours of the day and night, his rancorous rage rattling through the catacombs of Fantome until no one in Hugo's Passage could get a wink of sleep.

Despite the Daggers' nightly patrols, the rogues were still at large. They were making the Order look careless, sloppy. And after what Gaspard had done to Sylvie Marchant, the other smugglers were getting nervous. There was trouble in the catacombs. Trouble in Fantome.

Right now, Ransom's trouble was directly underneath him. After weeks of waiting, he was going to come face to face with her again, and this time, there would be no lullaby.

A bell sounded, unsettling a flock of river gulls. The tiles rattled under his feet as he stalked across the roof. He heard dogs barking. Trackers, most likely.

Girls' voices began to scream.

The back door burst open, sending a frightened fox skittering through the bushes. He peered over the roof and saw two girls hobbling through the garden. Cloakless. One redhead, one with purple hair. And ... was that a *tiara*? The girl was cursing and limping, while the redhead was crying so hard she couldn't speak.

No sign of Seraphine. But by the sickening growls in the building below him, Ransom guessed where she was. Though dead or alive, he couldn't tell. He watched the other two girls scramble over the railings with a ripple of disgust. He couldn't imagine leaving Lark or Nadia to such a grisly fate.

'Stay back!' Seraphine's voice cut through the night.

Ransom anchored himself to the drainpipe and looked down. He could trace her outline as she stood against the stained-glass window. Not only was she alive, she was fighting for her life.

The dogs were almost upon her. *Hell's teeth*, they were going to savage her.

A chair sailed through the stained-glass window, shattering it into a million pieces. It was followed, almost immediately, by Seraphine Marchant. She screamed as she leaped through the falling glass, soaring over a stone balustrade and skidding down the sloping roof.

The end of her cloak snagged on the horn of a gargoyle, bringing her to an abrupt stop in mid-air. For a moment, she hung half-choked from the sculpture, her feet dangling helplessly above the Verne. Then a look of determination came over her reddening face, so fierce it made Ransom laugh.

Here was a girl determined to live.

And ten feet above her stood the assassin who had been sent to kill her. He was not unaware of the unfairness of that. And he was impressed by her. He was compelled, despite himself, by the fire in her eyes and the hiss of her breath as she flung her arm up, reaching for the end of her cloak.

It seemed a shame to kill her.

The mark is just a mark. Dufort's voice echoed in his head.

Ransom set his jaw. This was about his survival, too.

She twined her fingers in her cloak, using the twisted material as a rope to pull herself up. To his mounting surprise, she managed to reach the gargoyle, grabbing its horn with one hand, and throwing her free arm around its neck. Her feet scrabbled for purchase as she clambered onto the balustrade, caught between the narrow walkway and the roof.

Ransom had hesitated long enough. With the Shade coursing through his veins, he reached inwards for that familiar mask, the cold impassivity he had spent years cultivating – the bravado that allowed him to be a Dagger. To be ruthless and unfeeling, and entirely in control.

Then he pulled a shadow from the roof and swung down to the balustrade.

It was a soundless landing, barely six feet from where his mark was kneeling with her cheek pressed against the gargoyle. He sauntered towards her, stepping into a shaft of moonlight.

He sensed the exact moment she saw him. Her body stiffened and she hugged the gargoyle closer, as though it could save her. He heard her breathing become fast and shallow, caught the whispered plea between her lips, but when she looked up at him, there was no fear on her face. Just that same fierce determination. And beneath it, a glowing ember of hatred.

'*You*,' she breathed.

Ransom rolled his neck, sinking into the game. 'Me,' he said, with a feral smile.

Chapter 11

Seraphine

The Dagger came from nowhere, stepping out of thin air as if Sera had conjured him with the strength of her own fear. He towered over her now, dressed head to toe in black. No cloak, but he didn't need one. Shade moved inside him. In the moonlight, she could see it writhing beneath his olive skin. A black whorl breached the collar of his sweater, and she cursed herself for not spotting the shadow-mark at the marketplace. A white scar sliced through his bottom lip. She had been too distracted by his eyes to notice that either.

Those eyes were quicksilver now, and hard as steel.

'Dancing swan,' he said, flashing his teeth. No sign of the warm, honey-gazed curiosity he had shown at the Rascalle. He cocked his head. 'Or is it dangling swan?'

She squared her jaw, summoning a mask of defiance. 'I'm not going to make this easy for you.'

His smirk grew. 'I like a challenge.'

Sera wanted to punch the smile off his smug face, then spit in it for good measure, but she was too busy clinging onto the gargoyle for dear life. 'My friends are coming for me.'

He tossed her a pitying look. 'Don't you know? There's no honour among thieves.'

'What would *you* know of honour?'

'You'd be surprised, Seraphine.'

She hated the way he said her name. Like a deadly caress. 'How long have you been following me?'

He narrowed his eyes, as if he was deciding whether to kill her outright or continue the conversation. A shadow curled around his arm, waiting to strike. More swarmed at his feet, straining to taste her. 'Quite a while,' he said. 'But you already know that.'

'For a Dagger, you're not exactly subtle.'

He leaned forward and plucked a shard of glass from her hair. 'For a Cloak, neither are you.'

She glowered up at him. 'Stalker.'

'I prefer the term assassin,' he said, tossing it aside.

'What about *gutless prick*?'

He stroked his stubbled jaw. 'No, I don't think I like that one.'

Sera's eyes darted. Above her, the dogs were still barking. Below her lay the cobbled street and beside it the rushing waters of the Verne, too far down to reach. And even then, the current would sweep her away. Or she could hop down onto the narrow walkway beside the balustrade, but she'd have to fight him for a foothold. And he had every advantage. He was a foot taller than her, broad-shouldered, with strong arms and long legs. Then there were those violent quicksilver eyes and the arsenal of shadows at his disposal.

He was Death itself.

But she was not dying tonight. No. She refused to let it end like this.

She just needed a second to think.

He flexed his fingers, shadows wreathing his knuckles as he stepped towards her. 'Now that we've dispensed with the pleasantries, we should come to the matter at hand,' he drawled.

'Wait.'

To Sera's surprise, he halted, a flicker of curiosity in his eyes. 'What for?'

'You killed my mother.' The words burst from her in a rush of desperation. 'You burned our home to the ground. You destroyed everything. *Why?*'

'That wasn't me.'

'So, you're a liar *and* a murderer.' She curled her lip, recalling all too easily the memory of him standing over Mama in the smoke. 'Aren't you proud of it?'

Shadows swelled at his back, blotting out the stars, and she could have sworn she'd managed to piss him off. 'I don't play with fire, Seraphine.'

'Stop saying my name.'

'What would you prefer, dancing swan? Angry swan, perhaps?'

He seemed to be enjoying their conversation. Or at the very

least, indulging in it. But the more she talked, the longer she lived. 'Tell me, Dagger,' she said, jutting out her chin. 'Do *you* have a name?'

That prompted a low chuckle. 'You haven't earned it.'

'And what will my death earn you? A pat on the back from Dufort? A kiss on the forehead at bedtime?'

He stiffened, smirk vanishing. 'Enough stalling. You're wasting time.'

Sera carefully released the gargoyle. 'And you're going to hell.'

'Maybe,' he said with a shrug. 'But not tonight.'

She shot to her feet and stumbled backwards along the narrow ledge, fighting for balance. He watched her struggle with mild interest.

'What *can* you be thinking, dancing swan? Are you really going to jump?'

She briefly considered it. 'Would that ruin your fun?'

'What part of this makes you think I'm having fun?'

'That stupid smirk on your stupid face.' The river wind rippled up Sera's cloak, reminding her of the drop below. She swallowed, thickly, reaching for another strand of courage. 'I am not dying tonight. This is not my destiny.'

'I think I'll decide that.' Shadows kissed her boots, rising to stroke her ankles.

'What right have you to decide anything for me?' she said, voice wavering as she watched them. 'To *hurt* me?'

The shadows stilled, as though pausing to consider her question. 'Don't drag this out, Seraphine,' the Dagger said, in a voice that was almost kind. 'I'll make it quick.'

She jumped, landing on the narrow walkway between the balustrade and the house. Her knees crunched upon landing, her teeth singing. He stepped down after her, filling up the space like an avenging angel. She backed up until she hit the end of the balustrade. Nowhere to run now. Overhead, the dogs had stopped barking. They had given up. She grabbed the letter opener from her pocket.

'I wouldn't do that if I was you,' he said, without breaking eye contact.

'Why? Don't monsters bleed?'

He gave her another pitying look. 'Only when you can actually strike them.'

'You shouldn't underestimate me.'

'What are you going to do, open me and read me?'

'Maybe I'll stick it in your eye.'

He barked a laugh. 'Go ahead, Seraphine. Do your worst.'

Sera brandished the letter opener. The Dagger struck, lightning fast, and before she could even blink, his hand was around her throat. Darkness swarmed around them, swallowing the moon. He lifted her up until she dangled like a marionette. Time slowed to an agonizing pace, his shadows closing in on her until she could see nothing beyond those silver eyes, gleaming like fallen stars. All too soon, it was here – the last moment of Sera's life, the finality of her own death rising to meet her like a great and terrible wave. There wasn't even time to be afraid.

Ten heartbeats, and she would be dead.

One. An agonizing coldness invaded her body. Frost filled her lungs, chasing away the last of her breath.

Two. Her eyes filled with tears, but she didn't blink. Didn't dare betray a hint of the dying plea that now ravaged her heart, *Help me, help me, help me.* Instead, she held his cruel silver gaze, determined that her death would haunt him.

Three. She opened her mouth, the word soundless on her lips. *Monster.*

Four. His grip wavered, dark brows knitting. Perhaps it was a trick of the moonlight or the addled thoughts of a dying brain, but he looked unsettled.

Five. A sudden shock of heat surged through Sera's body. For a heartbeat, it felt like her bones were bursting into flame. But the fire brought no pain. Only warmth.

Six. The Dagger's eyes went wide. Colour bloomed inside them, a soft autumnal glow swallowing the menacing silver.

Seven. He cried out, the air rippling with the scent of burning. And just beneath it, the faint tang of lemon blossom.

Eight. Sera gasped a new breath. With this strange warmth, came light. The shadows inside her fell away like ashes in the wind.

Nine. He released her, stumbling backwards. His gaze fell to the teardrop at her throat. It was glowing so brightly, it burned tears in her eyes. Seared every last shadow between them.

Ten. Emboldened by the shock of fear on the Dagger's face, Sera smirked.

'You're not dead,' he rasped. He stared, horror-struck, at her necklace, and it took everything in Sera not to do the same. '*How?*'

She had no answer for him. Whatever this strange fire inside her was, it had sprung up at his touch and ripped through his Shade.

Now the Dagger was just a man.

She was a flame.

And she refused to die tonight. But as for him ... The teardrop sizzled at her throat, sharing in the hurricane of her adrenaline. With a thundering cry, Sera leaped at the Dagger. She sank the letter opener into his gut, gritting her teeth as she pushed and *pushed*, through skin and blood and muscle.

He crumpled over with a sucking gasp.

When the blade was buried to its hilt, Sera's face was barely an inch from his, so close she could smell the wild mint on his breath. She twisted the handle, resting her forehead against his, so her eyes would be the last thing he saw. 'Bleeding swan,' she whispered.

He opened his mouth to respond, but blood poured out instead.

Sera reeled backwards, leaving the knife in his gut. 'Keep the souvenir. Courtesy of Sylvie Marchant.'

Then she turned on her heel and ran.

Buoyed by the roaring surge of adrenaline, she slipped over the end of the balustrade and leaped for a nearby trellis. She caught a vine, dragging her body close to the wall. The lattice groaned, but she was slight and nimble, not to mention well used to climbing the ruins of old farmhouses.

Sera scrambled down the side of Villa Roman, listening for any sign of disturbance. A barking dog, a patrolling nightguard, another assassin waiting in the wings. But there was only the gentle rush of the Verne and the fading groans of a Dagger who had fallen on his blade.

Good riddance.

When she was halfway down the building, Sera slipped, losing her footing on a cracked rung. But luck followed her down, and a lilac bush cushioned her fall. She rolled out of it, spitting petals as she headed for the iron railings.

It was only when her feet hit the cobblestones on the other side that she allowed her mind to reel. Triumph giving way to fear and confusion, as she tried to piece together what had happened up there. She stumbled towards the river, and only then realized she was still wearing her cloak. She wiped her bloodstained hands on it. Then, fingers trembling, she clutched the teardrop at her throat.

This strange, impossible thing.

She measured her breaths, trying to make sense of the magic that had just burst from her like a sunbeam and shredded all that Shade into ribbons.

In the distance, the Aurore guarded the city like a trusty soldier, casting its faithful glow across the slumbering streets. She gazed towards it now like it might hold the answer to this new mystery.

Mama's voice echoed in the back of Sera's mind. *And when the time comes, you will rise far above this wicked city, and become a flame in the dark.* The night wind kissed her cheeks, as though the saints were whispering to her too. *You will be the Aurore, Seraphine.*

The teardrop was no longer glowing, but Sera could feel the remnants of its magic humming in her bones. She sensed her mother's presence in its simmering warmth. And something else, too. A secret, revealed from beyond the grave. There was more to Sylvie Marchant than Shade. So much more.

'Thank you, Mama,' Sera whispered. 'For your love. For your magic.'

Wherever it had come from and whatever it meant, she would find out. But for now, she sighed with relief and pulled up her hood, disappearing into the dark.

Chapter 12

Ransom

Ransom was half-dead by the time Seraphine disappeared. High on the balcony of Villa Roman, he lay slumped in a pool of blood and shattered glass, trying to fight the blackness in his mind. Beneath the serrated edge of his pain, he felt a ripple of anger. Worse, *humiliation*. For nearly ten years he had stalked the streets of Fantome, without fear of anyone or anything. He was a weapon, honed by Shade. Unstoppable, unbeatable. And in less than ten seconds, a mouthy farmgirl had brought him to his knees.

With a letter opener.

Fuck.

He had felt bad about having to kill her before – hesitated, even, and more than once – but now ... *Now*, he really was going to murder her.

If he didn't die first.

He braced himself against the bloody stones, feeling a twinge in his right hand. The skin of his palm was smooth, but a moment ago it had sizzled. Something had flared out of her at his touch, shoving against him. It had burned him. *She* had burned him. One moment, he was holding her up like a ragdoll, willing her heart to stop quickly and painlessly, and the next, she was glowing like the sun.

She had looked just as surprised as he was.

And then she had stabbed him.

His head lolled dangerously, his sight fading. The night had grown dark again. Seraphine and her little magic trick had scoured the Shade from his bones. He fumbled in the pocket of his coat and found another vial. His spare. He pulled out the stopper with his teeth and tipped it all down his gullet.

His teeth chattered as the cold set in, familiar shadows spreading out inside him. They filled his veins, staunched the flow of his blood, just long enough for him to remove the knife lodged in his lower right side.

He hissed as it came free, the blade slick, then pulled up his shirt, examining the wound. The blood around it was so dark, it joined the whorls of his shadow-marks, congealing in a long narrow strip. He pressed his hands against the gash, sweat pouring from his brow as the Shade went to work. A temporary solution, but with any luck, it would be enough to get him off this balcony and back to Hugo's Passage.

'*Seraphine.*' Ransom muttered the name like a swearword. He had been a fool for hesitating, for talking to her at all. He cursed the primal instinct that had urged him to be gentle with her, that had roared at him as he curled his hands around her throat.

Never again. *Never.*

His gaze slid over the bloodied knife. That little spitfire was going to regret this.

He managed to drag himself to his feet. His body was weak, but the Shade was strong. He pulled a shadow from the roof and held onto it with both hands, carefully lowering himself into the garden. When he reached the ground his wound screamed but he stumbled across the garden before pulling himself over the railings and onto the street.

He stopped on the banks of the Verne, slowed by indecision. A part of him wanted to track Seraphine all the way back to the Hollows and finish what he started, tonight. Throw a brick through her window, scale the walls of House Armand, scream her name until his throat went raw. Pin her, kill her, make her suffer this time. Make her beg.

Get a hold of yourself, Ransom.

Pain was making him irrational, and the Shade was stoking his impulsiveness. If he set foot in House Armand tonight, in this state, he'd be in a cell by sunrise. Cordelia Mercure would make sure of it. And then Ransom would never untangle the mystery of this maddening spitfire and the magic she wore around her neck.

He thought fleetingly of her mother's farmhouse engulfed in flames, and wondered what other secrets Sylvie Marchant had hidden there. What other secrets Gaspard Dufort had tried to burn.

He hadn't destroyed them all.

But Ransom now understood this: Seraphine Marchant was no ordinary farmgirl. She was more dangerous than he could have imagined. More *infuriating*. He imagined her triumphant smile, that fleck of bronze glowing fiercely in her eye as she uttered those taunting words. *Bleeding swan.*

He bit off another swearword. He would have his revenge. But first, he had to survive the night. So, he set out on the long, agonizing walk home.

He was almost at the Bridge of Tears when a distant scream rang out. He snapped his chin up, just in time to catch the streetlamps flickering. A swathe of shadows moved up from the south. The air filled with a sudden putrid stench. It turned Ransom's stomach, setting him on high alert.

There was someone else here.

Something else.

He stalked in the direction of the scream, following the streetlamps as they faded, one by one. When he reached Merchant's Way, the taverns were dark, empty. The revellers had fled.

There was a body on the ground. An old woman in a ragged coat. A fresh kill. Her cerise lipstick was smeared along her cheek, and her papery skin was as grey as the Verne in winter. Her eyeballs were black.

His heart began to thunder, the Shade inside him surging to attention. It was not the body that unsettled him, but the thing he saw loping away from it. A darkness he could not see through. It moved like a man. Only it was taller, bigger. A beast.

A *monster*, he realized, with a sickening jolt.

Every instinct inside Ransom told him to turn on his heel and run in the opposite direction. But curiosity rooted him to the spot. Here was one of the monsters that had crawled up from the harbour or out of the sewers to terrorize the streets of Fantome. The rumours were true.

If Ransom could catch this beast – or better, *kill it* – he would curry favour with Dufort. And more importantly, he'd be able to rectify the damage that Seraphine Marchant had just done to his reputation.

As if it could hear the spiral of his thoughts, the beast turned, suddenly.

Ransom froze, trying to make sense of its face. Its silver eyes were far too large, its pinprick pupils lost in the searing brightness of the rest. Its wide mouth was slack and toothless, its long black tongue hanging out to one side. Its shadowed form looked *almost* human, but it had no hair and its long arms hung strangely, like its shoulders had been dislocated.

The beast cocked its head, pinning Ransom with those awful glowing eyes. Suddenly weak, Ransom searched for his voice and managed to say, 'What *are* you?'

The monster's nostrils flared. Then it charged.

If Ransom wasn't injured, he might have been quicker, smarter. But there was no time to reach for a shadow or even to leap out of the way as the monster thundered towards him and then, with a terrible ragged howl, passed right *through* him.

The agony was so startling, so corrosive, that Ransom's heart stopped. He collapsed on the banks of the Verne. This time, when the blackness swept in, he couldn't fight it.

Chapter 13

Ransom

When Ransom woke up, he thought he was ten years old again. He was in the alley beside Balthazar's tavern, sitting on an empty rum barrel. His lip was split, his left eye so swollen he couldn't see out of it. Fear curled like a fist in his stomach. Before him stood Gaspard Dufort, the man who had plucked him from the banks of the Verne like a discarded coin that very morning.

'Well, boy. Are you ready to take back your power?' It wasn't a question, but Ransom nodded anyway. He wanted Dufort to know he was serious, that he was brave. Even as his hands trembled.

Dufort removed a glass vial from his pocket. Ransom's throat went dry as he stared at the fine black powder, glimpsing raw magic for the very first time. All his life, he had heard stories about Shade, the inky dust that sustained the underworld of Fantome. Like most people, he harboured a morbid fascination with the Cloaks and Daggers, the thieves and assassins who made midnight in the city their playground. But he didn't fear them. He already lived with a monster, a man who needed no such black powder to move through their cottage like a shadow, instilling fear with the mere creak of his footstep.

Dufort held the vial out. 'Don't swallow more than half,' he said, looking Ransom up and down. 'You're barely bigger than that barrel. We don't want you overdoing it.'

Ransom snatched the vial quickly so that the Dagger wouldn't see his fingers trembling and tipped half of its contents down his throat, wincing at his split lip, which had been hastily sewn back together with twine.

The taste of ash on his tongue was a welcome distraction. The Shade was *cold*. It went through him like a shiver until it felt like his bones were coated in frost. He curled his arms around his stomach, weathering the chill.

Gaspard's laugh rippled through the dark alley. 'Embrace it,' he said, clapping Ransom on the back and nearly knocking him off the barrel. 'It will make you a man.'

Ransom felt more like a corpse than a man, his heart so cold now he wasn't sure it was even beating. He clenched his fists, waiting for the sensation to subside. He wasn't sure if it really did, or if his body simply acclimatized to the Shade, but after a while, a strange heat erupted behind his eyes and the alley lit up, as though someone had scorched the darkness away. The swelling over his eye abated, and he felt taller somehow, stronger. When he looked down, he glimpsed shadows darting across his hands.

His fingers twitched.

Gaspard laughed again. 'Careful with those. You'll find that Shade has a will of its own.'

Ransom was seized by the sudden urge to stalk straight into Balthazar's, flinging chairs and tables out of the way, and lay hands on his bleary-eyed, liquored-up violent brute of a father.

Dufort grinned like he could read his thoughts. 'Hold those reins, boy.' He removed a gold pocket-watch from his coat and glanced at the face. 'Ten more minutes.'

Almost closing time. Papa never left Balthazar's before he had to.

The minutes crawled by, every second longer than the one before, until at last, the tavern lanterns went out. Stragglers stumbled into the deserted street, and there, among them, was Papa. A towering beast at six foot six, red-cheeked and slow-footed, and reeking of brandy. He stumbled off in the direction of home. Ransom stepped out of the alley and followed him.

Shade quickened his footsteps, but Dufort pulled him back. 'Being a Dagger is as much about waiting as it is about killing,' he cautioned. 'Patience, Ransom. Wait for the opportune moment, and when it arrives, don't hesitate. Even for a second.'

Ransom nodded, trying to push down the Shade inside him. To walk when he wanted to run. To breathe when he wanted to roar.

They walked on, following his father through the sleepy village of Everell, where soon the only sound was the distant trill of a nightingale and the rustle of the wind in the trees. They came to a familiar stone cottage.

Ransom watched his father grapple with the gate, then curse as he kicked it open. The wood splintered as it fell away from the wall, and Ransom grimaced at the casual destructiveness he had come to know all too well. His father stumbled up the garden path.

Ransom paused at the broken gate. Now that the moment was upon him, he had the urge to turn around and flee, just as Mama and Anouk had. Was the Shade wearing off too soon, or was his conscience stronger than its magic?

Dufort came to his side. 'What did I tell you about hesitation?'

Ransom swallowed. 'What if this is a mistake?'

Dufort's eyes flashed, and in them, Ransom glimpsed a true Dagger: ruthless, impatient. Dangerous. 'The mistake here would be wasting that vial of Shade I gave you.' He spoke through his teeth. 'Is that what you're trying to tell me, boy? That I wasted my Shade?'

'No,' said Ransom quickly. A new fear was rising. His father was a known quantity – a brash man with heavy fists and a cruel tongue. But Gaspard Dufort was another beast entirely. 'What if I get caught?'

Gaspard barked a laugh. 'When was the last time you read about a Dagger in the penny papers?'

Ransom frowned. *Never*, was the answer. Daggers didn't get caught.

Dufort nudged him through the gate. Ransom stumbled, trampling his mother's tulips. His heart ached as he remembered the day they had knelt in the garden to plant them, how Mama had laughed when he got dirt on his nose and then, seeing his cheeks flame in embarrassment, grabbed some to draw a moustache on herself. Afterwards, Anouk had accidentally tracked mud through the house and Mama had run for the mop in a panic, shooing them both upstairs when their father came stomping up the garden path.

Ransom pictured her face yesterday morning, how the bruise on her cheekbone had looked like a thundercloud. He remembered the hope gleaming in her eyes when they made it to the gates of Everell, then the fear guttering inside them as Papa's voice cut through the air behind them.

One more step, Gisele, and it will be the last you'll ever take.

Ransom had taken one look at his mother and his sister, teetering on the precipice of freedom, and decided to fight. It was all over in the blink of an eye. He should have died then, but he didn't. Maybe the saints had taken pity on him. Perhaps Saint Oriel herself had reached through the veil of the afterlife to keep his heart beating, to offer him a destiny that reached beyond his father's rage.

Ransom never got to see Mama and Anouk run, so he liked to imagine they'd flown, high above Everell, soaring away from the life that had nearly buried them all. From the man who would still bury them if he could. And that was the sorry truth of it all. While Papa lived, they would never truly be safe. They would never come home to Everell. They would never come back to Ransom.

His anger flared, propelling him towards the house. Shadows followed him inside. His father was sitting on the stairs in a puddle of lamplight, trying to unlace his boots. When the door slammed, he looked up, their eyes meeting in the dimness.

Ransom hesitated.

His father didn't. '*You*,' he hissed, lumbering to his feet.

He swung blindly. Missed. Shade made it easy to dodge the blow. Another swing. Ransom leaped out of the way and Papa hit the wall, cracking the plaster. He howled in pain.

'Fool,' said Ransom, surprised by the callousness of his own voice. The Shade was speaking for him.

His father spun, but Ransom caught his fist, stopping the strike in mid-air. The shadows lunged, crossing the barrier between their bodies. Time slowed as they burrowed into his father. His eyes widened until Ransom could see all the red thorns inside them. Then they turned black. Ransom watched death crawl across his father's face with a curious sense of detachment, as if he was not in his body but floating somewhere above it, letting the Shade act in his stead.

His father had a heart after all. It only took ten beats to kill him.

And then it was over.

When Papa slumped to the floor, Ransom was still in a daze. He looked down at his father's lifeless face. His eyes had rolled back in his head, their whites now inky black. His lips were black, too, twisted in the throes of a final curse. Those cruel fists lay slack at his sides. The monster had been felled. But Ransom felt no relief.

As he stood in the narrow hallway, the Shade left his body like a terrible wind howling out of his bones. The night grew dark around him. Nausea roiled in his gut, and he pitched forward. The stitches in his lip split and blood trickled out, mixing with his vomit. He sank to the floor, choking on his sobs.

He might have stayed like that all night, curled in a ball beside Papa's lifeless body, if Dufort hadn't slipped through the door and scooped him up, carrying him away from the ashes of his childhood.

'It's all right, boy,' he soothed. 'It's done now.'

When they reached the street, Dufort set him down again. This time, when he vomited, the man rubbed his back. 'Here comes the gloom. It will pass.'

Ransom groaned. 'When?'

'When the last lick of Shade leaves your body.'

Dufort released him and walked on, humming softly to himself. 'That could only have gone two ways,' he said, over his shoulder. 'You were either going to kill your father, or that vial of Shade was going to kill you. Truth be told, I've never used it on a kid before.' When Ransom didn't answer – only retched again – Dufort turned on the heel of his boot. He was grinning so wide, Ransom counted three more gold fillings. 'Thanks to you, tonight has opened up a whole new world of possibilities.'

Ransom wiped his mouth. 'What does that mean?'

'It means you passed the test.' Dufort winked, and in that twinkle of silver, Ransom saw an entire future unfurl. A fate he had not bargained for. A destiny woven by a devil, not a saint. 'Welcome to the Order of Daggers, son.'

Son. The word was a life raft in a stormy sea. Ransom hurried after Dufort.

By the time they reached Old Haven, he was so tired, he could have curled up under the statue of Saint Lucille and slept for a week. In the flickering lamplight, he looked at his hands, tracing the slim black whorl that had appeared on his right knuckle. It ached.

'Your first shadow-mark,' said Dufort, guiding him past the statue. 'Take pride in it. There will be more to come.'

But the sight of that mark only filled Ransom with dread, his heart pounding as they descended into the bowels of Fantome, where ancient skulls peered after him.

Down, down, down, into the dark.

Ransom woke to find a familiar pair of green eyes staring down at him.

'*Hell's teeth,*' said Lark in a strained voice. 'What happened to you?'

Ransom's hand flew to his chest, searching for his heartbeat. It thrummed dully beneath his fingers. He blinked, willing the world into focus, and remembered where he was. When he was. He was lying half-dead on the banks of the Verne.

'There was a monster,' he said, with a rasp.

'We lost it,' came Nadia's voice from the other side of him. 'We were tracking another one, eastward, when we got word of this one. That makes three separate sightings tonight.' She grimaced as she examined the blood on his clothes. 'Where did all this come from?'

Ransom flinched as she lifted up his sweater, revealing the deep wound in his side. And then he remembered the rest. '*Seraphine,*' he hissed.

'What?' said Nadia. 'Who—?'

'It's the farmgirl,' said Lark, leaning over to examine the wound.

Ransom's breath shallowed as he tried to sit up. His head spun and the world blurred. He was losing consciousness again, his friends' voices fading as the darkness swept back in.

Chapter 14

Seraphine

Seraphine had barely made it back to the Hollows when she heard screaming up ahead. People were pouring from the Cathouse bordello and scattering in a panic, shouting about a pair of monsters that had come up from the sewers like a black mist.

She pulled her cloak tighter, quickly folding herself into a doorway as a huge dark shape came stalking down the street. She blinked furiously, but it was no illusion. The towering creature loosely bore the shape of a man, only it was taller and bent out of all proportion, a beast draped in shadow. A nightmare brought to life.

It growled as it bore down on a bumbling drunkard, who had tripped in his haste to flee. His cries tore through the night, before abruptly cutting out. And then he was dead, crumpled among the leaves on the cracked cobbles.

The silence that followed was deafening. Sera didn't dare move in case the monster caught wind of her. But she could smell it as it lumbered past, that awful sulphuric stench sticking to her nostrils.

She had never seen anything like it.

But— *no.* That wasn't right. She *had* seen something like this before, in her own back garden. Not a monster, but a cat that had transformed before her eyes, into a vicious creature draped in shadow. Mama had been the one to feed it. Seraphine had watched it all from her bedroom, had even seen it attack Mama.

Hadn't she? The memory was so strange, sometimes she wondered if it was a dream. But now the world was tilting, and she didn't know what to think. Only that she had to get back to House Armand and warn the others.

She held her breath, waiting for the monster's plodding footsteps to fade. She clutched the bead around her neck, searching for the same bravery that had found her on the balcony of Villa Roman. The teardrop warmed in her grip, and she sought comfort in the thrum of its magic, even if it made no sense to her. She didn't fully trust it yet. She didn't *know* it yet.

The monster disappeared, taking its reign of terror west towards the Scholars' Quarter, where some other unlucky soul would likely fall into its jaws. Sera didn't wait around to find out.

She darted out from the doorway and went east, only to halt

at the sight of another, larger creature halfway down the street. It snapped its head up, scenting her on the wind.

Shit.

Sera lunged for a nearby shadow but her necklace flared at the sudden rush of her panic. The beast stalked towards her. The bead had become a beacon at her throat, pulsing as though it was calling out to the creature.

She clamped her fist around the teardrop, smothering the light. Too late. The monster's eyes grew wider, its long black tongue snaking along the seam of its lips. A moth beholding a flame.

It pounced high, but she slid underneath it, coming quickly to her feet. She bolted into the night, her heart hammering at the sound of those loping footsteps behind her. They got louder, closer.

Her legs screamed, her lungs burning. She pushed on even as her body slowed, each laboured gasp searing her chest. Just when she thought the beast was going to lunge and catch her by the neck, a ragged howl rang out from the direction of the Scholars' Quarter. The monster skidded to a halt.

Sera didn't dare stop, even as she stole a glance over her shoulder. The creature was turning, starting to head towards that awful sound. Another monster, perhaps. Or another victim. Sera tried not to wince. Better them than her. She had fought too hard tonight to die.

She forged on, her head pounding as she raced through the midnight streets until at last, the lanterns winked out and the hedge that marked the boundary of House Armand feathered the darkness. She tugged her hood free as she rounded it, thundering down the garden path where she crashed straight into Theo, who was coming out of the front door.

'Sera!' He caught her by the shoulders, sweeping his startled gaze over her. 'You're here. I was just coming to—'

'Retrieve my corpse?' she said, half-breathless, half-wired with adrenaline.

He frowned. 'Well, the idea was to rescue you.'

'Then you're a hell of a lot braver than I thought,' she said, pushing him inside, and going with him. She kicked the door closed, then pressed her back against it.

He blinked. 'I don't know about bravery, but I've got a pocket full of chicken laced with valerian root. Every hound's weakness.'

Sera closed her eyes. So much had happened since the guard dogs at Villa Roman, she had almost forgotten about them entirely. Her fingers flew to her collar, where she grappled with the damn knot on her cloak. 'Can you help me with this?' she heaved. 'I feel like I'm choking.'

It was the panic, she knew. But Theo went to work anyway, deftly untying the cloak.

She closed her eyes and inhaled through her nose, smelling the sandalwood and vanilla that rolled off him, letting it anchor her. His hands brushed against her collarbone as he removed her cloak. It fell away, and whether it was the lightness it left behind or the warmth of the Shadowsmith standing with her in the safety of House Armand, she finally felt like she could breathe again.

'That's better,' she said, on a long sigh. 'Thank you.'

He flashed a grin. 'I'm always happy to help you undress.'

'And now you've ruined it.'

Bibi and Val were in the rec room on the third floor when Sera shuffled in. Bibi whimpered at the sight of her, then leaped from her chair and pulled her into a hug. Even Val, who was ordinarily averse to physical affection, hobbled over to join in.

'We're so sorry, Sera,' said Bibi, between sniffs. 'We thought you were right behind us, and then Val twisted her ankle and— and—'

'We left you there as dog fodder,' said Val, her face tight with regret. 'We should have stayed. We should have fought—'

'I'm glad you ran,' said Sera, pulling back to look at both of them. 'It was the smart decision.'

And more than that, she was relieved they hadn't witnessed the Dagger leaping from the roof of Villa Roman, or what she had done to him after. They might think her a monster after the way she gutted him.

'All home in one piece,' said Theo, leaning against the doorframe. 'Told you I'd rescue her.'

'We watched you from the window, Branch,' said Val flatly. 'You never even made it out of the house.'

'That's how good I am at heroism.'

Sera rolled her eyes, but a watery smile tugged at her lips. Theo and Bibi helped Val back into the armchair, propping her swollen ankle on a pile of cushions.

Now that the adrenaline was finally leaving Sera's body, anxiety was taking root. She clutched her necklace, wondering what the hell was inside it as she paced by the fireplace. She turned her gaze to the flames, thinking of all the times she had watched her mother tinkering with metals and powders at her bench in the garden, long after the work day was done. If only she had bothered to take interest in them. Maybe then she would know about this magic in her necklace, and why it seemed to repel Daggers but attract monsters. Both beings of Shade.

'Tell us how you got free of those hounds,' said Val. 'You must have sold your soul to Saint Oriel.'

'I jumped,' said Sera, offering the truth in its vaguest form for now. She wasn't ready to tell them everything, at least not until she made sense of it herself. 'I threw a chair through the window and leaped onto the balcony.' *Then I stabbed a Dagger to death.* She shook off the vision of his face from her mind, silenced the memory of the terror in his voice.

You're not dead . . . How?

Sera wished she knew.

'I climbed down the trellis and landed in a lilac bush.' She picked a twig from her hair and tossed it into the fire. 'I ran into a monster on my way home.' A pause as the enormity of what had happened finally settled over her like a thundercloud. 'Two, actually.'

Bibi and Val pitched forward in their seats. Theo stilled, his gaze falling to the teardrop at her throat. Sera hadn't realized she was still clutching it. She hastily tucked it under the collar of her sweater. There would be time for that later, but not now, not here. She went on, describing the monsters as best she could, confirming the rumours that had been swirling around Fantome for weeks. Her friends listened in horrified silence and when she finished, the room was so quiet she could hear Madame Fontaine's snores rattling from the floor above them.

'Where on earth are the monsters coming from?' pondered Bibi.

'I don't know,' said Sera, and that was the worst of it. She suddenly felt like she didn't know anything. About Fantome. About magic. About Mama.

Theo closed his eyes and scrubbed his hands through his hair, a skilled artificer trying to make sense of an abomination. But there was no sense to be found.

'Are you going to tell Madame Mercure?' said Val.

'No need,' came a voice from the doorway. Cordelia Mercure stepped into the room, wearing a black velvet robe and a thunderous expression. 'I heard everything. Grave tidings indeed.'

'Not all of it,' said Val, plucking the Rizzano tiara from a side table and waving it back and forth. 'At least we nailed the Heist.'

Mercure's nostrils flared as she snatched it, but her interest in the tiara quickly faded. 'We have far bigger matters to worry about now.' Her brows knitted, casting ripples along her forehead. 'I'm afraid I can see no way around it. I must speak with Gaspard Dufort and arrange a meeting of the Orders.'

Sera's stomach twisted violently. And though her necklace was tucked safely under her sweater, she didn't miss the way it flared at that name, sharing in the silent spike of her fear.

Part II

'When the world is at its darkest, we
must reach bravely through the shadows
to find where the light blooms.'

Lucille Versini,
SAINT OF SCHOLARS

Chapter 15

Ransom

Ransom stirred on and off until the early afternoon, when Lark and Nadia came banging on his bedroom door.

'Oh, good. You're still alive,' said Lark, striding inside.

'Barely,' croaked Ransom.

'It was touch-and-go there for a while,' said Nadia, peering down at him.

Ransom reached for the pitcher of water on his nightstand and drained it. 'Don't tell me,' he said, taking in the hesitant looks on his friends' faces. 'Dufort wants to see me.'

Lark nodded. 'Lisette overheard the commotion in here last night.'

'I really hate that snitch,' muttered Nadia.

Ransom rolled out of bed and flinched as pain flared all along his right side. Lark lunged to steady him.

Last night, after getting him home, Lark and Nadia had fetched a local physician and long-time ally of the Order. In the privacy of his bedchamber, she had seen to the wound in his side, treating it with alcohol and then a tincture of herbs, before sewing the skin back together. Thirty-six stitches of tough black thread, to match the whorls around it.

An inch to the left, and this would have been fatal, she'd told Lark and Nadia as Ransom bit down on his pillow to keep from screaming. It was an effort not to arch his back, to endure the stab and pull of the needle as it plunged deep, over and over again. *But the fever is still working on him. You need to get it to break.*

'Do you want Shade for the pain?' Lark asked him now, his voice laced with worry.

Ransom shook his head. Last night he had been in such agony he hadn't thought about anything else, but Lark had kept vigil at his bedside, counting his breaths as he slept, urging him to drink water every time he stirred and administering special tinctures every couple of hours. When his fever broke just after dawn, Ransom heard his best friend humming, gently guiding him through the fog of his nightmares.

Nadia had taken over from Lark at sunrise, laying a cool cloth on Ransom's brow and holding his hand in hers, chatting softy to him as he slept, as if they were two old friends taking a stroll along the Verne.

Ransom had survived the night, but he had not slept off his rage or humiliation. Although the scope of his feelings had since broadened to include a simmering relief at being alive, and a fierce gratitude for his two best friends. He didn't have the words to properly convey just how much they both meant to him, and when he tried, Nadia flinched.

'Ugh, no deathbed speeches,' she warned. 'You'll smudge my eyeliner.'

Lark helped him dress as quickly as his wound allowed, then knelt to lace up his boots. 'Have you decided what to tell Dufort?'

Ransom ground his teeth. He didn't know whether to admit his failure and suffer the consequences or say nothing of Villa Roman and redouble his efforts to pin down the girl.

'Are you going to mention Seraphine?' Nadia pressed.

Ransom bristled. 'Don't say that name.'

Lark raised his eyebrows. 'It won't make her magically appear.'

'No, but it still pisses me off.' Ransom knew he was being dramatic, petulant even, but that name conjured other things – visions of those dancing blue eyes, memories of the irritating smugness in her voice. *Bleeding swan.* And then there was the memory of the bead that had burned around her neck. The flame that had *burned* him. If he thought about it for too long it would drive him to violence and he couldn't afford to lose his composure in front of Dufort. Not after losing his mark.

Lark said no more. Ransom was glad of the silence as they walked to the Cavern, which was bustling with Daggers chatting over lunch. Dufort was in his usual spot at the back, with Lisette, the sharp-tongued, ambitious Dagger who was always clamouring for a shot at that gaudy ring on his left hand. At twenty-one, she was a couple of years older than Ransom, and possessed a hostile, feline beauty that matched her personality: that of a ruthless killer. She tossed her ice-blonde hair now, her grey eyes raking over him as he approached.

'You're limping,' she said, by way of greeting.

Dufort looked Ransom up and down. His eyes were clear today, his scowl deep. 'What happened last night?'

Lisette's red lips curled. 'Don't tell me your little farmgirl stuck you with her pitchfork.' She was teasing, but there was a note of hunger in her voice. Ransom's failure would bring her one step closer to claiming his role as Dufort's Second, the heir to the Order and all its riches, which included the favour of the king himself.

It was chiefly for this reason that Ransom decided to lie. 'I never got to the mark. I was on my way across the river when I ran into a monster.' He frowned at the memory. 'Well. It ran *through* me.'

Dufort sat up straight, the blood draining from his cheeks. 'So, the rumours are true.'

Ransom nodded. 'A beast of Shade. I plunged into a blackness so complete I couldn't remember my own name.' Without meaning to, his hands went to the wound in his side. 'I didn't think I'd ever wake up.'

The smile died on Lisette's face. 'Did this monster know you were a Dagger?'

'If it did, it didn't care.' A pause, then, 'I was lucky to have that Shade in my system.' Not that it lasted. 'It would have killed me if it had doubled back.'

Dufort's face tightened, his gaze falling to Ransom's side. Worry flickered there. 'Looks like it made a good attempt.'

Ransom didn't correct him.

Lark, who had been hovering close behind him, stepped forward. 'Nadia and I were following a lead down by the Scholars' Quarter when we heard the screams up on Merchant's Way. When we came across Ransom, he was half dead.'

'Tell me everything,' Dufort growled. 'Leave nothing out.'

Ransom left a lot of things out, but he gave Dufort what he most wanted: every detail he could recall about the monster; the way it moved, how it looked, even its sulphuric stench. Dufort sat in stony silence, while the other Daggers left their own conversations to listen in.

The story wasn't long – after all, Ransom had left out the first part entirely and he had been unconscious for most of the rest – but before he could finish, young Collette arrived in a clatter of footsteps.

'Mister Dufort! This just arrived for you.' She waved an envelope sealed with dark green wax. 'It's from House Armand.'

Dufort leaped to his feet, snatching the letter. Silence rippled through the Cavern as the Daggers watched him read it, Dufort's eyebrows lifting higher with each word. Then he crumpled the parchment with a rasping laugh. 'Looks like hell has frozen over,' he said, flinging it into the fireplace. 'Cordelia Mercure wants a meeting.'

Ransom got a proper look at himself when he went to bathe later that afternoon. His dark hair hung in damp tendrils across his forehead and there was a waxy sheen to his olive skin. Even his eyes looked tired. And yet, as he stood shirtless in front of the mirror, tracing the shadow-marks that marred his chest and shoulders, he saw that his right hand was different. He peered at the knuckle where a shadow-mark had once been. His *first* mark. For nearly ten years, that whorl had curled around his fingers like a branch of inky thorns. It had stung like them, too.

Now, it was gone. The skin there was unblemished, smooth and new, and when he pressed it, there was no pain. Not even the faintest tingle. He stared and stared, his heart swelling in his chest as he examined the hand that had killed so many, including his own father. The hand that had dangled Seraphine like a puppet on a string. The hand she had burned on that balcony. And now it was . . . clean.

He pressed it to his chest, inhaling deeply as he searched the dark reaches of himself, prodding at the heaviness that lingered there. Was it his imagination or had it lessened? Had some of the darkness inside him been burned away too? He traced his knuckle again, this new marvel before him, and remembered that bright light shining out of Seraphine's necklace. In her desperate haste to free herself had she accidentally healed some old wound of his without even realizing it?

Another question gripped him, so tight he couldn't breathe from the hope of it . . . Could she burn all the poison away, so that he could crawl out of this cruel place and leave behind the yawning hollow of darkness that would one day swallow him whole?

As Ransom watched himself in the mirror, his eyes grew,

the gold inside them hungry and bright, as though another version of himself was peering out of them. *What would you give for another chance at freedom? What would you risk to go all the way back?*

He dropped his head, caressing that little patch of unblemished skin.

Everything.

The meeting of the Orders took place the following Sunday at the bottom of the Aurore Tower, where the dusky autumn sky flickered with firelight. Dufort chose three Daggers to accompany him – Lisette, Lark and Ransom. By then, the pain in Ransom's side was less of a constant ragged shriek and more of a dull groan. Present but manageable. Still, it wracked him in the night whenever he turned on his side, or when his dreams conjured up that damn spitfire and her wicked little smile.

What an extraordinary secret she possessed. What life-changing power. It had come to plague his every thought.

When the Daggers arrived at Primrose Square, the rolling gardens within which the tower stood, Cordelia Mercure was already waiting for them. She was wearing a long violet coat, a wide-brimmed black hat and a scowl that could sink a ship. No cloak, but that was the rule. *No cloaks, no Shade.*

Dufort chuckled under his breath. 'If looks could kill . . .'

'That scowl is nearly as good as mine,' said Lisette, waggling her fingers in greeting.

Mercure stood with her arms folded, pretending not to see the gesture.

Ransom's heart pounded as he scanned the Cloaks on either side of Mercure. There was no sign of the spitfire. He chewed on his lip, unsure if he was relieved or pissed off. It wasn't like he could confront her, with an audience present.

'Surely you didn't think she'd be here,' whispered Lark, reading his mind like he always could. 'She's been a Cloak for all of a month.'

Behind Cordelia stood a tall, muscled man with cropped black hair, brown skin and keen brown eyes that assessed them with militant calm. To her right, a young tanned man with slicked-back silver hair and eyes so bright Ransom could see the hatred in them from all the way across the square. On her other side, a pale old woman with a cane, her face so wrinkled, she looked like a walking scowl.

'Fontaine,' muttered Dufort, voice rippling with disdain. 'I thought the old bat was dead.'

They came to a stop twenty feet from the Cloaks. High above them, three huge troughs of flames flickered along the stone scaffolds of the Aurore, the light from them melding into a single soaring glow.

'Beautiful,' murmured Lark, looking up at it. 'We should come here with Nadia some time.'

Ransom smirked. *Sap.*

'Gaspard,' said Cordelia in a cold voice.

'Cordelia,' he parried, colder still. 'Always a displeasure.'

Fontaine leaned on her cane. 'Hateful creature.'

Dufort sneered at her. 'Good of you to crawl out of your grave to join us.'

'I'll gladly take you back with me,' she croaked.

'All that bark and no teeth,' purred Lisette.

'That's enough,' said Cordelia Mercure sharply. 'Curb your odiousness, Gaspard. We have a serious matter to discuss.'

'And I thought this was a date,' he said, with a pout. 'I regret getting dressed up.'

She glared at him.

'Monsters,' she said, coming to the point. 'Have you encountered these beasts?'

Dufort gestured towards Ransom, and the other Cloaks turned to look at him. 'Ransom had a run-in with one. He barely got away with his life.'

'What a shame,' muttered Fontaine.

Lisette hissed at her. 'Play nice, old woman.'

'Fuck off,' said Fontaine.

Lark barked a laugh.

Dufort shot him a blistering glare.

Cordelia ignored the interruption. 'I lost a Cloak to one of these monsters.' She didn't elaborate. 'And three nights ago, another of mine almost met the same fate. She gave a chilling account. Up until then, we believed these indiscriminate killings to be the work of your Order.'

'You wound me,' said Dufort. 'I am many things, Cordelia. But sloppy is not one of them.'

She curled her lip. 'And yet you burned Sylvie Marchant's house to the ground.'

The silver-haired Cloak stiffened. Ransom wondered if he had known Sylvie. Or perhaps his loyalty was to her daughter. The thought made his nostrils flare.

'That was Dagger business,' said Dufort, evenly.

'Messy business,' said Fontaine.

He shrugged. 'Needs must.'

'The way I see it, *you* disrupted our trade and now we have monsters seemingly made of Shade stalking through our city, kidnapping and killing at will.' Mercure prowled closer until there was barely a foot between them. Despite their natural enmity, Ransom was impressed by her. There wasn't a hint of fear on her proud face. She must be the only person in Fantome who didn't cower from Dufort. Well, her and the old crone. 'You and I oversee all the Shade in this city, Gaspard, and these monsters are not *my* doing.'

'Careful with your conclusions, Cordelia,' he snarled. 'You don't want to make an enemy tonight.'

'You've been my enemy for nearly twenty years,' she scoffed. 'You murdered one of my best smugglers on what appears to have been a mindless whim and now everything is going awry. Disruption is growing across Fantome, a chaos that worsens with each passing day. If we don't find a way to contain it, the king's eye will soon fall on us. If we can't control this city, the underworld and the protection *both* our orders have enjoyed for centuries will fall away, and our power will be lost.'

Dufort appeared unmoved. 'If I wanted a lecture, I would have brought my Daggers to the Appoline.'

She glowered at him. 'Dagger or not, even you are not above reproach from the King of Valterre. A predator is only unassailable when they're at the top of the food chain. By the sound of it, you and your Daggers are no longer at the top. Which makes you as vulnerable as the rest of this city.' She raised a finger in warning. 'You would do well to remember that.'

Dufort caught her wrist.

Fontaine hissed in warning. The muscular Cloak lunged forward but Mercure raised her free hand, bringing him to a halt. 'It's all right, Albert. I clearly touched a nerve.'

Dufort's nostrils flared, but he did not deny it. She was right. The Daggers were ceding control of the underworld to something they did not understand. And no one here wanted the king breathing down their neck. 'Now that you've scrabbled your way to higher ground, Cordelia, why don't we set aside the threats and discuss a solution to our problem?'

She shook him off. 'I'm all ears.'

'We need to catch one of these monsters,' said Dufort, as if it was as simple as that. 'Only then can we figure out where they're coming from. And more importantly, how to kill them.' He cocked his head. 'Since you and your little pickpockets are averse to murder, if you get your nimble hands on one before me, I'll do the grisly part.'

'And then what?'

'And then your Cloaks can kiss my ring.'

She recoiled.

He stepped back, splaying his hands. 'And then we can go back to our much-enjoyed mutual enmity. Relatively unscathed.'

'What makes you think I trust you enough to work with you?'

'Because you have no alternative, Cordelia. For the first time in our lives, we face an enemy far greater than either of us.'

Cordelia crooked an eyebrow, her suspicion simmering. 'That depends on where these monsters are coming from. Mark my words, Gaspard, I intend to find out.'

'As you like,' said Dufort.

While Dufort and Mercure traded veiled threats, Ransom let his gaze wander. Something flickered up ahead. He blinked, sure he had imagined it, but then it happened again. Not a light, like the flames along the Aurore, but a shadow beneath it. A ribbon of darkness darted along the bottom of the tower, there and gone in a heartbeat.

He watched the shadows bend, and almost laughed. Of course there were other Cloaks here, hiding in plain sight. Cordelia Mercure was no fool. Three soldiers were not enough for a showdown with Gaspard Dufort, if it came to that.

But the question was: who else had come?

Ransom slipped a hand into his pocket and retrieved his vial of Shade. This was against the rules of the meeting, but he was standing so far behind Dufort, they'd hardly notice. No one was even looking at him. And he only needed a taste. A minute of sight to scour the shadows. To know if she was here, watching him. Gloating.

He turned away, tipping a morsel onto his tongue. He swallowed it down, stowing the vial before anyone noticed. The Shade shivered through him, quick and cold. It was almost as blistering as Fontaine's sharpening gaze. Had she seen what he'd done? Either way, he ignored her entirely. He tugged his sleeves down, hiding the whorls that moved across his hands. The world lit up, the shadows under the Aurore falling away like a curtain.

And there she was. His spitfire.

She was peering around a stone pillar in her long black cloak, staring right at him.

Ransom gave her a slow, lethal smirk.

She hugged the column, the shock on her face quickly blooming into horror. He almost felt sorry for her. But this was war, and she had drawn first blood. He had thirty-six stitches in his side to prove it.

So he dragged a finger across his neck, and mouthed, *I'm going to fucking kill you.*

Chapter 16

Seraphine

Seraphine was no lip-reader but it was hard to miss the Dagger's threat. Or the hatred glittering in his eyes. His words were as clear as if he had whispered them directly into her ear.

She drew back behind the pillar, scrunching her eyes shut, as if she could make him disappear.

'Who is *that*?' hissed Bibi, from behind the column next to hers.

'I have no idea,' she lied.

'He's staring at you.'

'He shouldn't even be able to see me.' She tugged her hood down until it brushed her eyebrows. *He shouldn't even be alive.* 'The rules said no Shade.'

'They also said no cloaks,' Bibi reminded her.

'That's different. We're not technically part of the meeting.'

An hour or so ago, after Madame Mercure, Madame Fontaine, Albert and Theo set out for the Aurore, Bibi and Sera had the bright idea to secretly follow them and eavesdrop on the meeting. Val had told them not to go, but Sera had rebuffed her warning, thinking she was just annoyed that her sprained ankle meant she couldn't join them.

But now, cowering under the lights of the Aurore, far too close to the menacing Head of the Daggers, she saw that Val had been right. Coming here was a mistake. It was dangerous to get this close to Gaspard Dufort, the man who had made marks of Mama and her. Sera was terrified by his nearness, her heart hammering so hard she could hardly think straight.

And then there was the matter of the Dagger she had stabbed at Villa Roman. She had been a fool to assume she had got rid of him that easily.

'Sera, this guy is *obsessed*,' said Bibi. 'He can't take his eyes off you. I can't tell if he wants to ravish you or murder you.'

The latter, thought Sera grimly.

'What did Dufort call him just now? Ransom? More like *handsome*.' Bibi chuckled to herself. 'I'm hilarious.'

Ransom. The Dagger's name was Ransom. Living, breathing, seething Ransom. What the hell kind of a name was Ransom?

'If the Cloaks and Daggers are serious about working together, then I suggest you use the time to explore this sizzling connection . . .' Bibi waggled her brows. 'If you get my meaning.'

Her meaning was as subtle as a sledgehammer to the face.

Sera shuddered. 'I'd sooner kiss a corpse.'

Ransom was supposed to *be* a corpse.

Saints, she had really messed this up. She clutched her necklace – a world of impossibility clenched inside her fist – and felt its magic buzzing faintly against her fingers, as if to say, *I am here.* It brought her little comfort. Despite her constant prodding at it these last few nights, she still had no idea what it was, or how she could use it again.

It had rebelled against the Dagger's attempts to kill her, shredding through his Shade, but it seemed not to mind when she donned Shade in the form of a cloak to hide herself. This little teardrop had a mind of its own. Or perhaps, somehow, it had come to know Seraphine's mind.

She shook off her frustration, tried to shove away her fear. They had lingered long enough in the lions' den. Gaspard Dufort didn't have the answers they were looking for, and the longer Sera remained in his presence, the more danger she was in. Especially now his Dagger had seen her. 'Let's get out of here, Bibi.'

She stepped back from the pillar, stealing one last glance at Ransom. His murderous eyes were still fixed on her, his jaw so tense it looked like stone.

Despite the disguise offered by her cloak, leaving the Aurore unnoticed was no easy feat. The glow of the firelight flooded Primrose Square, leaving shadows few and far between. The girls moved slowly and carefully, hopping from one to the next, like vines on a tree. Sera's heart thundered as she imagined Ransom tracking her, the Shade in his system blanching every speck of darkness in the square. She must look ridiculous to him, flailing and leaping about like a confused hare. But she would rather his ireful gaze on her back than his hand around her neck again.

At last, they reached the edge of the square, where the pale-stone promenade, Ambler's Walk, meandered south towards the heart of the city. Bibi slumped onto a bench and removed her hood. 'I'm sweating. I need a breather.' She untied her cloak and bundled it onto her lap.

Sera slipped off hers too. She had been wearing it for so long, the Shade had become heavy. Exhaustion tugged at her bones and made her head ache. She raked her hair back from her face, tying it into a knot at the nape of her neck.

'Gaspard Dufort is even more odious in person,' Bibi remarked. 'Did you see all the gold in his mouth? It looks like he swallowed a coin purse.' She paused, no doubt noticing the vacant look on Sera's face. She was miles away, back in the plains, watching the flames rise to lick the blue sky and smelling that awful, choking smoke as she rounded the hill . . .

Bibi's voice went quiet. 'Are you feeling all right? Seeing him tonight must have been really difficult. Especially after . . . well . . .' she trailed off.

'He ordered my mother's murder and then burned our farmhouse to the ground?' Sera's voice was hollow. *Difficult* was not the word for what she felt.

Bibi bit her lip. 'Perhaps we shouldn't have come.'

'I'm all right,' said Sera, putting her arm around Bibi, grateful for her new friend. At least she was not alone in her recklessness, even if they hadn't gleaned very much from the trip. 'Thank you for checking.'

They rolled to their feet, Sera tucking her cloak under her

arm as they walked on. Despite the clear evening, fear hung like a thick mist over the city, keeping everyone inside. The monster attacks meant most of the restaurants and taverns were closed, and the few that dared to remain open would lock up once night fell in earnest.

'We're almost at Ondine's,' said Bibi, pointing ahead to a small cobbled courtyard strung with garlands and paper lanterns. All but two of the black wrought-iron tables were empty. 'Do you fancy a quick bite to eat?'

Sera frowned, her trepidation warring with her hunger. She was starving, and the air smelled faintly like onion soup. Her favourite.

'We're miles from the harbour and it's barely dusk,' Bibi went on. 'I've never seen Ondine's so empty. I'd die for a slice of their bread-and-butter pudding. We wouldn't even have to queue.'

Sera wavered. Deciding for both of them, Bibi strode ahead, waggling her fingers at the waiter.

Sera was about to follow her when something struck her from behind. A whip of shadow curled around her waist and yanked her off her feet. She dropped her cloak as she was swept into a nearby alley, a strangled cry catching in her throat. The shadow snapped and she stumbled from its grip. The teardrop warmed at her throat, that unknowable magic fighting back. She turned to run but real hands caught her this time, pulling her against a body much larger than hers.

She bucked and thrashed, and one of those hands found her mouth, trapping her scream. The voice in her ear rippled down her spine. 'Hello, Seraphine.'

She knew that voice, that lilting promise of death. Fear roared in her ears. She kept fighting as she was dragged down the alley, hauled deep into the darkness, where water dripped from the peeling walls and the stench of refuse hung heavy in the air.

He spun her at the waist and pressed her back against the wall, a strong arm braced either side of her shoulders in case she tried to run.

Sera glared up into those all-too familiar eyes. The silver in them had faded, the last of it used on the shadow she had just shredded. Now, they were a perfect mix of hazel and rage.

'You and I have unfinished business.'

Sera's body flooded with adrenaline, but there was nowhere to run. She tilted her chin up, reaching for the only weapon she had left: the shield of her bravado. 'Yeah. I can't help but notice you're still alive.'

'Unlucky for you.' He gave a mirthless smirk, his gaze moving from her face to the hollow of her throat. She moved like lightning, grabbing the golden teardrop. His fist closed around hers a half-second too late.

'I'm flattered, but I'd rather not hold hands, Ransom. I don't think we're quite there yet.'

He frowned at his name in her mouth. 'Show me the necklace, Seraphine.'

Now, with only one arm pinning her in place, an escape route had opened up. Sera lunged to the left, but he pivoted, trapping her into the corner of the alley. She opened her mouth to scream for her friend. 'BI—'

He clapped his hand over it, stifling the sound. 'I wouldn't do that if I was you,' he threatened. 'Unless you want Dufort to come down here and personally pay you a visit?'

Sera squeezed the teardrop in her fist, willing it to do something – to fight him off her, to explode in another sunburst and help her resist his inexorable strength. It only flickered in her grasp, as if to say, *do it yourself.*

Her mind reeled, desperately trying to remember the manoeuvres Albert had taught her.

Ransom slowly removed his hand from her mouth, his fingers trailing along her jaw. 'Here's what's going to happen,' he said, leaning in. 'You're going to hand me that necklace. And then you're going to tell me how the hell it works.'

Through the mist of her rage, Sera remembered a move. He just had to come a little closer . . .

'Or what?' she challenged. 'You'll kill me?'

He cocked his head. 'Maybe I won't, if you co-operate.'

Such a bold-faced lie. She looked down at the wound in his side. 'Or maybe I'll kill you,' she said, trading a lie of her own.

His mouth twisted, stretching the scar that sliced his bottom lip. 'What do you have on you this time, Seraphine? A paperweight? A fountain pen?' His gaze roamed the length of her body. 'Do I need to pat you down?'

'Maybe you should. Just to be safe.'

His eyebrows rose, but he took the bait. Moved closer, the heat of his body searing the space between them. She jerked her knee up, found her mark between his legs. He hissed a curse, doubling over. She slammed her palm up, thrilling at the satisfying *crunch* of his nose.

He released a roar of fury. Blood gushed, striping his

mouth, his chin. Sera leaped to the side and bolted. Five paces passed in a blur, then five more. She was halfway to the street. Lamplight bloomed up ahead.

The air whistled, and a bottle clipped her ankle. She slipped, falling backwards. Her head smashed against the ground, causing a spiderweb of pain across her skull. She groaned. *Bastard.* She scrambled to her knees in a puddle of broken glass.

He was on her in the next breath, yanking her to unsteady feet, sealing the space between them with the hardness of his body. Immovable. Unyielding. Enraged. 'Nice try, spitfire.'

Black spots swarmed her vision. Blood trickled from her scalp, warm and slick on the back of her neck. She pretended not to notice. 'Nasty nosebleed you've got there, Ransom.'

'Plenty more glass bottles where that one came from,' he said, licking the blood from his lips.

Saints, her head was spinning awfully. 'Truce?' she said, weakly.

'No.' But he stalled, as though considering his next move. For a moment, they stared at each other, the rattle of their breath punctuating the silence. And then, he said, 'Let's talk.'

She raised her eyebrows. 'I thought you wanted to kill me.'

'Believe it or not, I'm trying *really* hard to resist.'

'What was all that mouthing about at the Aurore, then? Foreplay?'

He blinked, then offered the slash of a smile. 'Old habits.'

Too dizzy to attempt another escape, Sera curled her hand around her necklace, considering his words. The Dagger hadn't taken any more Shade. Here, in the narrow dark, he was just a man. Seething, but clear-eyed. Hesitant. She could sense it in the way he watched her, in how he let the silence stretch to allow her to speak. But *why?* 'Are you afraid to break that shiny new truce? So tightly wound around Dufort's baby finger that you're terrified of pissing him off?'

His lip curled. 'You don't know anything about me.'

'I know you're a Dagger,' said Sera. 'Which means you think the way Dufort tells you to. When he tells you to jump, you probably ask him how high.' Despite the blackness at the edge of her mind, she enjoyed the way he flinched, how the blood from his nose painted his lips crimson, the metallic tang of it mixing with his scent of woodsmoke and sage. 'I hope you know your days in those catacombs are numbered, that all the Shade you devour will eat through you long before your conscience does.'

There – a flash of emotion in his eyes, gone as quickly as it came.

'Perhaps it's foolish to assume you have a conscience at all,' she went on.

He inched closer, daring her to flinch. 'For your sake, you'd better hope I do, spitfire.'

'I'm not afraid of you.'

Lie, lie, lie. But he wasn't watching her eyes; he was watching her lips.

'Then why did you try and squawk your friend's name a moment ago?'

'I thought she might like to see the Dagger I skewered with my letter opener.'

He tapped the hand that clutched her necklace. 'What's in that thing?'

She tightened her grip on it, her words coming in a whisper. 'A tiny, ancient piece of paper ...'

His throat bobbed, his expression hungry. 'What does it say?'

'It says, *Fuck off, Ransom.*'

He glared at her. 'Are you always this immature?'

She smirked now that the Dagger's curiosity was plain to see. This was no longer a murder; it was a conversation, a careful trade of information. 'I have a better question. Why did you kill my mother and burn our house to the ground?'

For the second time since she had met him, the Dagger bristled at that question. 'I told you I didn't kill your mother. And I didn't burn your house.'

'So, what? You were just there to warm your hands on the bonfire of my life?' She had seen him, that tall, broad figure flickering through the flames. When he said nothing, only glared harder, she went on. 'Why did Dufort order my mother's murder?'

'I don't know.'

'Liar,' she hissed.

His attention returned to her own white-knuckled fist. It occurred to Sera that he probably believed she had discovered the magic herself, that she knew exactly how to use it. As far as Ransom was aware, she was a skilled artificer, a shredder of Shade, a force to be reckoned with. The thought made her laugh right in his face.

His frown hardened the edge of his jaw. It also dimly occurred to Sera that Bibi was right. He was murderously handsome. 'Something funny, Seraphine?'

'I told you I'm not scared of you,' she said, pressing her hand against his chest. She was surprised by the gallop of his heartbeat beneath her fingers. She shoved him back, and he let her do it. 'I'm laughing because *you* should be afraid of *me*.'

Maybe it was the wariness in his eyes, or perhaps it was the teardrop warming in her hand, but Sera really didn't feel afraid just then. She felt in control, so she made a blade of her fury and drove it home. 'You see, Ransom, you kill for coin. For praise from a rat like Gaspard Dufort. For a cold bed in a stone room far beneath the city. But me? My spirit – my fight – comes from my mother. And so does my magic.' A huff of breath at that word – *magic*. A dent in his composure. She went on, emboldened. 'My strength is your weakness. My secret is your nightmare. And that makes me a lot more dangerous than you.'

He nipped at the scar on his lip, his gaze never leaving her knuckles. She couldn't tell if it was fear or hunger that drew him closer, but she knew the balance of power between them had shifted to her.

'Even now, you can't take your eyes off it.' She knew she should stop – that taunting a Dagger was like waving a red rag at a bull – but she couldn't help herself. She wanted to frighten him just as he frightened her. She wanted him to cower at the thought of what she could do with Mama's magic, to scare him so badly that he left her alone for good. 'You're afraid of my magic. And you should be. Because sooner or later, it's going to—'

He pushed her back against the wall, his hand resting at the base of her throat. Her senses were scrambled, her breath punching out of her in sharp, shallow bursts. It was a threat – a demonstration of how easily he could choke the life out of her if he wanted to. He had knocked her from her pedestal with a casual sweep of his hand.

'Now who's afraid, spitfire?' he crooned, gazing down at her through a veil of black lashes. 'Look at that smart mouth tremble.'

She drew a shaky breath.

'Let's clear one thing up,' he said, his breath on her lips. 'I don't fear your magic, Seraphine. I *want* it.'

'Then let's talk,' she rasped. 'I'll talk.'

'Nice to see you return to your senses.' He slid his hand around the back of her neck, into the knot of her hair. It came loose, the long strands threading through his fingers. 'Must be the concussion,' he said, frowning. 'So much blood . . .'

Sera looked down and saw that he was right. The blood from the back of her head had run down her neck, staining the top of her sweater. There was blood on the cobbles too, his and her own, mingling in the dark grooves. The sight of it made her woozy. She closed her eyes, fighting the sudden tremble in her knees.

Get a grip.

She heard a soft *click.* Her eyes flew open as the clasp on her necklace opened beneath his deft fingers. Her hand dropped, and he grabbed her fist, working the teardrop free.

'*No.*' Sera would sooner lose her hand than the magic inside it. She struck out, slamming her fist into the wound in his side.

He cursed, grabbing her jaw.

She spat in his face.

He jerked backwards. There was a sudden clatter of footsteps, then a warning shout. A figure hurtled through the dark, tackling Ransom at the waist. They careened into a trash can, their fists flying so fast, it took Sera a second to spot the glint of silver hair. When they finally fell away from each other, Theo scrambled to his feet, his wild eyes finding hers.

He looked her over. 'You're bleeding.'

'I'm fine,' she said, shoving her necklace into her pocket.

Ransom leaped to his feet, rounding on Theo. 'Who the fuck are you?'

Theo spat out a glob of blood. 'Your worst nightmare.'

Ransom laughed. 'OK, Drama. The theatre is two streets over.'

'Keep laughing, tunnel rat.' Theo pulled a switchblade from his pocket just as Ransom brought out a vial of Shade. It was like bringing a toothpick to a swordfight.

'Leave him,' she said, pulling Theo away. 'Let's get out of here.'

'Go on, Drama.' Ransom bit the stopper off his vial. 'I'll give you a head start.'

They bolted for the mouth of the alley, then across the street to where Bibi was running towards them. 'Merciful saints!' she cried. 'I've been looking everywhere for you. I thought a monster took you!' She swept her hair from her face and Sera saw that her cheeks were blotchy, her eyes swollen from crying. 'When Theo found me, we ran up and down the river, shouting your name. Didn't you hear us?' Bibi looked at Theo, who was dishevelled and panting, then back at Sera, noting the blood on her sweater and in her hair. 'What happened to you?'

Sera's gaze darted back to the alley. 'I'll explain later.'

Sensing the urgency of the situation, Bibi reluctantly stayed her curiosity. They turned for home, their footsteps quickening as night fell and a gathering chorus of howls echoed through the city.

Chapter 17

Seraphine

Over dinner that night, Sera confessed everything to her friends. After what happened in the alley with Ransom – after what had *almost* happened to Theo when he came to save her – she couldn't stand the thought of lying to them any more. And more than that, she had come to trust them during her time at House Armand. She owed them the truth. If not for her own safety, then for theirs. She was marked, and becoming a Cloak hadn't changed that.

So, she told them everything about the day of Mama's murder when she had witnessed the Dagger standing over her dead body. Then her showdown with Ransom at Villa Roman, when her necklace had glowed like the sun, shredding his Shade and saving her life. She recounted the moment she had managed to stick him with her letter opener and get away in one piece, even confessing that she believed she had killed him up until today. If Theo hadn't found them in that alley when he did . . . She shuddered to imagine it.

But Saint Oriel had not yet deserted her. Once again, Sera had escaped with her life.

The others listened in horrified silence as she recounted it all, Theo's gaze fixed on that golden teardrop hanging from her neck.

'I knew there was something unusual about that thing,' he murmured when she had finished. He scrubbed a hand across his jaw, absently stroking the bruise blooming there. 'I wonder what it is.'

'I was hoping you might know,' Sera confessed. She had been wrestling with the idea of confiding in the Shadowsmith about it all week, hoping that the artificer might have some insight into its power.

But he only shook his head in bewilderment.

'I *knew* there was something going on between you and that Dagger,' said Bibi, leaning across her plate of roast chicken. 'You could have cut the tension with a knife. Though I admit, I didn't expect this . . .' She frowned, searching for the right word.

'Ongoing game of murder?' said Val, who was sitting with her ankle propped up on the windowsill.

'*Attempted* murder,' Sera corrected her.

'So far,' she countered. Then she frowned. 'You're a Cloak now. He's not supposed to go anywhere near you.'

'Unless Dufort cares more about getting rid of me than he does about Mercure's rules,' muttered Sera. Dufort didn't give a damn about rules that inconvenienced him.

Foolish was the Cloak who put their faith in the words of a man like Gaspard Dufort.

Sera sighed, taking in her friends' faces. She'd thought she would find relief in telling them the truth about Ransom but the fear in their eyes only made her feel worse. She picked at her food, trying to kindle her appetite. Pippin was curled up in her lap, as though the little terrier could sense the danger she had got herself into that evening and didn't want to let her out of his sight again. She sneaked him green beans and slivers of roast chicken as the conversation turned to the meeting at the Aurore, and the other pressing matter at hand: monsters.

'Do you reckon the Orders will really work together?' asked Val.

'Who knows?' said Bibi, biting the head off a sprig of broccoli. 'That Dagger attacked Sera right after the meeting. It's not like Dufort's word is worth anything.'

'I'm still not convinced he isn't behind the monsters.' Theo scowled into his wine glass. 'But I can't figure out the *why* of it.'

'The better question is, what are we supposed to do about the monsters?' said Bibi. 'Go out and catch them ourselves?'

'I can't say I'm itching to place myself in mortal danger,' said the Shadowsmith.

'It beats being cooped up in here all day.' Val glowered at her injured ankle. 'I want to catch a monster. Maybe you could fashion something to help us?'

'Like what?' he said, leaning back in his chair. 'A big net made of Shade?'

'Oh! Yes!' said Bibi.

He shot her a glare. 'That was a joke.'

Sera gripped her necklace, stroking it with the pad of her thumb until the bead warmed. She wondered what the magic inside it might do against a beast made of Shade, and if perhaps Mama had made the teardrop with that in mind. She shook off the thought as quickly as it formed. Experimenting on Fig was one thing. But these monsters that stalked the city . . . who could have foreseen such horrors?

And yet . . . Unease prickled along the back of Sera's neck, and she found her mind straining for a thought – an answer – that flitted just out of reach, like a firefly too quick to catch.

She wasn't the only one plagued by the mystery of her necklace.

I don't fear your magic, Seraphine. I want it.

The Dagger's words floated back to her.

Ransom hadn't killed her in that alleyway.

He *could* have killed her.

Now who's afraid, spitfire? He could have ended her with his bare hands and ripped the necklace from her corpse. *Look at that smart mouth tremble.*

He should have killed her.

Why didn't he kill her?

Her cheeks flared at the memory of his body pressed up against hers, his cruel mouth full of blood, the smell of wild mint on his breath. She shuddered, though she couldn't tell whether it was from revulsion or something far more dangerous. Something she did not dare to name. Even to herself.

Chapter 18

Seraphine

In a bid to put the horrors of yesterday behind them, Bibi asked Sera to accompany her on her next job. A small Break not far from the Hollows and better still, it paid well. Enough to cover next month's room and board, and to keep Sera in good standing with Madame Mercure and the other Cloaks.

They set out before sundown, Sera casing their surroundings to make sure Ransom wasn't lying in wait somewhere. But the sun was melting along the cracked rooftops, and the Dagger was nowhere to be seen. No monsters, either. She blew out a breath as they passed through the gate, leaving the grounds of House Armand.

'Don't worry,' said Bibi, turning to wave up at Val, who was watching them morosely from the window of the upstairs room where she was still resting her ankle. 'Whatever happens this evening, it can't possibly be worse than Villa Roman.'

Sera snorted. 'You are a master of perspective, Bibi.'

They wandered on, chatting as the narrow grey streets of the Hollows gave way to pretty squares lined with yellow-leaved trees and beautiful pale-stone buildings. When the sun set, they donned their cloaks, losing themselves in the shadows that crawled up the sides of those buildings and pooled beneath the awnings of bistros they passed by.

Sera's eyes darted all the while, watching the alleys and rooftops for a tell-tale glimmer of silver. She was so distracted by thoughts of Ransom that she didn't notice Pippin was tracking her until his wet nose tickled her ankle.

Sera yelped, leaping from a shadow to scoop him up. He darted out of reach.

'Get back here!' she shouted, but Bibi tugged on her arm.

'Don't make a scene,' she hissed, dragging her back into the shadows. 'We're trying to be inconspicuous, remember?' Their hurried footsteps were already too loud on the deserted streets. If they weren't careful, they'd round the next corner and run into a nightguard, or a monster, or a Dagger.

'He's supposed to be at home with Val. Not tracking *me*.' Sera groaned. 'He'll give us away.'

'He's fine,' said Bibi. 'No one will look twice at a terrier. And anyway, we're almost there.'

There was a small apothecary on a back street behind Merchant's Way. According to Madame Mercure, it was owned by a sour-faced man called Clement, who had fled the city after the first sighting of a monster several weeks ago. His sister, Clarice had approached House Armand with the job when she discovered he was not coming back any time soon.

'You never told me what we're looking for,' said Sera as they turned down a lane that was all too similar to the one Ransom had dragged her into yesterday. But the Dagger wasn't here. If he was, Pippin would surely catch his scent and right now he was trotting out in front, wagging his little tail as though he knew exactly where to go. 'Is it coin? Some kind of fancy herb?'

Bibi cleared her throat. 'Actually, it's ashes.'

Sera slowed. 'Ashes?'

'Lulu's ashes, to be exact. Their beloved childhood cat,' Bibi went on, as if that wasn't the most absurd thing she'd ever said. 'Clarice says Clement stole the urn from her during a fight five years ago and she wants it back. It used to sit on her mantlepiece.'

Sera stood still a moment. 'People are weird.'

Bibi gave a snort of agreement.

At the end of the lane, they came to a narrow green shopfront with a small cloudy window hung with tassels. Pippin reared up to sniff the flower box on the sill. He whimpered, coming to sit on Sera's feet. She saw then what had unsettled him. The trough wasn't full of flowers but heartsbane, the blood-red berries bulging from thin, thorny stalks.

'Poison,' muttered Sera, recalling the time she had picked a bush of heartsbane out in the plains, thinking they were redcurrants, only for Lorenzo to slap them out of her hands a half-second before she ate one. 'I wonder how many birds old Clement's killed with those.'

'At least now we don't have to feel bad about robbing him,' said Bibi lightly, though, as far as Sera knew, she never felt bad about robbing anyone. Sera stood back, watching the alley while Bibi went to work on the locked door. It yielded easily. She slipped her arm through the gap to dislodge the chain, and in a matter of seconds they were inside.

They crept through the cramped shop like mischievous ghosts, between rickety wooden shelves stuffed with all manner of herbs and spices that climbed all the way to the ceiling. It didn't take long to find poor Lulu, whose ashes were kept in a cat-shaped silver urn. It stood on a high shelf behind the till. Sera clambered onto the cluttered countertop, while Bibi stood at the shop window, peering out through the tassels.

'There's shouting outside.'

Pippin paced the shop floor, growling.

Sera tried not to think of monsters as she rose to her tiptoes, reaching for the topmost shelf. The shouting got louder, closer. A chorus of screams followed, raising the hairs on her arm. The urn almost toppled as she dislodged it, but she caught it in both hands, the counter trembling as she fought to regain her balance.

Pippin's growls became barks as Sera climbed down, passing the urn to Bibi as she went to wrangle Pip. He was pawing at the door, like he was desperate to investigate those terrified screams. Or perhaps he sensed something in the apothecary's shop that they had not.

Sera and Bibi exchanged a loaded glance, before hightailing it out of there. While Bibi locked the door behind them, Sera dumped the trough of heartsbane into a nearby bin. By the time they finished, Pippin was already at the bright end of the lane. The screams were getting further away but the approaching thunder of hoofprints meant the nightguards were coming. Perhaps they were looking to catch a monster, too, and had been alerted by the screams.

While Bibi struggled to tuck the urn under her cloak, Pippin darted from the alley. Instead of turning left for the Hollows, he turned right, running towards the oncoming clatter of hooves.

Sera took off at a sprint, flying out of the lane like a bat. Pippin was halfway to the street, running headlong at all those horses like he was going to fight them off. *Saints*, there were so many. At least forty mounted nightguards galloping down Merchant's Way, all of them riding too hard to spot the terrier darting right into their path.

'Pip!' Sera screamed, shrugging off her cloak to run faster, but it was too late to grab him. Too late for the horses to stop, even as a handful reared up in alarm.

Pippin froze, caught in the midst of a stampede as the horses closed around him, blocking him from Sera's view. She could only watch in wide-eyed horror as the horses thundered on, kicking up plumes of dust as they went, their white coats gleaming in the falling dark. She was about to launch herself into the fray when she spotted a cloud of shadows swirling right in the heart of the stampede.

A tornado of starless night, as hard and unyielding as any wall.

The horses parted around it, afraid of the swirling dark and the monster lurking within. Even the nightguards stiffened, kicking their heels and urging their steeds to gallop faster, harder, looking everywhere but at that wedge of darkness that refused to budge. It was like a boulder in the road, parting the king's horses into twin rivers of white until the last of them had passed. Then there was nothing left but the echo of their frantic hoofbeats and the dust swirling in their wake as they rode on towards the harbour.

Sera stood on the side of the street, staring at the blackness that had swallowed Pippin. It remained, even after the nightguards had moved on. Her eyes swam as she stumbled towards it, one hand outstretched in a silent plea, the other rising to cup her necklace. *Please do something*, she begged it. *Please help me save him.*

The shape shifted as she drew nearer, falling away in great black rivulets to reveal a hunched figure. A man, Sera realized, with a gasp of relief. Not a monster. As he stood up, he cast aside the last of his shadows, surrendering the shield he had fashioned. He raised his chin, revealing the gleaming silver eyes she had come to know far too well.

Ransom stared at her and she at him, nothing between them now but the clouds of their breath.

Pippin trembled in his arms.

Sera's heart hitched. She tried to sound brave, but her voice broke when she said, 'Please don't hurt him.'

The Dagger blinked, then frowned. 'What would be the point of saving him, only to hurt him?'

She swallowed thickly. She didn't know what kind of trick this was, but she refused to believe it was an act of kindness. Not from the Dagger who had killed her mother, then tried to kill her. She squeezed her necklace, silently begging for its protection, but it only offered a dim pulse of warmth.

'Please,' she said again. Her heart was a drum pounding in her chest. She was going to be sick if he didn't set Pip down. She was going to cry, her knees already threatening to buckle. 'Leave him out of this.'

Slowly, so slowly, as if he was trying not to startle her, the Dagger set Pippin down. If Sera hadn't witnessed the gentleness with which Ransom placed him on the street, she wouldn't have believed him capable of it.

Pippin bolted towards her, and she rushed to scoop him up, pressing her face into his scruff. The Dagger watched her all the while, shadows absently wreathing his ankles and crawling up his legs.

When Bibi's voice rang out behind her, Sera forced herself to speak. 'What do you want?' she demanded.

His eyebrows rose. 'Is that how you usually say thank you?'

She took a step away from him. He let her do it. She took another, slow and careful. And then a third.

'Consider this a peace offering, spitfire,' he said, casually digging those violent hands into his pockets. 'Next time, we're going to talk about that antidote.'

Sera frowned at the word. Not power. Not magic. *Antidote*. She wanted to call after him, but the Dagger was already gone, melting into the night as though he had never been there at all.

Chapter 19

Ransom

Down in the harbour, twenty-three ships floated in the moonlit dark. Their sails were furled, their lamps extinguished, as they tried to hide from the monsters of Fantome. Seawater lapped against the dock, casting the faint scent of brine into the air. A still night so far. Unlike yesterday, when the screams were so loud, Ransom could hear them all the way up on Merchant's Way.

'It's too quiet down here,' said Nadia, her stiletto-heeled boots clacking along the boardwalk. She tightened the belt on her black trench coat, her gaze darting around. 'Even the gulls have flown away.'

'Clever birds,' muttered Ransom, flipping his collar up to stave off the chill. Not for the first time in his life, he had the sudden, stirring desire to fly away from here too. Away from

Dufort and his endless demands, away from the spitfire that plagued his nightmares. Away from the monsters that seemed to spring up from nowhere. All this danger was beginning to feel like it was part of the same web, only Ransom couldn't figure out where he sat within it – was he the spider or a fly?

And what in hell's teeth was Seraphine Marchant?

Orphan and runaway.

Liar and artificer.

He cast his gaze out to sea, thinking of their conversation from last night, how she had begged him in the street, not out of fear for herself but the dog in his arms. The dog he had almost killed *several* nightguards to save. In her desperation to save the mutt, she had revealed a naked terror Ransom hadn't seen in her before. He had hated the sight of it.

It was dangerous territory he found himself in now. Too close to guilt, a hair's breadth from empathy. He should have killed her in that alleyway by the Aurore and buried his curiosity with her corpse. He had known it even then, but that smart mouth had got the better of him.

She had broken his nose for it. A reward for his stupidity. In a flare of panic, he had flung that rum bottle and she had tripped, falling backwards with a hard crack. They had stood, then, glaring at each other in the slick of their own blood. And when he saw that red line dripping down her neck, smelled the metallic tang mingling with the lemon blossom on her skin, it had turned his stomach. He had thought of Mama, sewing her own cuts closed over the sink too many times to count, and in that moment, as he towered over Seraphine Marchant, he didn't feel like a Dagger. He felt like his father.

For that reason alone, he was glad he saved the dog.

Not that it had garnered a shred of trust from her. That damn necklace remained a mystery he itched to untangle. Every time he glimpsed his reflection marred by all those black whorls, his thoughts returned to it. To what she could do for him, if she only stopped running. But then, perhaps she was smart enough to know that once she surrendered what he wanted from her, she was dead anyway.

Seraphine.

He was not yet done with her.

Lark, walking by Nadia's other side, picked up a rock and threw it into the sea. It soared over a sailing boat and landed with a *plonk*.

'What are you doing?' hissed Nadia.

'Seeing if there are any monsters who want to come out to play,' said Lark, firing another. 'Don't they usually come up from the sea?'

'They come from everywhere,' said Ransom.

And yet, they still hadn't caught one. Lisette was patrolling the north of Fantome with her own band of Daggers, while Caruso and Raphael took the quarters to the east and west. Tonight, Ransom had accompanied Lark and Nadia down to the harbour. They had come to investigate the Lucky Shell, a tavern at the far end of the boardwalk, where sailors congregated after long weeks at sea to listen to jaunty shanties and drink until the sun came up. Several nights ago, a monster had torn through it, sending its patrons fleeing in horror. The proprietor, Kipp, hadn't been seen since. And as a staunch ally of the Daggers, his fate – like his coin – was of great importance to Dufort.

The tavern was deserted. There wasn't a speck of light flickering at its windows, which had been shattered in the chaos.

'Not such a lucky shell after all,' remarked Lark as they wandered towards it. 'Even the rats have deserted it.'

They stood still a moment, peering up at the sorry façade, as if the tavern might tell them a secret. Wordlessly, they brought out their vials of Shade, downing them at the same time. Monster-hunting was dangerous enough as it was, but to do so without Shade was a fool's errand.

Ransom had learned that the hard way.

Lark shivered as the magic flooded him, his green eyes flickering to silver. Nadia's brown eyes changed a moment later, a shadow wreathing her neck as she flashed her teeth. Ransom blinked, and the night lit up. The darkness fell away, revealing the modest row of empty stalls and crooked taverns cowering along the edge of the sea.

Lark cracked his knuckles. 'Who wants to do the honours?'

Nadia kicked the door in. 'No time like the present,' she said, stalking inside.

'That was ... incredibly attractive,' said Lark, trailing after her.

She tossed her silky black braid. 'I know.'

The inside of the Lucky Shell was an even sorrier mess than the outside. The beams were broken, the tables had been tipped over and the floor was soaked in spirits. There were shattered bottles everywhere, the bar stained with spilled wine.

'What the hell was it even doing in here?' said Lark, picking up a stool to sit on.

Nadia shrugged as she rounded the bar. 'Maybe it needed something to take the edge off.'

Lark clucked his tongue. 'Nadia Raine. How can you possibly joke at a time like this?'

'It's how I cope with crippling uncertainty,' she said, flinging a coaster at him.

He caught it with one hand, then fired it at Ransom. It clocked him in the side of the head. 'Why have you gone quiet?'

'I'm thinking.' Ransom used a shadow to yank the stool out from under him. Lark fell with a clatter. 'Give it a try sometime.'

'Nah,' said Nadia, leaning across the bar like she was going to offer him a drink. 'You've got that faraway look in your eyes.'

Lark leaped back to his feet, unruffled. 'That's because he's thinking of his farmgirl.'

Ransom bristled. 'She's a mark.'

And that was the enduring truth of the matter. Dufort didn't give a rat's ass about Mercure's truce. At least not where it concerned the girl. He had dragged Ransom into his chambers not long after their meeting at the Aurore to tell him so.

Get it done and hide the corpse.

No body, no proof.

Nadia and Lark exchanged an amused glance. 'I'm curious,' said Lark. 'Have you ever spent this much time with a mark before?'

'You know ... *alive*,' added Nadia. 'Because mine tend to die right after they see me.'

'One last glance at paradise before they plummet straight to hell,' said Lark.

She turned to examine a tap, hiding the blush creeping into her cheeks.

Ransom picked up a bottle of wine and set it on the bar. The label was black like all the others here, with an emblem of a golden five-leafed clover. Underneath, the looping script read *Nectar of the Saints*.

Lark frowned at it. 'Huh. I've never seen a bottle like this one before. They serve *King's Sup* up on Merchant's Way.'

'I prefer *Queen's Kiss*,' said Nadia, turning to look at the label. 'It's cheap and tangy. But you only get it in the Hollows.'

Ransom hated wine but he had spent so much time in taverns, he could vaguely picture both labels. *King's Sup* and *Queen's Kiss* came from the royal vineyards of Valterre, which meant they bore the same royal insignia: two swords crossed beneath a rose in bloom. Not this strange five-leafed clover.

Nadia hopped up onto the bar. 'Poor old Kipp,' she said, surveying the destruction from her new vantage point. 'Do you really think he was kidnapped?'

Lark frowned. 'Kipp is the crankiest bastard I've ever met. A barrel of a man, six foot of muscle and swearing. Why would *anyone* want to kidnap him?'

'Then he's dead,' said Nadia, with a huff. 'This tavern was his one true love. He'd never leave it willingly.' She looked down at them, silver eyes dancing. 'Remember when we came here for your eighteenth birthday?'

'How could I ever forget?' Lark chuckled. 'We drank an entire bottle of whiskey and you danced a jig on this bar.'

He leaned back to look up at her, his eyes so soft they looked molten. 'You should have been a dancer, Nadia.'

'Maybe one day.' She smiled, shadows crawling to kiss those nimble, graceful feet. Not her shadows, but Lark's. They laced her ankles, as if coaxing her to dance again. For him.

Ransom had the sudden sense he was intruding on a moment. 'Every sailor in the place fell in love with you,' Lark went on. 'If I remember rightly, Kipp offered you a job on the spot.'

'Maybe I should have taken it,' she said, sinking back down. There was a note of wistfulness in her voice that Ransom recognized from his own thoughts, a sense that a part of her really did wish for a simpler life. A kinder life. 'Hung up my shadows for an apron ...'

'And then get eaten by a monster anyway?' Lark shook his head. 'I can't think of anything more tragic. You'd have been bored shitless. Your mind wanders every time you have to lace up your boots.'

She smirked. 'That's true.'

He grabbed the bottle Ransom had plucked from the floor and ripped out the cork. 'How about one last drink?' he said, pouring out three glasses of dark syrupy wine. 'To the people we left behind.'

'And the Daggers we became,' said Nadia, picking up a glass. She wrinkled her nose as she took a sniff. '*Ugh*. I'm not drinking this. It smells like my grandfather.'

'Your grandfather's dead,' said Lark.

'Exactly.'

Ransom didn't even reach for his glass. Even if he'd liked

the taste of wine, he was too restless to drink. While Lark shoved the bottle aside and grabbed the whiskey instead, Ransom stepped away from the bar entirely.

'I'm going to take a look upstairs.' He stalked across the tavern, to where a wooden door led to a narrow staircase. Their voices faded as he climbed. At the top, a familiar sulphuric stench hung in the air. The hairs on Ransom's arms stood up, the Shade inside him jerking to attention. Shadows darted along his knuckles, poised to strike.

There was only one room on the second floor of the Lucky Shell. Kipp used it mainly for storage, and to snatch sleep in the slow hours between dawn and dusk. It was filled with barrels of ale and crates of various other kinds of alcohol. There was an unmade bed over by the window, a nightstand littered with flakes of tobacco, a threadbare armchair and a fireplace that had been boarded up to keep out the rats.

Ransom stood on the threshold, his arms braced on the doorframe as he peered inside. It might have seemed ordinary to anyone else – an abandoned room in an abandoned tavern – but with Shade in his system, he noticed something that made his breath swell in his chest.

There was a shadow in the room. A gathering of darkness Ransom could not see through. It was crouched behind the barrels in the corner, and moaning softly, as though it was in pain. The sound was so human Ransom wondered if his mind was playing tricks on him. But the smell was even stronger now, the air so cold he could see his breath in it. There was a wrongness in here. A wrongness he had encountered once before on the banks of the Verne.

He stepped into the room. 'Hello?'

The shadow stilled. Shade was a second heartbeat inside Ransom, pushing him towards the darkness.

Go and look, he imagined it whispering. *Don't be afraid.*

A part of Ransom was afraid, but he was curious, too. If this truly was a wounded monster, hiding upstairs in the Lucky Shell, then he would capture it and drag it home to Dufort.

The creature trembled as Ransom approached. He peered at it, trying to make out a face in the shadow, but its misshapen head was bowed, its sinewy limbs pulled around itself until it was no bigger than the barrel it was hiding behind.

Another step, the floorboards creaking. It occurred to Ransom that he should alert Lark and Nadia to his find, but he was so close now he was afraid of spooking the creature. 'Hello?' he said, softer now. 'Can you hear me?'

He stopped at the barrel. The creature snapped its head up, revealing a gaping mouth of jagged teeth. Its lidless silver eyes flashed a half-second before it lunged.

Ransom let out a shout as the beast landed on him, pinning him to the floor. A terrible coldness swept through him. He swung his fist, searching for purchase in the sudden swarm of shadows, and it met bone with a sickening crack.

The monster howled.

Ransom bolted upright, grabbing its neck. He shuddered through another shock of cold. It was like staring into the face of Shade, watching Shade stare back. The monster bared its fangs, a growl coming on fetid breath. They wrestled, shadows folding around them until Ransom found himself in the darkness too. The room faded away until all he could see were those wide glowing eyes, inches from his own. Beneath their shine, there was something oddly familiar about them but Ransom's thoughts were turning sluggish, his heart slowing until it ached with every beat.

The Shade inside him was quickly fading. He knew, with chilling certainty, that he would have no protection against death without it. The monster knew it too.

Ransom flexed his fingers, trying to command the shadows that surrounded them, but they belonged to the monster – they were *part* of the monster.

The beast reared up, doubling in height as it shook itself free. It stood on Ransom's chest, crushing him into the floorboards. He kicked out as the creature's jaws unhinged, revealing the blackened hollow of its throat. That smell came again – barrelling into Ransom with such force it made him retch. He bucked and thrashed, pinned to the floor like a helpless moth.

'Ransom?' He heard his name through the swarm of shadows. 'What in hell's teeth is going on up there?'

The creature pitched forward, sinking its fangs into his shoulder. A scream ripped from his chest, taking the last of his breath with it. Blackness swept in, and Ransom knew if he closed his eyes, he would never open them again.

There was a crash and then an almighty hiss as the room exploded with firelight. The monster roared as it leaped off Ransom. The darkness went with it, the entire room flaring into focus. There were flames everywhere, bottles smashing and whiskey roaring as it went up in smoke.

'Move!' Lark yanked Ransom to his feet. 'It's coming down!'

Nadia was in the doorway, with a rag over her mouth. An

empty oil lamp swung from her hand. No prizes for guessing where she had thrown the first one. Ransom found his footing, and the two men stumbled towards her, their eyes on the monster as it lurched for the open window. It paused on the sill, and in the split second between flame and shadow Ransom glimpsed the ghost of a face. The remnants of what the monster had once been.

No, not *what*. But *who*.

A gasp stuck in his throat.

Lark stiffened in surprise.

And then the beast was gone, leaping from the window and disappearing like a breeze into the night. Smoke filled the room, the flames reaching so high they licked the ceiling.

'Run!' Nadia dragged them from the room as a beam fell and sliced the bed in two. The staircase was crumbling, the smoke so thick Ransom couldn't see through it. He covered his mouth with his sleeve and followed Lark and Nadia all the way down to the bar, where the ceiling was caving in.

They made for the exit, wheezing and coughing as the smoke spat them out onto the boardwalk. Lark tripped over a barrel and nearly face-planted on the ground. Ransom caught him by the collar, pulling him up. Nadia sank into a crouch to catch her breath while Ransom squinted into the night, looking for the monster. But the world was dark. His Shade was spent.

'It's gone,' said Nadia, rolling to her feet.

Lark looked down into the rippling water, as if he was expecting to see a face in the waves.

She pulled him away. 'Don't. We've already played with fire tonight.'

Behind them, the tavern roared and crackled, spitting smoke into the sky. Ransom could hear people shouting in the distance. The nightguards would be here soon, for all the good their quivering chins and paltry swords would do against a monster.

Still, the Daggers had to get out of here.

'Did you see its face?' said Lark, falling into step with him.

Ransom shuddered at the memory. He was still trying to make sense of it. 'I hoped I'd imagined it.'

Nadia looked between them. 'What was it?'

'Not what,' said Lark. 'Who.'

She jostled him. 'Stop talking in riddles.'

'It was Kipp,' said Ransom. 'The *thing* that attacked me was Kipp.'

Nadia stopped walking. 'You're wrong.'

He tugged her on. 'I wish I was.'

Lark's face was as grim as his own. It was the truth, plain and terrible. They hadn't come upon a creature in the Lucky Shell, but a man, who had somehow been changed into a monster. When the light had flared and the shadows flickered, Ransom had glimpsed a face he once knew. Lark had seen it too. They had found Kipp, after all.

'He didn't flee the monster, Nadia. He *became* the monster.'

The silence yawned as all three of them tried to untangle the mystery.

They reached the end of the boardwalk and headed for the Rascalle, taking cover under the awning of Florian's Emporium. The nightguards were already on their way. Ransom could hear the clatter of hooves, saw lanterns swinging in the distance.

Nadia wrapped her arms around herself, her voice quiet. 'If that thing really was Kipp, then that means all these monsters ... they're just ...'

'People,' said Lark. 'They're just people.'

'But how does it happen?' she whispered. 'How did Kipp turn into a monster in the first place?'

'It has to be Shade,' said Ransom, slumping onto the windowsill. 'All that darkness. The reek of it. I had no power over it.'

'Shade doesn't do *that*,' said Nadia, all three of them silently staring at the marks on their hands. Perhaps wondering if one day they might become monsters on the outside too.

Lark leaned back, touching his head against the window. 'The puzzle is before us,' he murmured. 'But half the pieces are missing.'

Nadia sighed. 'This is a brand-new coat. And now it reeks of smoke.'

Lark snorted. 'At least we're keeping things in perspective.'

'Here's a perspective,' said Ransom. 'We need to find out how ordinary people are being turned into monsters. And fast.'

Lark looked up at him. 'So, we can help them?'

'No.' It was Nadia who answered. 'So, we can destroy them.' She frowned as she looked to the flaming boardwalk. 'Because one thing's sure as shit. If we don't start killing them, they'll keep killing us.'

Chapter 20

Seraphine

As part of her nightly routine, Sera sat cross-legged on her bed, staring at the golden teardrop. Pippin sat beside her, wearing the same look of fierce concentration. *What are you made of? And what am I to do with you?*

The bead was dim tonight, hiding its power. Biding its time. Sera prodded it. Clamped it in her fist. Pressed it to her lips. Prayed to it. Threatened it. Threw it at the wall.

Still nothing.

'Wake up,' she hissed. 'Do something.'

She chewed on her frustration. She wished – *saints*, how she wished – she knew what this tiny bead was and why Mama had made it. What had she been working on all those late nights at her workbench when Sera was asleep, dreaming of far-flung adventures . . . ?

A part of Sera was afraid to dwell on it. Afraid to think of Fig's distorted body and compare it to the monsters she had seen in the Hollows. She was afraid of her mother's secrets, the good and the bad . . .

Next time, we're going to talk about that antidote.

She turned the Dagger's words over in her mind for the hundredth time. What did he mean by that? What did he *know*? And what the hell had possessed him to kill her mother but go to all that trouble to save her dog?

The bead warmed up, echoing the flicker of her frustration. She closed her eyes and held it against her heart. Sera knew Shade. She had known it all her life. The cold lick of that black dust beneath her fingers, the yawning hollow in every vial she used to bottle, as if the magic inside wanted to reach up through the stopper and take something vital from her.

But this teardrop was different. The magic inside it didn't feel cold or foreboding. It felt like a promise of hope, like a kiss from the saints. A shield against the rising dark.

It was a gift.

Sera wished she could go back to the day she had received it. She ached to return to the plains, to her mother and their quiet little life that had never seemed quite enough for either of them. Now it was all Sera wanted.

To return to the first snowfall of winter when they used to race their horses to the low forest and back, a cream bun for the winner. Always halved. To the spring when the daffodils bloomed in the garden, and they feasted on grapes and cheese until their bellies ached. To lazy summer evenings in Ploughman's Lake when they swam out on their backs to gaze at the stars, divining their futures in imaginary constellations. To autumn when the first leaves fell, amber and green and gold, and they made great piles of them to jump in.

All their wild and joyful living, Sera knew now, had unfurled under the dark shadow of Dufort's gaze. Yet she never felt it. And if Mama did, she never showed it. But this necklace . . . It said Mama knew something bad was coming. It said she was trying to prepare for it. Trying to protect Sera from it.

Maybe all that time Dufort was watching Mama, Mama was looking back at him.

Sera's cheeks prickled. 'I could go back,' she whispered. 'I should go back.'

Her farmhouse had been burned to cinders but she might find something in the ashes. A clue to this strange magic. A whisper of what she could do with it. The bead tingled against her fingers, a faint glow pulsing as if to say, *Yes, there is more to know. More to do.*

Sera returned it to her neck and went to extinguish the oil lamp on the wall. Something made her pause at the window. She turned, peering into the mouth of the Hollows.

She spotted him almost at once, that familiar pair of quicksilver eyes shining in the dark.

Her Dagger was pacing in the shadows just beyond the boundary of House Armand, as if he was hoping she would simply surrender her mistrust and stroll outside to meet him. Hand over her necklace and bare the column of her neck, let him rip her throat out and be done with it.

She raised her middle finger, hoping he could see it.

He stopped pacing, angling his head to one side.

She raised her other middle finger, for good measure. Then waved them back and forth.

His teeth gleamed in the dark. He raised his own hand, crooking his finger at her. She read the invitation in the slow taunt of his smile. *Come here, Seraphine.*

Like hell she would. Insufferable asshole.

She turned around and grabbed her book, refusing to be drawn into his obsessive little game. She started to read, eager to lose herself in someone else's adventure. It was no use. The Dagger was ruining her concentration, and *clearly* incapable of taking a hint. Every time she glanced up from her book, she saw that moon-bright gaze shining in the dark. She read the same page three times, and still had to go back over it.

Enough.

She grabbed her notebook from her dresser. It had been a gift from Bibi following their success at the apothecary, the cover engraved with an etching of Saint Oriel. She ripped out a page, grabbed her pen and wrote:

Get a hobby, stalker.

She folded the paper into a dart and opened her window, firing it with the skill she had honed back in the plains when she and Lorenzo used to exchange notes across the study room whenever their tutor was distracted. It glided over the garden path and across the hedge, disappearing into the shadows beyond.

She returned to her book, reading the same page for a fourth time. Three minutes went by, and embarrassment roared in her ears. What had she been thinking, trying to write to an actual *assassin*? Making a pen pal out of Mama's murderer and expecting him to reply! How utterly, completely—

There was a soft rap at the window. Pippin barked. Sera leaped to her feet. The paper dart had returned to the windowsill. He must have placed it there with a shadow.

She snatched it up, scanning the words scrawled beneath hers in small, neat script.

You are my hobby, Seraphine. Do you want to come out and play?

Sera slammed the window shut with such force, it rattled in its frame. She pulled the curtains, then leaped away from them for good measure. She crumpled the note and flung it at the wall, her cheeks so hot, she felt like an ember.

Bad idea. Terrible plan. Foolish game.

She flopped back into bed, setting her book aside. She pulled the duvet up to her chin, staring blankly at the ceiling. Trying not to think of his beautiful cruel face, hear the purr of those words in his gravelly voice. *Do you want to come out and play?*

'No,' she said, to the ceiling. And herself. 'I don't want to play.'

The teardrop at her throat tingled, reacting to the flood of her adrenaline.

She scrunched her eyes shut, willing sleep to find her. When it did, she was back in that alleyway by the Aurore. Ransom was there too, pressing her against the wall with the hard planes of his body, his broad hands on her waist, her blood on his lips.

Chapter 21

Seraphine

As the morning mist clung to the rain-spattered rooftops of the Hollows, smearing the greying dawn light, Seraphine grabbed her satchel and her dog and set off for the plains, Dagger be damned. He had to sleep some time.

She went by foot into the heart of the city before heading north, to where a towering stone arch marked the border between civilization and wilderness. There, she managed to hitch a ride on a passing milk wagon returning from the city. Soon, the plains unfurled before her, the sky rendered in lavish strokes of amber and pink, the yawning sun stretching its golden fingers over the horizon, beckoning her home.

When the farmer dropped her off a couple of hours later at a familiar fork in the road, Sera offered him three coppers and thanked him for the ride. The wagon trundled on, and so did she, letting Pippin lead her towards their little farmhouse which had, for many years, squatted amidst a patchwork of cornfields and vineyards, overlooked by rolling green hills that belonged to wandering sheep and bleating goats.

Sera knew it was gone. Burned to ash and embers. And yet, a small, wistful part of her hoped it might appear once they rounded the hill, her heart gladdening at the sight of its modest white frame and bright yellow door, the wooden porch-swing creaking in the wind. But when she cleared the hill, her heart sank. The blackened shell of her house marred the picturesque landscape behind it. The thatched roof was destroyed, the beams straining against the mild breeze.

Pippin stopped, sniffing at the air like he could smell the wrongness of what had happened here. She picked him up, holding him against her chest to soothe the ache in her heart as she drifted up the garden path.

Mama's body was long gone, burned to ash and swept away in the wind. All that remained was the burn mark in the wood, a reminder of where she had died with her hand flung out towards the garden as if, even in death, she was warning Sera to run.

Run little firefly, and never look back.

Sera sank to the floor beside that awful black mark, dropped her head into her hands and wept. Hours passed without her noticing. She wept until her tears ran out and her throat ached, until her eyes stung and her chest loosened. She wept until the little bead at her throat pulsed, its quiet warmth kissing the space above her heart until Sera remembered why she had come here. Until she remembered that she must go on.

She stood up and began carefully picking through the detritus of her former life. Everything was destroyed: their furniture and food, their clothes and books, even Pippin's chew bones. The fire had demolished Sera's favourite fairy-tale books and maps of the world as well as Mama's most treasured tomes on alchemy and artifice, greedily devoured the towering stack of encyclopaedias she had spent decades collecting.

Sera gripped the straps of her satchel as she followed Pippin into the back garden, where a handful of lavender bushes had survived the fire. Pip relieved himself in one. She turned away, and noted with some surprise that their garden shed was still standing.

She kicked the door until it yielded. Pippin scurried inside and she followed, leaving the door ajar. There wasn't much in here except for Mama's old tools: two shovels, a rake, a couple of trowels and a stack of baskets they had used to collect grapes in the vineyard. The rest was in the Vergas' barn a half-mile away. Save for a couple of misshapen wine bottles and crooked labels that bore the name of Mama and Maria's wine, *Nectar of the Saints,* there was little else to look at. Certainly no Shade. Though Sera doubted any of Mama's vials would have survived the fire. The Daggers weren't foolish enough to burn the house and leave the magic behind.

And anyway, Sera hadn't come back here for Shade. She frowned. What *had* she come for? Answers. A sign from Mama. A pathway out of the ruination around her, and a reason to walk it.

A flicker drew her eye to the teardrop glowing at her throat. Theo had forged her a better chain for it two nights ago, after inspecting it at length to no avail. It was double-clasped and made from true gold. Near-impossible to break. She smiled now at the gesture, relieved to have shared her secret with someone she could trust, even if it mystified him.

Pippin pawed at the threadbare rug, until a corner of it came away. Sera sank into a crouch. There was a crack in the floorboards, just wide enough to slide her thumb into. She did so, pulling until three of them gave away at once. A trapdoor.

She glanced up at Pippin. 'Clever mutt.'

The door hid a small crawlspace, just wide enough to fit a crate. Sera pulled it up, surprised to find it stuffed with five leafy heads. Boneshade. She might have mistaken them for cabbages had it not been for the golden glint of the bloom. The roots were gone, long ago ground into Shade, but strangely, the leaves were still perfectly intact, and glowing faintly in the half-light. Why had Mama kept them down here? How had they survived so long?

A better question: why had Mama hidden them in a place that not even Sera knew about? The bloom of the boneshade plant was always discarded. It wasn't remotely valuable.

Sera's frown deepened. It must have been valuable to Mama.

She stuffed the blooms into her satchel, then rifled through a set of jars until she came to the one Pippin was growling at. It was chock full of round berries. Pippin barked when she tried to open the lid so she set it aside, obeying the instinct that told her not to open it.

She continued her excavation, still unsure of what she was

looking for. She had the uncanny sense that she was peering into a secret pocket of Mama's life and she couldn't help hoping there might be something in here that was meant for her. A note, perhaps. Or an explanation for the magic she wore around her neck. A map of the world without Mama.

No such luck.

Nothing here meant anything to Sera. At the bottom of the crate, wedged between two slats, she found a narrow book that looked almost like a pamphlet. It was so old and well thumbed, the binding had come apart. Now it was more of a scattering of yellowed pages and faded ink. Sera had to squint to make out the title.

The Lost Days of Lucille Versini, Saint and Scholar

The book was ancient. At least two hundred years old judging by the print and size. Sera turned it over, examining it. Mama had often spoken of Lucille Versini, not as the saint she had become after her untimely death but as the scholar she had been – however briefly – in life. The youngest person to ever study at the Appoline, and to spearhead her own research. Sometimes, Sera got the sense that Mama was jealous of the young Versini girl, not for her fame but for the opportunity she had been given – to go to a place where knowledge was treasured, and innovation was celebrated.

Lucille's story had always struck Seraphine as unbearably tragic. She had barely scratched the surface of her own potential when her life had been cut short, her research extinguished as easily as blowing out a candle. What did Mama have to be jealous of?

She flicked through the pamphlet, intrigued by the pencil marks inside. Entire passages had been circled and underlined, sometimes two or three times. Most of the ink was too faded for words to be discerned, but her gaze snagged on one word – *Lightfire*.

The back of her neck began to prickle.

She heard a *crunch*. A sound she had heard a thousand times before. Someone was moving – no, *skulking* – through the flowerbed.

Ransom was here.

Sera slipped the tattered pages of Lucille Versini's life into her satchel with one hand, and, as she stood up, reached for a trowel with the other. Another crunch, closer now. She leaped outside and hurled the trowel.

There was a *clunk*, then a strangled shout. 'Agh! What the hell, Sera?'

She blinked the figure into focus. He was bent double, with one hand clasped over his eye and the other braced on his knee. She flinched as she noticed the generous crop of golden curls, his fraying blue plaid shirt, those long suntanned arms. They had wrapped around her more times than she cared to count.

She flung her hands up. 'I'm sorry, Lorenzo! I thought— Never mind. Are you all right?'

Lorenzo straightened. 'I figured you might be angry with me,' he said, dropping his hand to reveal an angry welt above his left eye. 'But I wasn't expecting assault.'

'It was an accident.'

He pressed his lips together. Full lips that tasted like sunlight and cider. 'There was nothing accidental about that aim.'

She swallowed. 'Pip—'

'Don't blame the dog. You always blame the dog.'

Lorenzo knew her too well. 'I wouldn't have thrown that trowel if you weren't sneaking up on me,' she snapped.

'I wasn't sneaking up on you,' he said, rising to the argument, like he always did. Lorenzo Verga was as fiery as the sun. 'Since when are you so jumpy?'

She folded her arms. 'Take a guess.'

Now it was his turn to flinch. His face fell, the fight seeping out of him. 'Sorry. I shouldn't have said that.' He passed a hand over the fair stubble on his jaw. 'It's good to see you, Sera. I've been so worried. By the time I saw those flames . . .'

'Mama was dead.'

'And you were long gone.' He dug his hands in his pockets. 'I'd hoped you'd made it to the city, found a place at House Armand like Sylvie wanted.'

She swallowed thickly, stung by a sense of betrayal. So he remembered what she had confided in him about Mama's fear, her warnings. He had known – or at least guessed – where she'd been all this time. 'And it didn't occur to you to come looking for me?'

A beat of hesitation. 'Mama said it was too dangerous to try and find you. You might have been marked too.' He looked at his boots, shame colouring his cheeks. 'The night of the fire, we left the vineyard and travelled to cousins in Farberg. We haven't been back long.'

'You ran away from me?' said Sera, blinking in disbelief.

He frowned, then offered weakly, 'Only for a little while.'

She gave a mirthless snort, no longer regretting the trowel. 'I should head back.' She whistled for Pippin, who was sniffing about in the lavender, then grabbed her satchel from the shed, before turning to leave.

Lorenzo slid in front of her, his hands coming to her shoulders. 'Wait.'

'Don't,' she said, quietly.

He dropped his hands, but didn't move out of her way. 'You have to understand that all of this ... this recklessness ...' He gestured to the burnt farmhouse, then the shed. 'There was always a chance it would end badly. Sylvie knew it. Mama knew it too. The risks ... If I had known then what I do now, I never would have let them go through with it.' He sucked on a tooth. 'It was only a matter of time before Gaspard Dufort got wind of it.'

Sera frowned, losing her footing in the conversation. 'What are you talking about?'

He stared at her blankly. In the sheen of his cornflower-blue eyes, she saw the reflection of her own confusion. 'Do you really not know what Sylvie was up to? I thought I was the only one out of the loop.'

Sera's blood chilled. Even Pippin had stopped his inspections, attuned to the sudden shift in her mood.

Lorenzo stepped in close and for a heartbeat she thought he was going to snatch her necklace. She covered it with her fist but he hardly noticed. Lorenzo was only a few inches taller than her, but as he pressed her back against the side of the shed, he covered her with his shadow. His voice dropped like he was afraid the lavender was listening in. 'The wine, Sera. You know what your mother was planning to do with the wine, don't you?'

She glanced around. Suddenly, the garden felt too quiet. She grabbed his shirt collar and pulled him into the shed, rounding on him in the dimness. 'What are you talking about?' she hissed. 'Stop dancing around it.'

'The wine,' he hissed back. 'Sylvie poisoned the latest batch!'

Sera blinked, the words rushing over her like floodwater. No, she must have misheard him. He snatched up a label and waved it around – the gilded words glinting in the half-dark: *Nectar of the Saints.* 'Haven't you heard about the monsters, Sera? Haven't you been wondering where they come from? All those twisted vicious creatures made of Shade. The stories have reached us even out in the plains.'

Sera shook her head, a manic laugh building in her throat. 'That's absurd, Lorenzo.' She used her foot to shove the crate back down into the crawl space. Pushing it away, just as fervently as she was pushing away his words. 'I've *seen* a monster with my own eyes. It was made of more than just Shade. It wasn't even human.' She shuddered at the memory of it chasing her down. 'It had no shape. No soul. Shade doesn't do that.' She tried to slam the trapdoor shut, but his foot shot out, stopping her.

'Not on its own,' he conceded. 'But what if it was mixed with something else?' He pulled the jar of berries from the crate. 'You know better than I do how Shade is made.'

'Of course I do,' she said, eager to prove her greater knowledge of the subject. 'You dry it out, then grind the root into a fine dust, shake the light particles loose and mix in a pinch of salt to stabilize the dust. Bottle and stopper immediately.' The words tumbled from her mouth in one breath, but her gaze never left the jar in Lorenzo's hand. This thing that was so significant – or perhaps dangerous – that Mama had hidden it in the shed, somewhere Seraphine – and Pippin – couldn't get at it.

She knew exactly what those berries were.

And then Lorenzo said it. 'Do you know what happens when you mix in heartsbane instead of salt? When you combine the purest of nature's poisons with the darkest of its magic?' When Sera said nothing, he went on. 'And then you decide to tip it into a cheap bottle of fruit wine?'

Sera slammed the trapdoor down, pulling the rug over it. 'You're making up fairy tales again. I forgot how you love to do that.'

He went on as if he hadn't heard her. 'It doesn't just poison the body, Sera. It poisons the soul. It *changes* you. It takes away the bridge between magic and mortality, until there's no going back to who you were before.' He set the jar down with a determined thud. A crack spiderwebbed across the glass. 'That is how you make a monster, Sera. That is what your mother intended.' His lips twisted. 'And for some reckless reason, my mother got sucked into her deranged plan.'

'You're lying,' fumed Sera.

'I *wish* I was lying,' he said, ruefully. 'Mama only admitted it to me when we got back from Farberg and found the poisoned batch gone from our barn. The delivery wagon must have come while we were away and taken it into the city. Mama was supposed to wait for the signal from Sylvie. She wasn't ready yet.' He raked his hands through his hair, and Sera watched fear flicker in his eyes. Fear for his mother, and fear of what their trip to Farberg had unwittingly set in motion. 'Now it's too late.'

Sera shook her head, hating that quiver in his voice. No, *no*, it couldn't be true. 'Why would Mama have any interest in making monsters?'

'You know why,' he said, softly.

Sera hated how her mind jumped back to last year when she had watched Mama experimenting on a stray cat in this very garden. Even now she could hear the echo of Fig's growl, then Mama's scream cutting through the night. By the way Lorenzo was looking at her, she knew he was thinking of it, too. She regretted ever confiding in him about it.

'Because sometimes it takes a monster to destroy a monster,' he said quietly.

Sera stared at him, and knew they were thinking of the same man. The only man her mother ever spoke about with spit and rage and fire.

'Your mother always longed to destroy the Daggers,' he went on, with a rueful smile. 'She talked about it more than the weather. But to do it, *really* do it, she had to find the kind of creature that even Dufort could not hope to kill. And when she couldn't find one, she decided to make one. We both know she was clever enough to do it.'

Sera swallowed back her revulsion, trying and failing to see her mother's grand vision. 'But the monsters aren't killing Daggers, Lorenzo,' she whispered. 'They're killing *everyone*.'

He rubbed the spot between his brows. 'I told you. She never finished her plan.'

Because Dufort got to her first.

The bead pulsed at Sera's throat, sharing her anger and confusion.

Silence hung like a storm cloud between them. In that moment, Sera hated Lorenzo. Not because of what he was saying, but because in her heart, she knew it was true. Her mother was capable of anything. And the teardrop around her neck was proof of that. If Sylvie Marchant had crafted a new kind of magic, then what was to say she hadn't made these monsters too? What was to say they weren't connected somehow?

'Mama hated the Daggers but she would never have endangered Fantome. Innocent people have died, Lorenzo. They're still dying. Mama would never have let that happen.' Of that, Seraphine was sure. She *had* to be sure. Because the alternative – that Mama was somehow a greater danger than even Dufort – was too sickening to consider. 'Whatever her plan was, she would have avoided that.'

Mercifully, Lorenzo nodded in agreement. 'Mama says Sylvie was working on an antidote too. Magic that would help the monsters.'

Sera's eyes widened at that word – *antidote*. The Dagger had used it too, had wanted to talk to her about it. But she had taunted him and sent him away.

Lorenzo was shaking his head. 'Then Dufort came for her and everything went wrong.'

She closed her eyes, trying to take it all in. But the enormity of his confession was so daunting, she was afraid it might overwhelm her.

'When he came over that hill, we grabbed the shotgun and ran,' he went on, his voice stricken. 'We didn't know how much he knew, what he was coming here for. We thought it was about the poison. About the wine. Mama was part of that too. For all we knew, he had marked us just the same.'

Sera's eyes flew open. 'You saw Dufort?'

Lorenzo stilled, realizing his mistake.

Out in the garden, Pippin started barking.

Sera ignored him. 'You just said it was Dufort that came over the hill. That Dufort killed Mama.' But that was not who she had seen in the house, standing over her mother's body. The man had been much taller and broader than Dufort. Had the smoke played tricks on her mind? Had Ransom told her the truth after all?

It didn't matter just then, because Lorenzo had let slip a graver truth. 'You knew she was going to die,' she said, reading the guilt on his face. 'You saw him come to kill her and you fled.'

His silence was answer enough, his expression so crestfallen she thought for a moment he was about to cry. But then he rolled his shoulders back and squared his jaw. 'She was marked. That's what happens when you mess with Dufort. Sylvie knew the risks and didn't care. In the end she . . .' he trailed off.

Pippin was pacing by the bushes, a growl rumbling in his throat.

'She what?' Sera prodded. 'Don't hold your tongue now; you've already said everything else.'

'She had it coming, Sera.'

Without thinking, she slapped him. His hand flew to his face, his eyes going wide. She shouldn't have done it, but she didn't regret it either. Silent tears streamed down her cheeks as she stormed away from the shed. He followed her across the garden where Pippin rushed to meet her. 'It's all right, Pip,' she said, scratching behind his ears to calm him down. 'We're going now. For good.'

Lorenzo lunged, grabbing her hand. 'Don't just walk away.'

She shook him off. 'This is what you want, isn't it? Nothing to do with Mama. Nothing to do with me. Well, your wish is my command.'

'There's no need to be so . . . so . . . *final* about this.'

'Move,' she fumed. 'Or I swear I'll choke down that jar of heartsbane just to get the hell away from you.'

'That's not funny,' he snapped.

'At least we agree on something.' She marched away from him, Pippin scurrying to keep up as she clenched her firsts, trying to shove down her grief, but it was becoming hard to see. She wiped her cheeks, scrubbing away the tears, but they kept coming.

'Seraphine! Wait!'

She paused to look over her shoulder. 'For what?'

Under the afternoon sun, Lorenzo's hair shone burnished gold, his boyish face a heartbreaking portrait of regret. Despite his fevered protestations, he was standing still. Watching her leave. Just as he had watched Gaspard Dufort come for Mama. He had done nothing then. And he was doing nothing now.

'To . . . talk?' he said, weakly. 'I miss you. I . . .'

'I'm done talking.' This time, when Sera turned away, she didn't look back. The truth was, Lorenzo was a coward.

And in this game of revenge – of strange magic and twisted monsters – there was no room for cowards.

When she reached the gate, she scooped Pippin into her arms. They turned for the hills, heading back towards Fantome.

'It's just you and me now, Pip,' she said, pressing a kiss to his shaggy head.

He licked a tear from her cheek and she smiled, adjusting her satchel. It was heavier now. At least their trip home hadn't been a complete waste of time. Sera hoped she had found a clue hidden in the floorboards. She intended to follow it, all the way back to the time of Lucille Versini if she had to. Because even in her despair, a glimmer of hope was flickering. She was going to find out if that faded word – *Lightfire* – meant what she thought it did: Magic.

Chapter 22

Ransom

I n the back garden of Seraphine Marchant's burnt-out
farmhouse, Ransom plucked a fig off a tree and ate it.
Delicious. It was soft and sweet as honey, the syrupy
liquid staining his lips. He licked them clean, then reached for
another.

Seraphine was in the shed, with the boy whose head looked
like a cabbage. Lorenzo. His shirt was too big and his trousers
were too long. All wide eyes and bumbling apologies. He
deserved that trowel to the face, though it had nearly revealed
Ransom when he had to clap his hand over his mouth to trap
his laughter.

After watching her cry for over an hour, kneeling on the
burnt floor with her arms wrapped around herself, he almost
cheered when that fire inside her sparked to life once more.

When her grief hardened into anger and sent that trowel whistling through the air. Meant, of course, for him. He would have taken ten trowels to the face over another minute of those deep, gasping sobs.

Ransom had come all the way out here to confront Seraphine, but the sight of her bent double on the floor had done something unexpected to his chest. It had tightened it to the point of pain and he could not now bring himself to face her, to intrude on an aching loss that so closely mirrored his own.

So he resolved to stay and watch her instead. To see what clues she might dig up for him in the rubble of her old life.

Now she was arguing with cabbage-head. Good. It made a welcome shift of mood from the moment he had pushed her up against the shed and covered her body with his. If Ransom had taken Shade today, he would have leaped at golden Lorenzo like a panther and torn him off her.

Threatening Seraphine was *his* job. This hapless farmboy had wandered into his territory. But without Shade, Ransom was a reasonable man. He had resolved to let the situation play out, to see if he might glean something from it. The spitfire had come back here for a reason, after all. He intended to find out what that was.

Her mutt glowered at him from the flowerbed. Ransom bit into his fig and tossed him the other half. The dog sniffed at the fruit suspiciously, then barked at him.

Ransom clucked his tongue. 'And after I went to all that trouble to save your life.'

The argument in the shed ended. Seraphine stomped out in

a rage, while cabbage-head shambled after her, pathetic as a lost puppy. The mutt went after her too.

While they continued sniping at each other in the front garden, Ransom crept behind the lavender bushes and slipped into the shed. He kicked the rug aside and rifled through the crate. Nothing of note. He frowned, unsure of what he was expecting to find down here anyway. Seraphine had already been through it, filling her satchel with whatever secrets Dufort had missed the first time.

He stood up and kicked the rug back into place. There was a cracked jar of berries on a nearby shelf. His eyes narrowed at the dark red juice smeared along the glass. Heartsbane. Ransom stilled, a part of him hurtling back to twelve years ago, when he had found a cluster of the same berries wrapped in cloth under one of Mama's flowerpots. He thought they were jam currants left by a kind neighbour who had heard Mama screaming the night before. Only the juice was darker, the same red as the cut on her lip.

He could still remember how her hands trembled when he brought the berries to her, how her eyes had rounded with horror as she snatched them from him. *Did you take any of these? Open your mouth, let me look inside.* Later, he watched her bury them in the garden, her fingers scrabbling in the dirt as she kept one eye on the door, sure Papa would come swaggering home at any moment. *We won't tell a soul about this, darling boy. Especially not Papa.* It was an easy thing to promise. Anouk was too young to understand, and Ransom never told Papa anything.

He wished his mother had found the courage to go through

with her plan. To use those berries instead of burying them. But fear was a noose around her neck even then, and the risk of failure was too great. If Papa had found out, he would have killed her for it. He would have killed them all.

Ransom set the jar down, blinking himself back to the present moment. What business did Sylvie Marchant, a Shade smuggler, have with a poison such as this? His gaze roamed, falling on the half-crumpled label beside it. He picked it up, recognizing the outline of a five-leafed clover. But – no. It was not a clover at all. It was boneshade, the golden bloom obvious to him now. *Nectar of the Saints.* The same wine they served at the Lucky Shell.

Ransom brushed his thumb over the emblem, thinking again of Kipp. The man, then the monster. He looked from the berries to the wine label, and back again.

'Who the hell are you?'

He jerked his chin up.

Cabbage-head was standing in the shed doorway, a hand braced on either side to block him in. Ransom remained wholly unthreatened. Even without Shade, he could knock this farmboy out in seconds.

He decided to greet him. 'I'm Ransom,' he said, flashing his teeth.

'Is that supposed to mean something to me?'

Ransom shrugged. 'I don't really care what it means to you.'

'What are you doing in Seraphine's shed?'

'I was just about to ask you the same thing.' Ransom held up the jar of heartsbane. 'Does this belong to you?'

'Who's asking?'

'I am,' said Ransom, waiting a beat. 'Or Gaspard Dufort, if you like.'

Lorenzo's throat bobbed.

Ransom offered him a bland smile. 'Shall I ask again?'

'The berries belonged to Sylvie.' He stepped back from the door, as though the sunlight might save him. Ransom remained where he was, allowing him the illusion of safety. 'The Shade, the poison. She sourced it all. The wine was the last ingredient, but the plan was Sylvie's. All of it was her idea . . .'

Ransom let the silence linger.

Lorenzo filled it with his own panic. 'She mixed the poison with the Shade to see what it could do.' It occurred to Ransom that this dithering farmboy thought he was here to kill him, and that talking might save his life. They always thought that. It had only ever worked for Seraphine. 'She had her sights on Dufort. Always did, as long as I knew her. She was obsessed with him, obsessed with making those monsters. She finally pulled it off.' His gaze flicked from the shed to the shell of the house, as if he was afraid Dufort would come stomping through it. 'She picked a fight with a dragon. I guess the dragon was smarter than she thought.'

Ransom raised his eyebrows. Was this why Dufort had killed Sylvie? Because in a fit of boredom out here in the plains, she had decided to fuck with the world order and make monsters more vicious than the Daggers of Fantome?

But— No. Dufort had been just as surprised by the monsters as anyone else. He was the last one to believe they even existed. Whatever she had died for, it was not this.

And yet, there was no denying that Lorenzo had handed over a huge piece of this strange puzzle. 'What about the girl?'

Lorenzo stiffened, finally showing a hint of courage. 'Seraphine had no idea about any of it. Not until today.'

'Nice of you to trample her mother's memory.'

'She deserves to hear the truth.'

'Well, that explains the lovers' quarrel.'

Lorenzo frowned. 'She's innocent. Leave her alone.'

'An admirable suggestion,' said Ransom drolly. 'I'll take it under advisement.'

Lorenzo was starting to sweat. He shifted from one leg to another, as if he was trying not to piss himself. Lately, Ransom had received so much smart-mouthed insolence from Seraphine Marchant, he had almost forgotten the effect he had on common folk. How terrifying he truly was.

'Are you going to kill me now?' said Lorenzo meekly.

'I'm thinking about it,' lied Ransom.

'Please. I have a life here. A family. A farm. A—' He stopped short.

'Vineyard?' prompted Ransom.

Lorenzo quailed. 'The b-b-batch is g-g-gone.'

Ransom almost laughed, but he didn't want to ruin the suspense. He was quite enjoying this feeling of being feared. Respected. It had been a while since he had experienced it. 'Why don't I count to ten, Lorenzo?' he said, indulgently. 'And if you've made it past that fig tree by the time I turn around, I'll let you live.'

Lorenzo was already running. He bolted across the garden,

making it to the fig tree in seven seconds. Ransom leaned against the doorframe, chuckling as he watched him flee, his plaid shirt billowing and long arms flailing, like a scarecrow cursed to life.

Chapter 23

Seraphine

When Sera returned to House Armand, most of the Cloaks were in the dining hall, enjoying a dinner of roast turkey with herb stuffing, spiced cranberry sauce and mashed potatoes. She ducked her head in to wave at Bibi and Val before continuing upstairs with Pippin, leaving him to tackle the giant turkey leg Rupert and Bianca had set aside for him. She didn't return to the dining room, instead heading to the basement to find Theo.

After several insistent knocks, the door opened to reveal the Shadowsmith in all his rumpled glory. His silver hair was ruffled and he was wearing loose-fitting trousers, a black vest, and his feet were bare. He blinked, rubbing the sleep from his eyes.

'Sorry to interrupt your nap,' said Sera, brushing past him. 'You missed dinner, by the way.'

Theo frowned. 'Not again.'

'If you ask nicely, Pip might share his turkey leg with you.' That earned her a sluggish smile. 'What are you working on down here anyway?'

'A hideous failure.' He sighed, gesturing to the mess of tools on the island. 'A compass that can detect unusually high concentrations of Shade. Spikes of magic.'

'You mean monsters.'

He nodded. 'It is not going well.'

Sera almost felt bad about adding another task to his workload. 'I went back to the plains today, to see if I could find out anything about Mama's necklace.'

His eyebrows shot up. 'That was reckless.'

'Everything I do these days is reckless.' She shrugged off her satchel, then crouched to rifle through it. She was glad not to have to look him in the eyes when she said, 'Today was . . . illuminating.' A colossal understatement. She had found answers in the plains, but they were not the kind she had been hoping for. At least, not the kind she could be proud of. To think that Mama decided to make monsters out of ordinary people . . . and all so she could punish Gaspard Dufort for his own depravity.

What good was an antidote now that the monsters were already scattered across Fantome, stalking and killing at will? How could they make the antidote if Mama had taken its secret to the grave?

Mama had gone too far. She had taken everything too far and made a mess she was no longer here to fix.

Lorenzo might have been a coward but he had been right

about one thing: Sylvie Marchant had had it coming. But this awful mess was not entirely Mama's fault. Dufort had murdered her, unwittingly setting her unfinished plan into motion. And Maria had fled instead of destroying that damn shipment of wine. She should have poured it into the river and been done with it all.

'Seraphine?' Theo was on his knees before her. 'You're a million miles away.'

She rolled back on her heels and buried her head in her hands. 'I'm spiralling.'

'I see that.' He gently removed her hands from her face. 'Can you be more specific? What did you find, out in the plains?'

Sera raked her hands through her hair, wishing she could forget everything Lorenzo had told her. But the truth was a storm in her heart, and it had grown wilder with every step towards home.

'Whatever it is, you can tell me,' said Theo. 'I promise I won't judge.'

Sera blew out a breath. 'I wouldn't be so sure about that.'

'You'd be surprised at the secrets people have spilled down here. Even Madame Mercure.' He winked. 'Try me.'

Despite her burgeoning shame and anger over what Mama had done, the burden was too great for Sera to shoulder alone. She found she did want to try with Theo. What else did she possibly have to lose?

'I'll be right here,' he said, kicking his legs out and leaning back against the glass island. 'Whenever you get done wrestling with your indecision.'

Sera sat beside him. In the falling quiet of the cloakroom, as night yawned across the city of Fantome and the distant sound of howls hitchhiked on the wind, she confessed everything that Lorenzo had told her about the monsters of Fantome, about Mama's role in their creation and how her plan had been set in motion too soon.

Theo listened in contemplative silence, his face a careful mask of impassivity.

When it was done, Sera didn't feel any better. She felt sick. As though she had stuck a knife in Mama's memory and drained all the goodness out. 'She wasn't a bad person,' she added, desperately. 'She just . . .' she trailed off.

'Wanted to destroy Dufort and his Daggers by any means necessary,' said Theo, with the kind of casual acceptance that made Sera want to hug him.

She nodded. 'I guess so.'

'Why?'

Sera chewed on her lip, unsure of how to answer him. There was so much uncomfortable truth between them that already the air felt heavier. She couldn't bring herself to add to it, to fully illuminate the long shadow Dufort had cast over their lives. But then Theo spoke again, muddling out his own answer. 'It's not like she was alone in that desire. Back where I come from, the villagers speak of Dufort like he's the devil himself. Most are too terrified to speak of him at all, to venture as far as Fantome in case they come face to face with a Dagger. To be a Cloak is one thing, but . . . .'

He frowned, and Sera sensed he had been wrestling with the immorality of his position here long before this conversation. 'But to be a Dagger . . . They're an abomination. A stain on the goodness of this city. They've turned the Age of Saints into an Age of Darkness. Your mother was hardly the first person ever to dream of destroying them. She was just the first to come up with an effective way to actually do it.' He paused, voice tightening. 'Only, the problem is, those monsters aren't killing Dufort's Daggers. They're killing . . .'

'Anyone,' said Sera grimly. 'Everyone.' She rolled to her feet. 'It's one big devastating mess. And now, she's not around to fix it.'

'So, we'll fix it,' said Theo, as if they were talking about repairing a ripped seam and not reversing the plague of monsters that now terrorized their city. He grabbed her satchel as he stood up and set it down on the glass island. A head of boneshade tumbled out. He set it aside, then peered in at the rest. 'Why do you have a satchel full of bloom?'

'I found them stashed in our shed back at home.' She turned her satchel upside down now and the pamphlet about Lucille Versini slipped out. 'I found this too,' she said, sliding it towards him. 'I think it might be a clue to the magic I wear around my neck. Mama was working on some kind of antidote to the monsters.'

He opened the pamphlet, squinting to make out the print. Much of it had been faded by time, some sentences trailing into nothing. But the Shadowsmith rose eagerly to the challenge, fishing a pot of ink from a drawer. As he unscrewed it, she caught the unmistakable whiff of Shade. 'I call this cloying ink,' he said. 'It clings to darkness, pushes the light away.'

He stoppered the bottle with his thumb, then tipped it over the pamphlet, letting the ink out, drop by drop. Sera watched it fall onto the lines of faded text, clinging to every word. In a matter of seconds, the entire page became legible, that word *Lightfire* so black, it seemed to leap from every paragraph.

'You really are clever,' she said, leaning closer until their heads touched.

'I know.'

They read a while in silence, Sera carefully turning the pages while Theo tipped cloying ink onto each new paragraph, painting the words back into place. 'Look. There.' She traced a paragraph that Mama had underlined almost in its entirety, reading the words aloud.

'In the last days of her young life, Lucille Versini was entrenched in her research, spending long nights in the library of the Appoline, edging ever closer to a new kind of magic. Not the Shade that her brothers had discovered almost a decade earlier. Rather, it was the antidote to such darkness, the secret of which, according to Lucille's journals, resided in the bloom of the very same plant. She called this magic Lightfire, and she sought to extract it, but the art of alchemy is never quite so simple.

The pursuit of Lightfire was to be her undoing. For there was nothing in all the world that frightened Hugo Versini so much as his little sister's avid mind. Some believe that Lucille discovered how to make Lightfire just before her death. A secret that Hugo Versini made sure to bury with her.'

'He killed her for it,' Sera murmured. 'His own sister.'

Theo curled his lip. 'There's nothing more dangerous than a frightened Dagger.' He reached for a head of bloom, holding it up to the light. It shone like a fallen sun. 'At least we know why your mother was storing these.'

'She was trying to make Lightfire.' Sera couldn't tear her gaze from the glinting bloom, caught suddenly in a surge of hope. 'She was trying to finish what Lucille Versini started.'

'Not just trying.' Theo looked meaningfully at Sera, his gaze falling to the bead at her throat. 'She had succeeded.'

She grasped her necklace, feeling the teardrop warm up in her fingers, as if agreeing with her. With a jolt, she remembered what Ransom had called her magic – an *antidote*. Mama had managed to make it after all – this little spark of Lightfire. It was not enough to protect Fantome, but it had protected Seraphine, hadn't it? It had fought the Dagger's Shade and saved her life at Villa Roman. 'But how did she do it?'

His face fell as he set the bloom down. He didn't need to say it – they both knew that the answer to that question had likely gone up in flames along with Mama.

Sera stilled, caught in the grip of another realization. 'He must have known.'

Theo cocked his head. 'Who?'

'Dufort,' she said, half-choking on the name. 'You said it yourself. There's nothing more dangerous than a frightened Dagger. When Hugo discovered what his sister was working on, he killed her for it. Lightfire was the only thing that could beat Shade. It was the same for Dufort. He knew the rediscovery of it would destroy his reign over the underworld.

It would destroy the entire legacy of Hugo Versini.'

Theo's face tightened. 'Do you think Dufort was watching her?'

'Yes,' said Sera, without a beat of hesitation. The truth was a horror inside her. Dufort had been watching them all their lives. Watching Mama, a lot more closely than she'd thought. Perhaps he had always known what Seraphine knew – that Mama's ambitions stretched far beyond the petty act of smuggling, that Shade was merely a gateway to another, greater dream – another, better, version of Fantome. 'Maybe the monsters evaded him. That wine was made on Maria Verga's land, bottled in her barn. But Lightfire . . .'

Lightfire was Mama's life's work.

Memories flooded Sera. All those hours spent in bookshops and libraries, the stacks of encyclopaedias that teetered in the corners back home, the smell of herbs and spices that always clung to her, the plants that lined their kitchen shelves, the stray cats that disappeared as quickly as they came. Those endless nights at her workbench where she tinkered beneath the light of the moon, the permanent hunch in her shoulders, the spark of every untried idea kindling in her eyes and tearing her away from conversations at dinner, from mugs of coffee and warm bubble baths, from bedtime stories and half-sung lullabies.

Those flashes of golden light that came in the dead of night, jostling Sera from her slumber, sending her to the window to search for falling stars. It was not the sky that sent those lights. It was Mama, always working, always reaching beyond the dark. Up, and up, and up.

Magic. It was all suddenly right there in front of Seraphine.

As loud and bright as the fire that had come afterwards. 'Mama spent her whole life chasing the memory of Lucille Versini. Chasing Lightfire. And ...' She tipped her head back, trying to breathe.

'And when she finally found it, Dufort killed her for it,' Theo finished quietly. There was a heavy beat of silence. 'But he didn't kill you.'

Sera started to pace. Trying to calm down, to subdue the sudden urge to scream and smash everything in sight. 'I'm going to kill him, Theo. I'm going to find him and I'm going to tear him apart. And I swear to Lucille and the rest of the saints that I'm going to do it with Lightfire.'

'Breathe, Sera,' he said, watching her battle through the storm of her emotions. 'Let's start with the magic. Once we figure that out, we can talk about the rest.'

She could have kissed him for his calmness, for not shaking her and telling her she was idiotic to consider moving against Dufort. But he had already returned his attention to the pamphlet, his brows knitting as he flicked through the rest of the pages. There was nothing more about Lightfire, no other clue beyond the bloom glowing dimly between them.

'I could try grinding the leaves,' he murmured after a while. 'Experiment with the dust.'

'That sounds like shooting an arrow in the dark,' she said, finally coming back to herself.

'But it's a start.'

The door flew open with a sudden *whoosh*, startling them from their conversation.

'Whatever this is, I'm part of it too,' said Val, hobbling

inside. 'Monsters. Lightfire. Revenge. I'm in.'

Theo released a long-suffering sigh. 'What have I told you about eavesdropping?'

'What have *I* told *you* about keeping secrets from me?' she shot back. 'If you two little whisperlings have found a clue to destroying these hell-born monsters then I want to know about it. I want to help.' She cleared her throat, looking a little sheepish. 'And honestly, I only crept down here because I wanted to catch you two making out.'

Sera glared at her. 'How is that any better than eavesdropping?'

Val shrugged. 'I was bored. I hardly expected to stumble upon a secret magical plot.' She hopped up onto the island, nearly creasing the pamphlet. 'And since I'm brain-meltingly clever, I have a killer suggestion.'

'Go on,' said Theo, snatching the pamphlet and placing it on a nearby shelf for safe keeping. 'Since apparently this is now a three-way conversation.'

'We should pay a midnight visit to the Grand Versini Library,' said Val. 'I bet you five silvers Lucille's journals are somewhere in the archives.'

Sera looked to Theo. 'Do you think it's worth a try?'

He chewed his lip. 'Well . . . What have you got to lose?'

Val blew a stray curl from her eye, lounging across the glass island like a cat. 'A better question is, what do you have to gain?'

Everything, whispered a voice inside Sera's head.

A short while later, Sera left the cloakroom, feeling emboldened. While Val took herself off to bed and Theo returned to his never-ending research, she went to the kitchens, where she devoured a bread roll stuffed with turkey in five bites. Her hunger sated, exhaustion crept in.

On her way up to bed, she took a detour to the music room, where she found Bibi sitting in a pool of firelight, playing the piano. Her long red hair was wound into a loose bun, and she was wearing her pyjamas. Long, pale fingers danced along the keys, filling the room – and the halls – with a melody so pleasant it made Sera smile. The chords were buoyant, embroidered with tinkling trills that reminded her of the dawn birds, singing to welcome the day.

She rested her head against the doorframe, every note a balm to her sore heart. *Hope*, they sang. *Hope dances along the horizon. And its name is Lightfire.*

Sera was going to reach for that hope with both hands.

The music stopped. Bibi looked at her over her shoulder. 'I'm afraid that's all I've come up with.'

It was only then that Sera noticed there was no sheet music. She edged into the room. 'You composed that yourself?'

Bibi nodded sheepishly. 'I couldn't sleep.'

'It's beautiful.'

'It's not finished yet,' she said, blushing at the compliment.

Sera shook her head, wonder warring with surprise. Bibi could have been a musician in another life. A composer to rival the best in Valterre. If this was the scope of her talent at barely seventeen, what would a handful more years do for her?

'You're frowning,' said Bibi, yanking her hands back from the keys. 'It's not supposed to be a sad song.'

'It's not sad,' said Sera quickly. 'It's incredible. It's joy in its purest form.' And it was joy, uncomplicated and uncompromising, exactly like Bibi herself. 'I was just thinking of how talented you are, how much you could learn in a place like the Appoline. Not the pitiful Hollows of Fantome, but somewhere that could truly nurture your creativity.'

Bibi smiled. 'I like it here, Sera. It inspires me just fine.'

She frowned. There was nothing on Bibi's face of the internal struggle that Theo dealt with, no sense of the restlessness Sera sometimes sensed in Val. 'What, stealing?'

'Living.' That smile remained. 'I have everything I could ever wish for at House Armand. Safety. Security. Beautiful clothes and a warm, cosy bed. Books to read and music to play. Food to savour and money to spend as I like. People to eat with, to laugh with. A family all of my own.'

Sera looked again at the piano, the ghost of her song still lingering in the air. She thought of the cool slick of Shade against her skin and the guilt that came with taking and *taking*, but never giving back, the risk of every Sleight and Break and Heist, and the grimy greyness of the Hollows. Then she pictured Bibi sitting at a grand piano in a sparkling ballgown, the notes of her song soaring through the oldest music halls in Valterre, gracing the ear of the king and winning the favour of the queen, and said, quietly, 'Is it enough?'

Bibi thought about it a moment. 'For me, it is.'

Sera nodded. She believed her. Bibi had come to this place as a child and found contentment here as she grew. She was happy, and it was simple, and a part of Sera envied her for it.

The truth was that for all the comfort and protection she had found at House Armand, Sera could not help the yearning in her heart to go further than Shade would take her. To eventually free herself from the darkness that had nipped at her heels her whole life. She wanted the brightness of tomorrow, complete freedom from the underworld, from Dufort and the price he had placed on her head.

For Bibi, freedom was House Armand. She wasn't straining for anything beyond these four walls. She had already found whatever peace she sought within herself.

'I'll let you return to your music,' said Sera softly. 'Let's chat tomorrow at breakfast? I've got a Heist in mind.'

'Can't wait,' said Bibi, smiling as she turned back to the keys. 'Goodnight, Sera.'

'Goodnight, Bibi.'

Sera was at the door when her friend called after her. 'You could be happy here too, Sera.' She ran her hands along the keys, sending a cheerful trill after her. It made Sera think of starlings, moving in a great ribbon across the sky. 'Home is not just a place. It's people. It's family.'

Sera knew that was true, but there could be no home without freedom. And while Dufort stalked this city, she would never truly be free.

Chapter 24

Seraphine

The Dagger was back. Standing in the darkness outside House Armand, his quicksilver eyes glowing like stardust. Sera glared at him through the gap in her curtains, hating the gnaw of her own curiosity.

Ransom had hesitated to kill her twice now. He had even gone out of his way to save Pippin. And *still*, he stalked her. Was he really that desperate to speak to her? Or did he know something vital about the magic in her necklace that she didn't? She reached for her pen.

What exactly do you want?

The paper dart soared into the night, and returned a minute later.

Come outside and I'll tell you.

No way. She was not walking into that spider's web without a damn good reason.

I would rather eat a bowl of my own hair.

The note came back again.

Charming. Did you enjoy your trip to the plains?

Dread prickled in Sera's cheeks as she imagined him following her all the way to the plains and lurking there in her garden, watching her cry. Watching her yell at Lorenzo. Oh, no. Her hand trembled as she wrote:

Did you kill Lorenzo?

The minutes stretched out, slow and agonizing. When the dart came soaring back to her, she snatched it from the air, feeling the cool brush of his shadows against her skin.

I spared your lover boy. But not before he pissed himself.

She laid her head against the window sash, letting relief wash over her. Lorenzo was alive. Never mind his cowardice, she didn't wish him dead. She grabbed her pen.

Thank you.

She regretted it the second she sent it. The Dagger hardly deserved applause for simply not killing someone. *Saints*, the bar was low. His reply came again.

> So, you *do* understand the concept of gratitude. Though you may save it on this occasion. I don't kill for free.

She should have left it at that, but she found herself reaching once more for her pen. Prodding the dark, just to see what it would do.

> In that case, moneybags, I've got a new assignment for you. Easy mark. Considerable compensation. Interested?

He took the bait.

> Amuse me.

Oh, she would.

> It appears I have a stalker. Obsessive, relentless, and wretchedly arrogant. Perfect, punchable teeth. I have it on good authority that he has a dodgy liver, as of recently.

She could have sworn she heard him laugh. A fleeting echo in the night. But no – she must have imagined it. Daggers didn't laugh. They were soulless, serious creatures. When the dart returned, she grabbed it far too eagerly. This time, when the shadow brushed against her hand, she didn't shiver.

You missed my liver, Seraphine. If you come outside, I'll let you trace my scar to prove it.

A violent heat erupted in her cheeks. She couldn't shake the image of him lifting his shirt to her, of her hands trailing across the muscled planes of his torso – *stop that*. What the hell was wrong with her? She turned from the window, afraid he might see the blush staining her cheeks. Even at a distance, he could so easily unsettle her. She snatched her pen up.

Careful, Dagger. I might burn you again.

The paper dart had barely left her hand before returning again.

Maybe I want to burn, spitfire.

Sera dragged her hands through her hair, trying to ignore the lick of heat in her ribcage, the parts of her that were burning at his words. She hated that, *hated* him. She snatched the pen, drove the nib so hard it cut through the paper. She ripped out a new page. Back to business. Back to the facts. He was an assassin and despite the curiosity simmering between them, she was still his mark.

What is the price on my head? I'll give you one hundred gold sovereigns to remove it.

Sera didn't have one hundred gold sovereigns. Or anywhere close. But he didn't know that. And she could get the money, if she had to. His reply came all too quickly.

I only negotiate face to face.

Liar. Murderer. Pain in her ass. She looked around her room. Snatched the vase of flowers Bibi had brought her last week. They were all but dead. She waved them in front of the window, then set them on the ledge.

Can I interest you in this charming bouquet? They're dead, like your soul.

Another laugh, echoing through the night. Impossible, surely. His reply hurtled straight through her open window, the shadow slung with such speed and precision, it knocked over the flowers. She caught the vase before it shattered.

Somehow, you're even more annoying in cursive.

Now, it was her turn to laugh. At least she was getting under his skin. A good night's work. She was about to shut the window and be done with it when she spotted the music box on her dresser. The one Bibi had pilfered for her at the Rascalle. The one he had returned to her in front of the statue of Saint Oriel. She had seen the memory of its lullaby shining in his eyes, had sensed it was important to him, though she couldn't guess why. She tore a clean page from her journal, and wrote:

What about a bribe?

She fired the dart into the dark, then stood at the window and opened the box, letting the lullaby trickle into the night. There came no reply. And yet she sensed he was still out there, listening to the lilting notes of 'The Dancing Swan'. Lost, perhaps, in whatever memories it conjured. After a while, she closed the box, regretting her decision. There was such melancholy in their air now, and she had lost that feeling of triumph. She set the box down on her dresser and turned to shut the curtains.

The paper dart had returned to her windowsill.

Her throat went dry as she opened it up. He had not replied to her with words this time, but with a drawing. A quick, assured sketch, the strokes as soft and sure as the lullaby. But the drawing filled her with horror.

It was of her. Not as she was now, gaping at the piece of paper in her hands, but at that moment not long before, when he had offered to let her trace his scar, the words sending a violent flush of heat through her and scrambling all the thoughts in her head. Somehow he had captured that moment, feasted on it.

The expression on the drawing – on her face – was not fear. Or anger.

It was desire.

And it made Sera want to fling herself out of the window. She sank to the ground and curled into a pathetic groaning ball, waiting for the roar of her embarrassment to pass. But it got louder, crueller.

Pippin woke from his slumber and went to check on her, pawing at her shoulder until she peeked at him through her fingers. 'I'm fine,' she whispered. 'Just drowning in a vat of shame.'

She couldn't let the conversation end like this – with his utter, unadulterated victory. So, one more time, she reached for her pen and wrote:

Go to hell, Ransom.

The paper dart returned almost at once, and though there were only three words on it, she could almost taste the sadness laced inside them.

Already there, Seraphine.

She knew then that he was gone. That the conversation was over, the game finished, and somehow, she had won.

And yet, for hours afterwards, she found she couldn't sleep.

Chapter 25

Seraphine

At breakfast the following morning, Sera filled Bibi in on everything she had missed the day before. She listened, enraptured, and by the end was more than eager to help Sera plunder the Grand Versini Library and uncover the lost recipe for Lightfire.

Later that day, they set off with Val in good spirits, leaving Theo behind to tinker with the bloom Sera had brought back from the plains.

It was dusk by the time they reached the Scholars' Quarter, where the Grand Versini sat in a pool of dying sunlight. Barely a stone's throw from the Marlowe, the library occupied its own sprawling courtyard, which boasted a magnificent fountain built in honour of Celiana, Saint of Song and Poetry, whose marble likeness spouted water into a large stone pool filled with copper coins.

Bibi fished a coin from her pocket. 'Shall we make a wish?'

'Personally, I'd rather pilfer that fountain than add my hard-earned copper to it,' said Val, frowning at the water like she really was considering it.

'If you steal those wishes, Saint Celiana will smite you.' Bibi chucked a copper in, closed her eyes and whispered under her breath. Then she smiled. 'I've got a good feeling about that one.'

After what had happened to Mama, Sera hardly believed in wishes, but she didn't believe in ruining the moment, either. So she fished a copper from her pocket and listened to the satisfying *plink* as it hit the water. Her wish was a single word: *Lightfire.*

A handful of people were milling about on the steps of the Grand Versini, but the patrolling dayguards were already cautioning them to hurry home before the sun set. For that was when the monsters came out to hunt, and judging by the number of dead bodies that had been turning up over the last few days, they were hungrier than ever.

Oh, Mama, what did you do?

In the shadows of a nearby lane, they slipped on their cloaks. Once they were folded safely into the dark, they crept out of the alley and up the imposing marble steps of the Grand Versini, slipping seamlessly from one shadow to the next.

They convened in the reading atrium on the third floor, where a balcony looked over the entryway three floors below, and waited for the stragglers to leave. The librarians packed up, stowing the last of their books and grabbing their satchels, eager to beat the darkness home. After one last patrol of every floor, they extinguished the lanterns and left through the front door, closing and locking it behind them.

Silence, then.

The last rays of sunlight slipped through the arched windows, setting the entire atrium aglow. Bibi pulled her hood down, her floating head appearing behind a nearby armchair. 'Too easy.'

'Don't get cocky,' warned Val. 'We're only halfway there.'

'Why can't we ever celebrate the small victories?' moaned Bibi.

'Because that's when things usually go to shit.'

They found a spiral staircase at the back of the fourth floor, and climbed it. Sera pressed her ear against the door at the top, listening for movement, but there was only the sound of her own heartbeat thundering in her ears and the tell-tale creak of the stairs as her friends climbed up behind her. She tried her lock pick, twisting and jiggling it just as Theo had taught her.

Click!

Her heart hitched as the door yielded. She slipped through the crack, into the sprawling darkness. The top floor was much larger than she was expecting, at least twice the size of the dining quarters at House Armand. The low ceiling was criss-crossed with wooden beams. The air up here was cold and stale, a faint ray of light spiralling down from a row of narrow windows.

Sera drew her cloak tighter as she drifted inside, listening for signs of life. But the stacks at the Grand Versini were deserted. And in total disarray. There were bookshelves and boxes everywhere, tattered chairs and broken tables, cracked lamps and even a disused printing press.

'What a dump.' Val's voice echoed in the silence. 'How are we going to find anything in here?'

'Divide and conquer,' said Sera, slipping off her hood and gloves, and removing a box of matches from her pocket. She grabbed three oil lamps from a nearby shelf, and handed one each to Val and Bibi. 'I'll start on this side. Bibi you start in the middle, and Val, you can begin at the other end of the stacks. Shout if you find anything useful.'

Bibi took off in a clatter of determined footsteps, with Val trailing close behind. Sera hovered near the door, craning her neck at the surrounding shelves. It was difficult to know where to begin. Most of the books up here were dusty and falling apart at the spine, and there were hundreds of old penny papers that had turned stiff and yellow with age.

She tried to be methodical with her search, clearing one section of shelves before moving on to the next, stacking and arranging books and pamphlets as she went.

Bibi hummed as she worked and every so often, Val announced her boredom with a long-suffering sigh. A couple of hours into the search, Sera was beginning to lose hope when Bibi's voice rang out. 'I found a cane! I think it belonged to Hugo! In a box of old penny-paper clippings about the Daggers. It was hidden under the stack.'

'Unless that stick is engraved with a recipe for Lightfire then it's irrelevant,' Val yelled back.

'I want to see,' said Sera, coming to meet Bibi halfway down the stacks.

Bibi presented the cane to her like it was the lost treasure of Valterre. Sera turned it in her hands, tracing the initials along the bottom: HRV. *Hugo Ralphe Versini.* How had such a valuable item accidentally ended up here? Along the top, a silver skull hid the sharp point of a blade.

'Keep it,' said Bibi, sliding the skull back into place. 'Might as well take something for our troubles.'

Sera took the cane back to her section, thinking it would make a nice gift for Theo.

Evening soon melted into night. Strands of moonlight slipped through the windows, illuminating the dust motes that spiralled around Sera's face. Her stomach growled as her disappointment grew. Val gave up entirely, leaving her section to join Bibi. By the sounds of it, they had happened upon a stack of love letters written by Armand Versini, and were taking turns doing dramatic readings between peals of hiccupping laughter.

Sera lingered over a bundle of penny papers dated from around the time of Lucille's death. One of the front pages was a black-and-white print of Lucille standing on the front steps of the Appoline. Sera lifted it to the moonlight, gazing up at the long-dead Versini girl like they were just now meeting for the first time.

'Come on, Lucille,' she whispered. 'Help me out.'

'I didn't know you could speak to ghosts,' said a voice in the dark. Low, and soft as honey. Lethal as a snake bite. 'You really are full of surprises.'

Sera bristled. 'Shit.'

Ransom clucked his tongue. 'Language, Seraphine. This is a sacred place.'

He was standing right behind her. She could feel the heat of his body rolling against hers, the air rippling as he chuckled under his breath. She tipped her head back and caught a glimpse of his eyes peering down at her. They were bright silver.

He had decided to kill her after all. She had pushed him too far last night, taunted him with that lullaby.

She was suddenly conscious of Val and Bibi giggling at the other end of the stacks. Unprotected. Unaware. She clasped her necklace in one hand, silently reaching for Hugo's cane with the other.

He crouched down, his mouth parting on a whisper that never came. She swung the cane, striking him on the side of the head. He groaned, slumping to one side.

She sprang to her feet and raced for the door.

Come on, asshole. Follow me.

She was down the spiral staircase in six seconds flat, her cloak and gloves forgotten. Ransom swung himself over the banister, landing right behind her. She bolted for the next staircase. He jumped that one just as easily, his silver eyes flashing. She shrank back from that menacing glare, until she was pressed against the railings of the third-floor balcony.

She brandished the cane like a sword. 'Aren't you tired of chasing me?'

He cocked his head. 'Aren't you tired of running?'

'Nope.' She wrenched the skull off the cane and flung it at him.

He caught it in his fist, returning it at such speed, it whistled past her left ear and struck the window behind her, cracking the pane.

'Warning shot,' he growled. 'Play nice.'

She snorted. 'Why? So you can kill me at your leisure?'

'There is nothing leisurely about you, spitfire.' He stuffed his hands into his pockets, and the shadows stopped advancing, instead forming a pool of darkness between them. A truce. Or a trap. 'I'm not here to kill you. I want to talk. Face to face.'

Sera kept her eyes on his shadows. 'Then why are your eyes bright silver?'

'Maybe I'm a little afraid of you.' He gestured to the exposed blade on the end of her cane. 'I know what you can do with a letter opener. I shudder to think what you'll do with that.'

'It's not the blade you should be worried about,' she said, hardening her voice. 'I have the power to destroy you. To destroy your entire Order.' Silence yawned. Not a single shadow moved. Not for the first time, she wondered what he knew about Lightfire. She watched him closely as she said, 'That power is why Dufort killed my mother. It's why he burned our house to the ground.'

Not even a twitch. 'So, you believe me, then.'

Sera frowned. 'What?'

'I told you I didn't kill her.'

She curled her lip, thinking again of that figure in the flames. 'Isn't the depravity all the same in the end? Who you are. What you do.'

His eyes flashed, but he held the line, even as his shadows strained against it. 'You want to talk about depravity? Then let's talk about the poison, Seraphine. What was it your mother called that wine of hers, *Nectar of the Saints*?' He sneered. 'Ironic choice.'

Sera quailed. He couldn't *possibly* know about the wine ... the *poison* ... Unless ... She winced. Of course he knew. He hadn't followed her all the way to the plains just to smell the lavender. He'd gone through the shed and found that damning label, those crimson berries. Heartsbane. But still, how had he managed to put it all together? It hit her, then – *Lorenzo*. He must have sung for his freedom.

'What's the matter?' he taunted, coming closer. 'Monster got your tongue? You can thank Sylvie for that.'

Slowly, almost tentatively, his shadows licked her shoes. The bead of her necklace flared, flooding her body with warmth.

His eyes widened, hunger thickening his voice. 'There you are.'

Sera's grip tightened on the cane. 'What the hell do you want from me?'

'I want you to touch me, Seraphine.'

She blinked, momentarily shocked into silence. The bead grew brighter, pulsing against her throat like it wanted to touch him too. 'You mean burn you,' she managed.

'Yes,' he said, reaching for her like a drowning man.

She watched the shadows darting across his knuckles and fear took over. She flung the cane at him. It struck his shoulder, ripping his shirt. His nostrils flared at the unexpected assault, his shadows rising in a sweeping black wave. In a panic, she reeled backwards and fell right over the railings.

'NO!' Her arms flailed, grasping at nothing. She was already plummeting. The ceiling fell away, her scream dying in her throat. She squeezed her eyes shut, bracing for the hard slap of marble.

Sera halted right before the moment of impact, as though someone had set the world to pause. The ceiling loomed high above her, reminding her of how far she had fallen, but she was alive. She was *floating*. She looked down to find herself in a cradle made of shadows. The second she noticed them, they frayed, shredded by the Lightfire at her throat.

She fell as they snapped and landed with a soft thud, releasing a strangled cry of relief.

Ransom arrived in the same breath, swinging down from the third floor and landing right in front of her. He extended his hand to her, and for an absurd moment, she thought about taking it.

She scrambled to her feet. Her legs were trembling badly. Her body was here, but her mind was still plummeting from the third floor, still reeling from the nearness of death. But there was no mistaking what had just happened. He had saved her life.

Maybe he was telling the truth after all. Maybe he really had come here to talk.

He frowned as he looked her over. 'What are you even doing here?'

'I'm researching Lucille Versini,' she said, because in the receding tide of her panic, she couldn't remember how to lie. She found she didn't want to. 'I was hoping to find her old journals.'

He blinked, showing his surprise before he masked it. 'Scholar, are you?'

'Something like that.'

His frown sharpened his cheekbones. In the moonlit dark, he looked like a statue cursed to life, a thing so cruelly perfect, he belonged in a museum. Somewhere far above them, Sera heard the distant echo of her friends' voices. Val and Bibi were looking for her, every step nudging them closer to danger.

The Dagger might have offered her a truce, but he had made no such assurances for her friends.

She had to move. Now.

'Lucille was buried with her journal,' he said, almost as an afterthought. 'You won't find anything of note in this dusty old place.' Seraphine blew out a careful breath, trying not to show her excitement at this new information. But he was watching her far too closely, his eyes gleaming in the darkness. 'Tell me, spitfire. What information do you seek?'

She smiled at him. 'I'll tell you if you catch me.' Then she turned on her heel and bolted for the door.

Chapter 26

Ransom

Seraphine Marchant was running from him again. Ransom had gone to the trouble of saving her life, and the ungrateful spitfire was already throwing it back in his face. Typical. He shouldn't have got his hopes up, shouldn't have expected her to trust him so quickly. He should have just lunged at her on the third floor and let her magic burn through him. Asking had been a mistake.

He had no intention of giving her up, though. He wanted to know everything about that damn necklace, about the magic that had scoured the shadow-mark from his hand and returned a vital piece of himself. The secret Dufort had already killed for and had been lying about ever since.

So, Seraphine ran, and Ransom chased her. She nearly crashed head-first into the door, her hands trembling as she unlocked it. It swung open and she launched herself into the night, her sun-bright hair flying out behind her as she took the marble steps two at a time. Ransom jumped the balustrade and landed at the bottom.

'Seraphine!' He skidded to a halt in the middle of the courtyard, shadows trailing in his wake. 'Don't make me drag you back to me!'

She spun around, wild-eyed and breathless. Beautiful. *Fuck.* Behind her, the statue of Saint Celiana spouted water into the air, the stream shimmering under the star-filled sky. Seraphine blew a strand of hair from her eyes, glaring at him with the heat of an inferno. 'Don't you dare.'

'Tell me about the monsters,' he said, daring a step towards her. 'If you made them, then you must know how to stop them.'

She tensed. 'I didn't make them.'

He was surprised at the relief he felt at those words. How they confirmed his suspicion that she was better than the murky games that played out in the underworld, that she was no more a monster than a maker of them. That she was good, and Dufort was wrong. That he had been right not to kill her. 'Fine,' he said. 'Then tell me about your magic.'

She hesitated, a frown knitting her brows like she was teetering on the precipice of confiding in him. Then the darkness behind her rippled. A shadow emerged, large and loping. Ransom couldn't see through it, and that told him exactly what it was. The bead glowing at her throat confirmed his guess.

'Seraphine,' he said, in a low voice.

She opened her mouth, but it was already too late to warn her.

The monster charged.

'MOVE!' Adrenaline flooded Ransom, propelling him towards her. She gaped in frozen horror as he pulled a shadow from the fountain and leaped clean over her, colliding with the monster in mid-air. The creature roared as Ransom tackled it. They crashed to the ground together, but the monster was bigger, faster. It jumped to its feet and drove him back into the fountain.

Seraphine's scream faded as they tumbled into the cold water. The monster came up for air and Ransom headbutted it, wincing at the thud of bone on bone. The creature fell backwards, dazed. Ransom leaped to his feet, claiming the higher ground, but the monster rose to its haunches, matching his height.

Ransom swung, finding its jaw, but even with Shade inside him he was no match for the hulking creature. It bared its fangs and lunged. Its gnarled hand found Ransom's throat, shoving him down, down, down, into the water, where there was no sound, no breath. Coppers shifted beneath him as he lay on a bed of spent wishes, trying to kick his way back to the surface, but the monster was a dead weight on his chest.

Ransom swung, but his fist moved in slow motion. He bucked as the creature added another hand to his throat, squeezing until he felt his eyes bulge. The world darkened as the last drops of Shade left his body. His breath followed, rising in a stream of bubbles.

Ransom had the sudden, unnerving realization that he was

about to die. After ten long years of clinging to life by his fingernails, of doing unthinkable things to survive, he had given it all up for the mark he was supposed to kill. For hair that shone like the sun rising over Everell, and eyes as bright as the sky he used to walk to school under. For a smart mouth and a brave heart. An unblemished soul. Like Anouk's. For a spirit fighting tooth and nail to survive. Like Mama's. And the secret of a magic that might have saved him too. The girl would live – and perhaps laugh – as he died. He might have laughed too if he had a morsel of breath left, but he was so cold now. So utterly, terribly cold.

And the world was fading away ...

In the blackness of his mind, Ransom saw his little sister. Anouk beckoned for him to follow as she turned to run, the old walls of their house crumbling away to reveal a field of wildflowers. Mama was there, too, wearing her favourite blue linen dress, the black coils of her hair falling to her shoulders. She was picking blackberries, her hand outstretched, reaching for his.

Come, my darling, Bastian. We've been waiting for you. She smiled as she uttered his name, the one he had surrendered nearly ten years ago on the banks of the Verne. Now it floated between them like a spell, calling him home. Ransom was dimly aware that none of this was real, that the vision dwelled in some unreachable pocket between his heart and his soul, but he didn't care.

He just wanted to go home. That's all he had ever wanted.

And he was close now, so very close ...

He reached for his mother's hand, his olive skin smooth

and unmarked once more ... and the meadow erupted into fire. Ransom blinked, and when he opened his eyes, he was drowning again in Saint Celiana's fountain. The weight on his chest was gone, and he was looking up at an angel wreathed in bright golden light.

For a fleeting moment, he thought Saint Celiana herself had come to rescue him from the precipice of death, but then a hand plunged into the water and curled inside his shirt. He was pulled from the stillness, up to starlight and air and the ragged sound of panic. 'Wake up! Breathe!'

Ransom coughed as he emerged from the water, convulsing as he tried to expel the fluid from his lungs. He collapsed over the side of the fountain, straining to breathe. Straining to think. Something was wrong. Although the night was dark around him, there was sunlight in the fountain.

He turned, resting his cheek on the stone rim, and tried to make sense of what he was seeing. The monster that had nearly killed him had not fled. It was still here, stuck in the same fountain, only it wasn't fighting now.

It was kneeling, head bowed, at the feet of Seraphine Marchant.

Chapter 27

Seraphine

Sera didn't even notice the monster until Ransom tackled it in mid-air. She thought he was charging at her, readying the final death blow, but then he leaped right over her head and for a baffling moment it seemed he had taken flight. Then he crashed to the ground behind her, dragging the monster with him. She had stood on the edge of it all, frozen in shock. For the second time that evening, the Dagger had saved her life.

Now he was scrapping in Saint Celiana's fountain. Or perhaps *dying* was a more accurate term.

Sera could have left him there to drown, let him succumb to the fate he deserved. She could have turned and run from the fight, back to the Grand Versini to bolt the door and wait for the creature to lope away, sated by its kill, but something stopped her. Perhaps it was honour. Or guilt. Or some other more dangerous feeling she did not wish to confront.

But as she watched Ransom fight a creature three times his size, kicking and swinging even as he went down into the water, even as the monster climbed on top of him, its shadows writhing like tentacles, she was seized by a rush of empathy. She recognized that same impulse inside herself – the urge to keep swinging even as the world shoved you underwater and choked the hope from your lungs.

It was that surge of understanding, that simmering connection dragged into the light, that made her fling all sense of self-preservation aside. She gripped her necklace, begging it to protect her as she climbed into the fountain. The light flared, bleeding through her fingers as she landed in the cold water and threw herself at the monster, knocking it off Ransom. They tumbled sideways together, Sera falling face-first in the water and drenching herself from head to toe. She sprang up, stance wide and fists raised, just like Albert had taught her, but the monster had stilled. Then it fell to its knees in the middle of the fountain and tilted its hideous face up to Saint Celiana.

But – no. The monster wasn't looking at the statue. The monster was staring at ... *her*. And the world was shining far too bright. Sera's necklace had erupted into such a blaze, it trailed along her skin, bathing her in golden light. It was a shield, an orb, a river of sunlight clinging to every inch of her.

'What the hell . . .'

At the sound of her voice, the monster bowed its head. Silence fell, the water stilling around them. Ransom had stopped struggling. He was staring up at her like a corpse, the silver of his eyes returned to their warm, hazel glow.

Panic ripped through Sera as she lunged, dragging him up from the water. 'Wake up!' she said, shaking him. 'Breathe!'

He shuddered as he coughed up a stream of water. Relief flooded her as he retched again, reaching for the rim of the fountain. When he found it, she turned to their other problem. There was a monster in the fountain. And for some reason, it was bowing to her, as though it were waiting for some kind of command. But . . . was it even possible?

The bead at her throat thrummed, as if to say, *Try it.*

'Look at me,' said Sera, her voice a rasp.

The monster raised its mighty head.

'Lift your hand.'

The monster's arm rose.

Holy. Shit.

Sera stared down at the misshapen creature, trying to make out the planes of its face. The true colour of its eyes and the slant of its lips, the shape of its nose.

'Who *are* you?' she whispered.

The monster groaned but it couldn't find the words, couldn't make its bloated tongue work properly. She came to her knees before it, the water climbing to her chest.

'Who are you?' she said again.

The monster closed its eyes, pressing its face forward. Sera reached for it without thinking, compelled by the need to peel away the shadows and find the wounded thing within. When she touched its face, the teardrop at her throat flared again, bathing both of them in its golden light.

'Fall away,' she whispered, not to the monster, but to the darkness that had mangled it.

The monster moaned, its face appearing through a haze of shadows. Its limbs shrank, its spine cracking as it untwisted. Slowly, painfully, the monster became a man. He was older than Sera was expecting. Grizzled and red-faced, with wide frightened eyes. He shuddered violently as the last of Mama's poison left his body. Sera knew then that he wouldn't survive. The Lightfire was his reprieve, but it was not going to save him. Too much time had passed. Nothing could save him now. By the look in his eyes, he knew it too, and he grasped for the bead at her throat, silently begging to be put out of his misery.

'It's all right,' she whispered, even though it wasn't. She took his hands, curling them inside her own. 'It's over now.'

The air hummed as the tiny bead of Lightfire fought those final tendrils of darkness. And then, at last, it was over. The man collapsed in the water just as Sera's necklace exploded. She grasped at the shattered teardrop as the force knocked her backwards.

She was unconscious before her head hit the water, and when it did, she sank like a stone.

Eons passed in the cold, wet dark. The Lightfire was gone, the teardrop cracked and wasted, and now there was nothing but blackness. No fear, nor thoughts. No voice. No breath.

But then – there was touch. Warm hands cupping her face. 'Seraphine?' Her name in his mouth, soft and searching. 'Can you hear me?'

She opened her eyes. Ransom was kneeling over her, the stars making a silver halo around his head. His dark hair was plastered to his face, and there were droplets sliding down his cheeks. He was soaked through, the remains of his shirt now clinging to his skin, the tears revealing the black whorls across his chest. His eyes were the colour of autumn, flickering between green and gold.

Sera blinked, half-wondering if she had died in that fountain, only to awaken in this strange afterlife where the Dagger that haunted her was a man capable of concern. A man soaked to the bone and handsome as hell.

'There you are.' His voice was hoarse, his lips twitching. 'Enjoying the view?'

Her eyelids fluttered as she searched for her sanity. 'You're touching me.'

'Just trying to restore your pulse.' He trailed a finger down her neck, kept it there. And smirked. 'It's racing.'

'Hands off the Cloak.' Her head spun as she tried to sit up. The sight of him kneeling over her practically half-naked was nearly enough to make her pass out again. 'And close your damn shirt.'

His chuckle warmed the space between them. 'So, you're fine, then.'

She glowered at him, hoping he couldn't see the heat rising in her cheeks. Three times tonight, she had faced death. Three times he had saved her. And this time, he had the nerve to do it looking like that. 'I'm not dead.'

'No.'

'Why?'

'Maybe Saint Oriel has a thing for you.' A half-smile. 'You do have a talent for cheating death.'

'Not death,' she said, quietly. 'You.'

He chewed on his bottom lip, nipping at that bone-white scar, like he couldn't fathom it himself. But after what they had just done for each other, without thought or explanation, she was beyond fearing him. Now she wanted to know him. To know what he wanted.

'Why did you ask me to burn you back there?' she said.

He dropped his gaze to the hollow of her throat, then her closed fist, which held her shattered necklace. 'Your magic is an antidote,' he said, quietly. 'It erases my shadow-marks.'

'Oh.' Of all the things she was expecting him to say ... Slowly, she trailed her gaze over those inky marks, lingering on the ones that wreathed his wrists and curled around his fingers, staining hands like those of an artist. Then she moved to the whorls on his chest, his shoulders, the strong column of his neck. Her throat was painfully dry, her heartbeat roaring in her ears, but she managed to say, 'And you want them gone?'

'Yes,' he said, with undisguised desperation. 'All of them.'

'Are they very painful?'

He nodded. 'In more ways than one.'

Understanding bloomed inside her. All these weeks, the Dagger hadn't just been seeking her. He was seeking freedom from himself, from all the terrible things he had done.

It was too late. The Lightfire was spent, the glass cracked inside her fist. But her skin was still glowing faintly, and she wondered if there was a kernel of that magic still inside her somewhere.

She sat up, closing the last sliver of space between them. 'I'm going to touch you now.'

His eyelids lowered, the word a whisper on his lips. *'Please.'*

She watched the breath swell in his chest as she slowly moved her hand to his cheek, touching him like she had the monster in the fountain. His skin was surprisingly warm, strands of his damp hair brushing against her fingers. She willed them not to tremble.

He closed his eyes, leaning into her touch.

The moment stretched until there was only this touch, this precious kernel of hope flickering between them. It was not enough. The Lightfire was gone, and when Sera lowered her gaze, the marks on his body remained.

'I'm sorry,' she whispered. 'It's too late.'

He hummed in response, then turned slightly, pressing a kiss to her palm.

Sera's heart stuttered. His lips were cool, but the soft press of them against her damp skin lit a fire inside her that devoured all thought.

He opened his eyes, finding hers. 'Thank you for trying.'

Sera swallowed, searching for words ... forgetting how to form them.

'SERA? WHERE THE FUCK ARE YOU?' Val's voice cut through the night.

With remarkable speed, the rest of the world crashed back in. Sera dropped her hand, pulling away from Ransom. He rolled back to his feet, downing a vial of Shade in one gulp as Val and Bibi came clattering across the square. He turned from Sera without another word, lifting the dead body from the fountain and cradling it to his chest like it was no heavier than a sack of grain. By the time Sera had got to her feet, he was already gone.

She stared after him as Val and Bibi rushed to meet her, so preoccupied by the phantom kiss on her one palm that she barely noticed the stinging in the other one. Then she opened her fist to examine the cracked bead inside it. She knew there wasn't a drop of Lightfire left, but she wasn't expecting to find something else inside the glass. It was a miniscule curl of parchment.

As her friends crowded around her, terror-struck and panting, Sera unfurled the note and held it up to the moonlight, squinting to make out the tiny, smeared handwriting. Her heart thudded painfully as she realized what it was – Mama's final message:

The monsters bow to the power of Lightfire. Become the flame and destroy the dark, Seraphine.

Part III

'Content are the souls who submit to the winding strands of fate.
Blessed are those who dare to spin their own.'

Oriel Beauregard,
SAINT OF DESTINY

Chapter 28

Ransom

With the body from the fountain in his arms, Ransom trudged back to the catacombs, damp and exhausted and full of thoughts of her. He couldn't stop replaying those final aching moments ... The gentle caress of her hand against his cheek, how her trembling breath had feathered his skin, her mouth so close he could almost taste her. He would not sleep easy tonight. Or perhaps ever again.

His legs were leaden as he walked, his shirt so torn that one of the sleeves had fallen off. It was the least of his concerns. He reached the catacombs and took the steps two at a time, passing under the blank-eyed stares of a hundred skulls and bumping right into Lark, who was on his way out for the night.

Lark stumbled backwards, nearly dropping the vial of Shade

in his hand. His gaze swept over the body in Ransom's arms, which was really more of a damp sack of skin and bones. 'What ... is that?'

'It's Kipp,' said Ransom, working to keep his voice even. Trying to pretend like he hadn't retched when he saw Kipp's hollow eyes staring up at him as he lifted him from the fountain. 'He's dead.'

'No shit,' said Lark.

They were interrupted by approaching footsteps. Nadia's voice floated down the tunnel. 'What are you two whispering about?' She stopped short, her brown eyes widening. 'Is that your mark?' She jostled Lark aside. 'The farmgirl?'

Ransom stiffened before he could help it. The thought of Seraphine Marchant dead in his arms was a whole new level of horror he couldn't afford to imagine. Not after tonight. Not after the fountain and what had come after.

Lark moved his hand to the small of Nadia's back. 'Take a closer look.'

'Oh, Kipp.' She clapped a hand over her mouth. 'He looks like hell.'

'Well, he is dead,' said Lark, unnecessarily.

'He looks more than dead,' she said, recoiling from the body. 'He looks *wrong*. Like someone plunged their hand down his throat and yanked out his soul.'

Ransom's Shade was wearing off. His head was beginning to pound, the body growing heavy in his arms. 'Is Dufort here?'

'He's drunk in the Cavern,' said Nadia. 'Piss-poor mood. As usual.'

'I bet this will cheer him up,' said Lark dryly. He pocketed his vial of Shade and followed Ransom down the north passage.

'I thought Kipp was a monster,' said Nadia, hurrying after them.

'He was,' said Ransom, flatly. 'He changed back.'

'*How*?' the other two chorused.

Ransom shrugged, trying to shake off the memory of Seraphine standing in that fountain, glowing like a human flame.

'Ransom.' Lark came to his side. 'How?'

'I don't know, Lark.'

'Why do you sound so angry?' said Nadia, coming to his other side.

'Maybe because I've been carrying the dead body of our friend around for the last hour,' said Ransom, all but spitting the words. His friends exchanged a loaded glance, and he fell silent, prickling with guilt.

A hush fell over the Cavern when he staggered in. Daggers stopped their conversations and set down their drinks, straining to see the dead body in his arms. He paid them no mind, striding straight to the back of the room, where Dufort was necking whiskey by the roaring fireplace, with a handful of older Daggers.

Lisette was perched on the arm of his chair, wearing a midnight-blue dress with a low neckline and a thigh-high slit. Her blonde hair was scraped into a tight bun and her eyes were bright silver. When she spotted Ransom, she rose from her seat. 'Are you drunk?' she hissed, through coral-stained lips. 'You know better than to bring a mark down here.'

'It's not a mark,' said Ransom. 'Clear the table.'

When nobody moved, Dufort barked, 'Clear the fucking table!'

The Daggers rushed into action, swiping away playing cards and sovereigns, dirty ashtrays and half-smoked cigars. Ransom laid Kipp's body down. In the flickering lamplight, they all stared at it, trying to make sense of the sunken cheeks and haunted eyes, the shrivelled skin and paper-thin lips. The silence stretched on and on. Ransom's fingers twitched as he watched Dufort. His body was flagging, fresh plumes of nausea rising inside him. He wanted to turn and rush back to his room, to sit alone in the dark and finally process everything he had seen tonight. Everything he had felt. But if he fled now, he would only arouse suspicion.

Dufort broke the silence with a grunt. 'There goes Kipp. Poor bastard.'

'Sad,' said Lisette, returning to her perch.

'Kipp was one of the monsters stalking the city,' said Lark. 'He attacked us a few days ago.'

'Well, now he's dead,' said Dufort.

'And damp,' said Lisette, wrinkling her nose.

'It wasn't the Shade that killed him,' said Nadia uneasily. 'There are no markers. Look at his eyes. His skin. And he doesn't have a single shadow-mark.'

Dufort looked at Ransom, his eyes cold. 'Where did you find him?'

'Saint Celiana's fountain.'

'And you were there why?' said Lisette.

'I was out for a walk.'

'And a swim?' she said, looking him up and down. 'New hobby of yours?'

He smiled tightly. 'I had no idea you were so fascinated by me, Lisette.'

She fingered her sleeve. 'Only since my sister *swore* she saw you leave the city the other day. She said you were headed to the plains.' She smirked. 'Isn't that where your mark used to live?'

Dufort snapped his chin up. 'The girl went back?'

'Not that I'm aware of,' said Ransom evenly. Then to Lisette. 'Your sister is mistaken.'

'Or *you* are lying.'

'Shut the fuck up, Lisette,' said Lark.

Dufort's eyes were still on Ransom. 'This isn't the body I asked you for.'

'You wanted a monster, Gaspard.'

'That's not a monster,' said Lisette.

'Not any more,' said Ransom. 'But maybe you can study it. Try to—'

'What the fuck do I look like?' snapped Dufort. 'A scholar?'

Ransom's face burned. 'Should I have left him in the fountain for a nightguard to find?'

'It depends on how he got in there in the first place,' mused Lisette. Still prodding. Insufferable bootlicker. 'And whether there was something else, some*one* else, you could have taken instead . . .'

Ransom inhaled.

She licked her teeth. Triumphant.

'What would you have preferred, Lisette? A fistful of

coppers?' said Nadia, glaring at her. 'In case you haven't noticed, the entire city's been under attack for weeks now. This is the closest we've come to finding out why.'

'Don't be such a smart-ass,' she hit back. 'I'm talking about the girl. The one he spends all his time following but not actually killing.'

'She's a Cloak,' snapped Ransom. 'It's not that simple.'

'Because you can't find her? *Or*,' Lisette purred, leaning forward, 'because you're enjoying the chase a little too much?'

'Watch it,' he said through his teeth.

The smirk returned. 'Have you screwed her?'

Ransom's temper flared, every muscle in his body going taut. If he had taken another vial of Shade, Lisette would be up against the cavern wall right now, with his shadows around her throat.

'Easy,' said Lark, laying a hand on his arm. 'She's just trying to rile you.'

'Remember your place, Lisette,' warned Lark.

She barked a laugh. 'Says one lapdog to another.'

'At least you're self-aware,' remarked Nadia.

'Not half enough,' said Lark. 'She's talking like a traitor.'

'Says who?' pressed Lisette. 'There's nothing more traitorous than screwing the mark. Especially if you forget to kill her afterwards.'

'*Enough!*' Dufort shattered his whiskey glass against the fireplace, bringing the entire Cavern to a standstill. 'Shut up, all of you, so I can hear myself think.'

'So, think,' said Ransom, stepping back from the table. 'I need to get changed.' His breathing was ragged as he hurried towards the north passage. Panic crested like a wave inside him, and he had the sudden feeling that he was going to throw up, right there in the cavern. And then everyone would know the truth.

He was a liar. A failure. A traitor. Seraphine Marchant was alive because he had saved her life. Not once, but three times in one night. Four, if he counted the lie of omission about that power she wore around her neck. The power that had shattered in a hail of golden light, freeing Kipp from the monster he had become, but too late to save him. If Dufort found out about any of it, he would cut Ransom's head from his body and mount it on the wall.

And what had Ransom done it for? The lure of Lightfire, and what it could do for his own soul? What he now knew it could do for the monsters of Fantome? Seraphine Marchant didn't just have the power to free Ransom. She had the power to free the entire city.

Or perhaps his unwillingness to harm her was born of something far simpler ... something far more dangerous. Perhaps, beneath the logic of it all, Lisette was right. He *did* want her. He wanted to take her more than he wanted to kill her.

It was all he could do not to think about kissing her. Tasting the fire of her just to see what it would do to him. What *she* would do to him. Ransom had been fighting for his life for as long as he could remember, trying to wrench power from men far stronger – and crueller – than him, and yet somehow, he felt most alive when he was standing in the glaring spotlight of that bronze-flecked gaze and sustaining insults from that sharp, lashing tongue.

Seraphine was a spitfire. And Ransom wanted to burn.

His footsteps echoed as he fled down the north passage, before turning east into a narrower tunnel. On and on he went, but it wasn't far enough. He couldn't outrun his panic, the lies churning in the pit of his stomach. He felt like the walls were closing in on him, the dark mouth of Fantome opening up to swallow him whole.

Traitor, traitor, traitor, chanted the skulls. *A blunt Dagger is a dead Dagger.*

Ransom swung into the nearest bathroom and vomited. He retched until his stomach ached and his breath came in dry heaves. When the worst of it was over, he collapsed against the cold stone wall and closed his eyes.

'Saint Oriel,' he whispered, though he knew she couldn't hear him down here. The saints did not service the needs of those already in hell. His wishes were not made to be answered. But he made one anyway. 'I want to go home.'

'You are home, Bastian,' came a familiar rumble. In that voice, his name – the one his mother had given him – sounded as threatening as a weapon. Ransom looked up to find Dufort towering over him, his arms folded across his barrel chest. 'Haven't I given you everything you've ever needed?'

It was not a real question.

'Safety. Security. Revenge. Riches. *Power.*' He growled the last word, but there was hurt beneath it. Hurt in his eyes. Frustration, too. He sighed through his nose. 'I raised you in my own likeness, Bastian. I raised you for greatness. But after all these years together, you're crumbling before my eyes and I can't understand why.'

'I'm not crumbling,' croaked Ransom.

Dufort squatted down. 'If I don't know what's wrong, I can't help you, son.'

Ransom looked at his feet. He couldn't tell him that he wanted out. That he wanted *her*.

'When you build a wall with lies, the lies will crack,' said Dufort. 'The wall will crumble. And you will find me, standing on the other side of it. As I am now.'

'I'm not lying,' said Ransom, raising his chin. 'You wanted a monster. I brought you one.'

'You brought me a husk.'

'It's more than anyone else has brought you.'

Dufort's lips twisted, another sigh heaving his shoulders. 'Forget about the monsters. If they can be killed as easily as they're formed, I don't care to waste my time on them. They'll die out eventually.'

Ransom frowned. 'The monsters are still killing people. More and more each day. They're making you look sloppy.'

Dufort snorted. 'I'm a Dagger, Ransom. Do you think I give a fuck what people think of me?'

Another non-question. Ransom knotted his hands, willing the conversation to end, but Dufort was only getting started. 'Let the beasts stalk. Let them kill. They'll wear themselves out.'

'Sure.' Ransom's voice was hollow. 'Whatever you say.'

Dufort grabbed his shoulder. 'I don't know what you're hiding from me, son, but I'm not made of patience. No one here is untouchable. Not even you. If I find out you've been with that girl, if you've betrayed my trust in you, I'll cast you out onto those streets just as quickly as I took you from them. I'll rip away everything you have.'

Ransom exhaled through his teeth, fighting the urge to swing at Dufort.

'The longer that girl lives, the more dangerous she becomes,' said Dufort. 'I won't tell you again. Get rid of her.'

He rolled to his feet, just as a shadow flitted by the door. Dufort reached out, yanking Lark in by the scruff of his neck. 'Stealthless, Delano. Even for you. I assume you heard that?'

Lark rubbed the back of his neck. 'Just the headlines, really.'

'Good,' said Dufort, with a grunt. 'Because now Seraphine Marchant is your mark, too.' He looked back and forth between them. 'If you two idiots can't get it done by the end of the week, you're both out on your asses.' He turned on Lark. 'I haven't appointed my Second yet. This is your chance to impress me.' Lark swallowed thickly, hunger glowing in his eyes. 'Don't screw it up, Delano. The next time Lisette barks at you, I'll have her lick your boots.'

He patted him roughly on the cheek, then stomped out of the chamber without so much as a backwards glance at Ransom. They listened for the fading echo of his footfall.

'Well, that was fun,' said Lark drolly. 'You should bring him dead monsters more often.'

Ransom summoned a smile. Even on his worst days, Lark always managed to make him feel less shitty. 'That'll teach me to go fishing in fountains.'

Lark looked down at him. 'Which, by the way, strikes me as *extremely* out of character for you.'

'Maybe I was making a wish.'

He raised his brows. 'What kind of wish?'

'Can't tell you,' he said, leaning his head back against the wall. 'Then it won't come true.'

'I thought Dufort was going to name you as his heir.'

Ransom's lips twisted. He was falling out of favour and he couldn't bring himself to care. 'I guess he's having second thoughts.'

Lark sat down beside him, bringing his knees up to his chest. 'We've never shared a mark before.'

Ransom hesitated, dread pooling in the pit of his stomach. 'No ...'

'Nothing wrong with a bit of healthy competition, though.' Lark paused. 'Right?'

'Right.'

Lark blew out a breath, dimple flashing. 'Well, then. Let the game begin.'

Chapter 29

Seraphine

Seraphine burst into the cloakroom at House Armand without bothering to knock. Theo, who was hunched over the glass island, glanced up at the intrusion, his eyes widening as he took in the sight of her, drenched and shivering from head to toe.

'What the—?'

'Any luck with the bloom?' she said, between heaving breaths. She stalked towards him, leaving damp footprints on the polished floor. The island was scattered with crushed leaves, scribbled-on pieces of paper and all manner of tinctures and vials. Theo was holding a jar of grey dust in his hand. 'Did you figure out the recipe for Lightfire?'

He stared at her. 'Why are you soaking wet?'

'I fell in a fountain,' she said, straining to see if he had made any progress. She was vaguely aware of her teeth chattering, but her heart was thundering so fast she barely noticed. She felt dangerously alive, like a lit fuse about to explode. 'With a Dagger. And a monster.'

Theo set the jar down, very slowly. 'Are you all right?'

Sera nodded. She was certainly alive. Her body was all right, but her mind was a different story entirely. It was still spiralling, trying to sort through everything – the sight of the monster kneeling at her feet; a helpless pawn . . . a willing soldier. Then the feel of its cold, mottled skin between her hands and that sigh of relief – so deep, so human – as she freed it – him – with her touch.

And then there was Ransom. Another puzzle she couldn't work out. His kiss burned like a brand against her palm. And *saints damn her*, she liked it. She wanted more of it.

Oriel, save me from myself.

Her breath quickened as she pictured his face inches from hers, the trail of his fingers along her cheek, the whisper of his worry as he said her name. Why was he worried? Why did he save her? Why did he *kiss* her?

Why did he look so achingly handsome soaking wet?

'Seraphine.' Theo was in front of her now, his hands braced on her shoulders. 'Sit down.' Sera sat, and he went to rifle through a nearby drawer. He returned with a sea-green sweater and soft grey trousers, both of which were far too big for her. 'Put these on before you catch your death.'

She barked a laugh. 'Death can't catch me,' she said, snatching them from him. 'No matter how hard it tries.'

'You sound . . . a little hysterical.'

'I feel hysterical.'

He turned around, affording her some privacy, and Sera clawed back her senses while slowly peeling her sodden clothes off.

'Start at the beginning. What happened to the monster?'

'I destroyed it,' said Sera, as her sweater landed in a sodden heap at her feet. 'Or the necklace did. I touched the monster and the darkness around it fell away. He turned back into a man.' She frowned at the memory. That poor helpless soul mangled by Mama's experiment. 'Then the necklace exploded. It must have used up all the magic.'

'So, the Lightfire is gone.'

'Yes.'

Theo groaned.

'There's something else,' Sera went on, as she wrestled with the laces on her boots. 'Lightfire doesn't just destroy the monsters. I think it . . . calls to them.' She yanked the boots off, and they fell with a clatter. 'I think the monster was drawn to me. Drawn to the magic in my necklace.'

'What makes you think that?'

'Before I killed it, it sort of . . . bowed to me.'

She watched him stiffen. 'And what about the Dagger?'

'The Dagger ran away with the monster's body.' Now, there was a sentence she never thought she'd say. She pulled her trousers off and told the story, deliberately leaving out the part where Ransom had saved her. Three times. Where she had saved him. That kiss. *Saints, that kiss.* 'After the necklace exploded, I found a note inside it from my mother.'

'Please tell me it contained the secret recipe for Lightfire?'

'Now, why would she ever think to be that helpful?' Sera sighed. 'She clearly thought she had more time. Or maybe she hid the useful part in my jewellery box, which went up in flames.' Sera pulled the trousers on and rolled them at her ankles, then pulled the sweater over her head, letting it swamp her. 'Here. See for yourself.'

He turned around and she passed him the note.

'*The monsters bow to the power of Lightfire*,' he murmured. '*Become the flame and destroy the dark*.' He gestured at the mess across the island. 'I've been working on the bloom all day. I can't crack the pathway to Lightfire. It's driving me up the wall.'

Just then, the door swung open, and Bibi and Val stalked inside. Val waved a bottle of brandy about. 'We swiped this from Fontaine's personal stash, so you know it's like a thousand years old. It's going to be good.'

'What happened to Cloaks not stealing from each other?' said Theo.

'Dire circumstances.' Bibi set down four glasses. 'Sera almost died tonight. Like, a *lot*.'

'Drink up,' said Val, pouring the brandy. 'I assume you've filled Theo in.' She looked between them. 'So, what do we know for sure?'

'That Lightfire kills monsters,' said Sera, drinking deeply. Though she had a sinking feeling that her mother's original intention had been to free them. After she used them against Dufort, presumably. But things had gone horribly wrong. By the time Sera had freed the monster in the fountain, his human body was too weak to survive. They had figured it out too late; the poison had burrowed too deep.

'And it also controls them,' said Theo uneasily.

'Why would anyone *want* to control them?' said Bibi, wincing as she sipped. 'Ugh. I feel like I'm drinking poison.'

'That means it's working,' said Val.

While the others talked among themselves, trying to unpick the mystery of Lightfire and its hold over the monsters of Fantome, Sera stared into her drink, tracing the whorls of amber.

Tonight had been a maelstrom of terror and confusion, but those parting words from Mama rang in her head now, and she knew at last, and for certain, what Sylvie Marchant wanted. It was what she had always wanted. To destroy Dufort's hold over her family, over this whole damn city.

Become the flame and destroy the dark.

Sylvie hadn't just made an army of monsters. She had found a way to control them, to *direct* them. She wanted Sera to take that army and use it to kill Dufort. Lorenzo had said it already: *Sometimes, it takes a monster to destroy a monster.* And Sylvie Marchant had made a whole lot of them, just to be sure.

Bibi waved her hand in front of Sera's face. 'What are you thinking about? The monster or the Dagger?'

'I've never heard of a Dagger this bad at his job,' muttered Theo.

'Maybe he doesn't want to kill her,' reasoned Bibi.

'No shit,' said Val, taking another swig of brandy. 'He wants to screw her.'

Sera nearly spat her drink out.

'You're drunk, Val,' said Theo flatly.

'Look at her,' said Val, smirking. 'Damp as a river rat and still drop-dead distracting. You know I'm right.'

Bibi giggled. Theo returned to his drink.

Val jabbed her finger at Sera. 'And *you're* blushing.'

'It's the brandy.'

'Which is nearly gone,' said Bibi, pouting at the dwindling bottle. 'Just like the Lightfire.'

'Cheers, everyone.' Val raised her glass. 'Looks like we'll soon be monster-fodder. See you all in hell.'

'Speak for yourself,' said Theo, clinking her glass. 'I'll be dancing with the saints.'

Sera drained her glass, coming to an uneasy realization. These monsters were Mama's responsibility. And now Mama was gone, they were Sera's problem. She hadn't just inherited a necklace, she had inherited a swarm of monsters. 'Nobody's going to hell. We'll make more Lightfire.'

'How?' said Bibi. 'We couldn't find a single word about it in the library.'

'That's because Lucille's journal isn't in the library,' said Sera slowly. 'The Dagger told me it was buried with her.'

There was a sobering silence.

'You mean it's in the catacombs?' said Val warily.

Theo snorted. 'It might as well be in hell itself.'

'Hell or not, I'm going down there.'

They all turned to stare at her.

'Now, *you're* drunk,' said Theo. 'How the hell are you planning to get inside Hugo's Passage?'

'I don't know yet,' admitted Sera, and perhaps she would have felt uneasy – scared even – if the brandy wasn't warm in her belly, stoking the flames of her courage. If her palm wasn't tingling with the memory of Ransom's kiss.

But now she knew the Dagger wanted that Lightfire just as badly as she did. Perhaps that meant he would help her.

Seeing her friends' matching looks of horror, Sera stood up, plucking her damp clothes from the floor. 'These monsters were made by my mother.' She picked up Mama's note, the weight of her task heavy in her fist. The guilt around what had become of this city just as heavy on her heart. 'It's up to me to get rid of them. One way or another.'

Bibi winced. 'Breaking into Hugo's Passage means crossing enemy lines, Sera.'

Sera almost laughed. After the way Ransom had looked at her tonight, after the way she had touched him, she was so far over enemy lines, she was nearly in Dufort's lap. 'That's tomorrow's problem,' she murmured. 'I'm going to sleep.'

A short while later, Sera was standing in the back garden, waiting for Pippin to relieve himself, when Theo appeared.

'Hey,' he said, slipping his hands in his pockets as he joined her on the back steps.

'Hey,' she replied, only now noting the dark circles under his eyes. 'I thought you'd be in bed.'

'I wanted to ask you a question.'

She raised her eyebrows.

'You plan to destroy them, don't you?' he said. 'The monsters, I mean.'

Sera hesitated. 'What else would I do with the Lightfire?'

He frowned, and she knew they were both thinking of the

note, of what Sylvie Marchant truly wanted of her. Not just to kill the monsters, but to first use them to destroy Dufort and his Daggers.

'Don't worry about it, Theo,' she said, rubbing his arm. 'You should get some sleep.'

But he lingered on the steps, both of them watching Pippin sniff around a hydrangea bush, pretending they weren't ruminating over the fate of Fantome. He sighed then, turning back into the house. 'Just remember what happened to Armand Versini. Daggers never lose, Sera.'

Not yet, she thought as she watched him go.

But there was a first time for everything.

Chapter 30

Seraphine

The following morning, Pippin went walkabout. Sera looked for him in his usual spots but he wasn't snoozing by the ovens in the kitchen or growling at squirrels through the windows of the rec room. She asked around until Blanche said she had seen him snoozing in the library after breakfast.

It was there Sera found him curled up under an armchair by the window. Madame Fontaine was sitting in the opposite chair, poring over a spread of tarot cards. Sera was about to turn around and come back later when the old lady looked up.

'I don't bite, Seraphine,' she said, beckoning at her. 'Your mutt likes me well enough.'

Sera edged inside. 'I didn't want to disturb you.'

Fontaine snorted. 'You were afraid I'd smell my brandy on your breath.'

Sera's cheeks flamed. She'd thought the three cups of coffee at breakfast had done enough to battle her hangover.

'I was saving the Laramie for a special occasion,' Madame Fontaine went on, gathering her cards back into the deck. For an old woman with gnarled hands, she shuffled them with surprising deftness. 'Not that those two urchins you run around with seemed to care.'

'It was a stressful night,' said Sera, vaguely wondering if the rumours were true, and Saint Oriel did in fact sometimes whisper to Fontaine. 'We had a run-in with a monster in the Scholars' Quarter.'

A card sprang from the deck and Fontaine caught it in mid-air, laying it face up on the table. It was an image of a woman in a gold mask, holding a silver one in her hand.

'The Deceiver,' said Madame Fontaine.

Sera stared at the card. *Well, shit.*

Fontaine continued shuffling. 'I knew your mother, you know. We had dealings many years ago when I was the head of this Order and she was a woman not much older than you.'

Sera didn't tear her gaze from the card. Was it meant to be her, or Mama?

The old woman wheezed a dusty laugh. 'Sylvie never could sit still, even back then. She refused to settle for the lot she was given in life. Was always reaching for something greater. Darker.' She looked up at Sera. 'When you go looking for trouble, trouble will find you first.'

'Funny thing for a Cloak to say,' remarked Sera. 'Isn't all trouble the same?'

'No.' The word was flat.

Sera avoided Fontaine's milky gaze, but she could feel it prickling the side of her cheek. It stirred unease inside her, and she got the sense that the longer she lingered here in the library, the more the old woman would pry, and Sera didn't want to tell her about her search for Lightfire. About Mama's note, or what she knew of the monsters of Fantome. She didn't trust the old crone. And it was clear the old crone didn't trust her.

'I need to take Pip for a walk,' she said, crouching to fish him out from under the chair. 'He ate way too much bacon at breakfast.'

Madame Fontaine kept shuffling. 'I knew your father too.'

Sera stilled. Then stood up, very slowly. She should have left then, run from those words the way she and Mama had tried to run from the man, but curiosity turned her feet to lead.

Fontaine hummed, her hands still working through the cards.

'He came to me some years before you were born. A street urchin with quick fingers, who wanted a better life. A richer life. He begged to be a Cloak.' Her lips twisted, the memory sour in her mouth. 'I turned him away.'

Sera was surprised by her flash of anger. It reminded her of the night she had come here begging for sanctuary, only to have the same door slammed in her face. 'Why?'

'For the same reason I turned you away.' Fontaine smiled, but there was no warmth in it. Just suspicion, laced with wariness. 'Only this time it wasn't up to me. You are no Cloak, Seraphine Marchant. Not in your heart.'

'You don't know me,' protested Sara.

Fontaine cocked her head. 'Do you know yourself yet?' Her fingers moved, quicker and quicker. 'You have an air of destiny about you.'

'You say that like it's a bad thing,' said Sera, at the scowl in her voice.

Fontaine didn't answer. She closed her eyes, frowning. Another card jumped. She let it flutter to the floor, where it landed face up. It was an old man in a reaping cloak, carrying a scythe.

'The Grim,' she said, with a grunt. 'Death lurks around the corner.'

'Whose death?' said Sera before she could help herself.

Madame Fontaine set the cards down. Perhaps it was Sera's imagination but she thought the old crone looked afraid. 'We will find out.'

Sera hugged Pippin closer, making for the door before another card jumped out bearing Mama's face or Dufort's scowl.

Fontaine's parting words followed her out into the corridor. 'You'd better replace that brandy, girl.'

Chapter 31

Ransom

Ransom sat on a wall in the Hollows, feeling like a prize fool. He had come here again, like a moth drawn to a flame, and she was asleep. Of course she was asleep. What did he expect? A face at the window, a hand waving to him? The clatter of her footsteps as she ran down the garden path and flung her arms around him, eager to unpick the events of last night and confide in him the secrets of Lightfire?

No. But he had come anyway. To know that she was safe, and to warn her about Lark, who he knew would eagerly rise to the challenge of killing her. The only reason Lark hadn't already tried was because he had gone with Dufort to Bellevue Castle in east Valterre. They had left that morning, after the Head Dagger was summoned by the king himself. It seemed their troubling monster problem, and the rising state of alarm in Fantome, had finally drawn the king's attention.

If Dufort hadn't been so angry at Ransom, he would have chosen him for company, but he had taken Lark instead, which sent a very particular message to Ransom: *Step up or fuck off.*

It had not had the desired effect. Ransom was glad to be rid of both of them, even if it was only for a couple of days.

He waited for an agonizing hour outside House Armand then turned for home. Just as a paper dart came floating overhead. He leaped to catch it, his heart beating hard as he read that messy, looping script.

I thought our little game was over ...

He reached for the pen he had stolen from the nearest brothel on that first night she had written to him, and scribbled his reply.

There are other players in the game now. You need to be careful.

He sent it back on a gusting shadow, sipping just enough Shade to do so and still keep his wits about him. There was a gap in her curtains, her face there peering out, trying to find him in the dark. He watched her write her reply.

I thought I was being careful.

He barked a laugh.

There is nothing careful about you, Seraphine.

He heard her answering laugh on the wind, and wished he could bottle it. That dart came again, veering too far to the left this time. He saved it from an open drain, scuffing his boots in the dive.

In the spirit of recklessness, I have a proposition for you, Ransom. Answer 'Yes' and see the outcome below (artist's rendering)...

He stared at the sketch underneath her words. A woefully out-of-proportion stick man, with a generous sweep of black hair and a giant goofy face. A little nick in the centre of his smile marked the scar on Ransom's lip. Something inside him glowed, warm and bright, and he knew if there was a mirror before him now, he'd find himself with that same goofy smile on his face. He wrote back.

You spent way too much time on my hair. And why is my head so massive?

He paced, waiting for her reply.

I know, right? I've been asking myself that since we first met.

Seraphine and that smart mouth. He tried not to think about claiming it.

Tell me your proposition.

He wanted to ask her to come outside and tell him to his face. To give him one stolen minute in the dark, but he was afraid of scaring her off.

Meet me at Our Sacred Saints' Cathedral tomorrow at dusk, and you'll find out.

He hated how his heart swooped, how easily she yanked it with her invisible string. If only she knew how desperately he wanted to say yes. To yell it at her window and wake every Cloak in House Armand.

I'll think about it.

He told himself there would be no reply, but he lingered another minute anyway, running to catch it when it came floating over the hedge.

It's a date.

Ruthless. She was teasing him. Tilting the whole damn game, and raising two fingers to Dufort. And he liked her even more for it. So much so that he folded the note to keep it. He turned away from her, grinning like that goofy stick man all the way back home.

Chapter 32

Seraphine

Sera wore her cloak as she walked across the river to the Saints' Quarter, with Ransom's warning still swirling in her head. She didn't know who the other players in the game were – or how many more Daggers Dufort had assigned to kill her – but she sure as hell didn't want to find out the hard way.

It was late afternoon when she set out from House Armand, the pale autumn sun gilding the city rooftops in soft amber light. There was a crispness to the air that made her draw her cloak tighter as she crunched through the leaf-strewn streets. Our Sacred Saints' Cathedral towered over the sleepy streets of west Fantome, formidable in its beauty. It was a remarkable feat of architecture, with a grand limestone façade and two rows of flying buttresses guarded by stern-faced gargoyles.

The church boasted twelve stained-glass windows at the front alone, one for each of the twelve original saints of Valterre. Seraphine peered up at them as she approached, catching the misted gaze of Saint Celiana, who had been painted on a floating seashell, playing a harp. In the window next to her, Maurius, Saint of Travellers and Seafarers, stood at the bow of a wooden ship, casting a fierce wind that blew the sails taut. Beside him stood a young, weeping Maud, Saint of Lost Hope, once worshipped for her ability to take on the sadness of others and unburden them of their worldly cares. She had been rendered with her shawl pulled tight around herself, her crystalline tears glistening in the dying sunlight.

Sera had never been inside Our Sacred Saints' Cathedral before. Mama used to joke that if they ever set foot inside it, the revered saints of Valterre would sniff out the Shade on the pads of their fingers and send them up in flames.

That joke was no longer funny to Sera.

A push on the large oak doors revealed the dimly lit sanctuary within. Puddles of blue and red and yellow light danced along the marble floors, while hundreds of candles flickered in the alcoves. The beauty of this place took Sera's breath away, and for a moment, she stood under the gazes of the saints and wished she was worthy of their attention. Wished she was a different sort of girl, from a different sort of life, where visiting a cathedral like this wouldn't set her teeth on edge.

You have an air of destiny about you.

Fontaine's words trickled down her spine.

The church was empty, save for a few people praying near

the back. Sera trailed her fingers along the wooden pews as she drifted towards the altar, where twelve statues stood peacefully. They watched over the dais where priests and priestesses gathered to worship them every week.

She removed her cloak and sat down, two rows from the statue of Frederic, Saint of Farmers and Hunters, and waited. She let her mind drift, back to lazy days out in the plains, when she and Lorenzo would sneak away from their tutor's cottage and hide in the cornfields, finding shapes in the clouds. They would stay like that for hours, making up stories, until they were laughing too hard to speak, or kissing too hard to breathe. Lorenzo had always wanted to be a farmer, to raise cattle in the plains, to keep chickens and in time, a brood of children, too. It was a simple life, but his eyes glowed whenever he spoke of it. Sera was too much of a daydreamer to settle so soon on what she wished to become, and she liked it that way – the future yawning out before her with a hundred different pathways to happiness.

Now, she felt all those possibilities slipping away, the destiny Mama had imagined for her closing around her like a vice. She thought of the Grim in Madame Fontaine's cards and wondered where this future would lead her – if there was a pathway left for her at all.

In the storm of her worries, the pew creaked.

The air warmed as a figure sat down beside her.

'I've always thought that statue of Saint Frederic makes him look constipated,' remarked an all-too-familiar voice.

Sera bit back her smile. 'Hello, stranger.'

Ransom turned to look at her. 'Hello, Seraphine.'

'You can't kill me in a church,' she said, meeting his gaze. Relieved to find it was not silver … Disconcerted to find it even more arresting in the flickering candlelight.

'Dagger's honour,' he said, pressing a palm to his chest. 'I thought we were past all that anyway.'

Sera hoped they were, but she couldn't help being wary. Better to remain on guard.

Ransom had no such concerns. He turned towards her, his forearm sliding along the back of the pew until his fingers brushed against her shoulder. She ignored the flare of heat in her body, the way her skin warmed at the nearness of his touch. He smirked at the rising blush in her cheeks. And what a smirk it was. *Saints, save me.* 'Tell me, spitfire. Why am I here?'

She drew a sharp breath, and his gaze dropped to her mouth. Lingered there. A black strand curled along his forehead and her fingers itched to push it back, to press her hand to his cheek and see if he might kiss it again. Ransom was distractingly handsome. He might not have his Shade, but he had that face, that voice. Other weapons. Other ways to disarm her.

She pulled back from him. 'Have you ever killed anyone in a church?'

He blinked. 'No. Have you?'

She shook her head. 'I've never killed anyone.'

'Not for lack of trying.'

She dropped her gaze to where she had stabbed him.

He followed her line of sight. 'Do you want to see my scar, Seraphine?'

Her throat tightened. 'You can't lift up your shirt in here,' she said in a strangled voice.

'So *pious*,' he said, with a chuckle. 'But you're probably right. I'd hate to scandalize our saints.'

She turned back to the statues, gathering her composure. 'If you're looking for unlucky number thirteen, Lucille Versini is not here,' he said, reading her confusion easily. 'For all his power, Hugo Versini never managed to get a statue of his sister into this place.' He clucked his tongue, tipping his head back. 'Not even a window pane. Her statue stands above his passage in Old Haven.'

'I doubt she'd care,' muttered Sera.

He hummed in agreement. 'And anyway, Lucille didn't possess any measure of magic. She wasn't blessed like the saints of old. She doesn't hold any lasting influence on this city.'

Not yet, thought Sera, working her way up to talking about the Lightfire. She was surprised he hadn't brought it up yet but she sensed he was waiting for her to show her hand.

He chewed on his bottom lip, nipping at that white scar. She was seized by the urge to trace it with her tongue. She blinked the thought away and returned her attention to the saints, giving her eyes a break from the terrible beauty of him. She was not here to lust over a Dagger, easy as it was. She was here to ask a favour of him.

She wrung her hands, preparing to come to the point, but he stood up abruptly and went to the bay of candles at the side of the altar. He lit one taper, and then another, setting them side by side, among a sea of other people's wishes.

Ransom dropped his head in silent prayer. Sera studied the towering shadow of his body flickering in the candlelight, the broad sweep of his shoulders and the curve of his biceps as he clasped his hands behind his back. Here was a devil standing under the eye of the saints, and he didn't seem to care. In fact, he was acting like he belonged in their company.

She laughed.

He looked up, frowning.

'Sorry,' she said quickly. 'Who are you praying for?'

He turned back to the candles as if he hadn't heard her, dipping his chin as he finished his prayer. Sera's curiosity only grew, but she pressed her lips together, waiting.

He returned to the pew, sliding so close his leg brushed against hers. 'What?' he said. 'No candles to light?'

She shook her head. 'I've had my fill of fire.'

'Right. Sorry.' He rubbed the spot between his eyebrows. 'That was tactless.'

She blinked at the sincerity of his tone. He dropped his hands on his knees, and she marvelled at how big they were next to hers. His olive skin shone golden in the candlelight, but the shadow-marks looked darker than ever. She tracked a black whorl that peeked out of his sleeve and curled around his left thumb, like a wreath of thorns. *The hands of a killer,* she reminded herself.

Then why did she want to touch them so badly?

He watched her study them, his mouth a hard line.

She sat back, looking at the melancholic statue of Saint Maud. 'Even if I did pray, I'm not sure anyone would hear me.' She didn't know why she was still speaking, but there was something about the silence in here that loosened her tongue. 'I'm not sure Mama is with the saints.'

He jerked his chin up. 'You don't believe that.'

She smiled ruefully. 'Have you forgotten who made all those monsters? And all the people they've killed?'

He frowned. 'Nothing in this world is ever black and white. What we do is not always who we are.'

She snorted. 'Is that what you tell yourself at night after you've murdered someone?'

There was a sudden whip of coldness between them. His lip curled and he leaned forward, bracing his elbows on his knees.

Behind them, pews creaked as worshippers left ahead of sundown. The church darkened, the candle flames flickering as if to fight the night sweeping in. Shadows danced around them, and idly Sera wondered how many times Ransom had ripped those same shapes off the wall and used them to choke the life out of someone. How many bad people he'd killed, how many good. She wondered if the regret in his eyes was a trick to snare her sympathies. If she should look at the marks on his hands instead.

She hadn't come here to wound him. And yet he seemed to care about what she thought of him. Perhaps she had echoed the things he thought about himself. Things like *monster, killer*. Maybe that's why he hated the shadow-marks on his body, why he wanted them gone.

'The candles are for my family,' he said, so quietly Sera had to lean forward to hear him. 'My mother. My sister. It's been almost ten years since I last saw them.'

'What happened to them?'

'They ran away ... We all did.' He scrubbed a hand across his jaw. 'My father was a violent man. He terrorized us for years, and when we ran, he chased us.'

'And he caught you?' she guessed, from the haunted look in his eyes.

He nodded, but said no more, leaving her to wonder about the kind of monster his father had been. What other things they had in common. Absently, he traced his finger along the scar on his lip, and she had the sudden sense she knew where it had come from. Or rather, *who.*

'Where is he now?'

'Dead.' The word was stone cold. And then, as though he couldn't quite hold in the rest, he said, 'He was my first kill. I was ten years old.'

Bile pooled in Sera's throat. She could scarcely imagine a child taking on such a heinous task, then bearing the weight of the guilt. She looked at all those shadow-marks and wondered which one was the first. How many had come after.

'I'm sorry you had to go through that,' she murmured, thinking now of her own father. How she wished him dead too. However many things she had judged Ransom for, she would not judge him for that.

He looked up at her. 'Why are you sorry? He was the victim.'

'No,' she murmured, holding his gaze. 'I don't think he was.'

He shrugged, looking away. 'The candles are an offering to Saint Maurius. I pray that wherever they went, they found a safe haven. Somewhere far beyond Fantome.'

Sadness slackened his shoulders. It was an effort not to reach for his hand, and offer a measure of comfort. So she said instead, 'I'm sure they did.'

He looked up at her again, something like hope catching in his eyes. And even though he was still a well-seasoned assassin and their truce teetered on the knife edge of their mutual curiosity, she felt like in that moment they were something else – two lost souls, left adrift in the same dark sea.

She went on, 'I bet they hired a wagon and went south, through the lavender fields of Florenne and the sun-kissed valleys beyond. They're probably in a white-stone village somewhere by the sea, living among the fisherfolk who sing to the waves to coax the shoals to shore.'

Ransom drew closer, his lips parted, as if to breathe in her story, and Sera continued, drawing them both deeper into the tale. 'In the morning, they rise with the sun to weave nets along the strand, and in the afternoon, when the heat of the day passes, they stroll along the beach and harvest mussels by the shoreline. They throw nets and catch crabs, watch the sea turtles slumbering just beyond the surf, where the jellyfish swim.'

Ransom's chuckle was low and breathy. 'Anouk is terrified of jellyfish. I threw one at her when we were children and she never got over the fright.'

'Anouk.' Sera smiled at the name. 'Maybe she's finally outgrown her fear. Maybe she has a pet jellyfish of her own that she's named after you.'

Ransom's laughter burst out of him, catching flight and soaring up to the roof. It was music she could listen to over and over again. 'Can't you picture it?' she said, joining in. 'Ransom the jellyfish. The Dagger of the Sea.'

'It has a certain terrifying ring to it,' he said, still chuckling. 'Although Anouk never called me Ransom. That's not my real name.'

'Oh.' She supposed that made sense. *Ransom* was an unusual name to give a child.

She could tell by the twist of his lips that he didn't like it. 'I was the price of my family's freedom.'

Ransom.

Sera bristled at the cruelty of it. 'Dufort gave you that name.'

'Dufort took me in. He saved my life. He can call me whatever he likes.'

Sera couldn't keep the bite from her voice. 'And he can have your soul while he's at it.'

He only shrugged. 'If that's the price of freedom.'

'And how is that freedom working out for you, *Ransom*? Are you enjoying your life as a Dagger?'

'Are you enjoying yours as a Cloak?' he parried.

The tension swelled, joining flame and shadow, as they stewed in the consequences of their decisions. 'You're not going to tell me your real name, are you?'

He looked at her – really looked at her – like he was considering it. It was like staring into the eye of the storm, trying to find the sunlight on the other side of it. 'Then I really would have to kill you.'

'Fine,' she muttered. 'I don't want to worsen my odds.'

'No,' he said quietly.

'The lullaby,' she said. 'How do you know it?'

'I used to sing it to my sister when our father came home drunk from the tavern. Anouk was training to be a ballerina. She used to call herself the dancing swan. She always wanted to fly.' His smile was edged with pain. Sera felt the same sadness inside her, that ache for a different, kinder life. 'In the end, she flew away.'

Sera reached into the pocket of her coat and removed the music box she had felt him covet the other night in the Hollows. The song they had come to share. She placed it on the pew between them. 'For you.'

He stared at it. Then at her. 'You're bribing me.'

'Maybe,' she said, tracing her finger along the wooden lid. 'Or maybe it's a gift.'

His fingers twitched like he wanted to take it. He resisted, and turned towards her, the fullness of his body blocking out the rest of the church, and all those statues watching over them. 'Tell me your proposition, Seraphine.'

'It's about the monsters.'

'I figured.'

'You know my mother made them. Whatever her reasons were, it doesn't matter.' She wouldn't tell him. Perhaps he had already figured it out. 'I have to destroy them. I have to free them. But to do that, I need to make more Lightfire.'

'So, make more,' he said.

'I intend to.' A breath of hesitation. 'But I need your help.'

'So that's why you lured me here.'

'*Lured* is a strong word. I'm hardly a siren,' she felt compelled to point out. His eyebrows rose, as if to say, *Aren't you?* Ridiculous. She couldn't make this Dagger do anything he didn't want to do, and they both knew it.

'What is it that you need from me, Seraphine? I don't know how to make Lightfire.'

'But you want it,' she said, quietly. 'Don't you?'

'Yes.' The word throbbed between them. He leaned closer, his scent surrounding her – woodsmoke and sage, and a hint of wild mint on his breath. His gaze dropped to her mouth. 'Badly.'

Sera scrambled for her words before they eddied away. 'Lucille Versini is the one who discovered Lightfire. Mama managed to crack the recipe but without her, I can't work it out. I need Lucille's journal,' she said, all in one hurried breath. 'I know it's buried with her in the catacombs.'

He cocked an eyebrow. 'You only know that because I told you.'

'For which I'm *very* grateful.' She flashed a smile. 'I have to read it, Ransom. I have to see if it holds the answers I need.'

'So, you would have me play Cloak?' he said, eyes flashing with amusement. 'You want me to thieve for you.'

She jutted out her chin. Too close to his face, those dancing eyes and teasing mouth. 'Do you want to rid Fantome of these monsters or not?'

'Of course I do,' he said, without missing a beat. 'But you're asking me to break into the sacred crypt of Lucille Versini. Which means going against the rules of the Order, and Dufort himself. And don't forget, I'm supposed to be killing you.'

Fair points.

'And all for the price of a lullaby,' he added.

'And Lightfire,' she reminded him. 'I have an artificer I trust. Whatever we make, I'll give you half of it. You can do what you want with it. Swallow it. Bathe in it.'

He cocked his head. 'Together?'

Her cheeks flamed. 'I'm serious, Ransom. Bring me the journal, and let me try.' At his silence, she went on, frustration sharpening her words. 'Or return to your hovel with the rest of the vermin and let this city rot. Let yourself rot, too, until those shadow-marks run so deep they eat your soul.'

'You're asking me to rob a crypt,' he said through his teeth. 'Can you give me a damn minute to consider the risks?'

'I'm asking you to do the right thing for once in your life,' she said, voice rising. 'Here's a tip, Ransom: if you want to actually atone for all the depraved shit you've done and be the kind of man your sister would be proud of, then it'll take more than erasing those marks on your hands.'

He recoiled as if she'd slapped him. 'And do you think killing all those monsters in one fell swoop will atone for the *depraved shit* your mother did?'

She prodded him in the chest. 'Don't talk about my mother.'

He caught her finger. 'Don't talk about my sister.'

She shook him off, glaring at him.

He glared right back. 'If you're not careful, spitfire, I'll go back to killing you.'

She didn't know what possessed her but before she could think better of it, she grabbed his hand and pressed it against the hollow of her throat. He let her do it, his calluses rough against her skin. Her pulse raced against them. His breath caught as he noticed, and she went utterly still, letting his fingers curl around her neck.

He watched her through lowered eyelids, waiting for her to flinch.

'Go ahead, Dagger.' She held his gaze, daring him to do it. Something feral burned in his gaze, and for a fleeting moment, she didn't know what he wanted: her body, or her corpse. His fingers twitched. Slowly, so slowly, he slid his palm up her neck and brushed his thumb along her jaw.

'Wicked game,' he breathed against her lips. 'Have you ever kissed anyone in a church, Seraphine?'

She closed her eyes, her chest aching, Her skin was so hot she felt like she would catch fire under his touch. She was putty in his hands. His to kill or kiss, to torture as he liked. When she opened her eyes to his molten gaze, she saw that she was torturing him too.

Something flitted across the back of her mind. 'The journal,' she remembered.

'I'll get you the journal,' he said at once, and she thought perhaps he had already intended to do it.

She smiled. 'There. Was that really so hard?'

His own lips curved. There was a slow beat of hesitation, and in the sliver of space that remained between them, she felt the heat of his desire raging against her own.

Then the church bells rang out, making her jump.

Ransom's face shuttered. 'I should go,' he said, more to himself than to her.

Seraphine nodded. 'The journal . . .'

'Yes. The journal.' He jumped to his feet, taking the music box with him. 'I'll let you know when it's done. In the meantime, go home and try to stay out of trouble.'

All she could do was stare after him as he strode from the church, clutching that little wooden box to his chest, like it was the other half of his heart. Her bribe accepted, their deal made, even if there was no kiss to seal it.

Seraphine couldn't help the crushing weight of her disappointment as she slid from the pew and followed him.

Chapter 33

Ransom

Ransom bolted from the Saints' Quarter with his self-control hanging by a single fraying thread. Heat flooded his veins and pounded in his chest, telling him to turn around, to go back and take Seraphine Marchant in that damn pew. To slide his fingers through her hair, crush his lips against hers and finish what they started in the shadows of that church. In the waters of Saint Celiana's fountain. On the day she had driven that blade into his gut and taunted him with those bronze-flecked cerulean eyes.

No, he could not go back. He could not afford to free-fall into lust. It would only damn them both. The full might of the Daggers was coming down on Seraphine Marchant, and if he wasn't careful, the hammer would fall on him too.

Curiosity had made Ransom come to the cathedral, but it was

desire that made him weak for her. It was desire that made him say yes. *Yes*, he would help her. *Yes*, he would plunder the crypt of Lucille Versini, and wrest that journal from her cold, dead hands. *Yes*, he would help Sera mine the secrets of Lightfire. *Yes*, he would help her destroy all those monsters, in the hope that she might destroy the monster that lived inside him too.

And if Dufort caught wind of it . . .

A violent shudder went through Ransom.

No. Dufort was away for another day and night. Lark had gone with him, leaving Ransom in charge of Hugo's Passage. There was something divine about the timing, as though Saint Oriel herself had plucked the strands of fate to allow him this one chance to help Seraphine.

To help himself, too.

The clangour of church bells soon faded into the distance. A light rain began to fall, the chill in the wind heralding winter. Overhead, a blanket of clouds smothered the moon, a gauzy mist smearing the light from the streetlamps until he felt like he had stumbled into a painting.

Before he knew it, Ransom had reached Old Haven. He was so lost in thought he hadn't noticed the graveyards crowding in on him as he walked long into the night. The world fell quiet, save for the distant howls reminding him of the monsters that now prowled taverns and homes, ripping innocents from their beds. Indiscriminate, sloppy kills. Terror sown by chaos.

And yet, a murder was a murder.

A killer was a killer.

Was he really so different from Sylvie's monsters? Did he deserve to be saved?

The question tormented him. He held his hands up to the streetlamp, studying the shadow-marks along his fingers. He was choosing to help Seraphine save this city, and that made him a man. Not a monster. Didn't it?

Up ahead, the statue of Lucille Versini gazed blankly towards the Aurore Tower. The sculpture once made for the cathedral now stood alone on a deserted street in Old Haven, guarding the entrance to Hugo's Passage instead. Even in death, Lucille could not outrun her brother.

Ransom unstopped a vial. A quick press of his lips against the glass rim gave him just enough Shade to pull the statue down. The entrance to Hugo's Passage groaned open and he ducked underneath the archway of skulls, making his way into the dimness. His feet led him down the north passage, then east. He ducked his head, nodding at Daggers as they stalked past him, preparing for their night's work.

At last, he reached the door to Dufort's bedchamber. He glanced around, then stripped a shadow from the wall and used it to work the lock free. It swallowed the last of his Shade, yielding with a soft *click*. Dufort might have taken better precautions if he ever thought a Dagger would be foolish enough to steal from him, or if he had anything in his room worth stealing, but the Shade here was stored in the vault at the end of the south passage, along with the rest of Dufort's riches.

A four-poster bed occupied one half of the chamber, while a set of leather armchairs and a grand bookshelf stood along the other, bracketing a fireplace full of ash. Ransom didn't linger. He grabbed the crypt keys from a hook on the wall and pocketed them, before slipping back out into the tunnel.

Shadows flickered on the wall and for a moment he stilled, but it was only his own fear playing tricks on him. Dufort was halfway across Valterre, summoned by the king himself. Ransom hurried on, down one passage and then another, until he came to a spiral of stone steps that wound deeper into the earth. The smell of damp clung to his skin as he descended into the bowels of the catacombs. Down, down, down he went, until the shadows thickened, fighting the oil lamps that hung widely spaced on the walls down here.

There were only two crypts in Hugo's Passage, one for Hugo himself, and the other for Lucille. Ransom went straight to the second, using the skeleton key in the ancient lock. The door yielded with a keening groan but he froze on the threshold, sure he heard the shuffle of footsteps. He spun around, his heartbeat thrumming in his throat.

'Who's there?' he called out.

His voice just echoed back at him. His mind must be more addled than he thought, the guilt of what he was doing weighing heavy on him. By coming here, he wasn't just helping Seraphine. He was betraying Dufort, stealing from the Daggers who had taken him in.

But he thought then of the monsters and the screams that filled Fantome night after night, and pushed on. Not just for Seraphine, but for the city. For his home.

He stepped inside the crypt. The darkness was cold and grasping. He lit the closest oil lamp, relieved as it sparked to life. The shadows fell away as the door closed behind him. The room was small and musty, hewn with exquisite stonework and hung with tapestries of a faraway mountain village.

In the middle of the crypt sat a small stone coffin with a golden plaque fixed to the lid.

HERE LIES LUCILLE VERSINI,
BELOVED SISTER AND CHERISHED DAUGHTER,
SAINT AND SCHOLAR

Ransom trailed his hand along the coffin, raising a spiral of dust.

Someone sneezed.

Ransom spun around, sparking another oil lamp to life. The darkness rippled and he lunged, catching the end of a cloak before it disappeared. He yanked and it fluttered to the ground, revealing the horrified figure of Seraphine Marchant.

Ransom closed the foot of space between them, and she flattened herself against the wall. Fear sparked in her blue eyes, making that bronze fleck shine.

'What the fuck are you doing?' he hissed through his teeth.

She opened her mouth, then closed it again. He could feel her leg trembling between his, her chest fluttering as she searched for her voice. 'Helping you?' she managed.

His face tightened. 'Are you trying to get us both killed?'

She shook her head. 'I was ... I just ... I was ... curious.'

'You and your damn death wish.' He pushed off the wall, needing to put some space between them before his anger warped into lust. He folded his arms, still glaring at her. 'A Cloak has never set foot inside these catacombs.'

'That you know of,' she said, with an awkward chuckle. Slowly, she peeled herself off the wall. 'But now that we're both here, we might as well work together. That lid looks heavy as hell.'

Ransom banked his anger, if only to keep himself from throttling her. The sooner it was done, the better. 'Fine. Let's just get this over with.'

She rounded the coffin, working her fingers under the lid. 'You pull, I'll push.'

As he worked to dislodge the ancient grave of Lucille Versini in order to commit a grievous robbery against his own Order, with the mark he was supposed to have murdered several weeks ago, Ransom dimly realized that he had completely lost his mind. The coffin lid was made of granite, and so heavy it was like moving the earth itself. Eventually, the lid yielded, but no more than six inches. A cloud of dust shot out, and Seraphine sneezed again.

'*Shh!*' he snapped, eyes darting around.

She pinched her nose, eyes streaming. 'Sorry. I've never been in a crypt before!'

'And you think I have?'

'You practically live in one,' she said, wiping the tears from her cheeks. 'Don't think I didn't notice all those freaky skulls on the way down here.'

'I suggest you keep your mouth shut if you don't want to become one of them.'

'Next time I have to sneeze, I'll just implode instead, shall I?'

'I wish you would.'

'No. You don't.'

And that was the problem.

They glared at each other over the length of the coffin.

Saints, she was infuriating.

Ransom raked his hair away from his face. 'Let's just . . . take a breath.'

'Fine by me.'

She tipped her head back. Her gaze fell on the tapestry over his shoulder, and he watched that tell-tale curiosity flare in her eyes. 'That must be Halbracht.'

'So I gather,' he said, still looking at her.

'Have you ever been?'

'To Halbracht? Of course not.'

'Is that such an odd question?' she said, letting her gaze fall to his. 'Your beloved leader Hugo grew up there.'

'I don't give a shit where Hugo Versini grew up.'

She quirked an eyebrow, a smirk dancing along her lips. Irritating. Beautiful. He truly was in hell. 'Careful what you say in these tombs, Dagger.'

'Careful what you ask, spitfire.'

'The time for being careful is long past.' Her eyes fell on the golden plaque. Her shoulders sagged and for a moment, there was such sadness in her gaze, he couldn't stand to look at her.

So he said the first thing he could think of. 'Halbracht is a notoriously secretive place. You can't just stroll up to the Pinetops and knock on the gates.' She looked up, distracted. 'It's heavily guarded.'

'Why?'

He shrugged. 'Maybe they're hiding something.'

'Everyone's hiding something,' she murmured.

Those three words raised the hairs on the back of his neck. 'What does that mean?'

'It means I want my journal. Let's just get this done,' she said, pushing against the coffin lid. This time, they didn't stop straining against the granite, both of them sweating and panting as the skeleton of Lucille Versini appeared between them inch by inch. She was little more than a collection of old bones, a small skull surrounded by white silk. Her bejewelled necklace remained, and Hugo had buried her in a tiara that still glittered under the lamplight.

But her greatest treasure was that journal. Now yellowed and crisp, it lay on her chest. Even in death, she was clutching it like a teddy bear.

Ransom looked up, wondering why Seraphine hadn't yet snatched it, but she was standing with her back against the wall now, and there were silent tears streaming down her cheeks. He went rigid, trying to work out what he had missed in the last thirty seconds of their excavation. 'Are you hurt?' he said, looking her up and down. 'If it was too heavy, you should have—'

'It's not that.' She shook her head, trying to swallow the crack in her voice. 'It's just ... she's real.' She scrubbed her cheeks, looking everywhere but at him. She was embarrassed, he realized. 'She's a skeleton.'

'Were you expecting her to sit up and shake your hand?' he said, striving for lightness, but it only worsened the discomfort on her face. 'Lucille has been dead for hundreds of years. Wherever her soul is, it's in a better place than this.'

'She was always a story to me. An untouchable ... A legend.' Her voice was small, frightened. 'I just wasn't expecting this ... *feeling*.'

He cocked his head, searching her face for the foolish bravado that had propelled her into the heart of Hugo's Passage to begin with, but there was no sign of it. It belatedly occurred to him that while Seraphine Marchant might have grown up in the house of a smuggler and had handled her fair share of Shade, she was not used to dead bodies.

Perhaps a part of her looked down at Lucille and saw herself. Someone young and clever and beautiful, with the world at her feet. Lightfire at her fingertips. Both of them hunted by the Head of the Order of Daggers. One dead, and one still just clinging to life. He saw that fear – knew it as intimately as his own. And he wanted to take it from her. To shoulder it, until she could breathe again.

'It wasn't right, what Hugo did to her. He was a terrible man.'

She looked up at him, eyes wide. 'Do you really believe that?'

He nodded without even thinking about it. 'I've always believed that.'

She frowned. 'That doesn't make sense. You don't make any sense.'

Ransom smiled, ruefully. 'Do you want the journal or not?'

'Yes.' But she hesitated.

'*This* is the part you can't do?' he said, leaning across the coffin. 'Do you want me to—?'

'No.' She rolled her shoulders. 'Keep your hands to yourself, Dagger.' He watched her prise the journal free, her skin taking on a definite greenish hue as she tried desperately not to touch the skeleton.

'Stop smirking at me,' she said, without looking up.

'I'm admiring your technique.'

She bit back her smile. When the journal came free, she leaped backwards, clutching it to her chest, just as Lucille had done.

'I did it,' she said, as if she couldn't quite believe it. She yanked up her sweater, tucking the journal into the waistband of her trousers, and Ransom stilled at the sight of her bare midriff. A familiar heat roared in his blood.

You lust-addled Neanderthal. You're standing in a fucking tomb.

'We should move the lid back into place,' she said, shoving it towards him. But the angle was off and now the lid had been loosened, it wobbled as she pushed.

'Careful!' He lunged to steady it, but skidded on her discarded cloak. He careened into the coffin, and the entire lid tilted. They tried to force it back into alignment but the stone was too heavy. It listed to the side, sliding to the ground with an earth-trembling thud.

The entire passageway shook, the lamps on the wall flickering as dust streamed down from the ceiling. Somewhere overhead, a chorus of shouts rang out. It was followed by the thrum of footsteps.

Seraphine swiped her cloak off the floor. 'Now what?'

He grabbed her shoulders and shoved her towards the door. 'Now, we run!'

Chapter 34

Seraphine

Seraphine flew out of the crypt so fast she lost her footing. Her knees had barely touched the ground before Ransom caught her, yanking her up by the waist.

'Move,' he hissed in her ear, but there was nowhere to run. There was only one way up and there were already footsteps coming down the stairwell.

She whirled on her heel. 'We're trapped.'

His gaze darted, then he tugged her down to the left, where the passage narrowed before ending at a stone wall. He swung her around, pressing her back against it and covering her body with his own. Sera tilted her chin up but she couldn't see beyond him, just the flickering dark and the warning in his eyes.

'Don't move, spitfire,' he said, peering down at her. 'Or we're both dead.'

Better to tilt those odds in their favour, then, thought Sera. She unfurled her cloak and flung it around his shoulders. He pulled the hood up, shadows falling across his face as he curled his arms around her, folding her into the cloak's magic. He walked her back into a shadow, where a breath of cool wind caressed her skin, raising the hairs on the back of her neck.

His arms tightened around her as the footsteps drew nearer. She looked up, caught in the firelight of his gaze. The tension thickened, her heart beating so hard she swore he must feel it against his chest. She opened her mouth, but he raised a finger to her lips and kept it there.

Behind them, there were footsteps. Then voices.

'What the hell happened in here?' demanded the first.

'Maybe Lucille's got unfinished business,' said another.

'You don't believe in ghosts, Nadia.'

'Good thing, as we'd all be screwed, living in this place.'

'Body snatcher, if you ask me.'

'Hardly, Caruso. What would someone do with the rotted corpse of Lucille Versini?'

'Says the girl who used to sneak skulls into other people's beds just to mess with them.'

'That was Lark, you prick.'

'Help me with this top stone, Lisette.'

Sera scrunched her eyes shut, wishing she was a million miles from here. Ransom rested his chin on the crown of her head, his breath ruffling her hair.

There was more grunting and shuffling. A lot of cursing.

Then the groan of stone on stone as the lid was slowly hoisted back into place. It slid home with a final thud, and the Daggers poured out of the crypt as quickly as they arrived. They paused in the passageway before heading in the other direction, deciding to inspect Hugo's tomb while they were down here.

Sera sagged with relief. 'That was close.'

Ransom tapped his finger against her lip. A warning. *Hush.* She snapped her teeth, nipping it.

He dipped his chin, his lips brushing against her ear. 'If you want to kiss me, just say so.'

A delicious thrill rippled down her spine. *Yes*, her body screamed. *Yes, yes, yes.* She rose to her tiptoes, her nose brushing against his. 'You're projecting, Ransom. You know I prefer stabbing you.'

'Maybe you're right,' he said, returning his finger to her lips. He pressed gently, parting them. 'Maybe I want to know what that smart mouth tastes like.'

Her lips curved against his touch.

He pulled back, just enough that she could see his eyes. Molten, golden.

She tilted her chin up. 'Are you afraid, Dagger?'

He flashed his teeth, that feral smile weakening her knees. 'Did you forget that you're the one who's marked, spitfire?'

Her gaze returned to the scar on his lip. She was a heartbeat away from licking it when the voices returned. The Daggers were coming their way.

'Who wants to tell Dufort when he gets back?' said Lisette.

'Forget Dufort,' said Nadia, who seemed like the most sensible of the bunch. 'I need a drink. A stiff one.'

Caruso chuckled. 'I've got something stiff for— *oof.*'

They took off, winding up the stairs and out of earshot. Sera held her breath, expecting more people to arrive, but silence fell. Ransom broke it with a whisper. 'Two more minutes.'

She frowned. They had the journal, and now the coast was clear. 'Why do we need to wait—?'

'For this,' he said, kissing her.

Her breath caught as his lips brushed against hers. The kiss was soft and far too fleeting, the sudden absence of his touch wrenching a sigh from her.

He looked down at her, a question burning in his eyes.

She rose up, twisting her fingers in his collar. 'Yes,' she whispered against his lips.

He smiled, seizing another kiss. This one was all hunger, hot and rough and crushing. She threw her arms around his neck, banking herself against him as he slid his hands into her hair, holding her there as he parted her lips, deepening the kiss. She opened her mouth and his tongue brushed against hers, slow and skilful. She moaned at the dizzying rush of his desire. He devoured the sound.

The kiss grew fast and frenzied, her body erupting as his lips crashed against hers, like they could feel every second running out. She pulled back, gasping. He laid his forehead against hers, catching his breath.

'Three minutes?' he said, in a rasp.

'Four?' She leaned in, gently nipping his scar.

He shuddered against her, sliding his tongue into her mouth. Her knees trembled and she sagged against the wall.

He pinned her there, claiming her lips again and drinking down her desire.

'Five minutes,' he said, between ragged breaths.

Sera would have given him a hundred minutes in the dark. He kissed her senseless, until she forgot where she was entirely, until there was only the heat of his tongue in her mouth and the sound of his groans in her ear. Time slipped away, and they didn't chase it.

She surrendered to the Dagger, relieved to be outside her own head and only in her body as his lips found the sensitive spot beneath her ear and his strong hands roamed the swell of her curves. He trailed his tongue down her jaw, branding the column of her neck, then the slope of her shoulder. He kissed her languidly, dragging his teeth across her skin and wrenching a shiver from her. She raked her fingernails down his back, tugging him closer until his hardness pressed between her legs, offering the promise of more. She wanted more, she wanted *all* of him.

'*Seraphine.*' Her name in his mouth was a ragged plea. He whispered it onto her skin, along the curve of her cheek, against her lips, into her mouth.

She was half a heartbeat from dragging him down onto the dusty floor when she heard the sound of crumpling paper. She froze.

He stilled, his hands tightening on her waist. 'What is it?'

She pushed him away as reality crashed back in. In the frenzy of her lust, she had almost crushed Lucille's journal. She raked her hands through her hair, gulping down the cool air, as though it might quell the fire raging inside her.

What the hell was she doing?

She looked up at Ransom, and saw the same wildness in his eyes. He sucked in a breath. 'That was ...'

'A slight deviation from the plan,' she said.

'You have to get out of here,' he said, coming back to himself. He slung the cloak around her shoulders. 'Here. Put this on.'

Sera didn't dare look at him as he fastened it at her collar, too afraid she would fall back into his arms. A familiar coldness reached for her as she stepped back into the shadows. Alone, this time.

Ransom hurried along the passage, leading her up the stairwell that returned them to the main crossway. She followed at a distance, leaping from one shadow to the next, winding her way back towards the entrance of the catacombs. Clear-eyed Daggers came and went, nodding at Ransom in the flickering half-light – just as before – none the wiser about where he had come from. What he had done in the shadows, and with whom.

Soon, the entrance to Hugo's Passage was before them, crowned with that sickening archway of skulls. For the second time that night, Sera shoved away her revulsion. Ransom twisted a skull on the wall and the doorway groaned open, letting in a welcome breeze.

'Go,' he said, under his breath. 'And don't come back here.'

Sera grabbed his hand. He looked down, momentarily stilling at the sight of her small, pale fingers interlaced with his.

She caressed the shadow-mark along his thumb, then lifted it to her mouth. 'Thank you for helping me.'

'Go,' he said again, his eyes softening.

For once, she did as he asked. With Lucille's journal in her arms and the shadow of his kiss on her lips, she smiled all the way home.

Chapter 35

Ransom

R ansom watched Seraphine run away from him with a curious mixture of longing and relief. Their flirting had always felt like a dangerous game, but that kiss . . . that *heat* . . . there had been nothing playful about that. The press of her tongue against his and her ragged moans in his mouth had unravelled something deep and primal inside him. His sense of caution had gone up in smoke, his loyalty to Dufort along with it. Hell, he would have spun her back into the crypt and finished what they started in the tunnel if she hadn't pulled away when she did.

If that journal in her waistband hadn't reminded him of who and what she was: trouble.

Trouble fled from him now, without looking back.

Mercenary little spitfire. The entrance to Hugo's Passage closed with a resounding thud, sealing him inside.

'I wish I hadn't just seen that.' Nadia's voice made him jump. Ransom turned to find her leaning against the wall.

He closed his eyes. *Shit.*

'What the hell are you doing, Ransom?' He heard her stomp towards him. 'Tell me your mark wasn't just inside these catacombs. Tell me you didn't bring a Cloak into the inner sanctum of Hugo Versini. Tell me—'

'I can't.' He snapped his eyes open. 'And please keep your voice down before Lisette hears and comes sniffing around.'

'Only if you can make sense of what I just witnessed,' she said, prodding his chest. In all the time he had known Nadia, he had never seen her so furious. 'You've got ten seconds.'

He raked his hands through his hair, trying to make sense of it himself. 'She followed me down here. I didn't know, Nadia. And then by the time I noticed—'

'You were already breaking into Lucille Versini's crypt?'

It was an effort not to flinch at the searing realization of his own stupidity. 'She needed Lucille's journal,' he tried to explain. 'There are secrets hidden in there about a new kind of magic. The kind that can destroy the monsters of Fantome.' Nadia's eyes widened, until Ransom could see his reflection in them. He was wide-eyed, his hair unkempt, lips swollen. The more he talked, the more unhinged he sounded. But the power of Lightfire was real. He had *seen* it. It had blanched away one of his shadow-marks, had destroyed a monster in front of his eyes. 'She's the one who turned Kipp back into himself in that fountain. She pulled the monster off me. Seraphine saved my life.'

She sighed through her nose. 'You've named your mark.'

Ransom was way past naming her, but he wasn't about to tell Nadia that. He was in enough trouble already.

'She's always had a name,' he said evenly. 'She and I want the same thing, Nadia. We all do. Lightfire is the secret to saving the city.'

'Saving it from *what?*' Nadia dropped her voice, stepping closer in case the walls were listening. 'Because by the sounds of it, this new kind of magic destroys Shade. And Shade is *our* business, Ransom.'

He frowned. She wasn't getting it.

'What else can *Lightfire* do?' she said, hissing the word.

He recalled the moment the monster had knelt in the fountain, its face upturned to Seraphine like she was the second coming of Saint Celiana herself. That sense of reverent worship, as though this cursed, hulking beast was a soldier kneeling for its general. Unease turned his stomach. But— No. Seraphine had cured the monster. Freed it. She had returned Kipp to his body. It was a kindness. 'I trust her, Nadia.'

'Even after she used you to sneak down here?'

'She needed the journal,' Ransom repeated.

'She could have got you killed. Why didn't you just take it to her?'

His lips twisted, that trickle of unease getting harder to ignore. That was the plan, the promise he'd made her, but Seraphine hadn't believed him.

'If you really trusted each other, she would have waited for you to bring it to her,' said Nadia, as though she could read his thoughts. Thank the saints she couldn't see the memory of their kiss. Or what it was still doing to his insides. 'Unless this was about more than a journal,' she went on. 'Unless she wanted to get an inside look at our home. Get an idea of the passages, the Cavern, learn how to get around. You know, in case she decides to come back here with whatever *secret magic* you're helping her make.' She bit off a curse. '*Saints,* Ransom. You're supposed to be smart.'

'If she wanted to kill me, she would have let me drown in that fountain, Nadia.'

She folded her arms. 'Did it ever occur to you that you're not the one she wants? That maybe you're a stepping stone?'

He opened his mouth, then closed it. He didn't have a comeback. He wished he had a damn comeback.

Maybe Nadia was right. Maybe Seraphine had just played him like a fiddle. Maybe by helping her tonight, he had created a monster of his own. But *no* – he was the monster . He looked at his hands, marred by shadow-marks. Proof of his own depravity.

Nadia followed his gaze, and sighed. 'You don't have to be a Dagger to be a villain, Ransom.' She folded her hand around his, eclipsing his markings with her own. 'But if you want to survive down here, you have to think with your head and not your heart.'

'What heart?' he muttered, shaking her off.

For the first time in his life, he saw pity in his friend's eyes. 'Don't let a thorn in your side ruin your life.'

Too late. He swallowed the words. Seraphine was so much more than a thorn in his side. She was a thorn in his soul.

There came the sudden clack of footsteps. Lisette was stalking down the tunnel like a bloodhound on the scent.

'I'd better go cover for you,' said Nadia, throwing him a warning look. 'For the *last* time.'

'I'm sorry you got dragged into this, Nadia.'

'Not as sorry as I am.'

'Are you going to tell Lark when he gets back?'

'I'm sure as hell going to think about it,' she said, turning from him before he could read her face. 'And then I'm going to do what's best for you, Ransom. I'm going to do what's best for all of us.'

Ransom stared after her, his words dissolving on his tongue. *What if that's not the same thing any more?*

In the quietening dark, he slid to the floor and buried his head in his hands.

Chapter 36

Seraphine

The cloakroom at House Armand was locked when Seraphine returned from Hugo's Passage. She restrained herself from bursting into Theo's bedroom and waving Lucille's journal in his face, deciding she'd better make sure there was something useful inside it first.

Down in the kitchens, Val was sitting on the windowsill nursing a cup of tea as she watched the midnight rain. Thankfully, Sera had missed the worst of it on her way home, and the journal had stayed safe and dry under her clothes.

Pippin, who was snoozing at Val's feet, raised his head when she arrived.

'That took a lot longer than you said it would,' said Val, looking her up and down. 'How did it go?'

Sera sank into a chair, resolving to skate over the details for both of their sakes. 'I got the journal. But I don't know how useful it is yet.'

'You *are* a good Cloak.' Val smirked. 'How was your Dagger?'

Seraphine's cheeks burst into colour. The memory of their kiss struck her like a bolt of lightning as it had many times on the way home, her footsteps so light she felt like she was floating.

Val chuckled into her tea. 'You need to work on your poker face.'

Poker body. Even her toes were curling.

'You'd better hope Mercure doesn't find out. You're not supposed to sleep with the enemy.'

'We didn't.'

She slurped her tea. 'How *exactly* did you get the journal?'

'Please don't interrogate me. I'll fold like a napkin.'

'I'm not sure I even want to know,' she said, chuckling. 'You certainly look exhausted.'

'I am,' Sera admitted.

'Don't let me keep you up.' Val rested her head against the window, turning her gaze to the crescent moon.

Sera stood up, and Pippin hopped off the bench to join her. She paused on the threshold of the hallway, drawn to the faraway look in Val's eyes. In the fractured moonlight, her tinted hair shone violet, her brown skin glowed softly.

'Are you all right, Val?'

She nodded, absently. 'Just daydreaming.' Then as if remembering herself, she shot Sera a warning glance. 'Do *not* tell Bibi.'

'I think she already knows you're human.'

'It's my birthday tomorrow.'

'Oh. I had no idea.'

'I hate birthdays. They just remind me that I'm still stuck here.' She blew a curl from her eye. 'When I would rather be anywhere else.'

'Really?' said Sera. 'You seem so at home here.'

'You get tired of it after a while. This place stops feeling like a castle and starts feeling like a prison. And all these riches . . .' She jerked her chin towards the chandelier, gestured at the priceless vase by Sera's left elbow. 'They don't make up for what we've lost.'

Sera edged back into the room, careful not to break the spell of vulnerability that seemed to shimmer between them. All this time, she'd thought Val was impenetrable, unshakable. That she was born to be a Cloak and loved every minute of it, but now she could see they were more alike than she thought. Both of them were stuck in a place they didn't truly belong. 'You don't have to be a Cloak if you don't want to be, Val. You're smart enough to make it anywhere in the city.'

Val huffed a mirthless laugh. 'I'm not talking about House Armand, Sera. I'm talking about Fantome.' She looked up, fear pooling in her eyes. 'Can't you feel it? These creeping tendrils of darkness. They were here long before the monsters. If you ask me, this whole city is rotten to its core. The Cloaks are just one part of the problem.'

Sera was struck by Val's candour, how her words sounded so much like the things her mother used to say. On the surface, Fantome glittered like gold dust, but beneath the gleaming façade, the city reeked of fear and avarice. After all these centuries, it still languished in the long shadow of the Versini brothers' legacy. It had been damned long before Mama made those monsters. All they did was drag the terror of this place into the light, made it so that people could no longer look away from it.

'I didn't know you felt that way.'

'Most people feel this way,' said Val, with a shrug. 'They just make do with their lot in life because they're too afraid to try to change anything.'

'Why don't you leave Fantome? You must have saved enough money by now.'

Val's lips twisted. 'Being a Cloak is the only thing I've ever been good at.'

'It's also the only thing you've ever tried,' said Sera gently.

'Maybe I'll move to the plains.' Val conceded a fleeting smile. 'Do you reckon I'd make a good farmer?'

'You could try your hand at being a scarecrow. Just wave your arms about and scream really loudly whenever you see a blackbird.'

Val snorted, then chewed on her lip, as if she was really considering it. 'I suppose I can't decide which is better,' she confessed. 'Being alone somewhere beautiful and free. Or being with the only people I've ever loved, here in the darkness.' She looked up at Sera, as if she was waiting for the answer.

'I don't know either, Val.'

'Never mind. I'm overthinking everything. Birthdays always make me misty-eyed.'

'I can stay a while,' offered Sera. 'If you want to talk some more?'

Val waved her off, reaching for that mask of invulnerability, the careful smirk and deadpan voice, the veneer that told the world everything was all right, even when it wasn't. 'Go get your sleep, monster slayer. Sounds like things are about to get interesting.'

'Tomorrow's going to be a big day,' said Sera. 'I've got to make Lightfire *and* a birthday cake.'

'I didn't know you could bake,' said Val, almost suspiciously.

'I grew up on a farm in the middle of nowhere. What do you think I was doing all that time while Mama was making Shade?'

'Poisoning the wine?'

'Ha ha.' Sera stuck her tongue out. 'Laugh it up, but tomorrow, I'm going to bake the best damn cake you've ever had.'

'Looking forward to it,' said Val, a smile, true and beautiful, blooming across her face. Sera turned to leave, when she spoke again. 'I'm glad you came to House Armand, farmgirl. For however long, for whatever reason. It was getting boring around here. I reckon we needed a bit of excitement.'

Sera smiled. 'Thanks, Val. You're a good friend.'

'You too, Sera. Sleep well.'

Upstairs, with the embers of Val's words still warm in her chest, Sera washed and got ready for bed. Then she turned on her lamp and began to flick through the journal. It appeared to be a mix of Lucille's personal musings as well as notes on her studies at the Appoline – the contents varying from daily observations of her new life in Fantome to feverish scribblings about magic.

In the village, the elders speak of boneshade in hushed tones as if they're terrified that my brothers will hear them from half a world away. The plant comes from Halbracht, but it does not belong to us any more. Even Papa does not whisper of it. His eyes have grown tired, wary. He is as afraid of Hugo now as he is of the brown bears that stalk the Pinetops. The boneshade grows all around us, but we are forbidden from touching it. Even Armand will not suffer my curiosity about it.

That's how I know there are more secrets to be found. Not in the root, where the dark magic grows. But in the bloom, golden as the summer sun.

When I was a girl, Mama used to cut and dry the leaves, and lay them out along the chicken coop, until they grew crisp at the edges. Then she ground them into dust and stored the vials in the back of her closet, along with her treasured pearl necklace and the sapphire Father gave her the day they married. 'We must take care to hide the light, my little firefly,' she whispered to me once. 'Just in case the darkness returns...'

I know now what darkness she meant. It only occurred to me after her death that Mama knew of the properties of boneshade long before the rest of us. She must have known about the power of its bloom, too. Only she took that secret to her grave.

Sera's fingers were trembling so badly, the pages shook as she turned them. Lucille Versini had spent her short life chasing the secrets her mother had taken to the grave. In her neat, looping scrawl, Sera saw her own frustration and determination reflected back at her.

In Athapales' Study of Ancient Alchemy, the truth is set out plainly: there must be balance in all things. Every force of magic has its equal and opposite. We have known that since the Age of Saints. If darkness can grow from an ancient plant, then so, too, can light. I am surer now than ever before that this light magic - this antidote - resides in the bloom of boneshade. And more than that, it can be extracted just as Shade is. All it takes is an enquiring mind and a dauntless spirit.

I will bring the truth into the light, and shatter the darkness that hangs over my family name. And when I find this secret - this old magic made anew - I will call it Lightfire.

Sera turned the pages until she found the next mention of Lightfire. It was near the end of the journal.

Each day brings me closer to Lightfire. Today, with this mix of charcoal and bloom, I'm sure I felt a spark between my fingers- the warmth of something more than just heat. It was magic. I almost caught it. Tomorrow I will try again.

She turned to the last page, its edges crumbling in her fingers. Her eyes darted around, scanning the final feverish scrawlings of Lucille Versini, while the last embers of hope flickered inside her. And then she saw it, a single word circled under a list of crossed-out ingredients. It was darker than the others, as if it was demanding to be read:

Sera reeled backwards, as a memory exploded into her mind. A cloudless summer's day, the sun beating down on the plains and bleaching the stones in the garden. Her mother was hunched over her workbench, sweat matting her dark curls. She was tinkering with a strand of gold wire, surrounded by the remnants of the day's experimentation. And there, by her elbow, the head of a boneshade plant. Bloom. The leaves were dried and curling, shining golden in the sunlight. The smell of gunpowder lingered in the air. Sera knew it from the shotgun Lorenzo used to scare off the crows in the cornfields, but she couldn't seem to place it in their garden between the peonies and the honeybees. *What's that strange smell, Mama?*

Mama had smiled, excitement trilling in her voice. *That, my little firefly, is the smell of creativity.*

'No,' Seraphine muttered, with a sudden shock of clarity, and Pippin looked up from the end of the bed, to see if she was talking to him. 'That was the smell of Lightfire.'

Gunpowder and bloom. It was beautifully, blessedly simple.

A manic laugh bubbled out of her. 'I think we've cracked it, Pip.'

Pippin blinked once, then promptly fell asleep. Still fizzing with the triumph of her discovery, Sera ran to the window and peered out into the night. All was quiet, still. She reached for her pen and paper and scribbled a note.

Are you out there?

The dart soared over the hedge. She waited for ten minutes, then ten more. His reply never came. Ransom was not there, and his sudden yawning absence might have unsettled Sera if her thoughts weren't already turning to tomorrow, to the beginnings of hope rising before her like a new sun.

But when she dreamed, it was not of Lightfire, but the solid darkness of the catacombs and the feverish heat of his lips moving against her own.

Chapter 37

Seraphine

Sera was sitting cross-legged outside the cloakroom when Theo came down after breakfast the following morning.

'Well, this is unnerving,' he said, by way of greeting.

She grinned up at him, and said, 'Gunpowder.'

He stared down at her. 'I haven't had enough coffee for whatever this riddle is.'

'The secret ingredient is gunpower!' said Sera, leaping to her feet. 'I found Lucille's journal last night. I read it cover to cover.' She grabbed his shoulders and pulled him close. 'I've cracked the recipe!'

Theo blinked slowly, taking in her words. Then he braced his hands on her arms to stop her from shaking him. 'Please wait for my breakfast to settle. And how do you know I'm not busy today with other important top-secret business?'

Sera frowned. 'Are you?'

'Obviously not,' he said, grappling for his keys. 'Let's make some damn Lightfire.'

Sera skipped inside after him. The Shadowsmith had every tool and herb and powder at his disposal but when he opened the safe, revealing rows upon rows of Shade vials lined up like soldiers, Sera's fingers didn't itch to take one.

The darkness no longer interested her. Now, she sought the sun.

As Theo set to work, mixing and measuring, she drifted around the cloakroom, trying to find somewhere to settle. When he retrieved a small jar of gunpowder, she peered over his shoulder and immediately sneezed into it. It sent a cloud right up into his face.

He turned to glare at her. 'You don't have to sit on my shoulder like a parrot, Sera. I know what I'm doing.'

'Right. Sorry. I'm just trying to support you. Morally.'

'Why don't you morally support me by passing me a cloth?' he said, as politely as he could manage with a face full of gunpowder. 'And maybe get us some snacks. It's going to be a long day.'

Sera gasped. 'That reminds me, I have to make a cake! I'll be back in a couple of hours.'

'You better bring me a slice!' he called after her.

Sera was in such a good mood, she skipped upstairs, where she found Bibi practising the piano in the music room. She roped her into helping, both of them giggling like children as they clattered their way through the kitchens, searching for cake tins. Bibi borrowed an apron from Alaina, who only surrendered it after they disappeared together into the storeroom for a suspiciously long time.

A couple of hours later, Sera sprinkled a final dusting of cocoa powder over a slightly lopsided fudge cake filled with chocolate buttercream and drizzled with ribbons of caramel. She carried it down to the cloakroom, while Bibi went to fetch Val.

When Sera nudged the door open, Theo was standing with his hands braced against the island. He was leaning over a clay bowl full of gold powder that was sparkling all on its own. Sera set the cake down. 'Is that—?'

'Lightfire,' he murmured.

She came to his side, not daring to breathe as she peered into the bowl. 'Can you hear that?' she said, leaning in. 'It's crackling.'

'Careful,' he said, tugging her back. 'It's raw. Which means it's volatile. I've already burned my fingers three times. We have to figure out what to do with it. And then how to use it to get rid of all those monsters.'

Absently, Sera reached for the ghost of her necklace, her mother's words ringing in her head: *And when the time comes, you will rise far above this wicked city and become a flame in the dark. You will be the Aurore, Seraphine.*

Her spine tingled as an idea unfurled, and she wondered if it had been there all along, hiding in the recesses of her soul, waiting to be discovered.

'We'll use the Aurore,' she said, looking at Theo.

His eyebrows rose, and he stared past her as he made sense of her idea, drawing a picture of it in his mind: the great tower of Fantome, a monument to the lost age of the saints, burning again with new magic. Three tiers glowing with Lightfire, and all those monsters turning their faces to it, finding their salvation.

'You are clever,' he murmured, a smile curling on his face.

Seraphine grinned right back. 'All we have to do is find a way to get them all to Primrose Square.'

A furrow appeared between his brow. 'I'll think of something. Just give me a few days.'

Sera nodded. A few more days and, if Saint Oriel smiled on them, it would all be over. The monsters would be destroyed at last, and Mama's legacy would be fulfilled.

Except . . . except that wasn't quite true.

There was one part of the plan that still needed to be . . . finessed. After all, Mama hadn't made all those monsters just to free them. She had made them to kill an even greater one:

Gaspard Dufort.

Seraphine did not yet know how she would deal with the Head of the Daggers, but one thing was cold and sharp and certain: for as long as Dufort drew breath, she would never truly be free. That meant he had to die, along with the monsters.

And one way or another, she would see to it.

The door flew open and Bibi hurried inside, unwittingly yanking Sera from her spiralling thoughts of revenge.

'The birthday girl is here!' she announced, just as Val stepped inside, looking rather embarrassed about the whole affair.

Sera grabbed the cake, holding it aloft. There wasn't time for candles, and if they chanced the Lightfire in its current crude form, the cake would probably explode.

'Happy birthday, Val!'

'Let's sing!' said Bibi, clapping her hands.

'This is so embarrassing,' said Val, but she couldn't fight her smile as they launched into song. When it was over, she pulled her curls back and mimed blowing out the non-existent candles, while Bibi produced a knife and several forks from her back pocket.

'The test is the taste,' said Val, shooting a smile at Sera as she cut the first slice. 'Let's see if it lives up to your word.'

'Just know that it's made with love,' said Bibi. 'And a sprinkling of my incompetence. There might be a few eggshells in there.'

'For luck,' added Sera, feeling a flurry of nerves as she watched Val take a bite. In such a short space of time, these people had become unimaginably important to her, and maybe it was silly, but she felt like this cake was her way of trying to show them that.

Val closed her eyes, licking the caramel from her lips. 'It's so good, I think I might levitate.'

Sera beamed. Theo and Bibi grabbed their forks, digging into the cake with gusto. They clustered around the island, feasting and chatting, and teasing Val, who despite her protestations, seemed to be enjoying her birthday – and the corresponding attention – very much. Theo fished a bottle of sparkling wine from a nearby cupboard, and sent the cork bouncing off the ceiling.

Val swiped the bottle, taking the first sip. 'You were right about that cake, farmgirl. It's the best I've ever had.'

'Don't tell Alaina that,' said Bibi, going for her second slice. 'I've been enjoying her good mood lately.'

'I know,' said Val pointedly. 'My room is right next to yours.'

Bibi's blush was so violent, it swallowed her freckles. 'Moving swiftly along . . . How goes the Lightfire?'

'See for yourselves.' Theo set the bowl down in the middle of the island, and they all leaned in, peering at the gold dust, as if they might find their futures glittering inside it.

'Whoa,' muttered Bibi.

'What are we going to do with it?' said Val, poking her finger inside the bowl.

Theo swatted it away. 'First, we have to find a way to use it without accidentally killing ourselves in the process. And then, we're going to destroy the monsters of Fantome and liberate the city.' He rolled back on his heels, looking at Sera. 'Easy enough, right?'

She told them about her idea of using the Aurore, and was relieved when they jumped at the chance to be part of her plan. It would be a thrill to be the heroes of Fantome for one night, and not just the thieves who crept about in its shadows.

The following day passed in torrential rain. While Theo flitted around the cloakroom in various states of stress, Sera, Val and Bibi came down to keep him company, chatting and laughing the hours away. Every so often, a wayward spark or minor explosion would yank them back to reality, but Theo would simply smile, assuring them it was all part of the process.

They broke for lunch and again for dinner, poring over their plan for the Aurore as more rain bucketed down. For three nights in a row Sera sat on her bedroom windowsill and waited for Ransom, tracing rivers of rainwater down the pane, but the ceaseless torrent kept him away. Meanwhile, down in the basement, Theo worked relentlessly into the night, brewing enough Lightfire to fill every flaming trough on the Aurore.

Sera didn't dare risk returning to Old Haven to tell Ransom of their progress but as her worry about Dufort – and what exactly she was going to do about him – festered, she found herself wondering if the answer to her problem might lie with the Dagger she had befriended. If the man who yearned for freedom just as sorely as she did, might help her one more time.

If he might help himself.

On the fourth night after dinner, while Bibi and Val joined the other Cloaks for music and dancing in the drawing room, Sera brought Pippin for a walk in the garden, taking advantage of a brief break in the foul weather. It was there that Theo found her.

'I thought you'd be upstairs dancing,' he called from the doorway. His silver hair was unkempt and dark circles pooled under his eyes. Even from across the garden, she could feel the adrenaline rolling off him. She knew that look, sensed the rattle of giddiness in his bones. She had sensed it in Mama more times than she could count.

'I felt guilty dancing while you were working,' she said, holding up a pine cone. 'Do you want to play fetch with us?'

His chuckle reached her on the wind. 'I have something better in mind. Come find me when you're done. I want to show you something.'

When Sera returned to the cloakroom, Theo was holding

a cloak in his hand. Only this one was different from the hundreds that hung around him. It wasn't true black. Rather, it shimmered softly under the lights, giving off the faintest glimmer of gold. When Sera brushed her fingers along it, they warmed, as though she was holding her hand up to a fire.

'Is that—?'

'Yes, it is,' he said, with a grin. A cloak of Lightfire. A cloak of flame. He nudged it towards her. 'I used your measurements.'

She practically leaped into the cloak, feeling like her heart might burst. A delicious thrill rippled up her spine as the material fluttered against her skin, warm and sure, and for the first time in forever, she felt utterly at peace, as though she was exactly where she was supposed to be. In this place, in this cloak.

'It feels incredible,' she said, drawing it tighter.

'Now, let's see what it can do,' Theo said eagerly.

Giddiness bubbled through her. 'Hide-and-seek?'

He was already slipping into his black cloak. He winked, then leaped into a nearby shadow and disappeared completely. 'Catch me if you can!'

Sera pressed her hand against the shadow and the darkness dissolved at her touch. He was standing before her again, grinning from ear to ear.

She grinned back. 'Easy.'

He lunged for another. She dissolved that one too. He ran and she chased, catching him over and over, until she was laughing so hard she couldn't stop. The exhilaration was dizzying. The cloak of Lightfire was far more powerful than the tiny teardrop she had worn around her neck. She was wrapped inside the magic now. Enveloping her, it became a part of her.

With the cloak around her shoulders, the shadows could not touch her. *Shade* could not touch her. The darkness was hers to destroy. The light hers to wield.

When she caught Theo for the ninth time, he threw his hands up, delighted by his own defeat. 'At least we know it works against the shadows in here,' he said, scanning the room as they slowly regathered on the walls. 'Let's hope it will work with the monsters, the same way your necklace did.'

'It will,' said Sera, every inch of her skin tingling with confidence. 'I really think our plan is going to work. I think we're ready.'

Almost, cautioned a voice in her head.

Concern flitted across Theo's face. 'Are you sure you want to be the one to lead the monsters—?'

'I'm sure,' she said. 'We'll do it tomorrow at nightfall.'

He retrieved a small wooden chest from a nearby shelf. 'I made these, too,' he said, removing the lid. 'Inspired by your mother's necklace. Just in case anything goes wrong and you need a little extra help.'

The chest contained fifteen or so unstrung pearls, each one emitting a soft glow. Sera plucked a single pearl and felt it warm in her hand. 'What exactly do they do?'

'I'm not entirely—'

She flung it at the wall.

'Sera!'

There was a sudden blinding flash of light. A gust of warm air rippled over them, the entire room flaring so bright, it stung tears into Sera's eyes. The darkness shattered, and for ten long heartbeats, it felt like the sun itself had exploded in front of them.

And then it was over.

She looked down to find Theo crouched on the floor, covering his eyes.

'Very cool,' she said.

He glared up at her. 'Don't ever do that again.'

She extended a hand to him. 'I won't. At least, not to you.'

He stood up, sweeping the hair from his forehead. Then he shut the chest and locked it. Sera removed her Cloak and laid it alongside the pearls.

'Tomorrow night, then,' he murmured.

'Tomorrow,' she said, blowing out a breath. She took courage in the glimmer of Lightfire between them, in Mama's words repeating like a mantra in her mind: *When the time comes, you will rise far above this wicked city and become a flame in the dark.*

Saint Oriel had got them this far. Sera just had to go a little further.

Chapter 38

Seraphine

Ransom came to her later that night, as though he could sense the threads of her plan coming together. Or perhaps it was the break in the torrential rain that let him finally venture beyond the shelter of Hugo's Passage. Whatever the reason, Seraphine's heart leaped when she spotted him outside her window, pacing in the dark.

Tonight, she didn't reach for her pen. Instead, she tugged a sweater on over her pyjamas and laced up her boots before hurrying downstairs. She ran for the gate, silently thanking Saint Maurius for holding off the rain.

Ransom was leaning against the wall across the street, his quicksilver eyes shamelessly drinking her in as she locked the gate behind her.

'You came back,' she called out.

He cocked his head. 'After that kiss, did you really think I could stay away?'

She grinned as she jogged to meet him.

He stiffened, raising his hands. 'Careful. I've taken Shade.'

'I can see that,' she said, stopping a foot in front of him. 'You look like you've swallowed the moon.'

'I wish I could spit it back out again,' he said, frowning. 'I didn't expect you to come outside. I thought you would write . . .' He bit off a swearword. 'Now, I can't even touch you.'

Sera almost laughed. How far they had come in just a few short weeks. From wanting to murder each other to wanting to . . . well, just *wanting*.

'I'll try not to tempt you too much,' she said, flashing him a wicked grin as she turned and beckoned him to follow her.

'Impossible task,' he said as he pushed off the wall. 'Even the back of your head is mesmerizing.'

Sera snorted, glad he couldn't tell how violently she was blushing. She led him to the end of the street, far from the glare of House Armand and through a thicket of trees so old they used to shed their leaves during the Age of Saints. They crowded in on her, tall and gnarled and creaking in the rising wind. Mulch clung to her boots as she wove between the trunks, seeking out the small clearing she had discovered not long ago with Pippin.

Ransom followed her, his shadows trailing behind him and upending the fallen leaves. 'If I didn't know better, I'd swear you were luring me into this forest to kill me.'

'I can think of far better things to do with you in this forest,' she tossed over her shoulder, swinging her hips for good measure.

He stifled a groan. 'You promised not to tempt me.'

She smirked at him. 'I was referring to the art of conversation.'

'Like hell you were.'

By the time they reached the clearing, a chill had settled into Sera's bones. Her breath clouded as she pulled her arms around herself, regretting not grabbing a coat on her way out.

Ransom frowned as he looked her over. 'I should be warming you up.'

'I'm fine,' she said, waving his concern away. She cleared her throat, coming to her news. 'We figured it out, Ransom. We cracked the recipe for Lightfire. I've been waiting to tell you.'

Waiting for you to come to me.

'Sorry. I've been avoiding the Hollows,' he said uneasily. 'Lark's been on my ass since he got back from Bellevue Castle and I was afraid he'd follow me here.'

Lark. Sera turned the name over in her mind, trying to imagine the pair of silver eyes that went with it. 'Is he another player in the game?'

A grim nod. 'You're his mark now too. And we have a deadline.'

Sera leaned against a tree to steady herself. Just when she had scrambled out from under one assassin, she found another waiting in the wings. She would never be free of the Daggers. She would never be free of Dufort. 'Ransom, there's something I—'

'I'm going to talk to Dufort,' he said at the same time. 'I'm going to ask him to let you go.'

Sera's eyes widened in horror. In three quick strides she was on him. If it hadn't been for the wall of shadows that surged up between them, she might have shaken him in her urgency. 'Have you lost your mind?'

'I think I've finally found it.' He set his jaw, resolute in his decision, and Sera got the sense he had spent the last few nights poring over it. 'Once the monsters are gone, the city will go back to the way it was. Whatever ... hatred Dufort held for your mother will die, along with the monsters she made. It doesn't have to damn you, too. I won't let it. When I speak to Dufort, when I reason with him—'

'He'll kill you too,' she cut in. 'You're not thinking clearly, Ransom.'

His frown sharpened. 'I'm thinking clearly for the first time in ten years, Seraphine.'

She was already shaking her head. 'It's not going to work. And if you try, you'll only damn yourself.'

'Then I'll damn myself.' He bit off a curse. 'Or maybe I'll tell him you're already dead. Leave the city, Seraphine, lie low somewhere up north. Eventually he'll forget about you.'

'He won't,' she said, with rising frustration.

'Of course he will,' he retorted, just as hotly. 'Do you know how many marks Dufort presides over at any given time? How many Daggers work under him? You're just one wayward farmgirl from the plains.'

'You don't know him like I do,' Sera snapped.

'I've known him for half my life,' he snapped back. 'He's like a father to me.'

Sera released a strangled laugh.

'In six months he won't even remember your—' Ransom began.

'STOP!' The word exploded from her with such force, he stumbled backwards. Shadows swarmed the clearing, flaring behind him like a terrifying pair of wings. But Sera was not afraid of him. She was afraid of his naivety. She was afraid of what Dufort would do to him because of it. 'Just . . . *stop*.'

He stared at her, hurt and confusion in his eyes.

'Gaspard Dufort is never going to forget about me,' she said again. Slowly. 'There's nowhere I can go that will ever be far enough away from him. Not while he has the king's ear. Not while he holds Fantome in his fist.'

Ransom stilled. 'Why?'

Such a small, quiet word.

Above them, the clouds opened, scattering rain across the clearing. A gauze of mist fell and it seemed to Sera that a part of Ransom already knew exactly what she was going to say. His body had already stiffened to weather the blow, his bright eyes wide and unblinking.

She made her tongue work, forcing the words out before shame got the better of her. 'Because Gaspard Dufort is my father.'

Silence swept through the clearing.

Ransom stood frozen. The only sign he had heard her at all was the pooling of shadows at his feet and the horror in his silver eyes.

'So if he truly is like a father to you,' she went on, in a cold voice, 'then you should know he likes to kill his own children when they get in his way.'

Ransom's eyelids fluttered.

Sera swallowed, ignoring the silent river of her tears as

he stared and stared at her. Waiting for her to take it back. To smile and say it was a sick joke. But the truth had sat in her heart for so long, it had begun to crush her. The man who had once held her as a baby, rocked her in her crib and sung lullabies to her at night, the man who had loved her to distraction – who had loved her mother to ruin – was the same man that Ransom thought of as a father.

But Dufort was no father. He was incapable of thinking beyond his own desire. The lure of the Daggers had snatched him away before Sera had learned to walk, and all those years he spent descending the ladder into darkness, her mother had fought to pull him back up. She had fought to scour away the shadows that barbed his heart, only to fail. Only to die.

Gaspard Dufort did not want to be saved. He wanted to rule, like a king. And he was willing to cut down anyone foolish enough to stand in his way.

'Aren't you going to say something?' said Sera, hating the yawning silence.

'If I *speak* ...' said Ransom very, very slowly. Darkness swarmed the clearing, the gathering tide of his anger. A branch snapped behind him, torn to the ground by one of his shadows. And he hadn't so much as blinked. 'If I even dare to *move* right now, I'm afraid I might tear this entire forest down so I can shove every fucking branch down that bastard's throat.'

The wind howled and the earth shook, the leaves trembling at their feet. But Sera wasn't scared. She marvelled at the fullness of his power, and how it tangled with his emotions. 'You're angry.'

His nostrils flared. 'There is no word for the depth of this feeling, Seraphine.' His voice was as cold as death, the forest so dark, she had to strain to see him. 'Rage. Horror. Betrayal … *Rage.*'

'Don't hide it,' she said, quietly. 'Let me see you.'

He opened his fist and the shadows receded in a rush, rustling the leaves as they scattered. His gaze softened as it found hers, and now the look on his face was one of pain.

'I don't understand,' he said, his voice barely more than a whisper. 'Please help me understand.'

She blew out a breath, the rain spattering her cheeks as she slumped against the tree. It was such a long and awful story, and she hated it almost as much as she hated her father. She hated that once upon a different lifetime, he might have been a good man. That the three of them might have lived a happy life together, far from the darkness that had destroyed them. She hated it so much she tried not to think of it at all. She certainly never spoke of it. But for this moment, and this man, she blew the cobwebs off the sorry tale her mother had told her only once, a very long time ago.

'My parents met over twenty years ago in a tavern in the Hollows,' she said with a sigh. 'A pair of orphans, both barely seventeen. They were runaways, searching for a better life. They saw each other across the bar and that was it. They danced all night and fell in love by morning.' She gave a little shrug. 'I suppose it was simple at the start.'

Ransom wasn't blinking.

'They found salvation in each other, a reprieve from the shitty childhoods they'd crawled their way out of. Two lost souls, bound up in each other. They decided they would make something of themselves together. A family. Then a fortune. But for a pair of orphans with no schooling or real-life experience, the only way to survive in the Hollows was to turn to Shade. So, that's what they did.' Sera didn't blame them for it, even now.

'Only my . . . Dufort wasn't content with smuggling. Every time he bottled Shade, his fingers itched to try it. To taste it.' She closed her eyes, cursing her father's avarice. 'It changed him. It changed who he wanted to become. It wasn't enough to be a good husband or a loving father any more. To have a house out in the plains, a good horse, and a field of sheep . . . He wanted a dynasty. He wanted to be remembered.'

She raked her damp hair from her face, turning her gaze to the shadows at Ransom's feet. They were creeping closer, as if they were listening to her story.

'So, my father became a Dagger. And he was good at it. Really good.' Her lip curled, and she didn't bother to hide her disgust. 'And then he changed some more. He stopped laughing and started shouting. He stopped kissing Mama and stared hitting her. Stopped playing teddies with me and started shaking me like one. He got cruel . . . violent.' A shudder wracked her, and Ransom jerked forward, his hands outstretched, before remembering the poison inside him.

He stalled a foot away.

'Mama kicked him out. She kept working but she refused to sell to his Order. She didn't want him anywhere near me. Near her. We moved again and again, but he always found us. He wanted her to know that no matter where we went or how far we travelled, we still belonged to him. Sometimes, I think it was a game to him. A chase.' Her voice broke and she pressed her fists against her eyes, trying to blanch away all those memories of him stomping back into their lives, sending the birds skittering to the skies with the boom of his voice. 'I wish we'd gone further. Gone north over the mountains and through the low hills, travelled until the road ran out and taken a boat over the horizon. But Shade was all Mama knew. It was our livelihood. And he would have found us eventually.'

Ransom was so still, he looked like a statue, but the sadness in his eyes told Sera he was listening, that he understood.

'At first, Mama thought she could save him from himself.' It was so crushingly obvious to Sera now, so heart-rendingly simple ... That light in her mother's heart, the flame that *he* had kindled in that tavern all those years ago had become the first spark of her ambition. 'When that didn't work, she tried to save us from him. I think that's why she became so obsessed with Lucille Versini, why she was so hell-bent on rediscovering Lightfire.'

'An antidote,' said Ransom, softly. 'All Lucille ever wanted was to save her brothers from the darkness.'

Sera nodded. 'But the closer Mama got to that recipe, the closer *he* got to her ...' She lifted her chin, finding the silver in his eyes fading, shards of green and gold shining through. 'My father didn't want to be free, Ransom. He didn't want to let go of his power.' She raked her gaze over the black marks on his neck, the inky spill across his hands, and knew that while Ransom had grown to hate his shadow-marks, Dufort wore his own like badges of honour.

'When he changed – when he got cruel – that hope in Mama turned to rage. She realized that the man she fell in love with was never coming back. That this new one, this Dagger, was a danger to us. And as long as he lived, we would never truly be free of him.'

Ransom was nodding now. Hadn't he lived through some version of this himself? Hadn't he killed his own father for the same reason?

'Mama knew she would have to destroy Dufort to save us. So, she made monsters to bring him to heel. Discovered the secret of Lightfire and set the stage for his demise.' Sera's heart felt so hollow now she pressed a hand against it just to feel it beat. 'But he got to her first.'

Ransom looked away, hissing a curse.

'And now he's going to kill me,' she finished, through chattering teeth. 'And there is nothing you can do to stop him.'

They were both soaked to the bone, the rain falling so hard she struggled just to make out his expression.

He raked his hands through his sodden hair. 'Seraphine.' Her name broke on his lips. She could feel him straining against the last of that Shade, aching to hold her. 'I'm sorry,' he whispered. 'I'm so sorry. I know that life you lived. That brand of fear is worse than any shadow. Stronger than any magic. I'm sorry for all of it. For my part in it.'

She inched closer. There was such anguish on his face now. It burned through the last of his Shade and then his eyes were clear, and he was looking at her as though he could see her – truly, fully – for the first time.

He reached for her and she went to him, crying as he folded her into his arms and pressed his lips to her hair. 'I won't let him hurt you again. I swear it.'

She laid her forehead against his chest and listened to the thunder of his heartbeat. 'Then bring him to me,' she said, against the damp planes of his chest. 'Tomorrow when the clock tower strikes ten, bring Dufort to the entrance to Hugo's Passage.'

She didn't say the rest – what she planned to do with all those monsters before she got rid of them, the freedom she intended to wrest from her father's cold dead hands. She didn't have to tell Ransom that. He heard it in her voice. He had done the same thing to his own violent father ten years ago.

'*Please,*' she said.

She scrunched her eyes shut, listening to the sawing of his breath as she waited for his answer . . . It seemed to take an age, the rain falling with a vengeance, the mud thickening beneath their boots. And then he sighed and gripped her tighter, whispering into her hair.

'I'll bring him to you.'

She curled her fists in his collar and dragged his mouth to hers, the press of her lips saying the words for her. *Thank you, thank you, thank you.*

He raised his hands to cup her face, drawing back from her just enough that she could look up at him. Droplets hung from his dark lashes and slid like tears down his cheeks.

'I'll help you,' he murmured, kissing her softly. 'We'll help each other.'

She traced the whorl of black along his collarbone, then pressed a kiss there. He groaned into her hair. She took his hands in hers, and brushed her mouth against those too. Slowly, gently, her lips skimmed his rain-spattered skin, every kiss a promise of freedom.

'Seraphine.' Her own name was a promise on his lips. 'My spitfire.'

Moonlight shone through a broken cloud and flooded the clearing, as though the saints themselves were peering down on them. As they stood together in the rain, shivering between soft, stolen kisses, Sera couldn't help but think there was an air of destiny about this moment too.

Chapter 39

Ransom

Ransom could have stood in that clearing with Seraphine all night, with nothing but the rain sliding between them, but by the time she finished her story, she was shivering so badly, she could hardly speak.

Nothing could have prepared him for her earth-shattering confession, the sickening truth that the man who had taken him in ten years ago and cared for him like a son was the same man who had terrorized his own daughter her entire life.

Seraphine was Dufort's daughter, and the rotten bastard had made a mark of her. Then he had handed that mark to Ransom, like a prize. The promise of the signet ring he wore on his left hand, and everything it stood for, because he was too much of a coward to do it himself.

The whole thing was so twisted that during the first half of

Seraphine's confession, Ransom had thought the bonfire of his rage would burn him to ash. It was an effort to stay and listen rather than stalk all the way back to Hugo's Passage and slam Dufort up against the wall to bleed the same confession from him.

Ransom was dimly aware he shouldn't care this much about their connection. The depth of his Order's depravity was hardly a surprise to him. He had seen enough, *doled out* enough, not to be surprised by anything. Lark wouldn't have batted an eyelid at Seraphine's confession, would have killed her anyway, but then, thoughts of Seraphine Marchant didn't haunt Lark to distraction.

Lark didn't know that she was quick-witted and sharp-tongued, that she was twice as foolhardy as she was headstrong, and more soft-hearted than she would ever admit. That she was reckless and beautiful in equal measure. That she kissed like it was her last gasp on earth, and moaned like a song.

Lark hadn't pressed her up against the walls of the catacombs and let her kiss him into oblivion. And he sure as hell hadn't just bartered a decade of loyalty to Dufort for the promise of freedom glowing in her eyes.

And besides all that, Lark's father had been a good man. Ransom's father had been just like Dufort. That was the worst part. The startling realization that Dufort was the very thing Ransom had run away from all those years ago. That for all his kindness to Ransom, he was no better than the brute who had torn Ransom's family apart.

Only the sight of Seraphine trembling like a leaf before him had pulled Ransom from the tornado of his anger. Her eyes had silvered with tears, her mouth quivering as she poured the truth at his feet. At the sight of her distress, all that anger inside him buckled.

It was a relief when the Shade left him so he could hold her. It was easy to promise he would help her, that he would bring Dufort to her tomorrow night and let her finish what her mother started.

But as Ransom walked Seraphine back to House Armand and turned for the long journey home, rain-soaked and shivering, he was needled by the depth of the betrayal he had agreed to and wondered if Dufort truly was beyond reason. If the only pathway to freedom was over his dead body.

He had to find out for himself.

Back in Old Haven, Ransom stalked into Hugo's Passage like a beast on the hunt. The catacombs were largely deserted, the hour so late now that even the Cavern was empty. No sign of Dufort, which was probably a kindness of fate. If Ransom ran into the Head of the Daggers right away, he would have lost that tenuous grip on his temper. And who would that have helped? Not Seraphine, and right now, she was the only person he cared about. He wanted to make sure she was safe.

Instead, he went to Lark's room, knocked twice, got impatient and barrelled inside. Lark cursed as he leaped out of bed, completely naked. He lunged for his robe, and Ransom blinked at another muffled sound of surprise, and belatedly realized there was someone else in his friend's bed. Another blink revealed Nadia, who had pulled the sheets up to the bridge of her nose, her wide brown eyes peering out over the top.

'Fuck— Sorry.' Ransom backed out of the room. 'I didn't realize— I didn't know.'

'One second.' Lark turned to mutter something to Nadia then joined Ransom in the hall, shutting the door behind him. 'What the hell happened to you tonight?' he hissed, looking him up and down. 'Don't tell me you went fishing for bodies in another fountain.'

Ransom frowned at the barb. 'It's raining.'

'No shit.'

There was an awkward stretch of silence.

'I knew you were taking tonight off,' said Ransom, slowly. 'But I didn't realize you two were ...'

'Living the dream?' Lark's tone was teasing but his green eyes were bright. He had been pining after Nadia for years, and now he wore the unmistakable look of a man in love.

Ransom couldn't keep the shock from his voice. 'How long have you two been ...?'

'A few months,' said Lark, his gaze softening. 'Best ones of my life.'

'Right.' Ransom couldn't keep the hurt from his voice. His two best friends had been sneaking around for *months* and they hadn't bothered to tell him.

'Don't look so bereft,' said Lark, clapping him on the shoulder. 'Even best friends lie to each other sometimes. I was going to tell you.'

'When?'

'When you came to tell me you were in love with your mark,' said Lark.

Ransom stared at him. Lark stared right back.

Of course Nadia had told him about the other night in the catacombs, probably sang for him like a canary the second he returned with Dufort. They had probably laughed over what a fucking idiot Ransom was.

'It's not like that,' said Ransom weakly.

'Whatever it *is* like, you better figure out a solution,' said Lark, prodding his chest. 'Either kill her or get her out of this city. If Dufort catches wind of what you're doing with *our* mark, it'll be your head *and* hers on a big fucking platter. And I'm not about to join that dinner party. One way or another, she has to disappear.'

Just a handful of minutes ago, Ransom had been teetering on the edge of telling Lark everything – about Seraphine and Dufort, and the life-altering promise he had just made her.

But now, looking at his friend in the dimness and realizing there were things about Lark and Nadia he didn't know – trust that he clearly hadn't earned from them – he decided he would say nothing. For his sake. And for Seraphine's.

Even best friends lie to each other sometimes.

He dipped his chin. 'Give me a few days, Lark. I'll figure it out.'

'You'd better,' said Lark, before turning on his heel and going back to Nadia.

Ransom went to his bedroom and opened Seraphine's music box. For a long time, he sat on the edge of his bed, watching that ballerina twirl as he listened to the music of his childhood, this lullaby of freedom. He wanted it now more than ever. Not just the freedom, but the girl as well.

They already shared a lullaby. Why not a dream, too?

He slept fitfully that night, the weight of his promise to Seraphine sitting like a tombstone on his chest. He awoke after midday, emerging bleary-eyed from his bedroom to forage for food.

There was no sign of Dufort anywhere, and short of knocking on every door in the passage or scouring the seedy streets of the city, Ransom could only wait for him to come back. Hours passed in the Cavern with only a deck of cards, a tumbler of brandy and his own addled thoughts as company, until Lisette came to bother him.

'You look even more haunted than usual,' she said, perching on the side of his armchair. 'Are the skulls beginning to frighten you?' She fingered the tassel of his cushion. 'Don't worry, when I become Head of the Order, I'll give this place a little sprucing up. Maybe plant a herb garden.'

When Ransom didn't bother to reply, only finished his drink and stared past her towards the door, she poked him in the shoulder. 'What's the matter? Farmgirl swallowed your tongue?'

It was an effort not to shove her off the armrest. 'Go back to your gossip mill, Lisette.'

'You used to be fun,' she said, flicking him in the cheek.

'Do you know where Dufort is?'

'Last I saw, he was in the graveyard,' she said, evidently deciding to be helpful for once. 'Being *pensive*. Meeting the king always puts him in a shit mood. I swear he's jealous of that big shiny crown.'

Ransom shot to his feet and made for the door, leaving her glowering at the back of his head. Above ground, dusk was sweeping through Fantome, the sky blooming like a fresh bruise. Though the rain had abated some time that afternoon, thunderclouds prowled overhead, the humidity so oppressive he felt like he was moving through steam.

Dufort was exactly where Lisette said he would be, perched at the far end of the graveyard, between weathered tombstones that jutted up from the earth like rotting teeth. He was sitting under a moss-eaten statue of Saint Calvin of Death, his eyes closed as though he was saying a prayer.

Dufort looked up at the sound of Ransom's footsteps and said, by way of greeting, 'There's a storm coming.'

Yes, there is.

Ransom looked down at the Head of the Daggers and was surprised at how swiftly his rage returned. The sight of those cornflower-blue eyes staring back at him, the wheat-blonde hue of that shorn hair – it was so obvious.

He blinked slowly.

I am such an idiot.

Seraphine had inherited few of her mother's characteristics, save for that shining fleck of bronze in her eye. The rest had come from Dufort, and it was so searingly obvious to him now that he couldn't have doubted her confession even if a small part of him desperately wanted to.

'Why do you look like you've swallowed a fucking thorn bush?' said Dufort, scrunching up his face to mock him.

'I want to talk to you about my mark,' said Ransom without preamble.

Dufort frowned. 'Is she dead?'

'No.' He watched Dufort swallow, noted his fingers twitching on his lap. 'Why do you want her dead, Gaspard?'

'What did Hugo Versini say about curiosity, Ransom?'

'Why do you want her dead?' Ransom said again.

Dufort scrubbed a hand across his face, so much calmer without Shade in his system. 'I'd rather not get into it.'

'Get into it,' said Ransom, holding his nerve. 'Please.'

Thunder rumbled in the distance as though the saints themselves were echoing his request.

Perhaps that's why Dufort gave in. 'Sylvie was working on something that could destroy everything our Order stands for. A kind of magic that can take the very core of our power and nullify it. Nullify us. She had been meddling from afar for years, and I suppose the fool in me let her get away with it.' He paused, a flicker of some unchartered emotion passing behind his eyes. Nostalgia . . . Or perhaps it was the remnants of love. He blinked the moment away. 'But Lightfire . . .' His lip curled. 'No. I could not abide it.'

Ransom was so surprised Dufort knew the name of Sylvie's magic that his eyebrows shot up.

'Destructive stuff, *Lightfire*,' he went on, spitting the word. 'Mark my words, Ransom, if it ever got out, it would be our undoing.'

Ransom had to work to keep his face neutral. 'What does any of that have to do with the girl?'

Dufort looked away. 'The girl holds her mother's secrets. She has to go too. The longer she stays at House Armand with Mercure, the more danger we're in.'

Ransom let the silence swell, giving Dufort the chance to fill it with the confession he had come for. That Seraphine Marchant was his daughter, that the thought of killing her filled him with guilt, or inspired even the slightest hesitation. Dufort conceded nothing.

'What if she left Fantome?' said Ransom, because he had to know if there was another way to free her. If Dufort could be reasonable, just this once, he could save his own life. 'What if she took those secrets and disappeared?'

'Then *you* would find yourself in a world of trouble.' Dufort's gaze sharpened as he rose from his seat. 'I need you to show me you can take care of this. Storm that damn house and drag her out by her cloak if you have to, but get it done. And do it *fast*.'

Go to hell.

Ransom slumped against a tombstone, swallowing his anger.

Dufort sighed as he returned his gaze to the statue of Saint Calvin, searching for a face beneath the skein of moss. 'The bravest of us carve out our own path in life, Bastian. Once we choose our destiny, there is no other way. There is no going back.'

Ransom grimaced at his words. They were not true – they could not be true. There were always other paths, other choices. Dufort had chosen his destiny for him at ten years old and now Ransom wanted a different one. He wanted to choose for himself.

'Wrangle that wayward conscience of yours, boy. We have graver matters to worry about.' Dufort turned for the gate, beckoning for Ransom to follow. 'The king is growing concerned about our little monster problem. If I don't get them out of this city, he'll send ten thousand soldiers to sweep the streets with all the brute force the royal purse can buy. His nightguards are already a nuisance. I don't want any more soldiers sniffing about in my city.'

Another growl of thunder tore through the night, and far across the Verne, the clock tower chimed eight.

They paused at the gate. Dufort sighed. 'I know what they say about me in the catacombs, you know. That all the Shade has eaten through my heart. I am not so far gone that I can't sense your restlessness.' He laid a heavy hand on Ransom's shoulder. 'You've been unhappy these past few months. I can see it. I have always been able to see it. Don't think that I've been content to watch you struggle, son. That I haven't thought to do something about it.'

Ransom frowned. 'What do you mean?'

'When I was at Bellevue Castle, I spoke to the king about your family. Your mother, Gisele. Your sister, Anouk. I know how much you've been missing them.'

Ransom's heart stuttered in his chest. 'You ... spoke to the king about *me*?'

'The smallest of asks,' said Dufort, with a wave of dismissal. 'He's put his best scouts on the case. Scattered them across the country like a fistful of marbles. There is nothing hidden in Valterre that cannot be found by the Crown.' He rolled back on his heels, offering a smile of lazy confidence. 'When we find them, you can bring them home, Bastian. Buy them a house and fill it with riches. Put all that coin you've earned to good use, perhaps remind yourself of the *blessings* this Order has given you. The blessings that *I* have given you.'

Ransom's throat tightened. 'How long?' he managed. 'How long until you hear back?'

Dufort shrugged. 'A week, maybe two? Stay close to me. When I hear something, you'll be the first to know.'

Ransom nodded, hope like a fist in his throat. He couldn't stop his eyes from misting over.

'It's a gift,' said Dufort as he nudged him through the gate, keeping that hand on his shoulder. 'You're not supposed to blubber.'

As the air crackled with the beginnings of a storm, Ransom looked up at the menacing lights of the Aurore and thought of Seraphine somewhere across the city, readying herself for battle.

It was too soon. Too soon to move against Dufort, too soon to slam shut that precious door to Ransom's past. He was so close now, closer than he'd ever been. He had to find out where his family was or the mystery of it would kill him. The *almost* knowing would drive him to ruin.

As thunder rolled across the darkening sky, he stalked from the graveyard and into the heart of the storm, hoping he was not too late.

Chapter 40

Seraphine

As night fell, Sera stepped out of the back door of House Armand. A canopy of clouds blotted out the rising moon and thunder grumbled across the city as though the saints knew what she was about to do. She couldn't tell if the storm was urging her on or warning her to turn back. She tried not to think about it as she embraced her friends in the garden, pressing a kiss to Bibi's cheek and squeezing Val's hand.

'Are you sure you're still up for this?'

'Surer than sure,' said Bibi, tightening the straps on her satchel. 'We'll see you at the Aurore.'

'For our great blaze of glory,' added Val, with a wink.

Sera smiled at her friends, ignoring her guilt. She hadn't told them about her plans for Dufort because she didn't want to worry them. And maybe, deep down, she was afraid they'd try and talk her out of it.

She turned to Theo, catching the worry on his face before he masked it with an easy smile. He stepped in, adjusting the hood of her Lightfire cloak. 'Time to become the flame, Sera,' he said, using her mother's words to strengthen her. 'Are you ready?'

She drew a steadying breath, relaxing into the brush of magic against her skin. She felt it reaching down inside her, warming the furthest depths of her soul.

'I'm ready,' she said.

Theo took her hand, folding a fistful of magical pearls inside it. 'Just in case.'

'Thanks,' she said. The pearls flickered as she slipped them into one of her pockets. She had a switchblade in the other. Another *just in case.* 'See you soon.'

Once she cleared the boundary of House Armand, she didn't look back. She marched on, into the dark heart of the Hollows. From there, she headed west, shattering the night as she went. Under the heaving sky, the city was darker than ever, but her cloak shone out like a light, guiding her through the deserted streets to the place where the monsters gathered.

By the time Sera reached the harbour, her heart was pounding in her chest. The sky growled and the wind stirred, carrying the odour of seaweed across the square. She stood at the end of the pier, where the reflection of her cloak shone back at her from the black water.

There were monsters here. She could *feel* them.

'Come out,' she whispered into the night.

Another gust cast her hood back, as lightning forked down

into the sea. Her hair tangled across her face, momentarily blinding her. She heard the water surge. It churned and thrashed as the deep answered her plea. Hands broke through the surface, followed by hunched shoulders, twisted arms and hulking bodies. The long dock creaked as it took the weight.

Her cloak flared as the monsters emerged, one after another after another. Each one was impossibly horrifying and utterly unique, a cursed creature mangled by poison and Shade. Mangled by Mama. They were groaning, hungry . . . *suffering*. As Sera stood among them, she felt their anguish sweeping over her like a scream.

Her stomach turned as they crawled towards her. She pressed her palm against her pocket, feeling the ridge of the pearls inside. Her switchblade wouldn't buy her much time against a monster, but if her cloak failed, the pearls might end up being the difference between life and death. She hoped it wouldn't come to that. The monsters crushed and fought each other in their thirst for magic, snapping jaws of needle teeth. She pulled her cloak tighter, fighting the urge to turn and flee.

'Stop!' she called out.

The monsters froze. Some dangled from the pier, mid-climb. Others halted less than ten feet from her, their silver eyes wide and unblinking. Just like that monster in Saint Celiana's fountain, they were waiting, all of them, for her command.

Power swelled inside Sera, fast and warm and dizzying. As her cloak shone out across the docks, she scanned the pier. There were forty or so monsters down here, and more skulking under the water. There would be others stalking the streets of Fantome, floating in the river, hiding in the sewers.

'Heel!' she cried.

The pier creaked as the monsters bowed, pressing their misshapen skulls to the wooden slats. Her jaw tightened as she stood before them, glowing like a saint. Seraphine Marchant, Saint of Monsters. She could almost hear Mama's laughter on the wind. Sera was so giddy she almost laughed too. Her cloak tingled along her skin, sharing in the unexpected trill of amusement.

It was so different to being cloaked in Shade – that strange heaviness that laced her bones and the headache that always lingered after she removed it. The cloak of Lightfire warmed her. Its magic nestled in her blood, sharing the swell of her emotions as though this strange, ancient power belonged inside her just as surely as her bones did. It stoked her confidence, telling her she could easily command this sea of monsters. That it was as simple as breathing.

'Come with me!' she called out, adrenaline making her bounce on the balls of her feet. The thud of lumbering footsteps followed her back across the pier. Two feet, then four, then so many it sounded like a fleet of wagons were trundling up the dock behind her. Sera sneaked a glance over her shoulder and saw bloated silver eyes flickering in the night.

Her lips spread into a slow smile.

The plan was working. The monsters were following her.

She looked north, to where the Aurore pierced the belly of a low-hanging storm cloud. The others would be there soon, but first, Seraphine and her monsters had a date with the devil of Fantome.

She walked on and the monsters followed, away from the

sea and into the heart of the city. As she went, more emerged from the lost alleys of Fantome, crawled up through sewers and dropped from the rooftops, falling into line behind her.

Soon, there were over a hundred creatures at her back, and their numbers kept growing.

She crossed the Verne and broke into a run, eager to be on the other side of this night, but when she neared Old Haven, her feet got heavier, slower. As she steeled herself for her final showdown with Gaspard Dufort, an old, festering fear emerged. It sat like a thorn in her chest, pricking at the thrall of her magic. Her cloak dimmed, responding to her dread.

She pushed on, refusing to be afraid. She was no longer a little girl cowering under the kitchen table while her parents screamed at each other, flinching as her father flung everything he could at the wall. She was a woman now, a living flame of power and vengeance, and she was done hiding.

Soon, only a handful of cobbled streets separated Sera from the entrance to Hugo's Passage. Dufort would be waiting there, led up the steps like a lamb to slaughter. In a matter of minutes, it would all be over, her father sacrificed to her mother's swarm of monsters, and his reign of terror at an end. Freedom waited just up ahead. Freedom at last . . .

Then the wind changed.

The air rippled as a shadow dropped from a nearby rooftop, and suddenly Ransom was before her. He landed in the middle of the narrow street, rising from a crouch with predatory grace. Dressed all in black and with those glittering silver eyes, he looked like a demon that had crawled straight out of hell.

Sera skidded to a stop. Twenty feet behind her, the monsters reared up at the sight of new prey. Her hand shot up. 'Fall back!'

The monsters froze mid-lurch. For a moment, it seemed like the entire city had fallen under a spell, but Ransom was still moving, closing the space between them in six strides.

Unease coiled in her gut. 'Where's Dufort?' she said, her eyes darting around.

'We have to wait, Seraphine.' His own eyes moved from her flaming cloak to the swarm of monsters at her back. A muscle ticced in his jaw but if he was afraid, it didn't show. 'Things have changed. I'm sorry. I need another week. Two, at the most.'

She blinked at him. 'Have you lost your mind? I've just dragged an army of monsters into Old Haven! It's too late, Ransom.'

He held his ground, his feet planted. 'I can't bring him to you,' he said, voice strained. 'Not yet.'

Sera flinched at the sting of his betrayal, but she was angrier at herself. It was her own fault for trusting a Dagger in the first place. For pouring her heart out to him and expecting him to care, for tricking herself into believing there was something real between them.

'Then get out of my way,' she said, hardening her voice. 'I'll go get him myself.'

Ransom didn't move. She tried to arc around him, but he slid in front of her. His hands curled into fists, and she wondered if he was thinking about throttling her, weighing his odds against her cloak of Lightfire and the army of monsters halfway down the street.

'Don't do anything rash,' he said in a low voice.

She spluttered a laugh. 'Look behind me, Ransom. We are *way* past rash.' Even without turning around, she could feel the monsters watching them, *straining* against her command to wait. Seeing the tightness in his jaw, she knew he could feel it too.

'You can't kill Dufort yet,' he said. 'He has something I need.'

'Then run home and kiss his feet.' Her cloak flickered at the hiss of her anger. 'Better yet, why don't I go with you?'

'Spitfire,' he said, a warning in his voice.

'Ransom, *move.*'

He flexed his fingers, shadows uncoiling from the nearby streetlamps. 'Do you truly expect me to let you rampage through Hugo's Passage and get yourself killed?'

'Worry about your friends, Dagger. I'm the one with an army of monsters.'

His shadows struck, curling around her arms, her waist. They snapped immediately, her cloak searing them into nothing.

'Good effort,' she said, shoving past him.

'Fuck it.' He lunged, grabbing her waist and spinning her into a nearby alley. Darkness swallowed them, the rest of the world falling away in a moment. By the time he released her, the silver in his eyes had softened. He heaved a breath, pinning her between his arms, a position that had become all too familiar to her. 'Listen to me. Dufort is looking for my family, Seraphine. He's enlisted the king's scouts. I need more time.'

She stared up at him in utter horror. 'Oh, Ransom,' she said, her anger dissolving into pity. 'You can't possibly believe that.'

He frowned. 'He has nothing to gain from it.'

She might have laughed if she didn't care so much about Dufort's clever little lie, how it was delaying her grand plan to flick him off the face of the earth. 'Doesn't he?'

Ransom's frown deepened, even as he shook off her words. 'I can't take the chance,' he whispered. 'What if it's real?'

'Dufort's words are never real, Ransom. His promises are as empty as his soul.' Sera huffed, fighting the urge to shake some damn sense into him. She understood now why he had reneged on his promise to her, and even in the depths of her frustration, she didn't begrudge him that fool's hope. But that didn't mean she would share in his delusion. She had her own promises to keep.

She raised her chin, meeting the determination in his gaze with her own. He loomed over her, so tall and broad in the narrow passage, and yet, he was no match for even one of Sera's monsters. They were barely a stone's throw from the mouth of the alley, waiting for her next order. She could destroy him with a single word, and they both knew it.

She didn't want to hurt him.

'Ransom,' she said, gently bracing her hands against his chest. He closed his eyes, shuddering as she shredded his Shade. He let her do it, wavering perhaps over his own foolish decision to trust Dufort, or simply unwilling to raise a hand to hurt her. He softened into her touch, and she could have pushed him away with ease, but she didn't.

Death waited around the corner. And with it, pain and grief and the sharp edge of revenge. It could wait a little longer. He laid his forehead against hers, as if he was having the same thought. Slowly, she moved her palms up his chest, twining her fingers in the collar of his shirt. He looked down at her beneath a veil of dark lashes, and something inside her came undone. She had never seen such raw, undisguised need.

His words were all gravel. 'How many minutes do you want, Seraphine?'

'As many as you can spare.'

He brushed his nose against hers. 'How about eternity?'

She laughed as he trailed his finger along her jaw, lifting her mouth to taste the sound. She rose on tiptoes and he moaned as the last of his Shade dissolved on her lips. She tasted the ash of it on his tongue as she opened her mouth to him. His arm tightened around her waist, the other cupping the nape of her neck as he crushed his lips against hers. She arched into him, sealing every inch of space between their bodies. Desire raged through her blood, chasing the rush of Lightfire.

'*Fuck*,' he hissed, between ragged breaths.

She pulled back, and beneath the glow of her cloak she saw that the shadow-mark on his collarbone was fading. She traced the skin there. 'Does it hurt?'

'*Yes*.' He traced his thumb along her bottom lip, his pupils so dilated she could see her own reflection in them. 'But don't stop.'

He kissed her again, his tongue moving slow and deep as he chased that agonizing pleasure. She met his hunger with her own, letting him drink from her magic like a man dying of thirst.

He slid his hands into her hair, their bodies melding as he pushed her up against the wall. She threw her arms around his neck, her hood falling back as she surrendered to her wild, growing need. She nipped his bottom lip and he swore, tipping her head back to take her mouth again. He laved her tongue, savouring the kiss. Savouring her.

It wasn't nearly enough. Sera wanted to rip his clothes off, to drag him down to the damp cobblestones, to taste every inch of his skin and lick the shadow-marks away one by one. The need to have more of him – to have *all* of him – was brutal.

He pulled back to kiss her neck, gently grazing her skin with his teeth. Her blood sang as he nipped and sucked there, marking her, before chasing the bite with his tongue. Sera's thoughts spun away from her as some frantic, baser part of her took control. She dropped her hand to the waistband of his trousers, pressing against the hardness she found there. His gasp dissolved into a low groan.

She palmed him through his clothes as he turned her cheek to the wall and traced the shell of her ear with his tongue. His other hand roamed under the folds of her cloak and then her sweater to find the swell of her breasts. He made a noise of ragged approval, thumbing her until she was limp in his arms. He took her mouth again, the hot brush of his tongue stoking the primal fire inside her.

She moved her hand faster, his breath shallowing as he braced himself against the wall.

'*Fuck*,' he grunted, pressing his knee between her legs to pin her there. He tore his other hand from her breasts, trailing his fingers along the bare skin of her midriff. Her cloak flickered, echoing her anticipation, and as his fingers dipped beneath her waistband she became vaguely aware that they were glowing now like twin flames.

She bucked her hips – grinding out a plea – and he chuckled against her lips. His fingers slipped lower, and he stifled a groan when he found her already wet for him. She cried out as he pushed deeper.

'*Good*, spitfire.'

She was so close already, she dropped her head to the crook of his neck, silently begging him to finish her. His fingers moved deeper, in a slow rhythm, his tongue expertly working her ear as he wrenched a string of moans from her.

She whimpered against his shoulder, her breath stuttering as she rode his hand. 'Ransom . . .' she gasped. 'I'm . . . going to . . .'

'*Yes*,' he growled. 'Give it to me.'

His command was her undoing. She shattered in his arms. Biting down on his shoulder as she fell apart, she buried her cries in his skin. He held her tight against him, his breath rough on her cheek as he watched her ride the swell of her pleasure. Her blood roared with ecstasy, the light from her cloak erupting and flooding the alleyway like a sunrise.

At the sound of his jagged gasp, she raised her head. His eyes were closed, his face slack with pleasure. She could still trace the hardness of him where they were pressed together. As he slipped his hand from her waistband, she saw that his knuckles were absent of shadow-marks. She grabbed the other hand, examining his wrist and forearm. There wasn't a single whorl left.

Her cloak – her *pleasure* – had obliterated every single one of them.

When she looked up at him, he was smiling at her, a faint dazed look in his eyes.

'I can't believe they're gone,' she whispered.

He only stared at her, as if she was the most precious thing he had ever seen. A slant of sunlight breaking through a storm. A lone star in a cloud-swept night.

He blinked the haze from his eyes. 'Run away with me, Seraphine.'

Her breath caught. 'W-what?'

'Run away with me,' he said, with devasting simplicity. 'Tonight. Tomorrow. Yesterday. I don't care.' He gently brushed the hair from her eyes. 'We have the same dream. Let's chase it together.'

Sera's heart thundered at his words, as if it was trying to crash through her chest to answer them. But in the afterglow of her pleasure, reality was filtering back in. She tugged her top down and pulled her cloak around her, trying to stop herself from screaming *yes!* to the man who had just made her shatter into pieces. She had a cloak of flame and an army of monsters and a plan to save the whole damn city, and she was standing in an alleyway with a Dagger and seriously considering pissing it all away.

She had to finish what she had started tonight. She had to go. She had to ask him to wait for her.

Then another shape dropped from the darkness, and Ransom's warning shout sounded just a moment too late. The blow came from behind, the force so blinding it knocked all thought from Sera's mind and sent her spiralling into blackness.

Chapter 41

Ransom

Ransom caught Seraphine before she hit the cobblestones. She flopped like a doll in his arms, her cheeks still pink from the rush of her climax, her full lips swollen from his kiss. The sight of the angry welt blooming on her temple kindled in him a quick and terrible rage. He rolled to his feet, cradling her against his chest.

Lark dropped the rock he had used to knock her out. 'Is this what you call *handling* it?' he demanded. 'You were supposed to get rid of her, not screw her in Dufort's front garden.'

Ransom rounded on him. 'Have you been following me?'

'Obviously,' said Lark, with a rare burst of anger. 'And a good thing, too. Otherwise I might not have noticed that giant army of monsters your murderous little girlfriend just dragged over here to kill us all. They're all standing frozen out in the damn street, like they're waiting for her next order. It's beyond terrifying.'

There was a distant flutter as Nadia swung down from the next rooftop, landing neatly between them. 'You have a lot of explaining to do,' she said, by way of greeting. She smoothed her dark hair back, her silver eyes flaring as she peered down at Seraphine. 'Is she dead?'

'Not yet,' said Lark, flexing his fingers. Shadows darted across his knuckles, but he kept his eyes on Ransom. 'But after she dragged all those monsters into our quarter, I don't see any way around it.'

Ransom stiffened as Lark stepped forward. It took every ounce of self-control not to maul him right there, to act like the sight of his oldest friend looming over the girl that had just obliterated every last shred of pain in his body and soul didn't make him want to rip the fucking walls down to bury him. But he was no fool. He was outnumbered, two to one, without an ounce of Shade to protect him. To protect her.

All they had left between them was that cloak, which so far, Lark had failed to question.

But when he curled his fingers around her throat, his Shade melted away. 'What the hell?' he hissed, stumbling backwards.

'It's that cloak.' Nadia stepped back. 'Get it off her.'

Ransom jerked away from Lark. 'If you touch her, I will fucking kill you.'

'Calm down, lover boy,' said Nadia, with a sigh. 'We're trying to help you.' She struck his shoulder with a whip of shadow. It was just enough to knock him off kilter, allowing Lark to dart in and rip the cloak off. It fluttered to the floor between them.

'Please don't make us hurt you to get to her,' she said, as more shadows gathered at her fingertips. 'Just . . . let me finish it. For all our sakes.'

Ransom met Nadia's glare with his own and knew she would go through him to get to Seraphine. She clearly thought she was doing the right thing, saving him from himself, from the thrall of the siren who had dragged a swarm of monsters into Old Haven with her.

With Shade at her fingertips, he couldn't fight Nadia off.

It was words, or nothing.

'If we kill her in this alley, her monsters will revolt,' he said quickly. 'And in case you haven't noticed, there are over a hundred of them less than twenty feet away from us, and I'm not looking to die tonight. With that Shade in your system, you can get back up on that roof but who says they can't climb up there after you? And if they go after either one of us, Lark and I are shit out of luck.'

Lark and Nadia exchanged a glance. In the loaded silence, a monster growled. Another pawed at the ground, its hackles raised. They were growing impatient. Whatever spell Seraphine had cast would not hold them much longer. Without her cloak, her command was wearing off.

'He's right,' said Lark, plucking the cloak off the ground. 'It's not worth the risk.'

'Let's go somewhere safe,' said Ransom. 'We can talk. I'll explain everything.'

'Fine,' said Nadia, her eyes darting back to where the creatures were waiting just beyond the alley mouth.

Ransom took off before they could reconsider, but the second they left the alleyway, the monsters began to lurch around. A ragged howl cut through the night, followed quickly by another.

'Do you hear that?' Nadia jerked her head at the growing thunder of footsteps.

'Hell's teeth,' hissed Lark, whirling on his heel. 'They're coming right at us!'

'Head for the catacombs!' yelled Nadia.

They broke into a run. Ransom glanced over his shoulder and released a litany of swears. He doubled his pace, his gaze darting. There was nowhere to hide here, nowhere to run but down into the darkness. And he had no choice but to take Seraphine with him.

Up ahead, the statue of Saint Lucille loomed through the mist.

Monsters spilled out across Old Haven, flooding the graveyards.

'Faster!' yelled Lark, but Nadia was already ahead of them, yanking a shadow off a streetlamp and making a lasso of it. She tossed it over Lucille's head and tugged. The entrance to Hugo's Passage groaned open and they raced down the stone steps.

Behind them, cobbles cracked under the stampede of monsters. Old Haven was trembling at its foundations, the force of their pursuit making skulls fall and shatter from the entryway. Ransom leaped across the threshold, twisting the skull to bring the door down as Lark and Nadia slid underneath it.

As the first monster reached the stairwell, the door thundered to a close, cutting off a gnarled hand wreathed in shadow. It flopped about on the ground before going still.

Nadia winced as she kicked it away. It hit the wall as the rest of the monsters pounded against the door. Bones fell from the ceiling, sending a shower of dust cascading over them.

'They're still after us,' said Nadia.

'Not us,' said Ransom, just now noticing the cloak glowing in Lark's hand. 'They're after *that*.'

Lark looked down at it. 'Well, shit.'

As the pounding worsened, the walls trembled. Daggers spilled out into the hallways to investigate the commotion. Nadia shoved Ransom headlong down the north passage, Lark coming round to his other side so he couldn't run away. 'Take your mark to the Cavern before tonight gets any worse,' said Nadia.

'It's already a horror show,' muttered Lark.

But as Ransom made his way to the Cavern, with Seraphine curled tightly in his arms, he had a terrible sinking feeling that the horror of this night had only just begun.

Down in the Cavern, Dufort was on his feet with the rest of the Daggers, trying to make sense of the dust falling from the ceiling. When he spotted Ransom, he went rigid. His silver gaze swept over the body in his arms. There was no smile. No pat on the back.

'Is she dead?' he said, in a strained voice.

Ransom went to a nearby table and laid Seraphine down. Then he stood over her like an avenging angel.

'No,' said Lark from behind him.

Dufort removed a vial of Shade from his pocket and tossed it to Ransom. 'Then kill her.'

Ransom batted it away, letting it shatter on the stone. 'Kill her yourself.'

There was a collective intake of breath. The other Daggers moved away, afraid to get caught in the crossfire.

Dufort's nostrils flared. 'I said, *kill her.*'

Ransom raised his chin. 'And I said no.'

Dufort stalked towards him. 'What the fuck did you just say?'

'*Ransom,*' hissed Nadia.

'I'll do it!' said Lisette, leaping up from her chair by the fireplace.

Dufort's hand shot out and shadows darted from the walls, shoving her back. He didn't take his eyes off Ransom. 'Ransom will do it.'

Lark stepped up. 'I can—'

'*No,*' growled Dufort.

Ransom was too revolted by Dufort to be afraid of him any more. The Dagger wasn't even looking at Seraphine – that was how little he cared about the life of his own daughter. This wasn't about her. It wasn't even about monsters or Lightfire. It was about ego and power, and control.

Dufort flexed his fingers. Shadows crawled towards Ransom.

'Look at her,' said Ransom.

'No.'

'*Look* at her.'

'*No,*' he hissed.

'What are you so afraid of, Dufort?' challenged Ransom.

Dufort's eyes darkened. But whatever he was about to say was lost to a distant bloodcurdling scream. It echoed all the way down the north passage, filling the cavern like a terrible aria.

It was followed by a warning cry. 'MONSTER IN THE PASSAGE!'

And then, an earth-shattering roar.

Chapter 42

Seraphine

Sera came to with a jolt, jarred back to life by the unmistakable bellow of her father.

'ALL DAGGERS TO THE NORTH ENTRANCE! BARRICADE THE DOOR!'

For a brief moment, it was like being nine years old again, hiding in the darkness under her bed. She kept her eyes shut, steadying her sawing breaths before they gave her away.

Breathe.

Don't react.

She lay perfectly still, listening to the thud of his footsteps around her, the bark of her father's voice, so familiar it raised the hair on her arms. She pushed her fear away, closed the door to her memories and bolted it shut.

Breathe.

Even with her eyes shut, she could feel the chaos all around her. The lingering mustiness of old bones and damp stone told her she was in the catacombs. Cloakless and concussed. And by the sound of things, there was a monster in here somewhere.

I hope it kills you, Dufort. Sera could feel his nearness, crackling in the air. One wrong move and he would strike her down. Which begged the question – why the hell wasn't she dead already? She tried not to frown and give herself away as she recalled those last moments in the alleyway, pressed up against Ransom, gasping between kisses ... then the blow on the side of her head.

Had he betrayed her after all?

She bit down on her tongue, fighting to keep her brow from furrowing.

'*MOVE*, YOU IMBECILES, BEFORE THEY TEAR THIS WHOLE PLACE DOWN!'

The patter of footsteps around her faded as more distant screams rang out.

It occurred to Sera that she should move, too. Mama's monsters might have followed her to the catacombs but she no longer had her cloak to command them. Which probably meant she was in just as much danger as the rest of them. She subtly flexed her hands, her feet. They were unbound. Apart from the dull ache in her head, she was in good shape. Fighting shape.

She cracked an eye open and slowly, carefully, turned her head. She was in a great cavernous room, which was all but deserted now. A small mercy. As a chorus of shouts echoed through the catacombs, the last of the Daggers scattered, making for the north passage.

Dufort stalled in the doorway, a hand braced on either side of the arch as he looked out on the chaos, listening to the screams of his Order as they died to defend him.

Rotten coward.

Sera's hand inched across her hip, finding the outline of the switchblade in her pocket. She exhaled in quiet relief. For the first time in her life, she had an open shot at Dufort. She would never again be this close to her father.

She sat up, slipping the knife from her pocket and flicking it from its sheath. She drew her arm back, angling it towards the back of his head.

A hand curled around her wrist.

She tipped her head back to see Ransom standing over her, a warning in his eyes. *Wait.*

No. *No.* She was done waiting.

Sera struggled against him, desperately trying to free her hand. It was reckless, she knew. An impossible shot. The signature on her own death warrant, but she might as well be dead already. *Please*, she screamed at him with her eyes. Silent tears burned, as eighteen years of pain and anger and frustration all bubbled to the surface. She was so close. So achingly *close*.

'It will take a lot more than a blunt pocket knife and your shitty aim, Seraphine.' Dufort's voice rose over the distant commotion. He had turned around, and was watching them struggle from the doorway. He smirked at Ransom. 'Impressive foresight, son.'

Son. Sera nearly retched at the word. She cut her eyes at Gaspard, channelling a lifetime of hatred and disgust into her glare. Here he stood at last – her constant nightmare, a terror far worse than the skulls that haloed him. 'You are no father.'

'Well, you would know, Seraphine.' He flashed his gold filling as he came towards her, but there was no warmth in his smile. Fury shone from the metallic sheen of his eyes, the Shade in his system smothering their soft cerulean blue. 'Let's not pretend you've been much of a daughter either.'

Sera felt Ransom stiffen.

'What kind of daughter did you expect?' she said, curling her lip. 'The kind that hugs you after you tried to strangle her mother on her ninth birthday? The kind that picks blackberries to make you a pie with the same wrist you broke in one of your Shade-fuelled rages?' Sera's voice hitched, matching the shrill of panic around her. She could hurl a hundred knives at him, and it still wouldn't be enough to equal the pain he had caused her. 'The kind that lies down at your feet to die after you murdered the only person – the only parent – who ever cared about her?'

'Dramatics,' he said, nostrils flaring. 'Just like your meddlesome mother. Everything is dark and bad and evil. And anyone who drinks from the darkness is evil, too.' He curled his lip, matching her expression with disconcerting ease. 'I secured an *empire* for her, and she turned her nose up at it.'

'You secured a fucking tomb,' spat Seraphine. 'Lie down and die in it.'

'That's exactly what your mother said,' he remarked, coldly. 'And tell me, little firefly, where is she now?'

Anger ripped out of Sera like a scream. 'I SWEAR I'LL KILL YOU!'

She bucked and thrashed but Ransom would not let her go. And yet she felt him trembling against her, the heat between them surging. Was it his anger or her own?

'I wouldn't have had to terrorize you if your mother could hack this world,' Dufort went on – like it mattered, this twisted narrative he told himself. 'But Sylvie never saw the beauty in the darkness, the possibility of what we could have been together. All she cared about was that fucking dead Versini girl and her dreams of *Lightfire*.' He spat the word. 'I wanted to make a name for myself – for *all of us* – and Sylvie wanted to destroy everything. She wanted to make a stand against Shade. Against the whole Versini legacy. Against *me*. And *you*—' He raised his finger, and shadows slithered from the walls around him. '*You* had the reckless stupidity to stand beside her.'

'I'm still standing beside her!' Sera yelled.

Dufort's silver gaze flicked to Ransom. 'Finish her.'

'Let go,' demanded Sera, at the same time.

'Ransom.' The walls trembled and a plume of dust clouded the air between them. 'Do your damn job.'

But Ransom didn't move, didn't tear his eyes from Dufort as the leader of the Daggers continued towards them, shadows billowing at his feet.

Silence. Defiance. Ransom's fury turned him into a predator. It squared his jaw and simmered darkly in his gaze. It curled his fists and his lips, made his teeth seem sharper somehow. In that moment, it felt more powerful than even Shade.

Dufort sensed it, and paused. Sera's fingers twitched on the hilt of her knife, and she wondered if Ransom had baited Dufort with his defiance, used his silence to lure him closer.

'Bastian.' Dufort uttered the name like a spell, and for a moment it hung between them, turning Ransom, this vicious, expertly honed Dagger, back into a ten-year-old boy. Bastian. Sera felt his hand tremble as he let her go, hissing through his bared teeth.

'Go to hell, you prick.'

Sera flung the dagger straight at Dufort's head. He jerked aside at the last second and it sliced into his cheek. Not a death blow, but she had drawn first blood. At least she would go down swinging.

Dufort lifted a hand to his cheek, and found it running with blood. 'That was your first and last shot at me,' he said, smearing it across his shirt. Shadows surged, the darkness coming at Sera like a swarm. But Ransom was quicker, grabbing her by the waist and swinging her off the table before they sheared her in two.

She landed on her hands and knees.

'You stupid little bastard!' roared Dufort.

When Sera looked up, the shadows had Ransom by the throat. He couldn't move. Couldn't speak. Dufort was choking the life out of him, heartbeat by heartbeat. Ten seconds was all it would take. Ten seconds and he would be dead. Sera was already moving.

One – Darkness plunged down his throat, tearing a silent shriek of pain from him.

Two – His eyes found Sera's, and she read the plea inside them. *Run.*

Three – The barricade at the north entrance failed, and a stampede of monsters barrelled inside.

Four – Sera spotted something twinkling in her peripheral vision. It was her Lightfire cloak, which had been discarded in the chaos.

Five – Sera lunged for the cloak, as fresh screams echoed down the north passage.

Six – Ransom stumbled to his knees, his skin turning grey.

Seven – Sera threw herself at him, slinging the cloak around his shoulders.

Eight – There was a blinding flash of light.

Nine – Ransom inhaled in a sucking gasp, his eyes glimmering with Lightfire.

Ten – Dufort's shadows shattered into a hail of darkness, and Ransom fell forward, into Sera's arms.

She curled herself around him, sharing in the buzz of Lightfire. Dufort downed another vial of Shade as he came towards them, but he was too late. She met his silver glare over Ransom's shoulder just as a swarm of monsters came crashing into the Cavern. 'Look, Papa,' she said, tossing him a cruel smile. 'It's a gift from Mama.'

And all hell broke loose.

Chapter 43

Ransom

Ransom knelt, half-spent, in Seraphine's arms, trying to gather the strength to stand and fight. She trembled against him as the monsters poured into the Cavern. They roared and thrashed, climbing the walls and smashing everything in sight. Some turned on each other, unable to tell the difference between the Shade inside each Dagger and the poisoned Shade in themselves.

Daggers rushed in after the monsters, bringing whatever weapons they could find in the tunnels. Shade was no good to them any more. The monsters ate through their shadows like air, so they hoisted swords and flung knives as they fought to defend their home.

Seraphine pulled back from Ransom, her eyes darting around. 'We have to move.'

He staggered to his feet, one hand clasping the Lightfire cloak at his throat, the other folding her body underneath it. The doorway was blocked, the cavern echoing with screams. Everywhere he looked, Daggers were fighting and falling, the monsters too caught up in bloodlust to find the Lightfire in their midst. 'This way,' he said, pulling her towards the stone fireplace. The fire was out, the last embers dying in the grate. He kicked ash over them, then pushed her inside it.

'What are you doing?' she said, stumbling backwards, into charcoal and ash.

He crawled in after her, making a shield of the cloak. A barrier through which the monsters couldn't pass. 'What does it look like? I'm hiding you.'

'I don't want to hide!' she cried, slamming her palms against his chest.

He trapped her arms with one hand. 'Can you not fight with me just this once?' This hot-headed spitfire was going to be the death of both of them. 'In case you haven't noticed, things have gone to shit around here.'

'That's because one of you assholes knocked me out,' she snapped. 'Now *move* out of my way, before Dufort flees like the rat he is.'

Hell's teeth, she was serious about going back out there. 'This is hardly the great spectacle of revenge you envisioned,' he said, shouting over the rising screams. 'Even *you* are not this reckless.'

She snorted. 'Want to bet?'

'*No*,' he hissed, resisting the urge to shake some damn sense into her. She was so hell-bent on revenge, she'd crawl through a bonfire just to get it. Burn herself along with Dufort, and the rest of them. 'I don't want to bet and I don't want to fight. I don't want to do anything right now, except come up with a really good plan to end this mess and get out of here alive.'

'Here's the plan. You take the cloak and the monsters. Stomp around, make a racket to draw their attention. Then get them out of the Cavern and up to the Aurore,' she said quickly. 'I'll go after Dufort.'

He scoffed in disbelief. 'With what weapon?'

'A pocket full of Lightfire,' she said, trying to climb past him. 'And whatever the hell I find on the floor.'

He braced a hand against her chest, kneeling on either side of her legs and pinning her hips with his own. He ignored the rushing urge to slam his lips against hers and wrench one more moan from those perfect lips.

Get a fucking grip.

He dragged his senses back to the unholy disaster unfolding around them. 'Can you not try and get yourself killed for one second?'

She glared up at him, her cheeks flushing. 'Stop getting in the way of my plans.'

'Then start making better ones. I'm trying to save your life!'

'I can save my own damn life.' She jutted her chin forward, until they were almost nose to nose. Teeth bared, breath heaving, both of them seething. Ransom didn't know if she wanted to kiss him or slap him, but one thing was certain, he was not about to let her go out there.

'Actually, historically, you can't.'

She cut her eyes at him, blowing a strand of hair from her

face. Fucking adorable. Even if she did want to throttle him. 'You must have a death wish.'

'Well, if I do, I'm certainly in the right place.' When she continued to glower at him, he sighed. 'Just … think with your head, please. Not your anger.'

'I'm going to kill him, Ransom,' she said, immediately ignoring his advice. 'It has to mean something – this awful night, the terrible mess of it all. I have to do what Mama asked of me. I have to finish what she started, so we can both know peace.'

'I'm not saying you can't kill him,' he said calmly. 'I'm just asking you not to kill yourself.'

'I know what I'm doing.' She squirmed beneath him, creating a distractingly lethal friction.

He rolled back on his heels before he stiffened between her legs. 'If we go back out there, we go together.'

'Fine,' she huffed.

A monster howled, far too close. There came the crack of bone and then the panicked gurgle of someone choking on their own blood.

Sera flinched, her gaze shifting to something over his shoulder. 'Ransom, there's a—'

A monster roared in his ear. It had jammed its misshapen head inside the grate, and now its shadowy tentacles were grasping at them. Seraphine screamed as one brushed her face.

Ransom twisted, trying to shove the monster out but it grabbed onto the end of the cloak, its glowing eyes so close, he could see his own terrified reflection in them.

'Free it!' cried Seraphine.

'How?' yelled Ransom, slamming his elbow into the monster's skull. Its jaw unhinged in an ear-splitting howl.

'Put your hands on its face! Release it!'

He grabbed the creature by the head. It went still, its chest heaving as they locked eyes. In that strange and deadly moment, Ransom didn't feel afraid. He felt ... hopeless. *Exhausted.* But this pain was not his own, he realized. And he had the power to do something about it.

'Rest,' he murmured, the word pouring from him like a prayer.

His hands tingled, his blood warming as the cloak's magic flowed through him. It was so different from the cold heaviness of Shade, the usual choking taste of ash and the awful twist of his stomach. Lightfire was a balm. It trickled through him like a sun-warmed stream, filling his bones with gentle, searching heat. It soothed his heart, laved the far, ragged reaches of his soul.

If Shade was death, then Lightfire was peace. It was freedom.

The monster groaned in relief. Its shoulders sagged as the shadows around it fell away, revealing the body of a woman with cropped white hair. She was barefoot and still wearing her sailor's uniform. She curled up on her side beside the grate, her final breath leaving her in a sigh.

A shiver passed through Ransom. Not Lightfire, but sorrow. 'I killed her.'

'No,' murmured Seraphine as she crawled to his side. 'My mother killed her. You freed her.'

He looked at her, and the agony in her face cleaved something in his chest.

He turned, scanning the cavern. It was thrumming with

monsters, and echoing with the screams of his friends, his family. Every monster that fell got back up again, more vicious and deadly than before. Lightfire was the one thing that could stop them but the creatures were now roaming throughout the catacombs and the humans only had a single cloak of it between them.

His thoughts spun, trying to come up with a plan. Seraphine stiffened at the sight of Dufort flitting across the cavern. The doorway to the north passage was clear and he was running for it.

'NO!' Forgetting the cloak and the promise they had just made, she shoved past Ransom and bolted from the fireplace, leaving him grasping at thin air.

'Seraphine!' He leaped to his feet and went after her, only to skid at the sound of Nadia's scream. She was ten feet away, trapped under a monster three times her size. Its jaws were inches from her neck, its shadows pinning her to the ground.

Ransom charged at the beast, sending it crashing into a broken table. It bucked beneath him, but Ransom struck fast, grabbing the creature's face. His palms buzzed, the flow of Lightfire filling his body as he gritted out, 'Let go.'

There was a flash of light and the shadows disintegrated. The monster twitched once, twice. And then it was no longer a beast. It was only a boy. He looked to be thirteen or so, wearing a stained T-shirt and a grubby bandana. A swabbie, Ransom guessed, and not long into his first taste of cheap wine. Poisoned wine.

He climbed off him, and helped Nadia to her feet. She stared at the cloak. 'That was ... effective.'

He tugged her close, casting it around her. 'Stick with me. We need to get these monsters out.'

She nodded, pushing the hair from her face with trembling fingers. 'Where's the girl?'

He turned on his heel, frantically searching the cavern. 'She's—*fuck*.'

Seraphine was on the ground by the doorway, fighting for her life.

Lark was killing her.

Chapter 44

Seraphine

The sight of Dufort running for the tunnels spurred Seraphine into action. She didn't even bother to wrestle the cloak from Ransom – it would only waste more time – as she vaulted past him, scrabbling to her feet.

Adrenaline pounded in her veins as she weaved across the room, narrowly avoiding a brawl of monsters tearing each other limb from limb. They snapped their heads up as she flew past, sniffing the air.

They must have sensed the handful of pearls in her pocket, the smallest shield of Lightfire now protecting her. She didn't know how potent they would be in a room of a hundred rabid monsters but she gathered half the pearls in her fist and, with her free hand, swiped a discarded blade from the floor, trying to ignore the dead Dagger bleeding out beside it. She hastily slid it into her waistband, replacing the one she had flung at Dufort.

Screams were a chorus around Sera, bouncing off the domed ceiling, the sound of bones shattering adding a sickening counterpoint. She pushed it all away – the noise and the panic and the fear paling against the blood-red promise of revenge. She darted between shadows and ducked under swinging punches as she made her way towards Dufort. He was ten steps from the doorway, and she was ten steps from him.

Nine steps. Eight. Seven. Hatred burned in her chest, quickening her pace. Six steps. Lightfire glowed in her fist, urging her on. Five steps. Dufort pivoted, flattening himself against the wall to dodge a stampeding monster. Four steps and she would be on him. She climbed onto an upturned chair, gaining the upper ground. He reached the doorway and Sera pounced.

For a heartbeat, she flew. Teeth bared and roaring, as if she was a monster herself. Then a figure swung in from her left, side-swiping her in mid-air. She landed on a broken table, the impact knocking the breath out of her.

She blinked, watching the skulls on the ceiling swim into focus. They were laughing at her.

You're delirious.

She sucked in air, trying to fill her aching lungs. Her back throbbed, and her leg was twisted underneath her body. The fall had cut her arm open, and there was blood everywhere.

She groaned, trying to sit up, but that figure came again, swinging through the air on a rope of shadow. At first, Sera thought it was a monster but then it landed above her, and she saw it was a man, not much older than her. Silver eyes flashing, pearlescent teeth bared in a savage smile. He was as tall and broad as Ransom, and for a delirious heartbeat, she thought she knew him. But she blinked, taking in his auburn hair and fair skin, and blamed the confusion on her concussion.

He straddled her torso, pinning her to the table. 'Try not to squirm.'

She spat in his face. 'Get off me, you prick.'

'Actually, it's Lark.' His shadows slithered over her. 'And if you could stay still while I'm killing you, I'd appreciate it.'

Seraphine crushed the pearls in her fist, willing the Lightfire to save her. A flash of heat, then a flare, and the shadows fell away.

Lark frowned. 'What the—?'

She swung her fist, slamming it into his cheek. He reeled backwards. She bucked, knocking him sideways. He rallied, lunging at her again. This time, he used both hands on her throat. 'Let's do this the old-fashioned way, shall we?'

Her eyes bulged as her throat closed. *Saint Oriel, help me.* He was strangling her with expert ease, the sides of her vision spotting as she tried to fight for a sip of breath. There was none. His thumbs pressed against her windpipe, crushing it, and for all Albert had taught her, Seraphine could not now think of a single move to free herself.

Lark brought his face close to hers, and she thought she glimpsed a flash of regret in his now-green eyes. 'I have to do it,' he said, quietly. 'He'll never be able to. And if he doesn't, Dufort will kill him. And he's like my brother. My only brother.'

Amid the sludge of her thoughts, Sera realized he was talking about Ransom. Lark was killing her to save Ransom. If she wasn't breathless, she might have laughed. But the thread of her life was fraying and her thoughts were slipping away.

In the end, it had all been for nothing. Lucille's life. Mama's life. Seraphine's life. The Versini legacy had smothered them all in a shadow so dark, not even Lightfire could fracture it.

Tears pooled in her eyes, the world growing quieter until there was only the slow thud of her heartbeat echoing in her head.

There was a ragged shout. Through a haze, Seraphine saw Ransom's fist connect with Lark's jaw with such force, his head spun around. Lark's grip on her slackened and her windpipe expanded. She gulped down air as both Daggers tumbled to the floor, swinging at each other.

A dark-haired girl rushed into the fray, trying to drag them apart.

Sera sat up just in time to see a monster charging at her. It was twice her size and three times as wide, its shadows lashing like whips. She rolled off the table, landing on top of Lark. '*Ooof.*'

He shoved her off and swung for Ransom again. Missed by an inch. 'Have you lost your mind?' Lark seethed.

'Keep your fucking hands off her!' said Ransom, dodging the next blow before landing one of his own with a sickening crack.

Lark roared in anger as the girl hooked her arm around his chest and dragged him away from Ransom. 'Cut it out, you idiots,' she snarled. 'We have bigger problems right now!'

Seraphine left them to their argument and made for the door, slipping into the north passage on the hunt for Dufort. The tunnel was deserted, save for several dead Daggers strewn across the ground. Sera winced as she stepped over them, making her way down the main passage.

Thanks to the night she had followed Ransom down here, she knew exactly where Dufort's chamber was. With any luck, she'd find him cowering inside it.

As she set foot in the smaller east passage, a frigid wind swept over her, extinguishing the oil lamps on the walls. There was a monster here. By the time she turned around, it was already leaping. It landed on her in a crushing heap, slamming her into the wall.

She slid to the ground, her teeth singing from the impact, the gash on her forearm ripped further open. Streams of blood were pouring out of her, making a puddle at her feet. She groaned as she lifted her head. The beast blurred as it rounded on her. It swept closer, the darkness around it rising like a wave. Sera whimpered, desperately flinging the pearls.

There was a snap of blinding light, magic swallowing the monster in a crackling gulp. The tunnel shimmered and for a moment it looked like a thousand fireflies were flitting around her. The scent of Lightfire hung heavy in the air, like lemon blossoms in the spring.

In the afterglow, Sera saw that the monster had become a young woman. She lay curled on her side, the skirts of her fine pink dress fanned out around her like fallen rose petals.

Sera struggled to her feet, and saw that she was drenched in her own blood. Her arm was bleeding badly and her head was starting to spin. She tipped it back, steadying herself against the rough stone. She had to make a tourniquet before she passed out from blood loss. Out here like this, she was monster-fodder. As good as dead.

But to turn back ... A chorus of howls rang out, warning her off.

She clamped her fingers around her arm above the wound and shuffled towards the entrance, following the flickering oil lamps. Every step was like wading through quicksand. She slumped against the wall, fingers catching at the rough stone for balance. She shoved herself along, one small step and then another, but her head was impossibly heavy and her vision was narrowing. She stumbled over a fallen body, her knees stinging as she hit the ground.

Shit.

She crawled onwards, leaving bloody handprints on the stones. She had no idea how far she'd come but the clash and clamour of fighting had faded and the only sound remaining was the rattle of her own breath.

How the hell had it all gone so wrong?

I will not die here.

I will not die tonight.

'Where do you think you're crawling to, little firefly?' A familiar voice crooned from the darkness. Sera closed her eyes, praying she had imagined it.

Dufort's nearness was punctuated by the tell-tale crunch of footsteps. He sneered as he walked towards her, kicking bodies aside without glancing at their ashen faces. His eyes were as blue as her own. He had surrendered his Shade – or perhaps the monsters had eaten through it all – but the silver glint in his hand told Sera he was not weaponless. He had a knife.

She was so weak she didn't trust her own legs to stand, let alone run. But she would not die cowering in the dirt like an animal. So she raised her head and met the hatred in his gaze with her own.

He stalled a few feet from her, taking in the blood pouring from her arm, then the crimson puddle in which she knelt. She was losing sensation in her body, and there were stars exploding in the sides of her vision. She patted her pocket desperately, but there were only four pearls left, useless against this particular monster. Her father. Her tormentor.

Dufort closed the space between them, then sank to his haunches. He took his signet ring off and dangled it before her, as though he were presenting a toy to a child. The ring was as ugly as the smirk on his face. 'Is this what you came for, Seraphine? My hard-earned legacy. All my gathered riches.'

She wished she had the strength to spit at him. 'I don't want anything from you,' she croaked. 'Go to hell.'

He smiled pityingly. 'We're already in hell, Seraphine. And in case you haven't noticed, it belongs to me.' He sighed. 'In another lifetime, it might have been yours. If only your mother had—'

She struck out, smacking the ring from his hand. It hit the wall with a clink. Dufort caught her by the throat.

She swung her fist again, but it was like moving through water. Too slow. Too heavy. He brought his knife to her neck. He hesitated, and she saw a ghost flitting behind his eyes. The shadow of the man he had been long, long ago. The one who had loved her.

He blinked and it was gone.

He leaned on the knife, and it bit into her skin.

Sera reached feebly for the collar of his shirt. She was too weak to fist it. Her hand slid down his chest, to the place where his heart should have been. She mouthed the word *Monster* as blood trailed down her neck.

Then that wind came again, cold and sweeping. It rippled up her spine and blew the stray strands of Dufort's hair back from his face. He froze with the knife at her throat, his eyes widening at something behind her. In the reflection of his pupils, Sera saw the monster loping towards them. It was haloed in the flickering lamplight, so big it took up the entire passage. So loud its footsteps made the ground rattle.

The monster roared as it lunged, and Sera's body reacted before her mind. She reeled backwards, flattening herself against the ground, as the beast leaped right over her and barrelled into Dufort.

Dufort screamed as the monster landed on his chest, but its shadows choked the sound from his throat. Its jaws unhinged in an awful screech as it pitched forward. It was all Sera could do to scrabble away from them, every part of her trembling as she clung to the wall as if the bones inside it could save her.

She watched in horror as the monster closed its jaws around her father's neck, plunging its reaching tentacles down his throat. Dufort twitched, his chest heaving as he tried in vain to fight the shadows inside him.

She knew she should run, or at least crawl, but she was rooted to the wall, unable to tear her gaze from her father. The man who proclaimed himself the lord of hell. Well, hell had other ideas. And as it bore down on Dufort, sucking the last drop of life from his body and turning the whites of his eyes black, Sera's entire body went cold.

She didn't know if it was shock or blood loss that stole the feeling from her face, but when the monster pulled back from Dufort, leaving him nothing but an ashen husk, she didn't even flinch.

The monster looked at her, and she at it. It cocked its head, as if it was curious. Then it loped towards her, slow and thudding, its eyes still glowing with the promise of death. Sera was not afraid of that promise. She had spent all her terror already. There was only purpose left.

I will not die here.

I will not die tonight.

She slipped a pearl of Lightfire from her pocket.

The monster opened its mighty jaws, its shadows filling up the passage until there was only darkness and within it, the gleam of its fangs. It screeched as it swooped down at her, and Sera rose up, meeting it head-to-head as she hurled the pearl into the blackness of its throat. Fire met darkness in an explosion of light. It splintered the darkness, and the monster along with it, scattering the last of its shadows into the walls.

She collapsed in a heap, tears streaming down her face as magic flickered around her like fireflies. They gathered around the body of an old man, still wearing his captain's hat. He looked so peaceful, he might have been sleeping. Sera prayed that somewhere on a different plane, Saint Maurius was folding him into his embrace and carrying him over a distant sea.

A few feet away lay her father. She wished for him only a deeper, darker hell than this.

Gaspard Dufort was dead. And as Sera studied his lifeless face and the awful twist of his lips, caught in a silent scream, she could not bring herself to mourn him. She did not have the strength for feeling at all. Only the relief that it was done, at last.

She slumped against the wall, listening to the shallow flutter of her own breath. She rolled her head around, the stone cool against her cheek as she fought the blackness in her mind. She flitted in and out of consciousness, not sure if she was dead or dreaming when she spied a figure flickering in the darkness.

She was so spent now, so delirious from blood loss, she thought she was imagining it. But then the figure swept towards her, and she saw that it was Ransom, wearing her cloak of Lightfire and a look of such crushing dread she hardly recognized him. '*Seraphine.*'

She blinked and he was closer now. He dropped to his knees and took her face between his hands, his nose brushing hers as he searched for life in her eyes. 'Can you hear me?' he said in a ragged whisper. Perhaps it was his nearness, or maybe it was the warm glow of Lightfire moving through him and into her; either way, Sera found new strength.

Enough to moan weakly in response.

He sagged against her. 'All right,' he said softly. 'All right, Seraphine.'

His hands left her face to trail across her body, searching for the source of the blood pooling between them. He swore when he found the gash on her arm. At another delicious spike of Lightfire, she reached up to smooth the lines on his forehead.

'Could be worse,' she croaked.

He gave her a flat look. 'How so?'

'Dufort is dead.'

'So I see,' he said, looking past her.

His face was like stone, those eyes unreadable.

'Are you angry?'

'Oh yes,' he said, brushing a knuckle along her cheek. 'But only because you got to do it without me.'

'I didn't do it at all,' she admitted.

'Good,' he murmured, looking past her again. Studying the husk of Dufort's body and then that of the captain, no doubt putting together what had happened. 'Then it was Saint Oriel.'

'Or Mama.' Sera felt herself smile. 'The Lightfire ... It's helping me.'

He moved in a blur, shrugging off the cloak and throwing it around her shoulders. Such instant relief. She felt like she had been swept into a warm hug, the searing pain in her arm quickly fading.

'I tried to free as many monsters as I could but there are too many,' he said, as he ripped a strip off the bottom of his shirt. 'This whole place is crawling with them. The cloak alone won't be enough.'

Sera watched him work, quickly and efficiently making a tourniquet for her arm. She had lost so much blood by now, she should be close to death but every second in that cloak filled her with new strength.

When it was done, he scooped her up, folding her into his arms and carrying her away from the body of her father. She turned her face into his chest, breathing in that heady mix of woodsmoke and sage. His heart thrummed beneath her cheek and she listened to the music of it, steeling herself for what would come next.

When they reached a fork in the passage, he set her down again. 'Can you stand?'

She showed him that she could. Her eyes darted back towards the common room, to that well of screams that went on and on. 'I'm going back in there, Ransom. I have to finish what I started.'

He nodded slowly, but when she turned, he grabbed her hand and tugged her back. She looked up at him, his drawn face lit by the glow of her cloak. He was covered in ash, his hands streaked with her blood. She was sure she looked even worse, but by the way he was gazing at her she'd never have guessed.

'You never gave me your answer,' he said.

It took her a minute, her sluggish mind sorting through the chaos of tonight, but she remembered – the thing he had asked of her in that alley before she got knocked out.

'You still want to run away with me?' she said, in quiet confusion. 'Even after everything that's happened?'

He was already nodding. 'For ten years, I've prayed to Saint Oriel,' he said, as if he was telling her a secret. 'Asking her for a better life than this one. For a kinder fate. The courage to chase it. I never really believed she could hear me down here in the dark, or that even if she could, she would ever bend her ear to the pleas of a Dagger. I almost gave up.' He laid his forehead against hers. 'And then you came barrelling over the horizon like a runaway sun. You shattered the darkness, Seraphine. And I realize now that all these years I wasn't wishing for freedom. I was wishing for you.'

His face blurred and Sera realized she was crying. She didn't know if her tears were born of grief or hope, or the soaring relief at having found a kindred soul in this dark circle of hell, who wanted to climb out of it with her. He swept his thumb across her cheek to catch them, and she smiled, and said, 'Yes, Bastian. My answer is yes.'

His name felt like another secret between them. She liked what it did to his face, filling it with light, and a kind of beauty that was different from the brooding handsomeness she had come to know. It was like sunlight on the plains, the first fall of snow in winter. It was hope for something beyond this night, beyond this place, and whatever that something turned out to be, she wanted to be a part of it.

'Tomorrow, when this is all over, we'll leave this city, Seraphine.'

'Together,' she said, kissing him.

'Together.' He answered her kiss with his own, his hands smeared with blood and ash as they cradled her face. His tongue swept in to meet hers as they held tightly to each other, blood-soaked and smiling at the mouth of hell.

And this kiss – the taste of it – was freedom.

Chapter 45

Seraphine

They broke apart as fresh cries filled the passage. This time, when Sera turned towards the sound, Ransom didn't tug her back. He fell into step beside her as, cloak glowing, she fished the final three pearls from her pocket.

When she breached the doorway to the Cavern, a gasp stuck in her throat. The room had been reduced to rubble and ruin, the floor strewn with ancient skulls, broken furniture and dead bodies. And still the monsters stalked and howled, lunging at anything that moved. Most of the remaining Daggers were either running or cowering in the alcoves.

Sera flung a pearl, setting off a bright flash. The monsters closest to her bellowed as they reared up, then convulsed as the poison inside them dissolved in the glow. A heartbeat later, they were dead, felled by the brief spectacle. It had the desired effect. The rest of the creatures snapped their chins up, turning their hungry eyes on Sera.

Now she had their attention.

'Follow me and I will free you!' she shouted.

One by one, the monsters left their mindless war and lumbered towards her, their black tongues lolling from their mouths.

'Don't stop until I command you,' she told them. 'Do not touch another soul.'

Daggers scrabbled out of the way, flattening themselves against the walls as the monsters stomped trance-like from the cavern, willingly surrendering their bloodlust for the promise of Lightfire.

Sera edged backwards into the passage, keeping her eyes on the mass of shadows.

Ransom's hand brushed along her spine. 'You are ... very good at this.'

She gave a grim smile. 'Mama always said I had a knack for bossing people around.'

'Oh, I know.'

She folded the last two pearls into his hand. 'Use these on any stragglers you find.' She glanced sidelong at him. 'Please be careful.'

'You took my line,' he said, leaning in to kiss her temple. 'I'll come for you when it's done.'

'Sacred Saints' Cathedral.' She grabbed his free hand and squeezed it, as though she could press the bargain into his skin. 'Meet me there at dawn.'

'I'll be there, Seraphine.'

He stepped away as monsters shoved through the doorway. Sera didn't give herself time to be afraid. She turned and led them down the long passage, grateful for the strength her cloak gave her and mindful not to trample the bodies in her way. The monsters made no such effort.

At the sound of the sudden exodus, more monsters crept out from the smaller tunnels, joining the others on their hunt for freedom. Sera didn't dare detour to find them all, hoping those pearls in Ransom's fist would be enough to deal with any that got left behind. She focused single-mindedly on the door at the end of the tunnel, following the rustle of wind that told her she was almost there.

Once outside, Sera took the steps to Hugo's Passage two at a time, conscious of every hulking shadow crowding at her back. At the top, she was greeted by an ominous clap of thunder and a sky so bruised, she felt the weight of it on her shoulders. In the distance, the top half of the Aurore had been swallowed by a thundercloud. There was no sign that her friends were still there waiting for her. She prayed they hadn't given up.

Raindrops kissed Sera's cheeks as she fled Old Haven. She was almost at the Verne when the bell of the clock tower rang out twelve times. Midnight. *Saints*, she was hopelessly late.

They'll be there, she told herself. *They made you a promise.*

Sera hugged her cloak tighter, letting the magic soak deep into her bones as she broke into a run. Footsteps rang out behind her as the monsters hurried to keep up. In the distance, lightning forked the skies around the Aurore, as if the saints themselves were urging her on.

Another crash of thunder welcomed Sera to Primrose

Square, the crack of lightning that followed so violent it split the sky. The rain was bucketing down with a vengeance now, blurring the outline of the Aurore and the troughs of ordinary flames fighting against the deluge. Some of them had gone out entirely. Others had been reduced to embers.

Sera ploughed towards the fading light, her heart throbbing with every step. The city was a symphony around her, the drumbeat of thunder joining with the low, keening wind, the rattle of rain against the tower giving way to the hiss of dying flames.

The night was getting darker, but Seraphine's cloak was a flame of its own and no amount of rain could snuff it out. The glow of her Lightfire reached towards three shadows peering out from under the Aurore.

Bibi's voice cried out beneath the grumbling of the sky. 'Sera! We've been so worried!'

Sera nearly cried with relief at the sight of her friends, sopping wet and up to their ankles in the squelching mud. When she reached them, she turned to face the monsters, commanding them to kneel at the base of the tower.

One by one, they obeyed, their shadows still straining towards her.

Val stared at them over her shoulder. 'This is the stuff nightmares are made of.'

Sera huffed. 'You have no idea.'

Her friends looked her over, no doubt noting the bloodstains on her clothes, the smears of ash on her cheeks, in her hair. Theo's gaze snagged on the tourniquet. 'What happened to you?'

'It's a long story.' And there was no time to tell it. 'Hand me a satchel. We need to start climbing.'

'Are you sure that's a good idea?' said Val. 'You look pretty beat up.'

'I'll be fine,' said Sera, grabbing a satchel full of powdered Lightfire. 'You two take the first tier. Your ankle is still weak and Bibi's balance is . . .' she trailed off.

'Non-existent,' supplied Bibi. 'No arguments here.'

The first tier was less than fifteen feet off the ground. A kinder fall, if there was to be one.

Theo frowned as he grabbed the next satchel. 'I'll take the highest tier.' He raised his hand before Sera could argue. 'I want the bragging rights.'

'All right,' she said gratefully. 'I'll take the second.'

'Race you!' Theo was halfway to the first tier before Sera even shouldered her satchel. She tipped her head back, watching in muted wonder as he scaled the first tier and then the second, angling for the topmost trough without a breath of hesitation. He simply addressed the challenge as if he'd been climbing towers his entire life. As if he cared more about this city – and its people – than himself.

Sera followed him up the tower, scrabbling for a foothold on the slick stone. She glanced back at the monsters as she climbed, unnerved to find them all watching her with a mixture of anguish and impatience.

Below her, Bibi gave Val a leg up, both girls grunting as they hauled themselves towards the lowest tier. It occurred to Sera that their plan was a hell of a lot more reckless in a thunderstorm, but it was way too late to turn back now. With a throng of hungry monsters at their feet, no one had even bothered to suggest it.

She turned her attention to the climb. Hand over hand, then foot over foot. Up and up she went, reaching the first tier with remarkable speed. She hauled herself onto the wide stone beam and hurried along the trough. Most of the flames here still flickered, shielded as they were by the two higher tiers above. But the rain was coming in sideways now, doing its best to extinguish them.

The sky boomed, and Sera flinched. Lightning forked into the far side of the square, sending a curl of smoke up from the burning grass. Rivers of rain poured down the tower as she made for the next scaffold, heaving herself up towards the second tier.

She was distracted by a howl from below. The monsters were growing impatient, no doubt addled by the storm and the frustration as they watched her retreating figure. Every step up the tower took the Lightfire further away from them. She had to move quicker, even as the storm rallied against her.

A glance below revealed Val and Bibi had made it onto the first tier, and had a jar of Lightfire in each hand. Above Sera, Theo was a shadow in the dark, shimmying up the narrowing tower into a hulking storm cloud.

Saints protect him. Sera reached the second tier and dragged herself onto the stone beam. She knelt at the trough, red-faced and panting, as a scream ripped through the night. She looked down to find Bibi swinging her satchel at a monster coming up from below. Three more had already begun to climb, the rest of the herd now circling the tower like they were thinking about tearing the whole thing down.

There were just enough of them to do it.

Shit.

Sera had climbed too high.

While Bibi faced off against the monster, Val unscrewed a jar of Lightfire and walked along the trough, dumping the powder on all those dying embers. Sera sucked in a breath, conscious of every crawling second. Either their plan would work or they would die.

No. She refused to watch her friends die. She refused to fail.

She held her breath and prayed to Saint Oriel of Destiny and Saint Calvin of Death, to Saint Maud of Lost Hope, to Lucille Versini and to Mama and to whatever damn force had decided to split the sky open and pummel them with rain.

We will live, her heart cried. *You will let us live.*

That handful of seconds felt like hours, but when the powder met those dying embers and set them alight again, the resounding crack of magic was so mighty even the sky paused to take a breath. The thunder stilled and the clouds parted, as though the moon wanted to watch too.

The trough erupted in Lightfire, the flames surging so high that Val fell backwards, shattering the empty jar. The monster on the scaffold fell too, leaving Bibi swinging at nothing. By the time the creature hit the ground, it was a person again, its shadows dissolving in the glow. Bibi grabbed her jar and tipped it into the other end of the trough, the Lightfire dancing – then joining together – in a glorious hiss.

'You did it!' cried Sera, as the monsters closest to the tower slumped to the ground, their howls fading to blessed silence. She looked up just as Theo's trough ignited, the explosion of

Lightfire illuminating the violet underbelly of the storm and the triumphant glint of his smile.

'You look like a saint!' Sera shouted.

'I feel like a saint!' he crowed, as he turned to clamber back down. 'Your turn!'

Sera didn't hear the thunder as it snarled at her back, barely noticed the rain as she unscrewed her jars and filled the final trough with a flourish. The entire tower went up in Lightfire, the flames burning through the rain, twisting and rising to kiss those menacing clouds. It was a magnificent spectacle, a triumph of magic and ingenuity, and as Sera stood proudly atop the Aurore looking out over the glowing city of Fantome, she wished more than anything that Mama was here to see it.

In the rumble of the storm she heard her promise. *When the time comes, you will rise far above this wicked city and become a flame in the dark. You will be the Aurore, Seraphine.*

Had Mama always known it would come to this? Had Saint Oriel whispered it to her in a dream?

Sera looked down at her friends as they walked among the scattered rain-soaked bodies. They were monsters no longer. Poor, helpless souls now at peace. Her stomach twisted as she thought of the ransacked catacombs and all the bodies that lay strewn across those tunnels. Her father's among them.

Had Mama seen that too? Was her own death the price of his demise?

Had she always known she would not be here to see this moment?

Sera's eyes streamed as she tipped her head back to stare

up at the glowing crown of the Aurore. She could not deny the beauty of the tower as she stood in its heart. This ancient monument to the lost Age of Saints burning with new magic. *Good magic.* Magic that would not go out. Light that would burn on and on, through every storm of darkness, through rain and shadow, through fear and despair and—

'Wow, you're really milking this, aren't you?'

Sera looked down just as another fork of lightning skewered the sky. It illuminated the outline of a figure standing on the other end of the beam. He was tall and broad-shouldered, with a sweep of tousled hair that made her think of Ransom at first. But she knew that menacing voice.

Lark.

She stiffened as he came towards her, trailing his fingers over the writhing flames. 'So Dufort was right. You really are trouble.'

A memory struck Sera like a fist. She had seen this same shadow once before, standing in a different fire. She had thought it was Ransom then too, and had later been told it was Dufort. But there was no mistaking the tilt of Lark's shoulders, the easy swagger with which he walked.

'You killed my mother,' she breathed.

Lark only shrugged. 'It was nothing personal.'

Sera was already swinging for him, striking his jaw with a crack to rival the lightning that followed.

Chapter 46

Seraphine

Sera dodged Lark's answering swing, leaping backwards along the stone beam. Her cloak was no good against a Dagger without Shade, but she could tell by the force of her punch that wearing it brought some benefits.

He turned to spit out a glob of blood. 'You're a lot stronger than I recall.'

'And you're a dead man walking,' she hissed, searching for a weapon to use against him. But Mama's monsters were gone, and her friends were down in the square, unable to see her plight through the wall of flames. Sera's great spectacle had trapped her. 'Who are you to measure the worth of every person who draws breath in this city?'

Lark glared at her. 'If you want to be a moralistic bitch, then give back the Rizzano tiara.'

'I hope Mama gave you hell,' she spat.

'Oh, she did,' he said with a chuckle. 'Cursed me in a hundred different ways. Cursed Dufort for not doing it himself. She swore she'd haunt him for it.'

Sera curled her lip. 'He always was a coward.'

'He wasn't scared.' Lark shook his head. 'He was in love with her.'

Sera stared at him, her stomach lurching so violently, she nearly retched.

'He went to that farmhouse of yours three times, you know. And three times, he turned back. In the end, he dragged me with him. Gave me a heap of coin to do it and then keep my mouth shut afterwards.' Another devasting shrug. 'If it helps, he couldn't stomach killing you either.'

It didn't help. It only made the roaring in her head worse. Sera was almost at the end of the beam now, and Lark was still prowling towards her. She had to shove him off, to keep her balance long enough to ruin his. Her mind reeled through all the manoeuvres Albert had taught her.

Focus ... Think.

'You won't get a reward for this,' she said, to keep him talking. 'Dufort is dead.'

If Lark cared he didn't show it. He lifted his hand, revealing the gaudy ring on his fourth finger. The same one Sera had slapped out of Dufort's grasp right before he died. 'I already have my reward.'

At her look of disgust, he went on. 'I'm hardly a graverobber, Marchant. He promised it to me when we went to Bellevue Castle together. He knew Ransom was wavering, losing interest in the Order. You were his final test, you know.' He sighed, raking his sopping hair back. 'Dufort was going to kill him if he didn't kill you. So Nadia and I decided to help him out.'

'You're not helping him,' said Sera. 'If you kill me, Ransom will never forgive you.'

Lark smiled. Without those violent eyes, the expression might have been beautiful. 'After you left Hugo's Passage with all your little monsters, how will he ever know it was me?'

Sera bared her teeth as she sank into a fighting crouch, the thunder adding its own growl. 'You'd better not miss.'

He mirrored her stance. 'I never do.'

Lark swung his fist as the sky ignited. Sera jerked backwards, and his knuckles grazed her jaw. He stole another foot of ground. Her fingers worked the knot at her collar, deftly freeing her cloak. He struck again and she ducked, swinging her foot around in an arc. It was a risk on the narrow walkway, but she caught his ankle.

He barely teetered. 'Pathetic.'

She leaped back to her feet, whipping her cloak free in one fluid movement. She raised it between them, taunting him like a bull.

Lark frowned, hesitating, and she seized the moment. She lunged, casting the cloak over him. It covered his head, momentarily scrambling his senses. Sera shoved with all her weight and he careened backwards, arms pinwheeling as his heels met the lip of the platform.

But Lark was not going down alone. His hand shot out, grabbing her injured arm. Without her cloak the pain surged, wrenching a scream from her. She reeled backwards, dragging him away from the precipice of death.

He ripped the cloak off, casting it away. Sera bucked against his grip but he slammed his head into hers, knocking her to the ground. He was on her in the next heartbeat, crushing her windpipe.

'Well, this feels familiar,' he said.

She fought with all the strength she had left, bringing her knees up to strike his lower back again and again. She fisted his hair and yanked. His head snapped backwards and his grip slackened. She hinged upwards, jamming her thumbs into his eyeballs.

He screamed, twisting away from her. She came up onto her knees, roaring. The sky roared with her. Years of pain and anger poured out of her like a battle cry. She freed it all from her heart: her lifelong hatred for her father, her disappointment that he had not been braver or better, that he hadn't fought hard enough against the thrall of Shade, that he hadn't loved them enough to come back. Then there was rage at her mother for ever loving him, for not running fast and far enough away, for falling into an obsession that killed her and so many others. And finally Sera's grief at the loss of both of them, the loss of what they might have been to each other in another lifetime, in a kinder city.

Sera was so lost in the storm in her soul that she didn't notice the lightning splitting the sky behind her. Not as it forked through the clouds and turned the world silver, not as the spike of all that blazing power reached towards the tower like a finger, towards the girl kneeling on the second tier.

It struck her spine like a hot poker. Sera screamed, the pain so devastating it arched her back and dragged her to her feet. She stumbled, gasping, as heat flooded her body, boiling her blood and searing her bones. She collapsed over the trough, desperately sucking air into her shrivelled lungs. Flames of Lightfire twisted to lick her arms, her neck, her face, as if they were trying to soothe the terrible inferno inside her.

And all the while, Lark dragged himself towards her, unharmed, although every hair on his head was standing on end. She was as good as dead anyway. The pain was already gone, and there was such peace inside her now, as if her body knew it was time to give up. It was all she could do to fling her palm out and hold it against his chest.

He choked on a gasp, and when she turned her head to look at him, she saw that his eyes were wide. Frozen. Her gaze fell to where her hand pressed against his chest. It was bare. She had burned his shirt away. Had burned his skin bright gold, *branded* it, and as he heaved a final strangled breath, she realized she had scoured his heart too. She *felt* it stop. A final judder and then – nothing.

She snatched her hand back. He swayed, then slumped onto the stone, his unseeing eyes staring past her. Slowly, Sera turned her hand, tracing the crackles on her palm. She watched the raindrops sizzle as they fell onto it, her brows knitting in confusion. There was silence in her head, as though a mist had fallen over her thoughts. She couldn't make her brain work. All she knew for certain was that she was breathing. She was *alive.*

How the hell was she alive?

She stood on trembling legs, and heard her name on the wind.

'SERA! GET DOWN!' Someone was yelling at her. Theo. Then Val. Bibi too. She looked out over the flames to see her friends frantically waving. 'IT'S GOING TO FALL!'

Sera's frown deepened. She realized too late that the rumbling she heard was coming from below, not above. And that the trembling she felt was not her legs. It was the stone. The lightning hadn't just struck her. It had travelled *through* her to strike the whole damn tower. She saw now it had cleaved the scaffolds, shattered two pillars at the base and blasted the entire third tier apart.

The Aurore was coming down.

By the time she realized, Sera was already falling.

Down, down, down she went, lost in a sea of rubble and rain, the world spinning about her in whips of black and gold. Light and dark, flame and shadow. Time moved so very slowly. The wind sang to her as she fell, that strange magic still crackling in her palms as great pillars of stone crashed to the earth and exploded into smithereens.

The sky shook and the city trembled. Sera closed her eyes, bracing herself for death, and in the sudden quiet of her mind, she heard a faraway voice.

Live, it whispered from the deepest reaches of her soul. *Live and burn the darkness away.*

The voice did not belong to Mama. It was older, softer ... born of another age entirely. As Sera hit the grass with a hard thud, blackness crashed over her like a wave, and in it, she swore she glimpsed the face of Saint Oriel.

She swore that she was smiling.

Chapter 47

Ransom

Ransom spent the pearls Seraphine gave him not long after she left. He used the first one on three monsters scrapping at the far end of the west tunnel, and the second on a straggler who had made it all the way down to the crypts.

After a thorough sweep of the catacombs, he returned to the Cavern, steeling himself for what he would find there. He had seen enough bodies in the tunnels, but he knew the true horror of tonight still awaited him.

It was too quiet in the Cavern, where the metallic tang of blood mixed with the sulphuric stench of Shade. While the surviving Daggers picked through the detritus of their home, clearing aside the fallen rubble and broken furniture, Ransom walked among the dead bodies, looking for his friends. Terrified of finding them.

He knelt to inspect the body of a woman crumpled on her side, her sleek black hair gleaming in the light of an oil lamp that had somehow survived the brawl. She flopped onto her back and he loosed a breath of relief. It wasn't Nadia, but a barmaid he vaguely recognized from the Lucky Shell. Another victim of Sylvie's poisoned wine.

He searched on. Most of the dead were Daggers much older than Ransom, their bodies marked by extensive black whorls. Most of the others were dressed like dockhands, merchants and fishermen still in their seal-skinned boots. Monsters, once. Corpses now.

Just like Dufort. Ransom's thoughts returned to the moment he had found Seraphine slumped in that tunnel beside her father, both of them so pale and still he'd thought she was dead too. Crushing, bone-deep terror had lanced through him at the sight. Even now, he could still feel it gnawing at the edges of his heart. The relief when her eyelids had fluttered had been so profound he had forgotten all about Dufort's body lying six feet away.

Dufort's death had not shocked or distressed Ransom as he once imagined it would. Even now, his thoughts skipped past the dead man to Seraphine, forging her way to the Aurore with a herd of monsters at her back. He tried not to dwell on the very real possibility they might turn on her at any moment. That a rogue creature could destroy the promise of freedom they had made to each other. The promise of tomorrow, and the adventures they would find beyond the darkness of Fantome.

He worried for his friends too. He regretted brawling

with Lark earlier, and was relieved that Nadia had hauled them apart. He had to find them to apologize, to explain everything.

Three Daggers carried Dufort's body into the Cavern, laying him down by the fireplace. An uncomfortable hollow yawned inside Ransom as he peered down at the Head of the Order, a man he'd once thought of as indestructible. He waited for a pang of guilt, of grief, but he felt neither.

What do you want to be, boy, brave or broken?

I want to be free. Ransom turned from the body. *Now I am.*

But at what cost?

Thirty-six dead Daggers so far, by Ransom's count, including those lying in the tunnels. A third of the Order destroyed in one night. His stomach twisted at the thought of Lark and Nadia, still missing. He turned on his heel, searching the faces of the figures moving around him.

Abel hobbled towards him, the lines on his face carved still deeper by worry. 'Have you seen Collette? I've searched all the tunnels.'

Ransom shook his head, and Abel staggered on, repeating the question to everyone he passed. Another pair of Daggers drifted over. Ren, with a deep gash on his cheek and Caruso, some of whose long black hair had been ripped out at the root. 'The Cloaks will answer for this bloodbath,' snarled Caruso.

More Daggers came until twenty or so of them were crowding around the body of Dufort, as if they were expecting him to rise from the dead and tell them what to do next.

'The bodies,' someone said at last. 'We need to start taking them out.'

'Good thing we're surrounded by graveyards,' muttered Caruso.

'Has anyone seen Lark and Nadia?' asked Ransom, but they shook their heads, pairing off to start carting out the bodies.

Ransom returned to the north passage, where he found Lisette pressed against the wall, as if she couldn't bear to go inside the Cavern. Her cheeks were streaked with tears and her blonde hair was caked with blood.

'So much death,' she murmured, holding her arms around herself. 'Why did they come here? Why did she do this to us?'

'It was Dufort,' said Ransom. All this death – this horror – started and ended with Dufort. 'He's dead.'

'Everyone is dead.' She stared past him. 'The Order is destroyed.'

'Have you seen Nadia? Or Lark?'

She slowly shook her head. 'Not since he went after the girl.'

Ransom froze. 'What?'

'He took Dufort's ring,' she said in a faraway voice. 'I suppose Nadia went after him when I told her . . .' She blinked herself from her stupor and glowered at Ransom. 'This is all your fault. You should have killed that meddlesome farm bitch when you had the chance.'

But Ransom was already running. Down the north passage and out into the storm. The roar of thunder paled against the roaring in his chest. He looked to the Aurore as he ran, praying he wasn't too late to stop Lark doing whatever he was about to do.

By the time he made it to the end of Old Haven, most of the lights on the Aurore had gone out. Shadows flitted across the stone, and a flash of lightning illuminated four figures climbing up the tower. And there among them, was a rippling golden cloak.

He was not too late.

Ransom was at the Verne when the whole Aurore went up in flames, sparking like a mighty torch. For a moment, the rain stopped entirely, the thunder ceasing its tirade as though the entire sky was watching in wonder.

Ransom's heart swelled as Seraphine's grand plan came to life, the glow of Lightfire crowning the ancient monument in a shimmering halo. Such magnificence. Such unbridled incandescence. It almost made him forget Lark and Nadia.

Then the thunder roared back to life. Ransom pushed on, towards the Aurore. Lightning danced around the tower. When it struck the stone, he had to shield his eyes from the glare. He slowed, blinking the spots from his vision. When the ground shook, he mistook it for thunder.

Then the tower crumbled right before his eyes.

Flames rained down like fireworks, huge chunks of stone following in a pounding hail.

Fast, so fast his feet barely touched the cobbles, Ransom ran, his chest heaving as he finally reached Primrose Square. He saw the bodies first, knew they were the monsters Seraphine had brought here, knew her plan had come off before the tower fell. It was not the plan he was worried about.

It was the girl. It was Lark and Nadia and the memory of that fork of lightning cleaving the tower in two. He shouted Seraphine's name, sending it up to the clouds. There came no answer. He called for Lark and Nadia, stalking towards all that rock and rubble, the shattered remains of the greatest monument in Valterre.

The clouds parted, scattering the last of their rain, as if they had seen enough. The moon poured its light onto the square, and after what felt like an eternity, Ransom spotted Nadia kneeling between two broken pillars.

His chest tightened at the sound of her sobs. They were deep and guttural, as if wrenched from her soul. Her head was bowed, and as he drew nearer, climbing over broken stone and ruined earth, he saw the reason for her tears and nearly fell to his knees too.

She was cradling Lark's body in her arms.

Ransom stumbled, all thoughts eddying away. Lark's face was paler than he'd ever seen it, the rosy hue of his cheeks lost to a strange, pearly sheen. His eyes were wide open, staring at nothing. They were no longer green, but gold. Like two gleaming coins.

Grief slammed into Ransom, making his legs buckle. Lark was gone. They had fought bitterly in the Cavern, their last words to each other some of the cruellest they had ever spat. Ransom hadn't meant them, but he couldn't take them back now. There would be no more jokes. No more laughter. No more singing, no more midnight adventures, no more rooftop conversations about love and loss and all that dwelled in between. There would be no more trips home to the farm, no more butter cake and brandy, no more chickens, no more . . . Lark.

No more Lark.

The loss spiralled through Ransom like a tornado. He braced himself against a fallen boulder, trying to find his breath.

'Ransom.' Nadia's voice broke on his name. He crawled to her, bringing his hand to Lark's cheek in vain hope. It was ice cold.

'What happened?' he managed.

'She murdered him,' said Nadia, in a cold, quiet voice. 'Right before she brought the whole tower down.'

No. That wasn't right. 'It was the lightning.'

'*She* was the lightning.'

He frowned.

'*Look,*' she hissed. And he followed her gaze, to the place where Lark's shirt had been scoured from his body. There, in the centre of his chest, was a small golden handprint, perfectly outlined by the shadow-marks around it. Scar tissue etched in gold. A type of burn Ransom had never seen before. It was like the sheer force of it had plunged right through Lark's body and stopped his heart.

Ransom couldn't tear his eyes away from that handprint. He knew those small, slender fingers, the palm he had kissed that night by Saint Celiana's fountain.

Fuck.

How had she done it?

And where the hell was she now?

'Ransom.' Nadia's voice again, pulling him back. He looked up at her, and nearly wept at the broken expression on her face. Her brown eyes were glassy and tear tracks smeared the dust on her cheeks. 'This is all her fault.'

'No.' His own voice was small. 'There must have been . . .' he trailed off. A reason? A mistake? He looked around, searching the mounds of rubble, but Seraphine was long gone. She had fled, and despite Nadia's fury, and the body of his best friend lying here beside him, Ransom was relieved she had escaped. 'She was just trying to survive.'

'*Survive?*' Nadia shoved him. 'Wake up. That girl dragged an army of monsters into Old Haven. She ransacked our home, killed our friends and murdered our leader. And *you* let her do it.'

Ransom was shaking his head. No, that wasn't what had happened. Nadia was twisting it.

'Dufort is dead. The Order is in ruins. Lark is *gone.*' Her voice cracked. She bowed her head, her hair making a shroud around Lark's face. 'Lark is gone. And you still won't admit it. You still can't see how dangerous she is.'

'She didn't mean for any of this ... It got out of hand ...' Seraphine was a fighter. She would have fought tooth and nail to get out of here alive, ripped the whole tower down to do it. Lark had come after her – tried to kill her.

Ransom raked the sodden hair from his face, his gaze flitting to that golden handprint. Or maybe he was a fool, after all. Maybe he had just sold out his Order for a chance to taste the sun. And the sun had burned him. Burned them all.

Nadia raised her head. 'Everything that happened tonight is because of her. *Everything.* She destroyed our home. She destroyed our family. Our best friend. My— my—' She surrendered a small whimper. 'She's taken everything from us and you're so lust-blind, you're sitting here beside your dead best friend defending her.' Another sob burst out, pouring from her like a scream. 'Look at *me.* Look at *him.* And then tell me it was worth it.'

Ransom's heart clenched as he looked at Nadia, then at his brother in her lap. Those eerie golden eyes. 'I didn't want this, Nadia.'

She gave a broken sigh. The light in her eyes had gone out and she was looking at Ransom as though he had extinguished it. He had. All of this horror and pain wasn't because of Seraphine. It was because of him. Because he had gone soft for her. Because he had lied to his friends about his intentions and kept the truth about Seraphine – about the monsters and the Lightfire and Dufort – from them until they had no choice but to take matters into their own hands. Until they thought they had to save him from himself.

'I'm sorry.' He reached for her. 'Nadia, I'm so sorry.'

'I can't breathe,' she whispered. 'How can I ever breathe again?'

He curled his arm around her and she buried her face in his shoulder and sobbed. Silent tears streamed down Ransom's face as he held her in his arms, Lark lying silently between them.

After a long while, Nadia pulled away again. She held up Dufort's ring, the skull gleaming in the moonlight. 'You have to make this right.' She pressed it into his hand. 'I swear to every blessed saint and dead Dagger in Fantome that if you don't kill her I will. I'll hunt that bitch to the far-flung corners of Valterre, to the end of my days, and when I catch her, I'll scour a handprint on her chest and hang her body from the Bridge of Tears, so every damn Cloak in Fantome knows what happens when you fuck with the Daggers.'

She stared hard at him, hatred burning in her eyes. Ransom

knew she meant every word. She would take that ring and make herself a reluctant leader, take the king's ear along with it and use his scouts to find Seraphine if it came to it. There was nothing Nadia wouldn't do to avenge her lover, to avenge her family.

And if Ransom walked away now, she would hunt him too. With the scorned might of a deadly Order, and the king himself.

But if he stayed … He stared at that ring in the palm of his hand and knew every terrible thing it symbolized. If he stayed and took that ring for his own, he would be able to stand between Seraphine and the Order of Daggers. Not just a leader, but a shield.

Only then, would she truly be free.

And he had promised her freedom, hadn't he?

'Do you hear me?' said Nadia.

Ransom nodded. Slowly, so achingly slowly, he closed his fist around the ring.

He stood up and, with Nadia's help, he lifted his friend from the rubble of the Aurore and carried Lark's body home.

Chapter 48

Seraphine

Sera was unconscious when Theo found her in the rubble. Dimly, she was aware of her name being called – no, *screamed* – somewhere far above the blackness in her mind, then, eons later, she felt the damp press of hands on her face. Strong arms lifted her from the rubble and more voices crowded in on her.

Is she breathing?

How the hell is she not dead?

It's all right, Sera. It's going to be all right.

Sera reached for those words like falling stars, only to plummet again into blackness.

When she woke up, she was in an infirmary, propped up on three pillows. Three tense faces stared back at her. She drank them in, one by one, looking for injuries. Satisfied, she surveyed her own battered body. She was covered in bruises and scrapes, but remarkably, nothing appeared to be broken.

'You are a marvel,' said Theo, as if he could read her thoughts. 'I don't know how you survived that fall.'

'Forget the fall,' said Val, perching on the edge of her bed. 'I don't know how you survived that lightning. You lit up like a firework, Sera.'

Yes. Yes, she remembered it now. The strike and the fall. The Dagger whose heart she had stopped. She clenched her palm shut, too afraid to look and see what crackled there. Was it a mix of lightning and Lightfire? Or some delusion she had imagined?

The gash on her arm had been mended by a nurse – seventeen stitches, bandaged up and set in a loose sling. Over a mug of sugary tea and six ginger biscuits, her friends told her what had happened after she fell, how they had fished her from the rubble and ran before the nightguards arrived.

They had passed a cavalry troop on their way to the infirmary, the king's soldiers riding hard and fast towards the broken Aurore, where they would find all those bodies strewn among the rubble. They would cart them away to be inspected, then buried, and there would be more questions for the city to answer. More fear and accusations, more whisperings about monsters and Lightfire and the changing face of Fantome.

Sera told her friends everything that had happened down in the catacombs, including her final showdown with Dufort, the man she had once called her father, as well as the things Lark had told her on the Aurore before that fateful lightning strike.

They listened in wide-eyed silence, fitting all the pieces of the night together until the jigsaw was complete.

'You can't go back to House Armand,' said Bibi. 'Not after what happened in the catacombs.' Sera hadn't just broken the truce, she had smashed it to smithereens, killing the Head of the Order and his second-in-command in the same night, saying nothing of the monsters and the Daggers they had killed.

'Mercure will hang you from the Bridge of Tears herself,' said Val.

Theo winced. 'You don't have to be so graphic about it.'

'I don't want to go back,' said Sera. 'When dawn breaks, I'm leaving this city.' She looked at each of them in turn. Her trio of stalwart, weary allies, as loyal and dauntless as the heroes of her favourite novels. 'Thank you for everything you did last night. And in all the days before that. I'd be dead without the three of you, and Fantome would be on its knees.' She summoned a watery smile. 'I'm really going to miss you.'

'It was the most exciting night of my life,' said Bibi, squeezing her hand. 'Despite all the almost-dying.' She paused. 'Or maybe because of it.'

Val scrunched her nose. 'Whoever said farmgirls were boring?'

Theo only frowned, as if he was working through some impossible problem in his head.

'I have one more favour to ask,' said Sera, wincing a little as she sat up. 'Could someone please fetch my dog for me?' She was not going anywhere without Pippin. And if it came to it, she would brave the threshold of House Armand and the furious swing of Fontaine's walking stick to get him.

But Bibi was already nodding. 'Of course!'

'Thank you,' said Sera, looking out of the window to keep from crying. The moon was fading from the paling sky, the night slowly giving way to dawn. Her thoughts turned to Ransom, and the promise they had made to each other in the catacombs.

It felt like a lifetime ago now.

But morning was coming, and at long last, freedom was dawning.

When dawn came, Sera was sitting on the bottom step of Our Sacred Saints' Cathedral in the middle of the deserted square. The rain had finally sputtered out, leaving a pearly sheen across the rooftops of Fantome. The sky was soft and pink, scattered with fluffy clouds edged in gold.

Across the square, three familiar figures appeared with a dog trotting out in front. She shot to her feet and Pippin yipped, hurrying towards her. She swept him into her arms, pressing kisses into his fur.

When the others caught up, Bibi slung a rucksack from her shoulder and handed it to Sera. It was filled with travelling clothes and provisions for the journey ahead.

'Thank you,' she said, setting Pippin down to hug her. Then she saw her friends were carrying three more rucksacks between them. 'What's all this?'

'We talked it over on the way home,' said Theo. 'We want to go with you.'

Sera blinked. 'What?'

'We want an adventure.' Val tugged at the straps on her rucksack. 'We want to see what lies beyond the Hollows.'

Sera's heart skipped a beat. 'But I don't even know where I'm going yet.'

'I'm more than ready to hurl myself into the unknown,' said Val, with a shrug. 'The sooner the better, frankly.'

'And what about you, Bibi?' said Sera. 'You love living at House Armand.'

'I love the people at House Armand,' said Bibi, with a smile. 'You are my people. And it's not like I'll be gone forever.'

Sera turned to Theo. 'What will House Armand do without its Shadowsmith? You love your craft. It's your passion.'

'*Creating* is my passion, Sera. Not Shade.' He looked past her to the empty space where the Aurore had stood. 'I just never thought there was anything beyond it. I've always believed that all the good magic died with the saints.' His eyes shone as they met hers. 'But after what I witnessed last night, after what we did with that Lightfire . . . we've only just begun to understand its true power. I can't give up my curiosity yet. I don't want to.' His smile grew, pressing a dimple into his cheek. 'And I don't want to give up our friendship either.'

Sera shook her head, marvelling at her luck. As the strands of this new unwritten destiny twisted around them, she looked up at the stained-glass windows of the cathedral and offered a prayer of thanks to Saint Oriel. Sera had discovered such radiant light in the heart of this ancient city, and for the first time in her life, she was not running away from a shadow, but towards a glimmering horizon.

'So, it's decided, then?' said Theo. 'We're going to be a travelling troupe?'

Val groaned. 'Why must you make it sound so uncool?'

Sera laughed as they began to bicker among themselves. She expected more of this in the days ahead, and she was eager to begin. But they had not yet completed their troupe – if that's what it was to be. 'Ransom will be here soon. I promised I would wait for him.'

Val and Bibi exchanged a look.

Theo frowned. 'Don't tell me you invited the tunnel rat?'

'It was his idea,' she said, shooting him a warning look. 'Ransom is a good person. He saved my life. We saved each other.'

'And he's *very* hot,' added Bibi gravely.

Val rolled her eyes. 'Fine. But he better bring a shit-ton of money with him.'

'He's a Dagger,' said Bibi. 'Of course he will.'

Sera didn't care about money. She only cared about the man with autumn-kissed eyes and ink-black hair whose smile knocked the breath from her lungs and whose kiss made her heart sing.

As the sun rose, he appeared at the other end of the square.

It was an effort not to run to him, but she managed to walk, slow and steady, leaving the others waiting for her by the steps.

It wasn't until Ransom drew closer that Sera realized something was wrong. Though the sun was rising, the morning was getting darker. Colder. Ransom had not come to the cathedral alone. He had brought all the shadows of Fantome with him, dragging them from buildings and streetlamps until they made a storm around him.

His eyes were as silver as the stars. With the dark rippling at his back, he looked like midnight incarnate.

Sera quailed at the sight of him stalking towards her. The wind kicked up, howling with the promise of death. The others drew back, sheltering around the side of the cathedral steps, taking Pippin with them. Sera did not retreat, instead surging forward. She marched into the swirling dark, searching for the man within.

But those silver eyes tracked her, and a rogue shadow struck like a whip, cutting a deep groove in the stones. A line which she was not to cross. She stood behind it, her heart hammering so hard she could barely breathe.

Ransom came to a stop ten feet away, night swarming at his back.

'What are you doing?' she said, embarrassed at the pathetic squeak of her voice.

He looked through her. 'Delivering this final message to you. Get out of this city and never come back.' His voice was as cold as the look on his face. 'If you set foot in Fantome again, it will be the last thing you ever do.'

Sera's mind reeled, trying to untangle how these last few hours had somehow changed everything. 'If this is about Lark, he came at me first. I never wanted to—'

'This is not about Lark.'

'I don't understand.' She tried again. 'You asked me to leave with you. You *wanted* this. You're free, Ransom.' She hated the plea in her voice. 'We're both free.'

He wouldn't look at her. 'It was a dream, Seraphine.'

'It doesn't have to be a dream.' Her eyes stung, her throat tightening painfully. 'It can be real. Let it be real.'

'Stop.' There was a hitch in his voice. 'I *can't*.'

Shadows arced over them, blotting out the world, until she was trapped in the storm of his darkness. She saw it then, a flash of silver on his left hand. Dufort's ring. Dufort's legacy. The Order of the Daggers had found its new leader. No— *No.*

The words lurched from her: 'What did you do?'

He said nothing.

'*Bastian!*' she called. 'Look at me!'

His hand shot out, firing shadows at the cathedral. The windows shattered in a hail of coloured glass. '*Don't* call me that.'

Sera refused to be afraid. 'Why are you doing this?'

He struck again, knocking a gargoyle from the eaves. It cracked the cobbles as it fell. He tore down another, ripping apart the cathedral piece by piece, just to show her he could. Somewhere behind Sera, Pippin was barking. The others were screaming at her to come away from Ransom.

But Sera stood her ground. He was trying to scare her – to frighten her off – but she had seen enough monsters to know Ransom was not one of them, and she refused to cower before this devastating spectacle.

Her heart was an anchor in her chest. It rooted her to that line in the earth, to the sight of that awful ring on his left hand and the matching quicksilver in his eyes. If she could just pierce his veneer, she could find the man beneath the Dagger. She could save him.

'Bastian!' she cried. 'You're *hurting* me.'

Perhaps it was the crack in her voice. Perhaps it was the tears on her face or the trembling of his hands; whatever the reason, he raised his chin. Their eyes met, and the agony she glimpsed there nearly punched through her soul.

She lurched towards him, walking right over the crack in the stones and into the heart of all that Shade. It rippled away from her, as if it was frightened. Sera didn't have time to wonder at the answering tingle in her blood. Or the magic that surged up through her ribcage. Without her cloak, her necklace, it made no sense, but the scent of lemon blossoms filled the air and Ransom's eyes widened, as if he could sense it too.

Lightfire.

She snatched his hand, her fingers crackling against his.

Yes, it was Lightfire. And it was thrumming in her blood.

His brow furrowed as the shadows around them fell away.

She watched the silver fade from his eyes. 'What are you doing?' she said softly.

He closed his eyes, denying her the sight of his humanity. 'Letting you go.' She moved her hands to his shirt but he caught them in his own. 'If I don't stay behind, the Daggers will come for you. They will hunt you every day of your life. They will chase you to the ends of the earth.'

'I don't care.'

'You will never be free, Seraphine. You will never know a minute of peace.'

'Bastian—'

'*Listen to me.*' He snapped his eyes open. 'They will find you and kill you and then they will string your corpse up by your fucking boots and *I* will have to cut you down—'

'Stop!' she pleaded.

'Go.' The word was a growl. 'Seraphine. *Go.*'

She trembled as he raised her hand to his mouth, pressing a parting kiss to her palm. His lips were soft and lingering. Her blood surged in answer and lightning crackled against his mouth. He raised his eyebrows, but said nothing as he released her.

He had said it all, already.

Sera opened her mouth to argue but he turned from her, taking a vial from his pocket and downing it in one gulp. His choice made, his path forking away from hers.

Tears streamed down her face, the words springing from her before she could stop them. 'You weren't the only one who prayed to Saint Oriel!' she called after him. 'I wished for you too, Bastian.'

She watched him stop. Flinch. For a moment she thought he would turn back, drop the act, cast aside his fear and go to her. Then shadows gathered at his back. He curled his fists and walked on, into the man-made dark.

Sera watched him go, her breath punching out of her in sharp bursts. Dimly, she became aware of the sun's warmth on the back of her neck, then the distant thrum of nightguards galloping through the streets, following her trail of destruction to another broken monument.

Sera turned around to find her friends hovering nearby. They stood in a puddle of stained-glass fragments, wearing matching looks of horror. Pippin was trembling in Bibi's arms.

Theo looked like he wanted to fling a dagger after Ransom.

Val broke the silence. 'What the hell was that?'

Sera wasn't entirely sure. She grimaced as she looked up at the cathedral, its empty windows gaping.

'The Daggers are going to come back stronger than before,' said Theo, following her gaze.

'And crueller,' muttered Val.

Bibi sighed. 'The city is as good as lost.'

'No,' said Sera. Perhaps it was Mama speaking through her, or the grand design of Saint Oriel herself, but the plan came to her so easily she felt it must have been at the back of her mind all along. 'We know their weakness now.' She could still feel it, the secret she had yet to unravel, crackling under her skin. 'Let's go away from here. To think and plan. *Create*. And when we're ready, we'll give the Daggers something to run from. We'll remake this city with Lightfire. And when we're done, everyone in Fantome will know the true meaning of freedom.'

Including the Dagger who had just banished her. She was not done saving him.

Theo cocked his head. 'Are you suggesting what I think you are . . . ?'

'A new Order,' said Sera. When Val snorted, she turned on her. 'Why not us?'

Theo stood a little taller, the light in his eyes kindling like the fire in her belly. 'The Order of Flames.'

'Now, that's an idea I can get behind,' said Bibi.

'All right, then,' Val relented, after a beat. 'We've taken so much from this city for so long, maybe it's time we finally gave something back.'

Even Pippin lifted his head, sniffing at the idea, like he approved of it, too.

As the sun rose over Fantome, the four founding members of the Order of Flames turned from the rubble and ruin of their city and went, side by side, into the unchartered wilds beyond.

Chapter 49

Ransom

R ansom climbed on to the rooftops to watch Seraphine
go. He couldn't help it. Couldn't help counting every
step she took away from him, as if they were his own
heartbeats running out.

It had taken every ounce of his self-control to push her away,
to kiss only her palm and not the gentle curve of her cheek,
the graceful column of her neck, that soft, smart mouth. For a
moment, he had thought about sweeping her into his arms and
damning it all. Damning them both.

He could not risk it. He could not risk her.

So, he had let her go, surrendering his first and final chance
of freedom. He couldn't bring himself to regret it, knowing
where the alternative would lead them. An Order run by a
vengeful Nadia, or worse, a cold-blooded, calculating Lisette.

The king's ear turned to her every whim, and Seraphine Marchant still running. Always running.

When she passed beyond his sight, under the towering stone arch that marked the exit from the city, out into the untamed reaches beyond, Ransom knew she was gone for good. No longer his spitfire, but a ghost like Mama and Anouk.

As the sun rose above the rooftops, crowning the city in syrupy golden light, he turned for the Hollows. The shadows came with him, and when they lagged, he downed another vial of Shade, welcoming the shiver that scoured away his grief. For Lark. For Seraphine. For the dream they had shared. The one he had sheared in half.

House Armand was silent as a tomb, save for the old woman sitting in the garden. Fontaine was perched on a windowsill, idly smoking a pipe, as though she was expecting him. When he came, dragging the darkness with him, and stood looking at her through the gate, she didn't even blink.

'You don't usually make such a spectacle of your arrival,' she remarked, by way of greeting. 'No paper darts today?'

'Dufort is dead.'

No inkling of surprise graced her wrinkled face. 'By whose hand?'

'Sylvie Marchant's.'

It was the truest answer. The monsters were her creation after all.

Fontaine gave a grunt of satisfaction. 'So, the lion has been slain at last. And here comes his cub, seeking comfort.' She blew a ring of smoke at him. 'The girl is long gone.'

Ransom's voice was as cold as the Shade in his bones. 'The girl is no longer welcome in my city.'

'So, you have finally surrendered your fascination with her.' A slow-curling smirk shifted the crevices in her face. 'I suppose fire is only mesmerizing until it burns you.'

He ignored the taunt, despite the unnerving awareness of those pale, milky eyes. 'I have a message for Cordelia Mercure.'

Fontaine glared at him through another ring of smoke. 'Then speak it, Bastian.'

He frowned. How the hell did she know his name? What *else* did she know about him?

'The monsters of Fantome are dead. The truce between our Orders is over. Tell your Cloaks to stay out of my way. If I catch one sniffing around Old Haven or sticking their nose in Dagger business, I'll kill them on sight.'

Her gaze flitted to the ring on his left hand. 'So, you have bartered your soul for the promise of power.'

His anger flared. Shade licked at his ribcage, dulling its heat. 'It wasn't worth much to begin with.'

A dry wheeze of laughter. 'And what of your bleeding heart?'

He didn't answer. His heart was lost to him, one piece of it buried with Lark in Old Haven, the other three scattered far beyond Fantome.

He turned from the gate.

'You know, she never was a true Cloak,' Fontaine called after him. 'Seraphine Marchant is something else entirely.'

He hated how her name went through him like sunlight. Too slowly, Shade licked it away. 'Whatever she was, it doesn't matter any more.'

'On the contrary, Bastian. I think it matters now, more than ever.' He shook off her words and walked on, even as they floated after him. 'The strands of destiny are not yet done with you.'

When he glanced over his shoulder, the old crone was gone, his shadows cresting as though to wash her warning away.

But it lingered, long after that.

Chapter 50

Seraphine

Seraphine and her friends travelled north through the plains, where vineyards and cornfields soaked up the sun's warmth, and onwards through a scattering of outlying villages that gave way to the Pinetops.

They went first on foot, and then by wagon, all four of them nestling into the wooden bed. Pippin slumbered between them, occasionally raising his bleary head to watch the flickering city lights get further away. Sera watched them, too, feeling a dull ache in her heart. She tried not to think of Ransom but as night swept in and her eyelids grew heavy, her thoughts betrayed her. She was haunted by the agony in his eyes, and that final press of his lips against her palm. *Seraphine, go.*

She turned those final moments over in her mind, trying to bury the feelings that came with them. She knew when they met again, he would not be able to show her the same kindness. They were enemies now, and one day soon, they would be rivals vying for control of the same city.

The travellers stopped to sleep in the first village they came to after the moon rose, exchanging coin for a room at the cheapest inn, where they ate their fill before bed. On the first night, in a fit of what felt now like utter wildness, they had decided to journey all the way to Halbracht, the ancient village that had birthed the Versini children and their obsession with magic. Shade, and later, Lightfire.

To four sleep-addled people drunk on cheap tavern wine, it had seemed like a grandly exciting idea, but by the fourth day, when Seraphine's back was aching and the hot sun had scalded her shoulders, she began to wonder if Halbracht was a dream beyond their grasp.

But despite their sunburnt sobriety, Theo remained sure of their destination, and, lacking an alternative, they let themselves be led by his confidence. Onwards they travelled, into the Pinetops, until the wagon could not withstand the terrain and they had to continue on foot. Pippin led them through the sloping hills, higher and higher, until the Silvercrest Mountains loomed on the horizon, and they heard the distant roar of the Hellerbend river. Sera's heart lifted as she glimpsed magnificent hawks swooping high above them, as if to draw them onwards.

'We're almost there,' Theo called, over his shoulder.

Val swiped a sweaty curl from her eye. 'What are you, a human compass? How the hell do you know that?'

Bibi was too out of breath to offer her usual optimism. But

Theo was sure-footed and smiling as he said, 'We're an hour out. Maybe less.'

For some reason, they all chose to believe him. And as it happened, the Shadowsmith was right. After another hour or so of trekking, Pippin caught a new scent, his tail wagging as he darted ahead.

Overhead, the jagged peaks of the Silvercrests rose to pierce the low-hanging clouds, and the travellers came at last to a narrow pass. A gate blocked their passage, its spires glinting menacingly in the afternoon sun.

A wooden signpost stood before the gate. It read:

Halbracht
Visitors unwelcome

Val dropped her rucksack with a groan. 'Well, it was fun while it lasted. Except I can't feel my ass and I smell like a sewer.'

Sera scowled at the sign while Pippin relieved himself against its foot.

Bibi slumped onto a nearby rock. 'Who wants to try sweet-talking our way in?'

Theo raised his fingers to his lips and whistled so loudly a hawk screeched in reply.

A minute passed, and then another, and just when Sera was going to fling a rock over the gate to see what might happen, a head popped up on the other side. The sunlight glinted off a mop of silver hair and for a second, she could have sworn it was Theo. Only he was standing beside her. And the boy climbing up the gate was younger than him by at least five years.

He gasped, then disappeared. A moment later, the gates groaned open and a woman slipped through. She had the same moon-silver hair braided down her back and eyes as bright as the south sea of Valterre. She took one look at Theo and shrieked with joy.

'Look at you, Theodore!' she cried as she flung her arms around him, squeezing until he wheezed. 'You're as tall as a damn beanstalk!'

They all turned to stare at Theo.

When the woman drew back from him, his cheeks were bright red. He cleared his throat, looking at his boots.

'You little snake,' said Val in disbelief. 'Between this and the identity of Sera's father, you two should start the Order of Liars.'

'Go easy on him,' chided Bibi. 'Who doesn't love a grand reveal?'

Sera was too shocked to say anything at all. She could only gape at the Shadowsmith, who was not from some unknown mountain village after all, but the infamous and secretive Halbracht.

The silver-haired woman clucked her tongue. 'Not like you to lose your tongue, Theodore. But I suppose I'm charming enough to make my own introductions.' She sketched a bow. 'I'm Paola Versini, Theo's extremely young and wildly attractive aunt.'

Val and Bibi exchanged a startled look. 'Did you just say—?'

'Wait. *Wait.*' Sera turned on Theo. 'Are you a Versini?'

'Only by blood.' He huffed an awkward laugh. 'We'll get to all that later.'

Oh, Sera would make sure of it. It was one thing to be related to Gaspard Dufort, but quite another to be related to Hugo Versini, the devil himself.

'So,' said Paola, her bright eyes roving between them. 'To what do we owe this totally unexpected and obviously ill-prepared visit?'

Theo looked to Sera, and she realized everyone was waiting for her to speak. After all, they had voted unanimously that she would be the head of their new order. It seemed that this moment – this explanation – was to be her first official task. So she rose to meet it, offering the cleanest, simplest truth. 'We are the Order of Flames, and we've come to finish what Lucille Versini started.'

Paola barked a surprised laugh, and Sera got the sense she knew exactly what she meant. And more than that, it did not unnerve her one bit. 'You'd better come in, then. Before the mountain goats think the invitation extends to them.'

With Pippin charting the way ahead, Sera passed through the gates of Halbracht and beheld a sprawling mountain village glittering with the promise of magic. Her palm crackled, the lightning inside her leaping to attention. Ready for this new adventure, this new destiny.

She smiled and opened her fist, letting the sparks dance.

ACKNOWLEDGEMENTS

The Dagger and the Flame is the enemies-to-lovers fantasy of my dreams and I have so many people to thank for bringing it to life in such an epic way.

Claire Wilson, thank you for a decade (and counting!) of sage advice, unerring kindness, and endless laughs. You are the most wonderful agent and friend.

Thank you, Pete Knapp, for representing me in the US – it has been a joy getting to know and work with you these past few years. Thanks, too, to Danielle Barthel and Stuti Telidevara at Park & Fine.

Thank you, Safae El-Ouahabi, and the rest of the team at RCW. Sam Coates, thank you for selling *The Dagger and the Flame* all over the world, and for finding the most perfect homes for Ransom and Seraphine. You are a machine!

Rachel Denwood, Head of the Order of Brilliant Books and Sparkling Charisma, thank you for helping me fan the first spark of this idea into a world that now burns so brightly. I can't wait to continue exploring it!

Thank you, Kate Prosswimmer, for your insightful edits and clear-eyed vision, which has helped make this book the very best version of itself.

Thanks, too, to the rest of the team at S&S for your hard work, creativity and infectious passion. Thanks Arub Ahmed, Olivia Horrox, Jess Dean, Sarah Macmillan, Miya Elkerton, Leanne Nulty, Hannah Taylor, Laura Hough, Danielle Wilson, Basia Ossowska, Justin Chanda, Karen Wojtyla, Nicole Fiorica, Bridget Madsen, Deb Sfetsios, Irene Metaxatos, Emily Ritter, Tatyana Rosalia, Samantha McVeigh and Caitlin Sweeney.

Thank you, Nina Douglas, for your brilliant work, inherent generosity, and all-round fantastic company.

The cover and special editions of *The Dagger and the Flame* are the stuff that dreams are made of. I am in awe and forever grateful to Micaela Alcaino for your incredible talent, and to Sean Williams for your design wizardry.

Thanks to Berni Vann at CAA and Emily Hayward-Whitlock at the Artists Partnership for working to bring *The Dagger and the Flame* to life on screen. Thank you to all the booksellers, librarians, teachers and readers, who have embraced my books over the years, and who work so tirelessly to spread their love of reading every day.

Lastly, thanks, as ever, to my incredible family and friends on both sides of the Atlantic. Special thanks to Jack, for everything (but especially the maps! We must never forget the maps!) and thank you Cali for the boundless love and infinite dog hair you bring into my life. 😊

ABOUT THE AUTHOR

Catherine Doyle grew up in the West of Ireland. She holds a BA in Psychology and an MA in Publishing.

She is an award-winning and bestselling author of several Middle Grade fantasy adventures including The Storm Keeper's Island trilogy, as well as the author of the Young Adult Blood for Blood trilogy (*Vendetta*, *Inferno* and *Mafiosa*), and the co-author of the Twin Crowns series.